"I'd be proud," she said quietly, lowering her head. "I'd be proud and happy to fight at your side."

"I believe that. But I'm not gallant enough. Nor valiant enough. I'm not suited to be a soldier or a hero. And having an acute fear of pain, mutilation and death is not the only reason. You can't stop a soldier from being frightened but you can give him motivation to help him overcome that fear. I have no such motivation. I can't have. I'm a witcher: an artificially created mutant. I kill monsters for money. I defend children when their parents pay me to. If Nilfgaardian parents pay me, I'll defend Nilfgaardian children. And even if the world lies in ruin—which does not seem likely to me—I'll carry on killing monsters in the ruins of this world until some monster kills me. That is my fate, my reason, my life and my attitude to the world. And it is not what I chose. It was chosen for me." . . . "But I don't want to die in a war, because they're not my wars."

Praise for Andrzej Sapkowski:

"Sapkowski has a phenomenal gift for narrative, for inventing sensational events, creating a suggestive mood, and building up the suspense. Along with a dazzling, slightly cynical sense of humor."

—Jacek Sieradzki, *Polityka*

"The character interplay is complex, unsentimental and anchored in brutal shared history. All bodes well for twisty plotting in future volumes."

—*SFX* on *Blood of Elves*

Books by Andrzej Sapkowski

The Last Wish

Blood of Elves

The Time of Contempt

BLOOD OF
ELVES

ANDRZEJ SAPKOWSKI

TRANSLATED BY DANUSIA STOK

www.orbitbooks.net

Original text copyright © Andrzej Sapkowski 1994
English translation copyright © Danusia Stok 2008
All rights reserved. In accordance with the U.S. Copyright Act of 1976, the scanning, uploading, and electronic sharing of any part of this book without the permission of the publisher is unlawful piracy and theft of the author's intellectual property. If you would like to use material from the book (other than for review purposes), prior written permission must be obtained by contacting the publisher at permissions@hbgusa.com. Thank you for your support of the author's rights.

Original title: *Krew Elfów*

Orbit
Hachette Book Group
1290 Avenue of the Americas, New York, NY 10104
Visit our website at www.orbitbooks.net

Orbit is an imprint of Hachette Book Group. The Orbit name and logo are trademarks of Little, Brown Book Group Limited.

The Hachette Speakers Bureau provides a wide range of authors for speaking events. To find out more, go to www.hachettespeakersbureau.com or call (866) 376-6591.

The publisher is not responsible for websites (or their content) that are not owned by the publisher.

Printed in the United States of America

Originally published in hardcover by Gollancz in the UK, 2008
First Orbit edition in the USA, May 2009

30 29 28 27 26 25 24 23 22 21

Verily I say unto you, the era of the sword and axe is nigh,
the era of the wolf's blizzard. The Time of the White Chill
and the White Light is nigh, the Time of Madness and the
Time of Contempt: Tedd Deireádh, the Time of End. The
world will die amidst frost and be reborn with the new
sun. It will be reborn of the Elder Blood, of Hen Ichaer, of
the seed that has been sown. A seed which will not sprout
but will burst into flame.

Ess'tuath esse! Thus it shall be! Watch for the signs!
What signs these shall be, I say unto you: first the earth
will flow with the blood of Aen Seidhe, the Blood of
Elves . . .

Aen Ithlinnespeath,
Ithlinne Aegli aep Aevenien's prophecy

CHAPTER ONE

The town was in flames.

The narrow streets leading to the moat and the first terrace belched smoke and embers, flames devouring the densely clustered thatched houses and licking at the castle walls. From the west, from the harbour gate, the screams and clamour of vicious battle and the dull blows of a battering ram smashing against the walls grew ever louder.

Their attackers had surrounded them unexpectedly, shattering the barricades which had been held by no more than a few soldiers, a handful of townsmen carrying halberds and some crossbowmen from the guild. Their horses, decked out in flowing black caparisons, flew over the barricades like spectres, their riders' bright, glistening blades sowing death amongst the fleeing defenders.

Ciri felt the knight who carried her before him on his saddle abruptly spur his horse. She heard his cry. "Hold on," he shouted. "Hold on!"

Other knights wearing the colours of Cintra overtook them, sparring, even in full flight, with the Nilfgaardians.

Ciri caught a glimpse of the skirmish from the corner of her eye – the crazed swirl of blue-gold and black cloaks amidst the clash of steel, the clatter of blades against shields, the neighing of horses—

Shouts. No, not shouts. Screams.

"Hold on!"

Fear. With every jolt, every jerk, every leap of the horse pain shot through her hands as she clutched at the reins. Her legs contracted painfully, unable to find support, her eyes watered from the smoke. The arm around her suffocated her, choking her, the force compressing her ribs. All around her screaming such as she had never before heard grew louder. What must one do to a man to make him scream so?

Fear. Overpowering, paralysing, choking fear.

Again the clash of iron, the grunts and snorts of the horses. The houses whirled around her and suddenly she could see windows belching fire where a moment before there'd been nothing but a muddy little street strewn with corpses and cluttered with the abandoned possessions of the fleeing population. All at once the knight at her back was wracked by a strange wheezing cough. Blood spurted over the hands grasping the reins. More screams. Arrows whistled past.

A fall, a shock, painful bruising against armour. Hooves pounded past her, a horse's belly and a frayed girth flashing by above her head, then another horse's belly and a flowing black caparison. Grunts of exertion, like a lumberjack's when chopping wood. But this isn't wood; it's iron against iron. A shout, muffled and dull, and something huge and black collapsed into the mud next to her with a splash, spurting blood. An armoured foot quivered, thrashed, goring the earth with an enormous spur.

A jerk. Some force plucked her up, pulled her onto another saddle. *Hold on!* Again the bone-shaking speed, the mad gallop. Arms and legs desperately searching for support. The horse rears. *Hold on!* . . . There is no support. There is no . . . There is no . . . There is blood. The horse falls. It's impossible to jump aside, no way to break free, to escape the tight embrace of these chainmail-clad arms. There is no way to avoid the blood pouring onto her head and over her shoulders.

A jolt, the squelch of mud, a violent collision with the ground, horrifically still after the furious ride. The horse's harrowing wheezes and squeals as it tries to regain its feet. The pounding of horseshoes, fetlocks and hooves flashing past. Black caparisons and cloaks. Shouting.

The street is on fire, a roaring red wall of flame. Silhouetted before it, a rider towers over the flaming roofs, enormous. His black-caparisoned horse prances, tosses its head, neighs.

The rider stares down at her. Ciri sees his eyes gleaming through the slit in his huge helmet, framed by a bird of prey's wings. She sees the fire reflected in the broad blade of the sword held in his lowered hand.

The rider looks at her. Ciri is unable to move. The dead man's motionless arms wrapped around her waist hold her down. She is locked in place by something heavy and wet with blood, something which is lying across her thigh, pinning her to the ground.

And she is frozen in fear: a terrible fear which turns her entrails inside out, which deafens Ciri to the screams of the wounded horse, the roar of the blaze, the cries of dying people and the pounding drums. The only thing which exists, which counts, which still has any meaning, is fear. Fear embodied in the figure of a black knight wearing a helmet decorated with feathers frozen against the wall of raging, red flames.

The rider spurs his horse, the wings on his helmet fluttering as the bird of prey takes to flight, launching itself to attack its helpless victim, paralysed with fear. The bird – or maybe the knight – screeches terrifyingly, cruelly, triumphantly. A black horse, black armour, a black flowing cloak, and behind this – flames. A sea of flames.

Fear.

The bird shrieks. The wings beat, feathers slap against her face. *Fear!*

Help! Why doesn't anyone help me? Alone, weak, helpless – I can't move, can't force a sound from my constricted throat. Why does no one come to help me?

I'm terrified!

Eyes blaze through the slit in the huge winged helmet. The black cloak veils everything—

"Ciri!"

She woke, numb and drenched in sweat, with her scream – the scream which had woken her – still hanging in the air, still vibrating somewhere within her, beneath her breast-bone and burning against her parched throat. Her hands ached, clenched around the blanket; her back ached . . .

"Ciri. Calm down."

The night was dark and windy, the crowns of the surrounding pine trees rustling steadily and melodiously, their limbs and trunks creaking in the wind. There was no malevolent fire, no screams, only this gentle lullaby.

Beside her the campfire flickered with light and warmth, its reflected flames glowing from harness buckles, gleaming red in the leather-wrapped and iron-banded hilt of a sword leaning against a saddle on the ground. There was no other fire and no other iron. The hand against her cheek smelled of leather and ashes. Not of blood.

"Geralt—"

"It was just a dream. A bad dream."

Ciri shuddered violently, curling her arms and legs up tight.

A dream. Just a dream.

The campfire had already died down; the birch logs were red and luminous, occasionally crackling, giving off tiny spurts of blue flame which illuminated the white hair and sharp profile of the man wrapping a blanket and sheepskin around her.

"Geralt, I—"

"I'm right here. Sleep, Ciri. You have to rest. We've still a long way ahead of us."

I can hear music, she thought suddenly. *Amidst the rustling of the trees . . . there's music. Lute music. And voices. The Princess of Cintra . . . A child of destiny . . . A child of Elder Blood, the blood of elves. Geralt of Rivia, the White Wolf, and his destiny. No, no, that's a legend. A poet's invention. The princess is dead. She was killed in the town streets while trying to escape . . .*

Hold on . . . ! Hold . . .

"Geralt?"

"What, Ciri?"

"What did he do to me? What happened? What did he . . . do to me?"

"Who?"

"The knight . . . The black knight with feathers on his helmet . . . I can't remember anything. He shouted . . . and looked at me. I can't remember what happened. Only that I was frightened . . . I was so frightened . . ."

The man leaned over her, the flame of the campfire sparkling in his eyes. They were strange eyes. Very strange. Ciri had been frightened of them, she hadn't liked meeting his gaze. But that had been a long time ago. A very long time ago.

"I can't remember anything," she whispered, searching for his hand, as tough and coarse as raw wood. "The black knight—"

"It was a dream. Sleep peacefully. It won't come back."

Ciri had heard such reassurances in the past. They had been repeated to her endlessly; many, many times she had been offered comforting words when her screams had woken her during the night. But this time it was different. Now she believed it. Because it was Geralt of Rivia, the White Wolf, the Witcher, who said it. The man who was her destiny. The one for whom she was destined. Geralt the Witcher, who had found her surrounded by war, death and despair, who had taken her with him and promised they would never part.

She fell asleep holding tight to his hand.

The bard finished the song. Tilting his head a little he repeated the ballad's refrain on his lute, delicately, softly, a single tone higher than the apprentice accompanying him.

No one said a word. Nothing but the subsiding music and the whispering leaves and squeaking boughs of the enormous oak could be heard. Then, all of a sudden, a goat tethered to one of the carts which circled the ancient tree bleated lengthily. At that moment, as if given a signal, one of the men seated in the large semi-circular audience stood up. Throwing his cobalt blue cloak with gold braid trim back over his shoulder, he gave a stiff, dignified bow.

"Thank you, Master Dandilion," he said, his voice resonant without being loud. "Allow me, Radcliffe of Oxenfurt, Master of the Arcana, to express what I am sure is the opinion of everyone here present and utter words of gratitude and appreciation for your fine art and skill."

The wizard ran his gaze over those assembled – an audience of well over a hundred people – seated on the ground, on carts, or standing in a tight semi-circle facing the foot of the oak. They nodded and whispered amongst themselves. Several people began to applaud while others greeted the singer with upraised hands. Women, touched by the music, sniffed and wiped their eyes on whatever came to hand, which differed according to their standing, profession and wealth: peasant women used their forearms or the backs of their hands, merchants' wives dabbed their eyes with linen handkerchiefs while elves and noblewomen used kerchiefs of the finest tight-woven cotton, and Baron Vilibert's three daughters, who had, along with the rest of his retinue, halted their falcon hunt to attend the famous troubadour's performance, blew their noses loudly and sonorously into elegant mould-green cashmere scarves.

"It would not be an exaggeration to say," continued the wizard, "that you have moved us deeply, Master Dandilion. You have prompted us to reflection and thought; you have stirred our hearts. Allow me to express our gratitude, and our respect."

The troubadour stood and took a bow, sweeping the heron feather pinned to his fashionable hat across his knees. His apprentice broke off his playing, grinned and bowed too, until Dandilion glared at him sternly and snapped something under his breath. The boy lowered his head and returned to softly strumming his lute strings.

The assembly stirred to life. The merchants travelling in the caravan whispered amongst themselves and then rolled a sizable cask of beer out to the foot of the oak tree. Wizard Radcliffe lost himself in quiet conversation with Baron Vilibert. Having blown their noses, the baron's daughters gazed at Dandilion in adoration – which went entirely unnoticed by the bard, engrossed as he was in smiling, winking and flashing his teeth at a haughty, silent group of roving elves, and at one of them in particular: a dark-haired, large-eyed beauty sporting a tiny ermine cap. Dandilion had rivals for her attention – the elf, with her huge eyes and beautiful toque hat, had caught his audience's interest as well, and a number of knights, students and goliards were paying court to her with their eyes. The elf clearly enjoyed the attention, picking at the lace cuffs of her chemise and fluttering her eyelashes, but the group of elves with her surrounded her on all sides, not bothering to hide their antipathy towards her admirers.

The glade beneath Bleobheris, the great oak, was a place of frequent rallies, a well-known travellers' resting place and meeting ground for wanderers, and was famous for its tolerance and openness. The druids protecting the ancient tree called it the Seat of Friendship and willingly welcomed all comers. But even during an event as exceptional as the world-famous troubadour's just-concluded performance the travellers kept to themselves, remaining in clearly delineated groups. Elves stayed with elves. Dwarfish craftsmen gathered with their kin, who were often hired to protect the merchant caravans and were armed to the teeth. Their groups tolerated at best the gnome miners and halfling farmers who camped beside them. All non-humans were uniformly distant towards humans. The humans repaid in kind, but were not seen to mix amongst themselves either. Nobility looked down on the merchants and travelling salesmen with open scorn, while soldiers and mercenaries distanced themselves from shepherds and their reeking sheepskins. The few wizards and their disciples kept themselves entirely apart from the others, and bestowed their arrogance on everyone in equal parts. A tight-knit, dark and silent group of peasants lurked in the background. Resembling a forest with their rakes, pitchforks and flails poking above their heads, they were ignored by all and sundry.

The exception, as ever, was the children. Freed from the constraints of silence which had been enforced during the bard's performance, the children dashed into the woods with wild cries, and enthusiastically immersed themselves in a game whose rules were incomprehensible to all those who had bidden farewell to the happy years of childhood. Children of elves, dwarves, halflings, gnomes, half-elves, quarter-elves and toddlers of mysterious provenance neither knew nor recognised racial or social divisions. At least, not yet.

"Indeed!" shouted one of the knights present in the glade, who was as thin as a beanpole and wearing a red and black tunic emblazoned with three lions passant. "The wizard speaks the truth! The ballads were beautiful. Upon my word, honourable Dandilion, if you ever pass near Baldhorn, my lord's castle, stop by without a moment's hesitation. You will be welcomed like a prince– what am I saying? Welcomed like King Vizimir himself! I swear on my sword, I have heard many a minstrel, but none even came close to being your equal, master. Accept the respect and tributes those of us born to knighthood, and those of us appointed to the position, pay to your skills!"

Flawlessly sensing the opportune moment, the troubadour winked at his apprentice. The boy set his lute aside and picked up a little casket which served as a collection box for the audience's more measurable expressions of appreciation. He hesitated, ran his eyes over the crowd, then replaced the little casket and grabbed a large bucket standing nearby. Master Dandilion bestowed an approving smile on the young man for his prudence.

"Master!" shouted a sizeable woman sitting on a cart, the sides of which were painted with a sign for "Vera Loewenhaupt and Sons," and which was full of wickerwork. Her sons, nowhere to be seen, were no doubt busy wasting away their mother's hard-earned fortune. "Master Dandilion, what is this? Are you going to leave us in suspense? That can't be the end of your ballad? Sing to us of what happened next!"

"Songs and ballads" – the musician bowed – "never end, dear lady, because poetry is eternal and immortal, it knows no beginning, it knows no end—"

"But what happened next?" The tradeswoman didn't give up, generously rattling coins into the bucket Dandilion's apprentice held out to her. "At least tell us about it, even if you have no wish to sing of it. Your songs mention no names, but we know the witcher you sing of is no other than the famous Geralt of Rivia, and the enchantress for whom he burns with love is the equally famous Yennefer. And the Child Surprise, destined for the witcher and sworn to him from birth, is Cirilla, the unfortunate Princess of Cintra, the town destroyed by the Invaders. Am I right?"

Dandilion smiled, remaining enigmatic and aloof. "I sing of universal matters, my dear, generous lady," he stated. "Of emotions which anyone can experience. Not about specific people."

"Oh, come on!" yelled a voice from the crowd. "Everyone knows those songs are about Geralt the Witcher!"

"Yes, yes!" squealed Baron Vilibert's daughters in chorus, drying their sodden scarves. "Sing on, Master Dandilion! What happened next? Did the witcher and Yennefer the Enchantress find each other in the end? And did they love each other? Were they happy? We want to know!"

"Enough!" roared the dwarf leader with a growl in his throat, shaking his mighty waist-length, red beard. "It's crap – all these princesses, sorceresses, destiny, love and women's fanciful tales. If you'll pardon the expression, great poet, it's all lies, just a poetic invention to make the story prettier and more touching. But of the deeds of war – the massacre and plunder of Cintra, the battles of Marnadal and Sodden – you did sing that mightily, Dandilion! There's no regrets in parting with silver for such a song, a joy to a warrior's heart! And I, Sheldon Skaggs, declare there's not an ounce of lies in what you say – and I can tell the lies from the truth because I was there at Sodden.

I stood against the Nilfgaard invaders with an axe in my hand . . ."

"I, Donimir of Troy," shouted the thin knight with three lions passant blazoned across his tunic, "was at both battles of Sodden! But I did not see you there, sir dwarf!"

"No doubt because you were looking after the supply train!" Sheldon Skaggs retorted. "While I was in the front line where things got hot!"

"Mind your tongue, beardy!" said Donimir of Troy flushing, hitching up his sword belt. "And who you're speaking to!"

"Have a care yourself!" The dwarf whacked his palm against the axe wedged in his belt, turned to his companions and grinned. "Did you see him there? Frigging knight! See his coat of arms? Ha! Three lions on a shield? Two shitting and the third snarling!"

"Peace, peace!" A grey-haired druid in a white cloak averted trouble with a sharp, authoritative voice. "This is not fitting, gentlemen! Not here, under Bleobheris' crown, an oak older than all the disputes and quarrels of the world! And not in Poet Dandilion's presence, from whose ballads we ought to learn of love, not contention."

"Quite so!" a short, fat priest with a face glistening with sweat seconded the druid. "You look but have no eyes, you listen but have deaf ears. Because divine love is not in you, you are like empty barrels—"

"Speaking of barrels," squeaked a long-nosed gnome from his cart, painted with a sign for "Iron hardware, manufacture and sale", "roll another out, guildsmen! Poet Dandilion's throat is surely dry – and ours too, from all these emotions!"

"—Verily, like empty barrels, I tell ye!" The priest, determined not to be put off, drowned out the ironware gnome. "You have understood nothing of Master Dandilion's ballad, you have learned nothing! You did not see that these ballads speak of man's fate, that we are no more than toys in the hands of the gods, our lands no more than their playground. The ballads about destiny portrayed the destinies of us all, and the legend of Geralt the Witcher and Princess Cirilla – although it is set against the true background of that war – is, after all, a mere metaphor, the creation of a poet's imagination designed to help us—"

"You're talking rubbish, holy man!" hollered Vera Loewenhaupt from the heights of her cart. "What legend? What imaginative creation? You may not know him, but I know Geralt of Rivia. I saw him with my own eyes in Wyzima, when he broke the spell on King Foltest's daughter. And I met him again later on the Merchants' Trail, where, at Gildia's request, he slew a ferocious griffin which was preying on the caravans and thus saved the lives of many good people. No. This is no legend or fairy-tale. It is the truth, the sincere truth, which Master Dandilion sang for us."

"I second that," said a slender female warrior with her black hair smoothly brushed back and plaited into a thick braid. "I, Rayla of Lyria, also know Geralt the White Wolf, the famous slayer of monsters. And I've met the enchantress, Lady Yennefer, on several occasions – I used to visit Aedirn and her home town of Vengerberg. I don't know anything about their being in love, though."

"But it has to be true," the attractive elf in the ermine toque suddenly said in a melodious voice. "Such a beautiful ballad of love could not but be true."

"It could not!" Baron Vilibert's daughters supported the elf and, as if on command, wiped their eyes on their scarves. "Not by any measure!"

"Honourable wizard!" Vera Loewenhaupt turned to Radcliffe. "Were they in love or not? Surely you know what truly happened to them, Yennefer and the witcher. Disclose the secret!"

"If the song says they were in love," replied the wizard, "then that's what happened, and their love will endure down the ages. Such is the power of poetry."

"It is said," interrupted Baron Vilibert all of a sudden, "that Yennefer of Vengerberg was killed on Sodden Hill. Several enchantresses were killed there—"

"That's not true," said Donimir of Troy. "Her name is not on the monument. I am from those parts and have often climbed Sodden Hill and read the names engraved on the monument. Three enchantresses died there: Triss Merigold, Lytta Neyd, known as Coral . . . hmm . . . and the name of the third has slipped my mind . . ."

The knight glanced at Wizard Radcliffe, who smiled wordlessly.

"And this witcher," Sheldon Skaggs suddenly called out, "this Geralt who loved Yennefer, has also bitten the dust, apparently. I heard he was killed somewhere in Transriver. He slew and slew monsters until he met his match. That's how it goes: he who fights with the sword dies by the sword. Everyone comes across someone who will better them eventually, and is made to taste cold hard iron."

"I don't believe it." The slender warrior contorted her pale lips, spat vehemently on the ground and crossed her chainmail-clad arms with a crunch. "I don't believe there is anyone to best Geralt of Rivia. I have seen this witcher handle a sword. His speed is simply inhuman—"

"Well said," threw in Wizard Radcliffe. "Inhuman. Witchers are mutated, so their reactions—"

"I don't understand you, magician." The warrior twisted her lips even more nastily. "Your words are too learned. I know one thing: no swordsman I have ever seen can match Geralt of Rivia, the White Wolf. And so I will not accept that he was defeated in battle as the dwarf claims."

"Every swordsman's an arse when the enemy's not sparse," remarked Sheldon Skaggs sententiously. "As the elves say."

"Elves," stated a tall, fair-haired representative of the Elder Race coldly, from his place beside the elf with the beautiful toque, "are not in the habit of using such vulgar language."

"No! No!" squealed Baron Vilibert's daughters from behind their green scarves. "Geralt the Witcher can't have been killed! The witcher found Ciri, the child destined for him, and then the Enchantress Yennefer, and all three lived happily ever after! Isn't that true, Master Dandilion?"

"'Twas a ballad, my noble young ladies," said the beer-parched gnome, manufacturer of ironwares, with a yawn. "Why look for truth in a ballad? Truth is one thing, poetry another. Let's take this – what was her name? – Ciri? The famous Child Surprise. Master Dandilion trumped that up for sure. I've been to Cintra many a time and the king and queen lived in a childless home, with no daughter, no son—"

"Liar!" shouted a red-haired man in a sealskin jacket,

a checked kerchief bound around his forehead. "Queen Calanthe, the Lioness of Cintra, had a daughter called Pavetta. She died, together with her husband, in a tempest which struck out at sea, and the depths swallowed them both."

"So you see for yourselves I'm not making this up!" The ironware gnome called everyone to be his witnesses. "The Princess of Cintra was called Pavetta, not Ciri."

"Cirilla, known as Ciri, was the daughter of this drowned Pavetta," explained the red-haired man. "Calanthe's granddaughter. She was not the princess herself, but the daughter of the Princess of Cintra. She was the Child Surprise destined for the witcher, the man to whom – even before she was born – the queen had sworn to hand her granddaughter over, just as Master Dandilion has sung. But the witcher could neither find her nor collect her. And here our poet has missed the truth."

"Oh yes, he's missed the truth indeed," butted in a sinewy young man who, judging by his clothes, was a journeyman on his travels prior to crafting his masterpiece and passing his master's exams. "The witcher's destiny bypassed him: Cirilla was killed during the siege of Cintra. Before throwing herself from the tower, Queen Calanthe killed the princess's daughter with her own hand, to prevent her from falling into the Nilfgaardians' claws alive."

"It wasn't like that. Not like that at all!" objected the red-haired man. "The princess's daughter was killed during the massacre while trying to escape from the town."

"One way or another," shouted Ironware, "the witcher didn't find Cirilla! The poet lied!"

"But lied beautifully," said the elf in the toque, snuggling up to the tall, fair-haired elf.

"It's not a question of poetry but of facts!" shouted the journeyman. "I tell you, the princess's daughter died by her grandmother's hand. Anyone who's been to Cintra can confirm that!"

"And I say she was killed in the streets trying to escape," declared the red-haired man. "I know because although I'm not from Cintra I served in the Earl of Skellige's troop supporting Cintra during the war. As everyone knows, Eist Tuirseach, the King of Cintra, comes from the Skellige Isles. He was the earl's uncle. I fought in the earl's troop at Marnadal and Cintra and later, after the defeat, at Sodden—"

"Yet another veteran," Sheldon Skaggs snarled to the dwarves crowded around him. "All heroes and warriors. Hey, folks! Is there at least one of you out there who didn't fight at Marnadal or Sodden?"

"That dig is out of place, Skaggs," the tall elf reproached him, putting his arm around the beauty wearing the toque in a way intended to dispel any lingering doubts amongst her admirers. "Don't imagine you were the only one to fight at Sodden. I took part in the battle as well."

"On whose side, I wonder," Baron Vilibert said to Radcliffe in a highly audible whisper which the elf ignored entirely.

"As everyone knows," he continued, sparing neither the baron nor the wizard so much as a glance, "over a hundred thousand warriors stood on the field during the second battle of Sodden Hill, and of those at least thirty thousand were maimed or killed. Master Dandilion should be thanked for immortalising this famous, terrible battle in one of his ballads. In both the lyrics and melody of his work I heard not an exaltation but a warning. So I repeat: offer praise and everlasting renown to this poet for his ballad, which may, perhaps, prevent a tragedy as horrific as this cruel and unnecessary war from occurring in the future."

"Indeed," said Baron Vilibert, looking defiantly at the elf. "You have read some very interesting things into this ballad, honoured sir. An unnecessary war, you say? You'd like to avoid such a tragedy in the future, would you? Are we to understand that if the Nilfgaardians were to attack us again you would advise that we capitulate? Humbly accept the Nilfgaardian yoke?"

"Life is a priceless gift and should be protected," the elf replied coldly. "Nothing justifies wide-scale slaughter and sacrifice of life, which is what the battles at Sodden were – both the battle lost and the battle won. Both of them cost the humans thousands of lives. And with them, you lost unimaginable potential—"

"Elven prattle!" snarled Sheldon Skaggs. "Dim-witted rubbish! It was the price that had to be paid to allow others to live decently, in peace, instead of being chained, blinded, whipped and forced to work in salt and sulphur mines. Those who died a heroic death, those who will now, thanks to Dandilion, live on forever in our memories, taught us to defend our own homes. Sing your ballads, Dandilion, sing them to everyone. Your lesson won't go to waste, and it'll come in handy, you'll see! Because, mark my words, Nilfgaard will attack us again. If not today, then tomorrow! They're licking their wounds now, recovering, but the day when we'll see their black cloaks and feathered helmets again is growing ever nearer!"

"What do they want from us?" yelled Vera Loewen-haupt. "Why are they bent on persecuting us? Why don't they leave us in peace, leave us to our lives and work? What do the Nilfgaardians want?"

"They want our blood!" howled Baron Vilibert.

"And our land!" someone cried from the crowd of peasants.

"And our women!" chimed in Sheldon Skaggs, with a ferocious glower.

Several people started to laugh – as quietly and fur-tively as they could. Even though the idea that anyone other than another dwarf would desire one of the excep-tionally unattractive dwarf-women was highly amusing, it was not a safe subject for teasing or jests – especially not in the presence of the short, stocky, bearded individ-uals whose axes and short-swords had an ugly habit of leaping from their belts and into their hands at incredible speed. And the dwarves, for some unknown reason, were entirely convinced that the rest of the world was lech-erously lying in wait for their wives and daughters, and were extremely touchy about it.

"This had to happen at some point," the grey-haired druid declared suddenly. "This had to happen. We forgot that we are not the only ones in this world, that the whole of creation does not revolve around us. Like stupid, fat, lazy minnows in a slimy pond we chose not to accept the existence of pike. We allowed our world, like the pond, to become slimy, boggy and sluggish. Look around you – there is crime and sin everywhere, greed, the pursuit of profit, quarrels and disagreements are rife. Our traditions are disappearing, respect for our values is fading. Instead of living according to Nature we have begun to destroy

it. And what have we got for it? The air is poisoned by
the stink of smelting furnaces, the rivers and brooks are
tainted by slaughter houses and tanneries, forests are being
cut down without a thought . . . Ha – just look! – even on
the living bark of sacred Bleobheris, there just above the
poet's head, there's a foul phrase carved out with a knife
– and it's misspelled at that – by a stupid, illiterate vandal.
Why are you surprised? It had to end badly—"

"Yes, yes!" the fat priest joined in. "Come to your
senses, you sinners, while there is still time, because the
anger and vengeance of the gods hangs over you! Remember Ithlin's oracle, the prophetic words describing
the punishment of the gods reserved for a tribe poisoned
by crime! 'The Time of Contempt will come, when the
tree will lose its leaves, the bud will wither, the fruit will
rot, the seed turn bitter and the river valleys will run with
ice instead of water. The White Chill will come, and after
it the White Light, and the world will perish beneath bliz-
zards.' Thus spoke Seeress Ithlin! And before this comes
to pass there will be visible signs, plagues will ravish the
earth – Remember! – the Nilfgaard are our punishment
from the gods! They are the whip with which the Immor-
tals will lash you sinners, so that you may—"

"Shut up, you sanctimonious old man!" roared Sheldon
Skaggs, stamping his heavy boots. "Your superstitious rot
makes me sick! My guts are churning—"

"Careful, Sheldon." The tall elf cut him short with a
smile. "Don't mock another's religion. It is not pleasant,
polite or . . . safe."

"I'm not mocking anything," protested the dwarf. "I
don't doubt the existence of the gods, but it annoys me
when someone drags them into earthly matters and tries

to pull the wool over my eyes using the prophecies of some crazy elf. The Nilfgaardians are the instrument of the gods? Rubbish! Search back through your memories to the past, to the days of Dezmod, Radowid and Sambuk, to the days of Abrad, the Old Oak! You may not remember them, because your lives are so very short – you're like Mayflies – but I remember, and I'll tell you what it was like in these lands just after you climbed from your boats on the Yaruga Estuary and the Pontar Delta onto the beach. Three kingdoms sprang from the four ships which beached on those shores; the stronger groups absorbed the weaker and so grew, strengthening their positions. They invaded others' territories, conquered them, and their kingdoms expanded, becoming ever larger and more powerful. And now the Nilfgaardians are doing the same, because theirs is a strong and united, disciplined and tightly knit country. And unless you close ranks in the same way, Nilfgaard will swallow you as a pike does a minnow – just as this wise druid said!"

"Let them just try!" Donimir of Troy puffed out his lion-emblazoned chest and shook his sword in its scabbard. "We beat them hollow on Sodden Hill, and we can do it again!"

"You're very cocksure," snarled Sheldon Skaggs. "You've evidently forgotten, sir knight, that before the battle of Sodden Hill, the Nilfgaard had advanced across your lands like an iron roller, strewing the land between Marnadal and Transriver with the corpses of many a gallant fellow like yourself. And it wasn't loud-mouthed smart-arses like you who stopped the Nilfgaardians, but the united strengths of Temeria, Redania, Aedirn and Kaedwen. Concord and unity, that's what stopped them!"

"Not just that," remarked Radcliffe in a cold, resonant voice. "Not just that, Master Skaggs."

The dwarf hawked loudly, blew his nose, shuffled his feet then bowed a little to the wizard.

"No one is denying the contribution of your fellowship," he said. "Shame on he who does not acknowledge the heroism of the brotherhood of wizards on Sodden Hill. They stood their ground bravely, shed blood for the common cause, and contributed most eminently to our victory. Dandilion did not forget them in his ballad, and nor shall we. But note that these wizards stood united and loyal on the Hill, and accepted the leadership of Vilgefortz of Roggeveen just as we, the warriors of the Four Kingdoms, acknowledged the command of Vizimir of Redania. It's just a pity this solidarity and concord only lasted for the duration of the war, because, with peace, here we are divided again. Vizimir and Foltest are choking each other with customs taxes and trading laws, Demawend of Aedirn is bickering with Henselt over the Northern Marches while the League of Hengfors and the Thyssenids of Kovir don't give a toss. And I hear that looking for the old concord amongst the wizards is useless, too. We are not closely knit, we have no discipline and no unity. But Nilfgaard does!"

"Nilfgaard is ruled by Emperor Emhyr var Emreis, a tyrant and autocrat who enforces obedience with whip, noose and axe!" thundered Baron Vilibert. "What are you proposing, sir dwarf? How are we supposed to close ranks? With similar tyranny? And which king, which kingdom, in your opinion, should subordinate the others? In whose hands would you like to see the sceptre and knout?"

"What do I care?" replied Skaggs with a shrug. "That's a human affair. Whoever you chose to be king wouldn't be a dwarf anyway."

"Or an elf, or even half-elf," added the tall representative of the Elder Race, his arm still wrapped around the toque-wearing beauty. "You even consider quarter-elves inferior—"

"That's where it stings," laughed Vilibert. "You're blowing the same horn as Nilfgaard because Nilfgaard is also shouting about equality, promising you a return to the old order as soon as we've been conquered and they've scythed us off these lands. That's the sort of unity, the sort of equality you're dreaming of, the sort you're talking about and trumpeting! Nilfgaard pays you gold to do it! And it's hardly surprising you love each other so much, the Nilfgaardians being an elven race—"

"Nonsense," the elf said coldly. "You talk rubbish, sir knight. You're clearly blinded by racism. The Nilfgaardians are human, just like you."

"That's an outright lie! They're descended from the Black Seidhe and everyone knows it! Elven blood flows through their veins! The blood of elves!"

"And what flows through yours?" The elf smiled derisively. "We've been combining our blood for generations, for centuries, your race and mine, and doing so quite successfully – fortunately or unfortunately, I don't know. You started persecuting mixed relationships less than a quarter of a century ago and, incidentally, not very successfully. So show me a human now who hasn't a dash of Seidhe Ichaer, the blood of the Elder Race."

Vilibert visibly turned red. Vera Loewenhaupt also flushed. Wizard Radcliffe bowed his head and coughed. And, most interestingly, the beautiful elf in the ermine toque blushed too.

"We are all children of Mother Earth." The grey-haired druid's voice resounded in the silence. "We are children of Mother Nature. And though we do not respect our mother, though we often worry her and cause her pain, though we break her heart, she loves us. Loves us all. Let us remember that, we who are assembled here in this Seat of Friendship. And let us not bicker over which of us was here first: Acorn was the first to be thrown up by the waves and from Acorn sprouted the Great Bleobheris, the oldest of oaks. Standing beneath its crown, amongst its primordial roots, let us not forget our own brotherly roots, the earth from which these roots grow. Let us remember the words of Poet Dandilion's song—"

"Exactly!" exclaimed Vera Loewenhaupt. "And where is he?"

"He's fled," ascertained Sheldon Skaggs, gazing at the empty place under the oak. "Taken the money and fled without saying goodbye. Very elf-like!"

"Dwarf-like!" squealed Ironware.

"Human-like," corrected the tall elf, and the beauty in the toque rested her head against his shoulder.

"Hey, minstrel," said Mama Lantieri, striding into the room without knocking, the scents of hyacinths, sweat, beer and smoked bacon wafting before her. "You've got a guest. Enter, noble gentleman."

Dandilion smoothed his hair and sat up in the enormous carved armchair. The two girls sitting on his lap quickly jumped up, covering their charms and pulling down their disordered clothes. The modesty of harlots, thought the poet, was not at all a bad title for a ballad. He got to his feet, fastened his belt and pulled on his doublet, all the while looking at the nobleman standing at the threshold.

"Indeed," he remarked, "you know how to find me anywhere, though you rarely pick an opportune moment. You're lucky I'd not yet decided which of these two beauties I prefer. And at your prices, Lantieri, I cannot afford them both."

Mama Lantieri smiled in sympathy and clapped her hands. Both girls – a fair-skinned, freckled islander and a dark-haired half-elf – swiftly left the room. The man at the door removed his cloak and handed it to Mama along with a small but well-filled money-bag.

"Forgive me, master," he said, approaching the table and making himself comfortable. "I know this is not a good time to disturb you. But you disappeared out from beneath the oak so quickly . . . I did not catch you on the High Road as I had intended and did not immediately come across your tracks in this little town. I'll not take much of your time, believe me—"

"They always say that, and it's always a lie," the bard interrupted. "Leave us alone, Lantieri, and see to it that we're not disturbed. I'm listening, sir."

The man scrutinised him. He had dark, damp, almost tearful eyes, a pointed nose and ugly, narrow lips.

"I'll come to the point without wasting your time," he declared, waiting for the door to close behind Mama. "Your ballads interest me, master. To be more specific, certain characters of which you sang interest me. I am concerned with the true fate of your ballad's heroes. If I am not mistaken, the true destinies of real people inspired the beautiful work I heard beneath the oak tree? I have in mind . . . Little Cirilla of Cintra. Queen Calanthe's granddaughter."

Dandilion gazed at the ceiling, drumming his fingers on the table.

"Honoured sir," he said dryly, "you are interested in strange matters. You ask strange questions. Something tells me you are not the person I took you to be."

"And who did you take me to be, if I may ask?"

"I'm not sure you may. It depends if you are about to convey greetings to me from any mutual friends. You should have done so initially, but somehow you have forgotten."

"I did not forget at all." The man reached into the breast pocket of his sepia-coloured velvet tunic and pulled out a money-bag somewhat larger than the one he had handed the procuress but just as well-filled, which clinked as it touched the table. "We simply have no mutual friends, Dandilion. But might this purse not suffice to mitigate the lack?"

"And what do you intend to buy with this meagre purse?" The troubadour pouted. "Mama Lantieri's entire brothel and all the land surrounding it?"

"Let us say that I intend to support the arts. And an art-ist. In order to chat with the artist about his work."

"You love art so much, do you, dear sir? Is it so vital for you to talk to an artist that you press money on him before you've even introduced yourself and, in doing so, break the most elementary rules of courtesy?"

"At the beginning of our conversation" – the stranger's

dark eyes narrowed imperceptibly – "my anonymity did not bother you."

"And now it is starting to."

"I am not ashamed of my name," said the man, a faint smile appearing on his narrow lips. "I am called Rience. You do not know me, Master Dandilion, and that is no surprise. You are too famous and well known to know all of your admirers. Yet everyone who admires your talents feels he knows you, knows you so well that a certain degree of familiarity is permissible. This applies to me, too. I know it is a misconception, so please graciously forgive me."

"I graciously forgive you."

"Then I can count on you agreeing to answer a few questions—"

"No! No you cannot," interrupted the poet, putting on airs. "Now, if you will graciously forgive *me*, I am not willing to discuss the subjects of my work, its inspiration or its characters, fictitious or otherwise. To do so would deprive poetry of its poetic veneer and lead to triteness."

"Is that so?"

"It certainly is. For example, if, having sung the ballad about the miller's merry wife, I were to announce it's really about Zvirka, Miller Loach's wife, and I included an announcement that Zvirka can most easily be bedded every Thursday because on Thursdays the miller goes to market, it would no longer be poetry. It would be either rhyming couplets, or foul slander."

"I understand, I understand," Rience said quickly. "But perhaps that is a bad example. I am not, after all, interested in anyone's peccadilloes or sins. You will not slander anyone by answering my questions. All I need is one small piece of information: what really happened to Cirilla, the Queen of Cintra's granddaughter? Many people claim she was killed during the siege of the town; there are even eye-witnesses to support the claim. From your ballad, however, it would appear that the child survived. I am truly interested to know if this is your imagination at work, or the truth? True or false?"

"I'm extremely pleased you're so interested." Dandilion smiled broadly. "You may laugh, Master whatever-your-name-is, but that was precisely what I intended when I composed the ballad. I wished to excite my listeners and arouse their curiosity."

"True or false?" repeated Rience coldly.

"If I were to give that away I would destroy the impact of my work. Goodbye, my friend. You have used up all the time I can spare you. And two of my many inspirations are waiting out there, wondering which of them I will choose."

Rience remained silent for a long while, making no move to leave. He stared at the poet with his unfriendly, moist eyes, and the poet felt a growing unease. A merry din came from the bawdy-house's main room, punctuated from time to time by high-pitched feminine giggles. Dandilion turned his head away, pretending to show derisive haughtiness but, in fact, he was judging the distance to the corner of the room and the tapestry showing a nymph sprinkling her breasts with water poured from a jug.

"Dandilion," Rience finally spoke, slipping his hand back into the pocket of his sepia-coloured tunic, "answer my questions. Please. I have to know the answer. It's incredibly important to me. To you, too, believe me, because if you answer of your own free will then—"

"Then what?"

A hideous grimace crept over Rience's narrow lips.

"Then I won't have to force you to speak."

"Now listen, you scoundrel." Dandilion stood up and pretended to pull a threatening face. "I loathe violence and force, but I'm going to call Mama Lantieri in a minute and she will call a certain Gruzila who fulfils the honourable and responsible role of bouncer in this establishment. He is a true artist in his field. He'll kick your arse so hard you'll soar over the town roofs with such magnificence that the few people passing by at this hour will take you for a Pegasus."

Rience made an abrupt gesture and something glistened in his hand.

"Are you sure," he asked, "you'll have time to call her?"

Dandilion had no intention of checking if he would have time. Nor did he intend to wait. Before the stiletto had locked in Rience's hand Dandilion had taken a long leap to the corner of the room, dived under the nymph tapestry, kicked open a secret door and rushed headlong down the winding stairs, nimbly steering himself with the aid of the well-worn banisters. Rience darted after him, but the poet was sure of himself – he knew the secret passage like the back of his hand, having used it numerous times to flee creditors, jealous husbands and furious rivals from whom he had, from time to time, stolen rhymes and tunes. He knew that after the third turning he would be able to grope for a revolving door, behind which there was a ladder leading down to the cellar. He was sure that his persecutor would be unable to stop in time, would run on and step on a trapdoor through which he would fall and land in the pigsty. He was equally sure that – bruised, covered in shit and mauled by the pigs – his persecutor would give up the chase.

Dandilion was mistaken, as was usually the case whenever he was too confident. Something flashed a sudden blue behind his back and the poet felt his limbs grow numb, lifeless and stiff. He couldn't slow down for the revolving door, his legs wouldn't obey him. He yelled and rolled down the stairs, bumping against the walls of the little corridor. The trapdoor opened beneath him with a dry crack and the troubadour tumbled down into the darkness and stench. Before thumping his head on the dirt floor and losing consciousness, he remembered Mama Lantieri saying something about the pigsty being repaired.

The pain in his constricted wrists and shoulders, cruelly twisted in their joints, brought him back to his senses. He wanted to scream but couldn't; it felt as though his mouth had been stuck up with clay. He was kneeling on the dirt floor with a creaking rope hauling him up by his wrists. He tried to stand, wanting to ease the pressure on his shoulders, but his legs, too, were tied together. Choking and suffocating he somehow struggled to his feet, helped considerably by the rope which tugged mercilessly at him.

Rience was standing in front of him and his evil eyes glinted in the light of a lantern held aloft by an unshaven ruffian who stood over six feet tall. Another ruffian, probably no shorter, stood behind him. Dandilion could hear his breathing and caught a whiff of stale sweat. It was the reeking man who tugged on the rope looped over a roof beam and fastened to the poet's wrists.

Dandilion's feet tore off the dirt floor. The poet whistled through his nose, unable to do anything more.

"Enough," Rience snapped at last – he spoke almost immediately, yet it had seemed an age to Dandilion. The bard's feet touched the ground but, despite his most heartfelt desire, he could not kneel again – the tight drawn rope was still holding him as taut as a string.

Rience came closer. There was not even a trace of emotion on his face; the damp eyes had not changed their expression in the least. His tone of voice, too, remained calm, quiet, even a little bored.

"You nasty rhymester. You runt. You scum. You arrogant nobody. You tried to run from me? No one has escaped me yet. We haven't finished our conversation, you clown, you sheep's head. I asked you a question under much pleasanter circumstances than these. Now you are going to answer all my questions, and in far less pleasant circumstances. Am I right?"

Dandilion nodded eagerly. Only now did Rience smile and make a sign. The bard squealed helplessly, feeling the rope tighten and his arms, twisted backwards, cracking in their joints.

"You can't talk," Rience confirmed, still smiling loathsomely; "and it hurts, doesn't it? For the moment, you should know I'm having you strung up like this for my own pleasure – just because I love watching people suffer. Go on, just a little higher."

Dandilion was wheezing so hard he almost choked.

"Enough," Rience finally ordered, then approached the poet and grabbed him by his shirt ruffles. "Listen to me, you little cock. I'm going to lift the spell so you can talk. But if you try to raise your charming voice any louder than necessary, you'll be sorry."

He made a gesture with his hand, touched the poet's cheek with his ring and Dandilion felt sensation return to his jaw, tongue and palate.

"Now," Rience continued quietly, "I am going to ask you a few questions and you are going to answer them quickly, fluently and comprehensively. And if you stammer or hesitate even for a moment, if you give me the slightest reason to doubt the truth of your words, then . . . Look down."

Dandilion obeyed. He discovered to his horror that a short rope had been tied to the knots around his ankles, with a bucket full of lime attached to the other end.

"If I have you pulled any higher," Rience smiled cruelly, "and this bucket lifts with you, then you will probably never regain the feeling in your hands. After that, I doubt you will be capable of playing anything on a lute. I really doubt it. So I think you'll talk to me. Am I right?"

Dandilion didn't agree because he couldn't move his head or find his voice out of sheer fright. But Rience did not seem to require confirmation.

"It is to be understood," he stated, "that I will know immediately if you are telling the truth, if you try to trick me I will realise straight away, and I won't be fooled by any poetic ploys or vague erudition. This is a trifle for me – just as paralysing you on the stairs was a trifle. So I advise you to weigh each word with care, you piece of scum. So, let's get on with it and stop wasting time. As you know, I'm interested in the heroine of one of your beautiful ballads, Queen Calanthe of Cintra's granddaughter, Princess

Cirilla, endearingly known as Ciri. According to eye-witnesses this little person died during the siege of the town, two years ago. Whereas in your ballad you so vividly and touchingly described her meeting a strange, almost legendary individual, the . . . witcher . . . Geralt, or Gerald. Leaving the poetic drivel about destiny and the decrees of fate aside, from the rest of the ballad it seems the child survived the Battle of Cintra in one piece. Is that true?"

"I don't know . . ." moaned Dandilion. "By all the gods, I'm only a poet! I've heard this and that, and the rest . . ."

"Well?"

"The rest I invented. Made it up! I don't know anything!" The bard howled on seeing Rience give a sign to the reeking man and feeling the rope tighten. "I'm not lying!"

"True." Rience nodded. "You're not lying outright, I would have sensed it. But you are beating about the bush. You wouldn't have thought the ballad up just like that, not without reason. And you do know the witcher, after all. You have often been seen in his company. So talk, Dandilion, if you treasure your joints. Everything you know."

"This Ciri," panted the poet, "was destined for the witcher. She's a so-called Child Surprise . . . You must have heard it, the story's well known. Her parents swore to hand her over to the witcher—"

"Her parents are supposed to have handed the child over to that crazed mutant? That murderous mercenary? You're lying, rhymester. Keep such tales for women."

"That's what happened, I swear on my mother's soul,"

sobbed Dandilion. "I have it from a reliable source . . . The witcher—"

"Talk about the girl. For the moment I'm not interested in the witcher."

"I don't know anything about the girl! I only know that the witcher was going to fetch her from Cintra when the war broke out. I met him at the time. He heard about the massacre, about Calanthe's death, from me . . . He asked me about the child, the queen's granddaughter . . . But I knew everyone in Cintra was killed, not a single soul in the last bastion survived—"

"Go on. Fewer metaphors, more hard facts!"

"When the witcher learned of the massacre and fall of Cintra he forsook his journey. We both escaped north. We parted ways in Hengfors and I haven't seen him since . . . But because he talked, on the way, a bit about this . . . Ciri, or whatever-her-name-is . . . and about destiny . . . Well, I made up this ballad. I don't know any more, I swear!"

Rience scowled at him.

"And where is this witcher now?" he asked. "This hired monster murderer, this poetic butcher who likes to discuss destiny?"

"I told you, the last time I saw him—"

"I know what you said," Rience interrupted. "I listened carefully to what you said. And now you're going to listen carefully to me. Answer my questions precisely. The question is: if no one has seen Geralt, or Gerald, the Witcher for over a year, where is he hiding? Where does he usually hide?"

"I don't know where it is," the troubadour said quickly. "I'm not lying. I really don't know—"

"Too quick, Dandilion, too quick." Rience smiled ominously. "Too eager. You are cunning but not careful enough. You don't know where it is, you say. But I warrant you know what it is."

Dandilion clenched his teeth with anger and despair.

"Well?" Rience made a sign to the reeking man. "Where is the witcher hiding? What is the place called?"

The poet remained silent. The rope tightened, twisting his hands painfully, and his feet left the ground. Dandilion let out a howl, brief and broken because Rience's wizardly ring immediately gagged him.

"Higher, higher." Rience rested his hands on his hips. "You know, Dandilion, I could use magic to sound out your mind, but it's exhausting. Besides, I like seeing people's eyes pop out of their sockets from pain. And you're going to tell me anyway."

Dandilion knew he would. The rope secured to his ankles grew taut, the bucket of lime scraped along the ground.

"Sir," said the first ruffian suddenly, covering the lantern with his cloak and peering through the gap in the pigsty door, "someone's coming. A lass, I think."

"You know what to do," Rience hissed. "Put the lantern out."

The reeking man released the rope and Dandilion tumbled inertly to the ground, falling in such a way that he could see the man with the lantern standing at the door and the reeking man, a long knife in his hand, lying in wait on the other side. Light broke in from the bawdy-house through gaps in the planks, and the poet heard the singing and hubbub.

The door to the pigsty creaked open revealing a short

figure wrapped in a cloak and wearing a round, tightly fitting cap. After a moment's hesitation, the woman crossed the threshold. The reeking man threw himself at her, slashing forcefully with his knife, and tumbled to his knees as the knife met with no resistance, passing through the figure's throat as though through a cloud of smoke. Because the figure really was a cloud of smoke – one which was already starting to disperse. But before it completely vanished another figure burst into the pigsty, indistinct, dark and nimble as a weasel. Dandilion saw it throw a cloak at the lantern man, jump over the reeking one, saw something glisten in its hand, and heard the reeking man wheeze and choke savagely. The lantern man disentangled himself from the cloak, jumped, took a swing with his knife. A fiery lightning bolt shot from the dark figure with a hiss, slapped over the tough's face and chest with a crack and spread over him like flaming oil. The ruffian screamed piercingly and the grim reek of burning meat filled the pigsty.

Then Rience attacked. The spell he cast illuminated the darkness with a bluish flash in which Dandilion saw a slender woman wearing man's clothes gesticulating strangely with both hands. He only glimpsed her for a second before the blue glow disappeared with a bang and a blinding flash. Rience fell back with a roar of fury and collapsed onto the wooden pigsty walls, breaking them with a crash. The woman dressed in man's clothing leapt after him, a stiletto flashing in her hand. The pigsty filled with brightness again – this time golden – beaming from a bright oval which suddenly appeared in the air. Dandilion saw Rience spring up from the dusty floor, leap into the oval and immediately disappear. The oval dimmed but, before it went out entirely, the woman ran up to it shouting incomprehensibly, stretching out her hand. Something crackled and rustled and the dying oval boiled with roaring flames for a moment. A muffled sound, as if coming from a great distance, reached Dandilion's ears – a sound very much like a scream of pain. The oval went out completely and darkness engulfed the pigsty again. The poet felt the power which gagged him disappear.

"Help!" he howled. "Help!"

"Stop yelling, Dandilion," said the woman, kneeling next to him and slicing through the knots with Rience's stiletto.

"Yennefer? Is that you?"

"Surely you're not going to say you don't remember how I look. And I'm sure my voice is not unfamiliar to your musical ear. Can you get up? They didn't break any bones, did they?"

Dandilion stood with difficulty, groaned and stretched his aching shoulders.

"What's with them?" He indicated the bodies lying on the ground.

"We'll check." The enchantress snicked the stiletto shut. "One of them should still be alive. I've a few questions for him."

"This one," the troubadour stood over the reeking man, "probably still lives."

"I doubt it," said Yennefer indifferently. "I severed his windpipe and carotid artery. There might still be a little murmur in him but not for long."

Dandilion shuddered.

"You slashed his throat?"

"If, out of inborn caution, I hadn't sent an illusion in

first, I would be the one lying there now. Let's look at the other one . . . Bloody hell. Such a sturdy fellow and he still couldn't take it. Pity, pity—"

"He's dead, too?"

"He couldn't take the shock. Hmm . . . I fried him a little too hard . . . See, even his teeth are charred— What's the matter with you, Dandilion? Are you going to be sick?"

"I am," the poet replied indistinctly, bending over and leaning his forehead against the pigsty wall.

"That's everything?" The enchantress put her tumbler down and reached for the skewer of roast chickens. "You haven't lied about anything? Haven't forgotten anything?"

"Nothing. Apart from 'thank you'. Thank you, Yennefer."

She looked him in the eyes and nodded her head lightly, making her glistening, black curls writhe and cascade down to her shoulders. She slipped the roast chicken onto a trencher and began dividing it skilfully. She used a knife and fork. Dandilion had only known one person, up until then, who could eat a chicken with a knife and fork as skilfully. Now he knew how, and from whom, Geralt had learnt the knack. *Well*, he thought, *no wonder. After all, he did live with her for a year in Vengerberg and before he left her, she had instilled a number of strange things into him*. He pulled the other chicken from the skewer and, without a second thought, ripped off a thigh and began eating it, pointedly holding it with both hands.

"How did you know?" he asked. "How did you arrive with help on time?"

"I was beneath Bleobheris during your performance."

"I didn't see you."

"I didn't want to be seen. Then I followed you into town. I waited here, in the tavern – it wasn't fitting, after all, for me to follow you in to that haven of dubious delight and certain gonorrhoea. But I eventually became impatient and was wandering around the yard when I thought I heard voices coming from the pigsty. I sharpened my hearing and it turned out it wasn't, as I'd first thought, some sodomite but you. Hey, innkeeper! More wine, if you please!"

"At your command, honoured lady! Quick as a flash!"

"The same as before, please, but this time without the water. I can only tolerate water in a bath, in wine I find it quite loathsome."

"At your service, at your service!"

Yennefer pushed her plate aside. There was still enough meat on the chicken, Dandilion noticed, to feed the innkeeper and his family for breakfast. A knife and fork were certainly elegant and refined, but they weren't very effective.

"Thank you," he repeated, "for rescuing me. That cursed Rience wouldn't have spared my life. He'd have squeezed everything from me and then butchered me like a sheep."

"Yes, I think he would." She poured herself and the bard some wine then raised her tumbler. "So let's drink to your rescue and health, Dandilion."

"And to yours, Yennefer," he toasted her in return. "To health for which – as of today – I shall pray whenever the occasion arises. I'm indebted to you, beautiful lady, and I shall repay the debt in my songs. I shall explode the myth which claims wizards are insensitive to the pain of others, that they are rarely eager to help poor, unfortunate, unfamiliar mortals."

"What to do." She smiled, half-shutting her beautiful violet eyes. "The myth has some justification; it did not spring from nowhere. But you're not a stranger, Dandilion. I know you and like you."

"Really?" The poet smiled too. "You have been good at concealing it up until now. I've even heard the rumour that you can't stand me, I quote, any more than the plague."

"It was the case once." The enchantress suddenly grew serious. "Later my opinion changed. Later, I was grateful to you."

"What for, if I may ask?"

"Never mind," she said, toying with the empty tumbler. "Let us get back to more important questions. Those you were asked in the pigsty while your arms were being twisted out of their sockets. What really happened, Dandilion? Have you really not seen Geralt since you fled the banks of the Yaruga? Did you really not know he returned south after the war? That he was seriously wounded – so seriously there were even rumours of his death? Didn't you know anything?"

"No. I didn't. I stayed in Pont Vanis for a long time, in Esterad Thyssen's court. And then at Niedamir's in Hengfors—"

"You didn't know." The enchantress nodded and unfastened her tunic. A black velvet ribbon wound around her neck, an obsidian star set with diamonds hanging from it. "You didn't know that when his wounds healed

Geralt went to Transriver? You can't guess who he was looking for?"

"That I can. But I don't know if he found her."

"You don't know," she repeated. "You, who usually know everything, and then sing about everything. Even such intimate matters as someone else's feelings. I listened to your ballads beneath Bleobheris, Dandilion. You dedicated a good few verses to me."

"Poetry," he muttered, staring at the chicken, "has its rights. No one should be offended—"

"'Hair like a raven's wing, as a storm in the night . . .'" quoted Yennefer with exaggerated emphasis, " '. . . and in the violet eyes sleep lightning bolts . . .' Isn't that how it went?"

"That's how I remembered you." The poet smiled faintly. "May the first who wishes to claim the description is untrue throw the first stone."

"Only I don't know," the Enchantress pinched her lips together, "who gave you permission to describe my internal organs. How did it go? 'Her heart, as though a jewel, adorned her neck. Hard as if of diamond made, and as a diamond so unfeeling, sharper than obsidian, cutting—' Did you make that up yourself? Or perhaps . . . ?"

Her lips quivered, twisted.

". . . or perhaps you listened to someone's confidences and grievances?"

"Hmm . . ." Dandilion cleared his throat and veered away from the dangerous subject. "Tell me, Yennefer, when did you last see Geralt?"

"A long time ago."

"After the war?"

"After the war . . ." Yennefer's voice changed a little.

"No, I never saw him after the war. For a long time . . . I didn't see anybody. Well, back to the point, Poet. I am a little surprised to discover that you do not know anything, you have not heard anything and that, in spite of this, someone searching for information picked you out to stretch over a beam. Doesn't that worry you?"

"It does."

"Listen to me," she said sharply, banging her tumbler against the table. "Listen carefully. Strike that ballad from your repertoire. Do not sing it again."

"Are you talking about—"

"You know perfectly well what I'm talking about. Sing about the war against Nilfgaard. Sing about Geralt and me, you'll neither harm nor help anyone in the process, you'll make nothing any better or worse. But do not sing about the Lion Cub of Cintra."

She glanced around to check if any of the few customers at this hour were eavesdropping, and waited until the lass clearing up had returned to the kitchen.

"And do try to avoid one-to-one meetings with people you don't know," she said quietly. "People who 'forget' to introduce themselves by conveying greetings from a mutual acquaintance. Understand?"

He looked at her surprised. Yennefer smiled.

"Greetings from Dijkstra, Dandilion."

Now the bard glanced around timidly. His astonishment must have been evident and his expression amusing because the sorceress allowed herself a quite derisive grimace.

"While we are on the subject," she whispered, leaning across the table, "Dijkstra is asking for a report. You're on your way back from Verden and he's interested in hearing what's being said at King Ervyll's court. He asked me to convey that this time your report should be to the point, detailed and under no circumstances in verse. Prose, Dandilion. Prose."

The poet swallowed and nodded. He remained silent, pondering the question.

But the enchantress anticipated him. "Difficult times are approaching," she said quietly. "Difficult and dangerous. A time of change is coming. It would be a shame to grow old with the uncomfortable conviction that one had done nothing to ensure that these changes are for the better. Don't you agree?"

He agreed with a nod and cleared his throat. "Yennefer?"

"I'm listening, Poet."

"Those men in the pigsty . . . I would like to know who they were, what they wanted, who sent them. You killed them both, but rumour has it that you can draw information even from the dead."

"And doesn't rumour also have it that necromancy is forbidden, by edict of the Chapter? Let it go, Dandilion. Those thugs probably didn't know much anyway. The one who escaped . . . Hmm . . . He's another matter."

"Rience. He was a wizard, wasn't he?"

"Yes. But not a very proficient one."

"Yet he managed to escape from you. I saw how he did it – he teleported, didn't he? Doesn't that prove anything?"

"Indeed it does. That someone helped him. Rience had neither the time nor the strength to open an oval portal suspended in the air. A portal like that is no joke. It's clear that someone else opened it. Someone far more powerful.

That's why I was afraid to chase him, not knowing where I would land. But I sent some pretty hot stuff after him. He's going to need a lot of spells and some effective burn elixirs, and will remain marked for some time."

"Maybe you will be interested to hear that he was a Nilfgaardian."

"You think so?" Yennefer sat up and with a swift movement pulled the stiletto from her pocket and turned it in her palm. "A lot of people carry Nilfgaardian knives now. They're comfortable and handy – they can even be hidden in a cleavage—"

"It's not the knife. When he was questioning me he used the term 'battle for Cintra', 'conquest of the town' or something along those lines. I've never heard anyone describe those events like that. For us, it has always been a massacre. The Massacre of Cintra. No one refers to it by any other name."

The magician raised her hand, scrutinised her nails. "Clever, Dandilion. You have a sensitive ear."

"It's a professional hazard."

"I wonder which profession you have in mind?" She smiled coquettishly. "But thank you for the information. It was valuable."

"Let it be," he replied with a smile, "my contribution to making changes for the better. Tell me, Yennefer, why is Nilfgaard so interested in Geralt and the girl from Cintra?"

"Don't stick your nose into that business." She suddenly turned serious. "I said you were to forget you ever heard of Calanthe's granddaughter."

"Indeed, you did. But I'm not searching for a subject for a ballad."

"What the hell are you searching for then? Trouble?"

"Let's take it," he said quietly, resting his chin on his clasped hands and looking the enchantress in the eye. "Let's take it that Geralt did, in fact, find and rescue the child. Let's take it that he finally came to believe in the power of destiny, and took the child with him. Where to? Rience tried to force it out of me with torture. But you know, Yennefer. You know where the witcher is hiding."

"I do."

"And you know how to get there."

"I know that too."

"Don't you think he should be warned? Warned that the likes of Rience are looking for him and the little girl? I would go, but I honestly don't know where it is . . . That place whose name I prefer not to say . . ."

"Get to the point, Dandilion."

"If you know where Geralt is, you ought to go and warn him. You owe him that, Yennefer. There was, after all, something between you."

"Yes," she acknowledged coldly. "There was something between us. That's why I know him a bit. He does not like having help imposed on him. And if he was in need of it he would seek it from those he could trust. A year has gone by since those events and I . . . I've not had any news from him. And as for our debt, I owe him exactly as much as he owes me. No more and no less."

"So I'll go then." He raised his head high. "Tell me—"

"I won't," she interrupted. "Your cover's blown, Dandilion. They might come after you again; the less you know the better. Vanish from here. Go to Redania, to

Dijkstra and Philippa Eilhart, stick to Vizimir's court. And I warn you once more: forget the Lion Cub of Cintra. Forget about Ciri. Pretend you have never heard the name. Do as I ask. I wouldn't like anything bad to happen to you. I like you too much, owe you too much—"

"You've said that already. What do you owe me, Yennefer?"

The sorceress turned her head away, did not say anything for a while.

"You travelled with him," she said finally. "Thanks to you he was not alone. You were a friend to him. You were with him."

The bard lowered his eyes.

"He didn't get much from it," he muttered. "He didn't get much from our friendship. He had little but trouble because of me. He constantly had to get me out of some scrape . . . help me . . ."

She leaned across the table, put her hand on his and squeezed it hard without saying anything. Her eyes held regret.

"Go to Redania," she repeated after a moment. "To Tretogor. Stay in Dijkstra's and Philippa's care. Don't play at being a hero. You have got yourself mixed up in a dangerous affair, Dandilion."

"I've noticed." He grimaced and rubbed his aching shoulder. "And that is precisely why I believe Geralt should be warned. You are the only one who knows where to look for him. You know the way. I guess you used to be . . . a guest there . . . ?"

Yennefer turned away. Dandilion saw her lips pinch, the muscles in her cheek quiver.

"Yes, in the past," she said and there was something

elusive and strange in her voice. "I used to be a guest there, sometimes. But never uninvited."

The wind howled savagely, rippling through the grasses growing over the ruins, rustling in the hawthorn bushes and tall nettles. Clouds sped across the sphere of the moon, momentarily illuminating the great castle, drenching the moat and few remaining walls in a pale glow undulating with shadows, and revealing mounds of skulls baring their broken teeth and staring into nothingness through the black holes of their eye-sockets. Ciri squealed sharply and hid her face in the witcher's cloak.

The mare, prodded on by the witcher's heels, carefully stepped over a pile of bricks and passed through the broken arcade. Her horseshoes, ringing against the flagstones, awoke weird echoes between the walls, muffled by the howling gale. Ciri trembled, digging her hands into the horse's mane.

"I'm frightened," she whispered.

"There's nothing to be frightened of," replied the witcher, laying his hand on her shoulder. "It's hard to find a safer place in the whole world. This is Kaer Morhen, the Witchers' Keep. There used to be a beautiful castle here. A long time ago."

She did not reply, bowing her head low. The witcher's mare, called Roach, snorted quietly, as if she too wanted to reassure the girl.

They immersed themselves in a dark abyss, in a long, unending black tunnel dotted with columns and arcades. Roach stepped confidently and willingly, ignoring the impenetrable darkness, and her horseshoes rang brightly against the floor.

In front of them, at the end of the tunnel, a straight, vertical line suddenly flared with a red light. Growing taller and wider it became a door beyond which was a faint glow, the flickering brightness of torches stuck in iron mounts on the walls. A black figure stood framed in the door, blurred by the brightness.

"Who comes?" Ciri heard a menacing, metallic voice which sounded like a dog's bark. "Geralt?"

"Yes, Eskel. It's me."

"Come in."

The witcher dismounted, took Ciri from the saddle, stood her on the ground and pressed a bundle into her little hands which she grabbed tightly, only regretting that it was too small for her to hide behind completely.

"Wait here with Eskel," he said. "I'll take Roach to the stables."

"Come into the light, laddie," growled the man called Eskel. "Don't lurk in the dark."

Ciri looked up into his face and barely restrained her frightened scream. He wasn't human. Although he stood on two legs, although he smelled of sweat and smoke, although he wore ordinary human clothes, he was not human. *No human can have a face like that*, she thought.

"Well, what are you waiting for?" repeated Eskel.

She didn't move. In the darkness she heard the clatter of Roach's horseshoes grow fainter. Something soft and squeaking ran over her foot. She jumped.

"Don't loiter in the dark, or the rats will eat your boots."

Still clinging to her bundle Ciri moved briskly towards

the light. The rats bolted out from beneath her feet with a squeak. Eskel leaned over, took the package from her and pulled back her hood.

"A plague on it," he muttered. "A girl. That's all we need."

She glanced at him, frightened. Eskel was smiling. She saw that he was human after all, that he had an entirely human face, deformed by a long, ugly, semi-circular scar running from the corner of his mouth across the length of his cheek up to the ear.

"Since you're here, welcome to Kaer Morhen," he said. "What do they call you?"

"Ciri," Geralt replied for her, silently emerging from the darkness. Eskel turned around. Suddenly, quickly, wordlessly, the witchers fell into each other's arms and wound their shoulders around each other tight and hard. For one brief moment.

"Wolf, you're alive."

"I am."

"All right." Eskel took a torch from its bracket. "Come on. I'm closing the inner gates to stop the heat escaping."

They walked along the corridor. There were rats here, too; they flitted under the walls, squeaked from the dark abyss, from the branching passages, and skittered before the swaying circle of light thrown by the torch. Ciri walked quickly, trying to keep up with the men.

"Who's wintering here, Eskel? Apart from Vesemir?"

"Lambert and Coën."

They descended a steep and slippery flight of stairs. A gleam was visible below them. Ciri heard voices, detected the smell of smoke.

The hall was enormous, and flooded with light from a huge hearth roaring with flames which were being sucked up into the heart of the chimney. The centre of the hall was taken up by an enormous, heavy table. At least ten people could sit around that table. There were three. Three humans. Three witchers, Ciri corrected herself. She saw nothing but their silhouettes against the fire in the hearth.

"Greetings, Wolf. We've been waiting for you."

"Greetings, Vesemir. Greetings, lads. It's good to be home again."

"Who have you brought us?"

Geralt was silent for a moment, then put his hand on Ciri's shoulder and lightly pushed her forward. She walked awkwardly, hesitantly, huddled up and hunched, her head lowered. *I'm frightened*, she thought. *I'm very frightened. When Geralt found me, when he took me with him, I thought the fear wouldn't come back. I thought it had passed . . . And now, instead of being at home, I'm in this terrible, dark, ruined old castle full of rats and dreadful echoes . . . I'm standing in front of a red wall of fire again. I see sinister black figures, I see dreadful, menacing, glistening eyes staring at me—*

"Who is this child, Wolf? Who is this girl?"

"She's my . . ." Geralt suddenly stammered. She felt his strong, hard hands on her shoulders. And suddenly the fear disappeared, vanished without a trace. The roaring red fire gave out warmth. Only warmth. The black silhouettes were the silhouettes of friends. Carers. Their glistening eyes expressed curiosity. Concern. And unease . . .

Geralt's hands clenched over her shoulders.

"She's our destiny."

Verily, there is nothing so hideous as the monsters, so contrary to nature, known as witchers for they are the offspring of foul sorcery and devilry. They are rogues without virtue, conscience or scruple, true diabolic creations, fit only for killing. There is no place amidst honest men for such as they.

And Kaer Morhen, where these infamous beings nestle, where they perform their foul practices, must be wiped from the surface of this earth, and all trace of it strewn with salt and saltpetre.

Anonymous, *Monstrum*, or *Description of the Witcher*

Intolerance and superstition has always been the domain of the more stupid amongst the common folk and, I conjecture, will never be uprooted, for they are as eternal as stupidity itself. There, where mountains tower today, one day there will be seas; there where today seas surge, will one day be deserts. But stupidity will remain stupidity.

Nicodemus de Boot, *Meditations on life,*
Happiness and Prosperity

CHAPTER TWO

Triss Merigold blew into her frozen hands, wriggled her fingers and murmured a magic formula. Her horse, a gelding, immediately reacted to the spell, snorting and turning its head, looking at the enchantress with eyes made watery by the cold and wind.

"You've got two options, old thing," said Triss, pulling on her gloves. "Either you get used to magic or I sell you to some peasants to pull a plough."

The gelding pricked up its ears, snorted vapour through its nostrils and obediently started down the wooded mountainside. The magician leaned over in the saddle, avoiding being lashed by the frosty branches.

The magic worked quickly; she stopped feeling the sting of cold in her elbows and on her neck, and the unpleasant sensation of cold which had made her hunch her shoulders and draw her head in disappeared. The spell, warming her, also muffled the hunger which had been eating at her for several hours. Triss cheered up, made herself comfortable in the saddle and, with greater attention than before, started to take stock of her surroundings.

Ever since she had left the beaten track, she had been guided by the greyish-white wall of mountains and their snow-capped summits which glistened gold in those rare moments when the sun pierced the clouds – usually in the morning or just before sunset. Now that she was closer to the mountain chain she had to take greater care. The land around Kaer Morhen was famous for its wildness and inaccessibility, and the gap in the granite wall that was a vital landmark was not easy for an inexperienced eye to find. It was enough to turn down one of the numerous gullies and gorges to lose sight of it. And even she who knew the land, knew the way and knew where to look for the pass, could not allow herself to lose her concentration for an instant.

The forest came to an end. A wide valley opened before the enchantress, strewn with boulders which ran across the valley to the sheer mountain-slope on the other side. The Gwenllech, the River of White Stones, flowed down the heart of the valley, foam seething between the boulders and logs washed along by the current. Here, in its upper reaches, the Gwenllech was no more than a wide but shallow stream. Up here it could be crossed without any difficulty. Lower down, in Kaedwen, in its middle reaches, the river was an insurmountable obstacle, rushing and breaking against the beds of its deep chasms.

The gelding, driven into the water, hastened its step, clearly wanting to reach the opposite bank as quickly as possible. Triss held it back lightly – the stream was shallow, reaching just above the horse's fetlocks, but the pebbles covering the bed were slippery and the current was sharp and quick. The water churned and foamed around her mount's legs.

The magician looked up at the sky. The growing cold and increasing wind here, in the mountains, could herald a blizzard and she did not find the prospect of spending yet another night in a grotto or rocky nook too attractive. She could, if she had to, continue her journey even through a blizzard; she could locate the path using telepathy, she could – using magic – make herself insensitive to the cold. She could, if she had to. But she preferred not to have to.

Luckily, Kaer Morhen was already close. Triss urged the gelding on to flat scree, over an enormous heap of stones washed down by glaciers and streams, and rode into a narrow pass between rocky outcrops. The gorge walls rose vertically and seemed to meet high above her, only divided by a narrow line of sky. It grew warmer, the wind howling above the rocks could no longer reach to lash and sting at her.

The pass broadened, leading through a ravine and then into the valley, opening onto a huge depression, covered by forest, which stretched out amidst jagged boulders. The magician ignored the gentle, accessible depression rim and rode down towards the forest, into the thick backwoods. Dry branches cracked under the gelding's hooves. Forced to step over fallen tree trunks, the horse snorted, danced and stamped. Triss pulled at the reins, tugged at her mount's shaggy ear and scolded it harshly with spiteful allusions to its lameness. The steed, looking for all the world as though it were ashamed of itself, walked with a more even and sprightly gait and picked its way through the thicket.

Before long they emerged onto clearer land, riding along the trough of a stream which barely trickled along the ravine bed. The magician looked around carefully, finally finding what she was looking for. Over the gully, supported horizontally by enormous boulders, lay a mighty tree trunk, dark, bare and turning green with moss. Triss rode closer, wanting to make sure this was, indeed, the Trail and not a tree accidentally felled in a gale. But she spied a narrow, indistinct pathway disappearing into the woods. She could not be mistaken – this was definitely the Trail, a path encircling the old castle of Kaer Morhen and beset with obstacles, where witchers trained to improve their running speeds and controlled breathing. The path was known as the Trail, but Triss knew young witchers had given it their own name: The Killer.

She clung to the horse's neck and slowly rode under the trunk. At that moment, she heard stones grating. And the fast, light footsteps of someone running.

She turned in her saddle, pulled on the reins and waited for the witcher to run out onto the log.

A witcher did run out onto the log, flitted along it like an arrow without slowing down, without even using his arms to aid his balance – running nimbly, fluently, with incredible grace. He flashed by, approaching and disappearing amongst the trees without disturbing a single branch. Triss sighed loudly, shaking her head in disbelief.

Because the witcher, judging by his height and build, was only about twelve.

The magician eased the reins, nudged the horse with her heels and trotted upstream. She knew the Trail cut across the ravine once more, at a spot known as the Gullet. She wanted to catch a glimpse of the little witcher once again – children had not been trained in Kaer Morhen for near to a quarter of a century.

She was not in a great hurry. The narrow Killer path meandered and looped its way through the forest and, in order to master it, the little witcher would take far longer than she would, following the shortcut. However, she could not loiter either. Beyond the Gullet, the Trail turned into the woods and led straight to the fortress. If she did not catch the boy at the precipice, she might not see him at all. She had already visited Kaer Morhen a few times, and knew she saw only what the witchers wanted her to see. Triss was not so naïve as to be unaware that they wanted to show her only a tiny fraction of the things to be seen in Kaer Morhen.

After a few minutes riding along the stony trough of the stream she caught sight of the Gullet – a leap over the gully created by two huge mossy rocks, overgrown with gnarled, stunted trees. She released the reins. The horse snorted and lowered its head towards the water trickling between pebbles.

She did not have to wait long. The witcher's silhouette appeared on the rock and the boy jumped, not slowing his pace. The magician heard the soft smack of his landing and a moment later a rattle of stones, the dull thud of a fall and a quiet cry. Or rather, a squeal.

Triss instantly leaped from her saddle, threw the fur off her shoulders and dashed across the mountainside, pulling herself up using tree branches and roots. Momentum aided her climb until she slipped on the conifer needles and fell to her knees next to a figure huddled on the stones. The youngster, on seeing her, jumped up like a spring, backed away in a flash and nimbly grabbed the sword slung across his back – then tripped and collapsed between the junipers and pines. The magician did not rise from her knees; she stared at the boy and opened her mouth in surprise.

Because it was not a boy.

From beneath an ash-blonde fringe, poorly and un-evenly cut, enormous emerald eyes – the predominant features in a small face with a narrow chin and upturned nose – stared out at her. There was fear in the eyes.

"Don't be afraid," Triss said tentatively.

The girl opened her eyes even wider. She was hardly out of breath and did not appear to be sweating. It was clear she had already run the Killer more than once.

"Nothing's happened to you?"

The girl did not reply; instead she sprang up, hissed with pain, shifted her weight to her left leg, bent over and rubbed her knee. She was dressed in a sort of leather suit sewn together – or rather stuck together – in a way which would make any tailor who took pride in his craft howl in horror and despair. The only pieces of her equipment which seemed to be relatively new, and fitted her, were her knee-high boots, her belts and her sword. More pre-cisely, her little sword.

"Don't be afraid," repeated Triss, still not rising from her knees. "I heard your fall and was scared, that's why I rushed here—"

"I slipped," murmured the girl.

"Have you hurt yourself?"

"No. You?"

The enchantress laughed, tried to get up, winced and swore at the pain in her ankle. She sat down and carefully straightened her foot, swearing once more.

"Come here, little one, help me get up."

"I'm not little."

"If you say so. In that case, what are you?"

"A witcher!"

"Ha! So, come here and help me get up, witcher."

The girl did not move from the spot. She shifted her weight from foot to foot, and her hands, in their fingerless, woollen gloves, toyed with her sword belt as she glanced suspiciously at Triss.

"Have no fear," said the enchantress with a smile. "I'm not a bandit or outsider. I'm called Triss Merigold and I'm going to Kaer Morhen. The witchers know me. Don't gape at me. I respect your suspicion, but be reasonable. Would I have got this far if I hadn't known the way? Have you ever met a human on the Trail?"

The girl overcame her hesitation, approached and stretched out her hand. Triss stood with only a little assistance. Because she was not concerned with having help. She wanted a closer look at the girl. And to touch her.

The green eyes of the little witcher-girl betrayed no signs of mutation, and the touch of her little hand did not produce the slight, pleasant tingling sensation so characteristic of witchers. Although she ran the Killer path with a sword slung across her back, the ashen-haired girl had not been subjected to the Trial of Grasses or to Changes. Of that, Triss was certain.

"Show me your knee, little one."

"I'm not little."

"Sorry. But surely you have a name?"

"I do. I'm . . . Ciri."

"It's a pleasure. A bit closer if you please, Ciri."

"It's nothing."

"I want to see what 'nothing' looks like. Ah, that's what I thought. 'Nothing' looks remarkably like torn trousers and skin grazed down to raw flesh. Stand still and don't be scared."

"I'm not scared . . . Awww!"

The magician laughed and rubbed her palm, itching from casting the spell, against her hip. The girl bent over and gazed at her knee.

"Oooh," she said. "It doesn't hurt any more! And there's no hole . . . Was that magic?"

"You've guessed it."

"Are you a witch?"

"Guessed again. Although I prefer to be called an enchantress. To avoid getting it wrong you can call me by my name, Triss. Just Triss. Come on, Ciri. My horse is waiting at the bottom. We'll go to Kaer Morhen together."

"I ought to run." Ciri shook her head. "It's not good to stop running because you get milk in your muscles. Geralt says—"

"Geralt is at the keep?"

Ciri frowned, pinched her lips together and shot a glance at the enchantress from beneath her ashen fringe. Triss chuckled again.

"All right," she said. "I won't ask. A secret's a secret, and you're right not to disclose it to someone you hardly know. Come on. When we get there we'll see who's at the castle and who isn't. And don't worry about your muscles – I know what to do about lactic acid. Ah, here's my mount. I'll help you . . ."

She stretched out her hand, but Ciri didn't need any help. She jumped agilely into the saddle, lightly, almost without taking off. The gelding started, surprised, and stamped, but the girl quickly took up the reins and reassured it.

"You know how to handle a horse, I see."

"I can handle anything."

"Move up towards the pommel." Triss slipped her foot into the stirrup and caught hold of the mane. "Make a bit of room for me. And don't poke my eye out with that sword."

The gelding, spurred on by her heels, moved off along the stream bed at a walking pace. They rode across another gully and climbed the rounded mountainside. From there they could see the ruins of Kaer Morhen huddled against the stone precipices – the partially demolished trapezium of the defensive wall, the remains of the barbican and gate, the thick, blunt column of the donjon.

The gelding snorted and jerked its head, crossing what remained of the bridge over the moat. Triss tugged at the reins. The decaying skulls and skeletons strewn across the river bed made no impression on her. She had seen them before.

"I don't like this," the girl suddenly remarked. "It's not as it should be. The dead should to be buried in the ground. Under a barrow. Shouldn't they?"

"They should," the magician agreed calmly. "I think so, too. But the witchers treat this graveyard as a . . . reminder."

"Reminder of what?"

"Kaer Morhen," Triss said as she guided the horse towards the shattered arcades, "was assaulted. There was a bloody battle here in which almost all the witchers died. Only those who weren't in the keep at the time survived."

"Who attacked them? And why?"

"I don't know," she lied. "It was a terribly long time ago, Ciri. Ask the witchers about it."

"I have," grunted the girl. "But they didn't want to tell me."

I can understand that, thought the magician. *A child trained to be a witcher, a girl, at that, who has not undergone the mutations, should not be told such things. A child like that should not hear about the massacre. A child like that should not be terrified by the prospect that they too may one day hear words describing it like those which were screamed by the fanatics who marched on Kaer Morhen long ago. Mutant. Monster. Freak. Damned by the gods, a creature contrary to nature. No, I do not blame the witchers for not telling you about it, little Ciri. And I shan't tell you either. I have even more reason to be silent. Because I am a wizard, and without the aid of wizards those fanatics would never have conquered the castle. And that hideous lampoon, that widely distributed* Monstrum *which stirred the fanatics up and drove them to such wickedness was also, apparently, some wizard's anonymous work. But I, little Ciri, do not recognise collective responsibility, I do not feel the need to expiate the events which took place half a century before my birth. And the skeletons which are meant to serve as an eternal reminder will ultimately rot away completely, disintegrate into dust and be forgotten, will disappear with the wind which constantly whips the mountainside . . .*

"They don't want to lie like that," said Ciri suddenly. "They don't want to be a symbol, a bad conscience or a warning. But neither do they want their dust to be swept away by the wind."

Triss raised her head, hearing a change in the girl's voice. Immediately she sensed a magical aura, a pulsating and a rush of blood in her temples. She grew tense but did not utter a word, afraid of breaking into or disrupting what was happening.

"An ordinary barrow." Ciri's voice was becoming more and more unnatural, metallic, cold and menacing. "A mound of earth which will be overgrown with nettles. Death has cold blue eyes, and the height of the obelisk does not matter, nor does the writing engraved on it matter. Who can know that better than you, Triss Merigold, the Fourteenth One of the Hill?"

The enchantress froze. She saw the girl's hands clench the horse's mane.

"You died on the Hill, Triss Merigold." The strange, evil voice spoke again. "Why have you come here? Go back, go back at once and take this child, the Child of Elder Blood, with you. Return her to those to whom she belongs. Do this, Fourteenth One. Because if you do not you will die once more. The day will come when the Hill will claim you. The mass grave, and the obelisk on which your name is engraved, will claim you."

The gelding neighed loudly, tossing its head. Ciri jerked suddenly, shuddered.

"What happened?" asked Triss, trying to control her voice.

Ciri coughed, passed both hands through her hair and rubbed her face.

"Nn . . . nothing . . ." she muttered hesitantly. "I'm tired, that's why . . . That's why I fell asleep. I ought to run . . ."

The magical aura disappeared. Triss experienced a

sudden cold wave sweeping through her entire body. She tried to convince herself it was the effect of the defensive spell dying away, but she knew that wasn't true. She glanced up at the stone blocks of the castle, the black, empty eye-sockets of its ruined loop-holes gaping at her. A shudder ran through her.

The horse's shoes rang against the slabs in the courtyard. The magician quickly leaped from the saddle and held out her hand to Ciri. Taking advantage of the touch of their hands she carefully emitted a magical impulse. And was astounded. Because she didn't feel anything. No reaction, no reply. And no resistance. In the girl who had, just a moment ago, manifested an exceptionally strong aura there was not a trace of magic. She was now an ordinary, badly dressed child whose hair had been incompetently cut.

But a moment ago, this child had been no ordinary child.

Triss did not have time to ponder the strange event. The grate of an iron-clad door reached her, coming from the dark void of the corridor which gaped behind the battered portal. She slipped the fur cape from her shoulders, removed her fox-fur hat and, with a swift movement of the head, tousled her hair – long, full locks the colour of fresh chestnuts, with a sheen of gold, her pride and identifying characteristic.

Ciri sighed with admiration. Triss smiled, pleased by the effect she'd had. Beautiful, long, loose hair was a rarity, an indication of a woman's position, her status, the sign of a free woman, a woman who belonged to herself. The sign of an unusual woman – because "normal" maidens wore their hair in plaits, "normal" married women hid theirs beneath a caul or a coif. Women of high birth, including queens, curled their hair and styled it. Warriors cut it short. Only druids and magicians – and whores – wore their hair naturally so as to emphasise their independence and freedom.

The witchers appeared unexpectedly and silently, as usual, and, also as usual, from nowhere. They stood before her, tall, slim, their arms crossed, the weight of their bodies on their left legs – a position from which, she knew, they could attack in a split second. Ciri stood next to them, in an identical position. In her ludicrous clothes, she looked very funny.

"Welcome to Kaer Morhern, Triss."

"Greetings, Geralt."

He had changed. He gave the impression of having aged. Triss knew that, biologically, this was impossible – witchers aged, certainly, but too slowly for an ordinary mortal, or a magician as young as her, to notice the changes. But one glance was enough for her to realise that although mutation could hold back the physical process of ageing, it did not alter the mental. Geralt's face, slashed by wrinkles, was the best evidence of this. With a sense of deep sorrow Triss tore her gaze away from the white-haired witcher's eyes. Eyes which had evidently seen too much. What's more, she saw nothing of what she had expected in those eyes.

"Welcome," he repeated. "We are glad you've come."

Eskel stood next to Geralt, resembling the Wolf like a brother apart from the colour of his hair and the long scar which disfigured his cheek. And the youngest of the Kaer Morhen witchers, Lambert, was there with his usual ugly, mocking expression. Vesemir was not there.

"Welcome and come in," said Eskel. "It is as cold and blustery as if someone has hung themselves. Ciri, where are you off to? The invitation does not apply to you. The sun is still high, even if it is obscured. You can still train."

"Hey." The Enchantress tossed her hair. "Politeness comes cheap in Witchers' Keep now, I see. Ciri was the first to greet me, and brought me to the castle. She ought to keep me company—"

"She is undergoing training here, Merigold." Lambert grimaced in a parody of a smile. He always called her that: "Merigold," without giving her a title or a name. Triss hated it. "She is a student, not a major domo. Welcoming guests, even such pleasant ones as yourself, is not one of her duties. We're off, Ciri."

Triss gave a little shrug, pretending not to see Geralt and Eskel's embarrassed expressions. She did not say anything, not wanting to embarrass them further. And, above all, she did not want them to see how very intrigued and fascinated she was by the girl.

"I'll take your horse," offered Geralt, reaching for the reins. Triss surreptitiously shifted her hand and their palms joined. So did their eyes.

"I'll come with you," she said naturally. "There are a few little things in the saddle-bags which I'll need."

"You gave me a very disagreeable experience not so long ago," he muttered as soon as they had entered the stable. "I studied your impressive tombstone with my own eyes. The obelisk in memory of your heroic death at the battle of Sodden. The news that it was a mistake only reached me recently. I can't understand how anyone could mistake anyone else for you, Triss."

"It's a long story," she answered. "I'll tell you some time. And please forgive me for the disagreeable moment."

"There's nothing to forgive. I've not had many reasons to be happy of late and the feelings I experienced on hearing that you lived cannot compare to any other. Except perhaps what I feel now when I look at you."

Triss felt something explode inside her. Her fear of meeting the white-haired witcher, which had accompanied her throughout her journey, had struggled within her with her hope of having such a meeting. Followed by the sight of that tired, jaded face, those sick eyes which saw everything, cold and calculating, which were unnaturally calm but yet so infused with emotion . . .

She threw her arms around his neck, instantly, without thinking. She caught hold of his hand, abruptly placed it on the nape of her neck, under her hair. A tingling ran down her back, penetrated her with such rapture she almost cried out. In order to muffle and restrain the cry her lips found his lips and stuck to them. She trembled, pressing hard against him, her excitement building and increasing, forgetting herself more and more.

Geralt did not forget himself.

"Triss . . . Please."

"Oh, Geralt . . . So much . . ."

"Triss." He moved her away delicately. "We're not alone . . . They're coming."

She glanced at the entrance and saw the shadows of the approaching witchers only after some time, heard their steps even later. Oh well, her hearing, which she considered very sensitive, could not compete with that of a witcher.

"Triss, my child!"

"Vesemir!"

Vesemir was really very old. Who knows, he could be even older than Kaer Morhen. But he walked towards her with a brisk, energetic and sprightly step; his grip was vigorous and his hands strong.

"I am happy to see you again, Grandfather."

"Give me a kiss. No, not on the hand, little sorceress. You can kiss my hand when I'm resting on my bier. Which will, no doubt, be soon. Oh, Triss, it is a good thing you have come . . . Who can cure me if not you?"

"Cure, you? Of what? Of behaving like a child, surely! Take your hand from my backside, old man, or I'll set fire to that grey beard of yours!"

"Forgive me. I keep forgetting you are grown up, and I can no longer put you on my knee and pat you. As to my health . . . Oh, Triss, old age is no joke. My bones ache so I want to howl. Will you help an old man, child?"

"I will." The enchantress freed herself from his bear-like embrace and cast her eye over the witcher accompanying Vesemir. He was young, apparently the same age as Lambert, and wore a short, black beard which did not hide the severe disfigurement left behind by smallpox. This was unusual; witchers were generally highly immune to infectious diseases.

"Triss Merigold, Coën." Geralt introduced them to each other. "This is Coën's first winter with us. He comes from the north, from Poviss."

The young witcher bowed. He had unusually pale, yellow-green irises and the whites of his eyes, riddled with red threads, indicated difficult and troublesome processes during his mutation.

"Let us go, child," uttered Vesemir, taking her by the arm. "A stable is no place to welcome a guest, but I couldn't wait to see you."

In the courtyard, in a recess in the wall sheltered from the wind, Ciri was training under Lambert's instructions. Deftly balancing on a beam hanging on chains, she was attacking – with her sword – a leather sack bound with straps to make it resemble a human torso. Triss stopped to watch.

"Wrong!" yelled Lambert. "You're getting too close! Don't hack blindly at it! I told you, the very tip of the sword, at the carotid artery! Where does a humanoid have its carotid artery? On top of its head? What's happening? Concentrate, Princess!"

Ha, thought Triss. *So it is truth, not a legend. She is the one. I guessed correctly.*

She decided to attack without delay, not allowing the witchers to try any ruses.

"The famous Child Surprise?" she said indicating Ciri. "I see you have applied yourselves to fulfilling the demands of fate and destiny? But it seems you have muddled the stories, boys. In the fairy-tales I was told, shepherdesses and orphans become princesses. But here, I see, a princess is becoming a witcher. Does that not appear somewhat daring to you?"

Vesemir glanced at Geralt. The white-haired witcher remained silent, his face perfectly still; he did not react with even the slightest quiver of his eyelids to Vesemir's unspoken request for support.

"It's not what you think." The old man cleared his throat. "Geralt brought her here last autumn. She has no one apart from— Triss, how can one not believe in destiny when—"

"What has destiny to do with waving a sword around?"

"We are teaching her to fence," Geralt said quietly, turning towards her and looking her straight in the eyes. "What else are we to teach her? We know nothing else. Destiny or no, Kaer Morhen is now her home. At least for a while. Training and swordsmanship amuse her, keep her healthy and fit. They allow her to forget the tragedy she has lived through. This is her home now, Triss. She has no other."

"Masses of Cintrians," the enchantress said, holding his gaze, "fled to Verden after the defeat, to Brugge, Temeria and the Islands of Skellige. Amongst them are magnates, barons, knights. Friends, relations . . . as well as this girl's subjects."

"Friends and relations did not look for her after the war. They did not find her."

"Because she was not destined for them?" She smiled at him, not very sincerely but very prettily. As prettily as she could. She did not want him to use that tone of voice.

The witcher shrugged. Triss, knowing him a little, immediately changed tactics and gave up the argument.

She looked at Ciri again. The girl, agilely stepping along the balance beam, executed a half-turn, cut lightly, and immediately leaped away. The dummy, struck, swayed on its rope.

"Well, at last!" shouted Lambert. "You've finally got it! Go back and do it again. I want to make sure it wasn't a fluke!"

"The sword," Triss turned to the witchers, "looks sharp. The beam looks slippery and unstable. And Lambert looks like an idiot, demoralising the girl with all his shouting. Aren't you afraid of an unfortunate accident? Or maybe you're relying on destiny to protect the child against it?"

"Ciri practised for nearly six months without a sword," said Coën. "She knows how to move. And we are keeping an eye on her because—"

"Because this is her home," finished Geralt quietly but firmly. Very firmly. Using a tone which put an end to the discussion.

"Exactly. It is." Vesemir took a deep breath. "Triss, you must be tired. And hungry?"

"I cannot deny it," she sighed, giving up on trying to catch Geralt's eye. "To be honest, I'm on my last legs. I spent last night on the Trail in a shepherd's hut which was practically falling apart, buried in straw and sawdust. I used spells to insulate the shack; if it weren't for that I would probably be dead. I long for clean linen."

"You will have supper with us now. And then you will sleep as long as you wish, and rest. We have prepared the best room for you, the one in the tower. And we have put the best bed we could find in Kaer Morhen there."

"Thank you." Triss smiled faintly. *In the tower*, she thought. *All right, Vesemir. Let it be the tower for today, if appearances matter so much to you. I can sleep in the tower in the best of all the beds in Kaer Morhen. Although I would prefer to sleep with Geralt in the worst.*

"Let's go, Triss."

"Let's go."

* * *

The wind hammered against the shutters and ruffled the remains of the moth-eaten tapestries which had been used to insulate the window. Triss lay in perfect darkness in the best bed in the whole of Kaer Morhen. She couldn't sleep – and not because the best bed in Kaer Morhen was a dilapidated antique. Triss was thinking hard. And all the thoughts chasing sleep away revolved around one fundamental question.

What had she been summoned to the fortress for? Who had summoned her? Why? For what purpose?

Vesemir's illness was just a pretext. Vesemir was a witcher. The fact that he was also an old man did not change the fact that many a youngster could envy him his health. If the old man had been stung by a manticore or bitten by a werewolf Triss would have accepted that she had been summoned to aid him. But "aching bones" was a joke. For an ache in his bones, not a very original complaint within the horrendously cold walls of Kaer Morhen, Vesemir could have treated with a witchers' elixir or – an even simpler solution – with strong rye vodka, applied internally and externally in equal proportions. He didn't need a magician, with her spells, philtres and amulets.

So who had summoned her? Geralt?

Triss thrashed about in the bedclothes, feeling a wave of heat come over her. And a wave of arousal, made all the stronger by anger. She swore quietly, kicked her quilt away and rolled on to her side. The ancient bedstead squeaked and creaked. *I've no control over myself*, she thought. *I'm behaving like a stupid adolescent. Or even worse – like an old maid deprived of affection. I can't even think logically.*

She swore again.

Of course it wasn't Geralt. Don't get excited, little one. Don't get excited, just think of his expression in the stable. You've seen expressions like that before. You've seen them, so don't kid yourself. The foolish, contrite, embarrassed expressions of men who want to forget, who regret, who don't want to remember what happened, don't want to go back to what has been. By all the gods, little one, don't fool yourself it's different this time. It's never different. And you know it. Because, after all, you've had a fair amount of experience.

As far as her erotic life was concerned, Triss Merigold had the right to consider herself a typical enchantress. It had began with the sour taste of forbidden fruit, made all the more exciting by the strict rules of the academy and the prohibitions of the mistress under whom she practised. Then came her independence, freedom and a crazy promiscuity which ended, as it usually does, in bitterness, disillusionment and resignation. Then followed a long period of loneliness and the discovery that if she wanted to release her tension and stress then someone who wanted to consider himself her lord and master – as soon as he had turned on his back and wiped the sweat from his brow – was entirely superfluous. There were far less troublesome ways of calming her nerves – ones with the additional advantages of not staining her towels with blood, not passing wind under the quilt and not demanding breakfast. That was followed by a short-lived and entertaining fascination with the same sex, which ended in the conclusion that soiling towels, passing wind and greediness were by no means exclusively male attributes. Finally, like all but a few magicians, Triss moved to affairs with other wizards, which proved sporadic and frustrating in their cold, technical and almost ritual course.

Then Geralt of Rivia appeared. A witcher leading a stormy life, and tied to her good friend Yennefer in a strange, turbulent and almost violent relationship.

Triss had watched them both and was jealous even though it seemed there was little to be jealous of. Their relationship quite obviously made them both unhappy, had led straight to destruction, pain and yet, against all logic . . . it had lasted. Triss couldn't understand it. And it had fascinated her. It had fascinated her to such an extent that . . .

. . . she had seduced the witcher – with the help of a little magic. She had hit on a propitious moment, a moment when he and Yennefer had scratched at each other's eyes yet again and had abruptly parted. Geralt had needed warmth, and had wanted to forget.

No, Triss had not desired to take him away from Yennefer. As a matter of fact, her friend was more important to her than he was. But her brief relationship with the witcher had not disappointed. She had found what she was looking for – emotions in the form of guilt, anxiety and pain. His pain. She had experienced his emotions, it had excited her and, when they parted, she had been unable to forget it. And she had only recently understood what pain is. The moment when she had overwhelmingly wanted to be with him again. For a short while – just for a moment – to be with him.

And now she was so close . . .

Triss clenched her fist and punched the pillow. *No*, she thought, *no. Don't be silly. Don't think about it. Think about . . .*

About Ciri. Is she . . .

Yes. She was the real reason behind her visit to Kaer Morhen. *The ash-blonde girl who, here in Kaer Morhen, they want to turn into a witcher. A real witcher. A mutant. A killing machine, like themselves.*

It's clear, she suddenly thought, feeling a passionate arousal of an entirely different nature. *It's obvious. They want to mutate the child, subject her to the Trial of Grasses and Changes, but they don't know how to do it.* Vesemir was the only witcher left from the previous generation, and he was only a fencing instructor. The Laboratorium, hidden in the vaults of Kaer Morhen, with its dusty demijohns of elixirs, the alembics, ovens and retorts . . . None of the witchers knew how to use them. The mutagenic elixirs had been concocted by some renegade wizard in the distant past and then perfected over the years by the wizard's successors, who had, over the years, magically controlled the process of Changes to which children were subjected. And at a vital moment the chain had snapped. There was no more magical knowledge or power. The witchers had the herbs and Grasses, they had the Laboratorium. They knew the recipe. But they had no wizard.

Who knows, she thought, *perhaps they have tried? Have they given children concoctions prepared without the use of magic?*

She shuddered at the thought of what might have happened to those children.

And now they want to mutate the girl but can't. And that might mean . . . They may ask me to help. And then I'll see something no living wizard has seen, I'll learn something no living wizard has learned. Their famous Grasses and herbs, the secret virus cultures, the renowned, mysterious recipes . . .

And I will be the one to give the child a number of elixirs, who will watch the Changes of mutation, who will watch, with my own eyes . . .

Watch the ashen-haired child die.

Oh, no. Triss shuddered again. *Never. Not at such a price.*

Besides, she thought, *I've probably got excited too soon again. That's probably not what this is about. We talked over supper, gossiped about this and that. I tried to guide the conversation to the Child Surprise several times to no avail. They changed the subject at once.*

She had watched them. Vesemir had been tense and troubled; Geralt uneasy, Lambert and Eskel falsely merry and talkative, Coën so natural as to be unnatural. The only one who had been sincere and open was Ciri, rosy-cheeked from the cold, dishevelled, happy and devilishly voracious. They had eaten beer potage, thick with croutons and cheese, and Ciri had been surprised they had not served mushrooms as well. They had drunk cider, but the girl had been given water and was clearly both astonished and revolted by it. "Where's the salad?" she had yelled, and Lambert had rebuked her sharply and ordered her to take her elbows off the table.

Mushrooms and salad. In December?

Of course, thought Triss. *They're feeding her those legendary cave saprophytes – a mountain plant unknown to science – giving her the famous infusions of their mysterious herbs to drink. The girl is developing quickly, is acquiring a witcher's infernal fitness. Naturally, without the mutation, without the risk, without the hormonal up-*

heaval. But the magician must not know this. It is to be kept a secret from the magician. They aren't going to tell me anything; they aren't going to show me anything.

I saw how that girl ran. I saw how she danced on the beam with her sword, agile and swift, full of a dancer's near-feline grace, moving like an acrobat. I must, she thought, *I absolutely must see her body, see how she's developing under the influence of whatever it is they're feeding her. And what if I managed to steal samples of these "mushrooms" and "salads" and take them away? Well, well . . .*

And trust? I don't give a fig for your trust, witchers. There's cancer out there in the world, smallpox, tetanus and leukaemia, there are allergies, there's cot death. And you're keeping your "mushrooms", which could perhaps be distilled and turned into life-saving medicines, hidden away from the world. You're keeping them a secret even from me, and others to whom you declare your friendship, respect and trust. Even I'm forbidden to see not just the Laboratorium, but even the bloody mushrooms!

So why did you bring me here? Me, a magician?

Magic!

Triss giggled. *Ha,* she thought, *witchers, I've got you! Ciri scared you just as she did me. She "withdrew" into a daydream, started to prophesy, gave out an aura which, after all, you can sense almost as well as I can. She automatically reached for something psychokinetically, or bent a pewter spoon with her will as she stared at it during lunch. She answered questions you only thought, and maybe even some which you were afraid to ask yourselves. And you felt fear. You realised that your Surprise is more surprising than you had imagined.*

You realised that you have the Source in Kaer Morhen.

And that, you can't manage without a magician.

And you don't have a single friendly magician, not a single one you could trust. Apart from me and . . .

And Yennefer.

The wind howled, banged the shutter and swelled the tapestry. Triss rolled on to her back and, lost in thought, started to bite her thumb nail.

Geralt had not invited Yennefer. He had invited her. *Does that mean . . . ?*

Who knows. Maybe. But if it's as I think then why . . . ? Why . . . ?

"Why hasn't he come to me?" she shouted quietly into the darkness, angry and aroused.

She was answered by the wind howling amidst the ruins.

The morning was sunny but devilishly cold. Triss woke chilled through and through, without having had enough sleep, but finally assured and decided.

She was the last to go down to the hall. She accepted the tribute of gazes which rewarded her efforts – she had changed her travel clothes for an attractive but simple dress and had skilfully applied magical scents and non-magical but incredibly expensive cosmetics. She ate her porridge chatting with the witchers about unimportant and trivial matters.

"Water again?" muttered Ciri suddenly, peering into her tumbler. "My teeth go numb when I drink water! I want some juice! That blue one!"

"Don't slouch," said Lambert, stealing a glance at Triss

from the corner of his eye. "And don't wipe your mouth with your sleeve! Finish your food; it's time for training. The days are getting shorter."

"Geralt." Triss finished her porridge. "Ciri fell on the Trail yesterday. Nothing serious, but it was because of that jester's outfit she wears. It all fits so badly, and it hinders her movements."

Vesemir cleared his throat and turned his eyes away. *Aha*, thought the enchantress, *so it's your work, master of the sword. Predictable enough, Ciri's short tunic does look as if it has been cut out with a knife and sewn together with an arrow-head.*

"The days are, indeed, getting shorter," she continued, not waiting for a comment. "But we're going to make today shorter still. Ciri, have you finished? Come with me, if you please. We shall make some vital adjustments to your uniform."

"She's been running around in this for a year, Merigold," said Lambert angrily. "And everything was fine until . . ."

". . . until a woman arrived who can't bear to look at clothes in poor taste which don't fit? You're right, Lambert. But a woman has arrived, and the old order's collapsed; a time of great change has arrived. Come on, Ciri."

The girl hesitated, looked at Geralt. Geralt nodded his agreement and smiled. Pleasantly. Just as he had smiled in the past when, when . . .

Triss turned her eyes away. His smile was not for her.

Ciri's little room was a faithful replica of the witchers' quarters. It was, like theirs, devoid of almost all fittings and furniture. There was practically nothing there beside a few planks nailed together to form a bed, a stool and a trunk. Witchers decorated the walls and doors of their quarters with the skins of animals they killed when hunting – stags, lynx, wolves and even wolverines. On the door of Ciri's little room, however, hung the skin of an enormous rat with a hideous scaly tail. Triss fought back her desire to tear the stinking abomination down and throw it out of the window.

The girl, standing by the bed, stared at her expectantly.

"We'll try," said the enchantress, "to make this . . . sheath fit a little better. I've always had a knack for cutting and sewing so I ought to be able to manage this goatskin, too. And you, little witcher-girl, have you ever had a needle in your hand? Have you been taught anything other than making holes with a sword in sacks of straw?"

"When I was in Transriver, in Kagen, I had to spin," muttered Ciri unwillingly. "They didn't give me any sewing because I only spoilt the linen and wasted thread; they had to undo everything. The spinning was terribly boring – yuk!"

"True," giggled Triss. "It's hard to find anything more boring. I hated spinning, too."

"And did you have to? I did because . . . But you're a wi— magician. You can conjure anything up! That amazing dress . . . did you conjure it up?"

"No." Triss smiled. "Nor did I sew it myself. I'm not that talented."

"And my clothes, how are you going to make them? Conjure them up?"

"There's no need. A magic needle is enough, one

which we shall charm into working more vigorously. And if there's a need . . ."

Triss slowly ran her hand across the torn hole in the sleeve of Ciri's jacket, murmuring a spell while stimulating an amulet to work. Not a trace remained of the hole. Ciri squealed with joy.

"That's magic! I'm going to have a magical jacket! Wow!"

"Only until I make you an ordinary – but good – one. Right, now take all that off, young lady, and change into something else. These aren't your only clothes, surely?"

Ciri shook her head, lifted the lid of the trunk and showed her a faded loose dress, a dark grey tunic, a linen shirt and a woollen blouse resembling a penitent's sack.

"This is mine," she said. "This is what I came in. But I don't wear it now. It's woman's stuff."

"I understand." Triss grimaced mockingly. "Woman's or not, for the time being you'll have to change into it. Well, get on with it, get undressed. Let me help you . . . Damn it! What's this? Ciri?"

The girl's shoulders were covered in massive bruises, suffused with blood. Most of them had already turned yellow; some were fresh.

"What the hell is this?" the magician repeated angrily. "Who beat you like this?"

"This?" Ciri looked at her shoulders as if surprised by the number of bruises. "Oh, this . . . That was the windmill. I was too slow."

"What windmill? Bloody hell!"

"The windmill," repeated Ciri, raising her huge eyes to look up at the magician. "It's a sort of . . . Well . . . I'm using it to learn to dodge while attacking. It's got these paws made of sticks and it turns and waves the paws. You have to jump very quickly and dodge. You have to learn a lefrex. If you haven't got the lefrex the windmill wallops you with a stick. At the beginning, the windmill gave me a really terribly horrible thrashing. But now—"

"Take the leggings and shirt off. Oh, sweet gods! Dear girl! Can you really walk? Run?"

Both hips and her left thigh were black and blue with haematomas and swellings. Ciri shuddered and hissed, pulling away from the magician's hand. Triss swore viciously in Dwarvish, using inexpressibly foul language.

"Was that the windmill, too?" she asked, trying to remain calm.

"This? No. This, this was the windmill." Ciri pointed indifferently to an impressive bruise below her left knee, covering her shin. "And these other ones . . . They were the pendulum. I practise my fencing steps on the pendulum. Geralt says I'm already good at the pendulum. He says I've got . . . Flair. I've got flair."

"And if you run out of flair" – Triss ground her teeth together – "I take it the pendulum thumps you?"

"But of course," the girl confirmed, looking at her, clearly surprised at this lack of knowledge. "It thumps you, and how."

"And here? On your side? What was that? A smith's hammer?"

Ciri hissed with pain and blushed.

"I fell off the comb . . ."

". . . and the comb thumped you," finished Triss, controlling herself with increasing difficulty. Ciri snorted.

"How can a comb thump you when it's buried in the ground? It can't! I just fell. I was practising a jumping pirouette and it didn't work. That's where the bruise came from. Because I hit a post."

"And you lay there for two days? In pain? Finding it hard to breathe?"

"Not at all. Coën rubbed it and put me straight back on the comb. You have to, you know? Otherwise you catch fear."

"What?"

"You catch fear," Ciri repeated proudly, brushing her ashen fringe from her forehead. "Didn't you know? Even when something bad happens to you, you have to go straight back to that piece of equipment or you get frightened. And if you're frightened you'll be hopeless at the exercise. You mustn't give up. Geralt said so."

"I have to remember that maxim," the enchantress murmured through her teeth. "And that it came from Geralt. Not a bad prescription for life although I'm not sure it applies in every situation. But it is easy to put into practise at someone else's expense. So you mustn't give up? Even though you are being thumped and beaten in a thousand ways, you're to get up and carry on practising?"

"Of course. A witcher's not afraid of anything."

"Is that so? And you, Ciri? You aren't afraid of anything? Answer truthfully."

The girl turned away and bit her lip.

"You won't tell anybody?"

"I won't."

"I'm frightened of two pendulums. Two at the same time. And the windmill, but only when it's set to go fast. And there's also a long balance, I still have to go on that . . . with a safety de— A safety device. Lambert says I'm a sissy and a wimp but that's not true. Geralt told me my weight is distributed a little differently because I'm a girl. I've simply got to practise more unless . . . I wanted to ask you something. May I?"

"You may."

"If you know magic and spells . . . If you can cast them . . . Can you turn me into a boy?"

"No," Triss replied in an icy tone. "I can't."

"Hmm . . ." The little witcher-girl was clearly troubled. "But could you at least . . ."

"At least what?"

"Could you do something so I don't have to . . ." Ciri blushed. "I'll whisper it in your ear."

"Go on." Triss leaned over. "I'm listening."

Ciri, growing even redder, brought her head closer to the enchantress's chestnut hair.

Triss sat up abruptly, her eyes flaming.

"Today? Now?"

"Mhm."

"Hell and bloody damnation!" the enchantress yelled, and kicked the stool so hard that it hit the door and brought down the rat skin. "Pox, plague, shit and leprosy! I'm going to kill those cursed idiots!"

"Calm down, Merigold," said Lambert. "It's unhealthy to get so worked up, especially with no reason."

"Don't preach at me! And stop calling me 'Merigold'! But best of all, stop talking altogether. I'm not speaking to you. Vesemir, Geralt, have any of you seen how terribly battered this child is? She hasn't got a single healthy spot on her body!"

"Dear child," said Vesemir gravely, "don't let yourself get carried away by your emotions. You were brought up differently, you've seen children being brought up in another way. Ciri comes from the south where girls and boys are brought up in the same way, like the elves. She was put on a pony when she was five and when she was eight she was already riding out hunting. She was taught to use a bow, javelin and sword. A bruise is nothing new to Ciri—"

"Don't give me that nonsense," Triss flared. "Don't pretend you're stupid. This is not some pony or horse or sleigh ride. This is Kaer Morhen! On these windmills and pendulums of yours, on this Killer path of yours, dozens of boys have broken their bones and twisted their necks, boys who were hard, seasoned vagabonds like you, found on roads and pulled out of gutters. Sinewy scamps and good-for-nothings, pretty experienced despite their short lives. What chance has Ciri got? Even though she's been brought up in the south with elven methods, even growing up under the hand of a battle-axe like Lioness Calanthe, that little one was and still is a princess. Delicate skin, slight build, light bones . . . She's a girl! What do you want to turn her into? A witcher?"

"That girl," said Geralt quietly and calmly, "that petite, delicate princess lived through the Massacre of Cintra. Left entirely to her own devices, she stole past Nilfgaard's cohorts. She successfully fled the marauders who prowled the villages, plundering and murdering anything that still lived. She survived on her own for two weeks in the forests of Transriver, entirely alone. She spent a month roaming with a pack of fugitives, slogging as hard as all the others and starving like all the others. For almost half a year, having been taken in by a peasant family, she worked on the land and with the livestock. Believe me,

Triss, life has tried, seasoned and hardened her no less than good-for-nothings like us, who were brought to Kaer Morhen from the highways. Ciri is no weaker than unwanted bastards, like us, who were left with witchers in taverns like kittens in a wicker basket. And her gender? What difference does that make?"

"You still ask? You still dare ask that?" yelled the magician. "What difference does it make? Only that the girl, not being like you, has her days! And bears them exceptionally badly! And you want her to tear her lungs out on the Killer and some bloody windmills!"

Despite her outrage, Triss felt an exquisite satisfaction at the sight of the sheepish expressions of the young witchers, and Vesemir's jaw suddenly dropping open.

"You didn't even know." She nodded in what was now a calm, concerned and gentle reproach. "You're pathetic guardians. She's ashamed to tell you because she was taught not to mention such complaints to men. And she's ashamed of the weakness, the pain and the fact that she is less fit. Has any one of you thought about that? Taken any interest in it? Or tried to guess what might be the matter with her? Maybe her very first bleed happened here, in Kaer Morhen? And she cried to herself at night, unable to find any sympathy, consolation or even understanding from anyone? Has any one of you given it any thought whatsoever?"

"Stop it, Triss," moaned Geralt quietly. "That's enough. You've achieved what you wanted. And maybe even more."

"The devil take it," cursed Coën. "We've turned out to be right idiots, there's no two ways about it, eh, Vesemir, and you—"

"Silence," growled the old witcher. "Not a word."

It was Eskel's behaviour which was most unlikely; he got up, approached the enchantress, bent down low, took her hand and kissed it respectfully. She swiftly withdrew her hand. Not so as to demonstrate her anger and annoyance but to break the pleasant, piercing vibration triggered by the witcher's touch. Eskel emanated powerfully. More powerfully than Geralt.

"Triss," he said, rubbing the hideous scar on his cheek with embarrassment, "help us. We ask you. Help us, Triss."

The enchantress looked him in the eye and pursed her lips. "With what? What am I to help you with, Eskel?"

Eskel rubbed his cheek again, looked at Geralt. The white-haired witcher bowed his head, hiding his eyes behind his hand. Vesemir cleared his throat loudly.

At that moment, the door creaked open and Ciri entered the hall. Vesemir's hawking changed into something like a wheeze, a loud indrawn breath. Lambert opened his mouth. Triss suppressed a laugh.

Ciri, her hair cut and styled, was walking towards them with tiny steps, carefully holding up a dark-blue dress – shortened and adjusted, and still showing the signs of having been carried in a saddle-bag. Another present from the enchantress gleamed around the girl's neck – a little black viper made of lacquered leather with a ruby eye and gold clasp.

Ciri stopped in front of Vesemir. Not quite knowing what to do with her hands, she planted her thumbs behind her belt.

"I cannot train today," she recited in the utter silence, slowly and emphatically, "for I am . . . I am . . ."

She looked at the enchantress. Triss winked at her, smirking like a rascal well pleased with his mischief, and moved her lips to prompt the memorised lines.

"Indisposed!" ended Ciri loudly and proudly, turning her nose up almost to the ceiling.

Vesemir hawked again. But Eskel, dear Eskel, kept his head and once more behaved as was fitting.

"Of course," he said casually, smiling. "We understand and clearly we will postpone your exercises until your indisposition has passed. We will also cut the theory short and, if you feel unwell, we will put it aside for the time being, too. If you need any medication or—"

"I'll take care of that," Triss cut in just as casually.

"Aha . . ." Only now did Ciri blush a little – she looked at the old witcher. "Uncle Vesemir, I've asked Triss . . . that is, Miss Merigold, to . . . that is . . . Well, to stay here with us. For longer. For a long time. But Triss said you have to agree forsooth. Uncle Vesemir! Say yes!"

"I agree . . ." Vesemir wheezed out. "Of course, I agree . . ."

"We are very happy." Only now did Geralt take his hand from his forehead. "We are extremely pleased, Triss."

The enchantress nodded slightly towards him and innocently fluttered her eyelashes, winding a chestnut lock around her finger. Geralt's face seemed almost graven from stone.

"You behaved very properly and politely, Ciri," he said, "offering Miss Merigold our ongoing hospitality in Kaer Morhen. I am proud of you."

Ciri reddened and smiled broadly. The enchantress gave her the next pre-arranged sign.

"And now," said the girl, turning her nose up even higher, "I will leave you alone because you no doubt wish to talk over various important matters with Triss. Miss Merigold. Uncle Vesemir, gentlemen . . . I bid you good-bye. For the time being."

She curtseyed gracefully then left the hall, walking up the stairs slowly and with dignity.

"Bloody hell." Lambert broke the silence. "To think I didn't believe that she really is a princess."

"Have you understood, you idiots?" Vesemir cast his eye around. "If she puts a dress on in the morning I don't want to see any exercises . . . Understood?"

Eskel and Coën bestowed a look which was entirely devoid of respect on the old man. Lambert snorted loudly. Geralt stared at the enchantress and the enchantress smiled back.

"Thank you," he said. "Thank you, Triss."

"Conditions?" Eskel was clearly worried. "But we've already promised to ease Ciri's training, Triss. What other conditions do you want to impose?"

"Well, maybe 'conditions' isn't a very nice phrase. So let us call it advice. I will give you three pieces of advice, and you are going to abide by each of them. If, of course, you really want me to stay and help you bring up the little one."

"We're listening," said Geralt. "Go on, Triss."

"Above all," she began, smiling maliciously, "Ciri's menu is to be more varied. And the secret mushrooms and mysterious greens in particular have to be limited."

Geralt and Coën controlled their expressions wonderfully, Lambert and Eskel a little less so, Vesemir not at all. *But then,* she thought, looking at his comically embarrassed expression, *in his day the world was a better place. Duplicity was a character flaw to be ashamed of. Sincerity did not bring shame.*

"Fewer infusions of your mystery-shrouded herbs," she continued, trying not to giggle, "and more milk. You have goats here. Milking is no great art. You'll see, Lambert, you'll learn how to do it in no time."

"Triss," started Geralt, "listen—"

"No, you listen. You haven't subjected Ciri to violent mutations, haven't touched her hormones, haven't tried any elixirs or Grasses on her. And that's to be praised. That was sensible, responsible and humane. You haven't harmed her with any of your poisons – all the more so you must not cripple her now."

"What are you talking about?"

"The mushrooms whose secrets you guard so carefully," she explained, "do, indeed, keep the girl wonderfully fit and strengthen her muscles. The herbs guarantee an ideal metabolic rate and hasten her development. All this taken together and helped along by gruelling training causes certain changes in her build, in her adipose tissue. She's a woman, and as you haven't crippled her hormonal system, do not cripple her physically now. She might hold it against you later if you so ruthlessly deprive her of her womanly . . . attributes. Do you understand what I'm saying?"

"And how," muttered Lambert, brazenly eyeing Triss's breasts which strained against the fabric of her dress.

Eskel cleared his throat and looked daggers at the young witcher.

"At the moment," Geralt asked slowly, also gliding his eyes over this and that, "you haven't noticed anything irreversible in her, I hope?"

"No." She smiled. "Fortunately, not. She is developing healthily and normally and is built like a young dryad – it's a pleasure to look at her. But I ask you to be moderate in using your accelerants."

"We will," promised Vesemir. "Thank you for the warning, child. What else? You said three . . . pieces of advice."

"Indeed. This is the second: Ciri must not be allowed to grow wild. She has to have contact with the world. With her peers. She has to be decently educated and prepared for a normal life. Let her wave her sword about for the time being. You won't turn her into a witcher without mutation anyway, but having a witcher's training won't harm her. Times are hard and dangerous; she'll be able to defend herself when necessary. Like an elf. But you must not bury her alive here, in the middle of nowhere. She has to enter normal life."

"Her normal life went up in flames along with Cintra," murmured Geralt, "but regarding this, Triss, as usual you're right. We've already thought about it. In spring I'm going to take her to the Temple school. To Nenneke. To Ellander."

"That's a very good idea and a wise decision. Nenneke is an exceptional woman and Goddess Melitele's sanctuary an exceptional place. Safe, sure, and it guarantees an appropriate education for the girl. Does Ciri know yet?"

"She does. She kicked up a fuss for a few days but finally accepted the idea. Now she is even looking forward to spring with impatience, excited by the prospect of an expedition to Temeria. She's interested in the world."

"So was I at her age." Triss smiled. "And that comparison brings us dangerously close to the third piece of advice. The most important piece. And you already know what it is. Don't pull silly faces. I'm a magician, have you forgotten? I don't know how long it took you to recognise Ciri's magical abilities. It took me less than half an hour. After that I knew who, or rather what, the girl is."

"And what is she?"

"A Source."

"That's impossible!"

"It's possible. Certain even. Ciri is a Source and has mediumistic powers. What is more, these powers are very, very worrying. And you, my dear witchers, are perfectly well aware of this. You've noticed these powers and they have worried you too. That is the one and only reason you brought me here to Kaer Morhen? Am I right? The one and only reason?"

"Yes," Vesemir confirmed after a moment's silence.

Triss breathed an imperceptible sigh of relief. For a moment, she was afraid that Geralt would be the one to confirm it.

The first snow fell the following day, fine snowflakes initially, but soon turning into a blizzard. It fell throughout the night and, in the early morning, the walls of Kaer Morhen were drowned beneath a snowdrift. There could be no question of running the Killer, especially since Ciri was still not feeling very well. Triss suspected that the witchers' accelerants might be the cause of the girl's menstrual problems. She could not be sure, however, knowing practically nothing about the drugs, and Ciri was, beyond doubt, the only girl in the world to whom they had been administered. She did not share her suspicions with the witchers. She did not want to worry or annoy them and preferred to apply her own methods. She gave Ciri elixirs to drink, tied a string of active jaspers around her waist, under her dress, and forbade her to exert herself in any way, especially by chasing around wildly hunting rats with a sword.

Ciri was bored. She roamed the castle sleepily and finally, for lack of any other amusement, joined Coën who was cleaning the stable, grooming the horses and repairing a harness.

Geralt – to the enchantress's rage – disappeared somewhere and appeared only towards evening, bearing a dead goat. Triss helped him skin his prey. Although she sincerely detested the smell of meat and blood, she wanted to be near the witcher. Near him. As near as possible. A cold, determined resolution was growing in her. She did not want to sleep alone any longer.

"Triss!" yelled Ciri suddenly, running down the stairs, stamping. "Can I sleep with you tonight? Triss, please, please say yes! Please, Triss!"

The snow fell and fell. It brightened up only with the arrival of Midinváerne, the Day of the Winter Equinox.

On the third day all the children died save one, a male barely ten. Hitherto agitated by a sudden madness, he fell all at once into deep stupor. His eyes took on a glassy gaze; incessantly with his hands did he clutch at clothing, or brandish them in the air as if desirous of catching a quill. His breathing grew loud and hoarse; sweat cold, clammy and malodorous appeared on his skin. Then was he once more given elixir through the vein and the seizure it did return. This time a nose-bleed did ensue, coughing turned to vomiting, after which the male weakened entirely and became inert.

For two days more did symptoms not subside. The child's skin, hitherto drenched in sweat, grew dry and hot, the pulse ceased to be full and firm – albeit remaining of average strength, slow rather than fast. No more did he wake, nor did he scream.

Finally, came the seventh day. The male awoke and opened his eyes, and his eyes were as those of a viper . . .

Carla Demetia Crest, *The Trial of Grasses and other secret Witcher practices, seen with my own eyes*, manuscript exclusively accessible to the Chapter of Wizards

CHAPTER THREE

"Your fears were unfounded, entirely ungrounded." Triss grimaced, resting her elbows on the table. "The time when wizards used to hunt Sources and magically gifted children, tearing them from their parents or guardians by force or deceit, is long gone. Did you really think I might want to take Ciri away from you?"

Lambert snorted and turned his face away. Eskel and Vesemir looked at Geralt, and Geralt said nothing. He continued to gaze off to the side, playing incessantly with his silver witcher medallion, depicting the head of a snarling wolf. Triss knew the medallion reacted to magic. On such a night as Midinváerne, when the air itself was vibrating with magic, the witchers' medallions must be practically humming. It must be both irritating and bothersome.

"No, child," Vesemir finally said. "We know you would not do such a thing. But we also know that you do, ultimately, have to tell the Chapter about her. We've known for a long time that every wizard, male or female, is burdened with this duty. You don't take talented children from their parents and guardians any more. You observe such children so that later – at the right moment – you can fascinate them in magic, influence them—"

"Have no fear," she interrupted coldly. "I will not tell anyone about Ciri. Not even the Chapter. Why are you looking at me like that?"

"We're amazed by the ease with which you pledge to keep this secret," said Eskel calmly. "Forgive me, Triss, I do not mean to offend you, but what has happened to your legendary loyalty to the Council and Chapter?"

"A lot has happened. The war changed many things, and the battle for Sodden Hill changed even more. I won't bore you with the politics, especially as certain issues and affairs are bound by secrets I am not allowed to divulge. But as for loyalty . . . I am loyal. And believe me, in this matter I can be loyal to both you and to the Chapter."

"Such double loyalty" – Geralt looked her in the eyes for the first time that evening – "is devilishly difficult to manage. Rarely does it succeed, Triss."

The enchantress turned her gaze on Ciri. The girl was sitting on a bearskin with Coën, tucked away in the far corner of the hall, and both were busy playing a hand-slapping game. The game was growing monotonous as both were incredibly quick – neither could manage to slap the other's hand in any way. This, however, clearly neither mattered to them nor spoiled their game.

"Geralt," she said, "when you found Ciri, on the Yaruga, you took her with you. You brought her to Kaer Morhen, hid her from the world and do not let even those closest to the child know she is alive. You did this because something – about which I know nothing – convinced you that destiny exists, holds sway over us, and guides us in everything we do. I think the same, and have always done so. If destiny wants Ciri to become a magician, she will become one. Neither the Chapter nor the Council have to know about her, they don't have to observe or encourage her. So in keeping your secret I won't betray the Chapter in any way. But as you know, there is something of a hitch here."

"Were it only one," sighed Vesemir. "Go on, child."

"The girl has magical abilities, and that can't be neglected. It's too dangerous."

"In what way?"

"Uncontrolled powers are an ominous thing. For both the Source and those in their vicinity. The Source can threaten those around them in many ways. But they threaten themselves in only one. Mental illness. Usually catatonia."

"Devil take it," said Lambert after a long silence. "I am listening to you half-convinced that someone here has already lost their marbles and will, any moment now, present a threat to the rest of us. Destiny, sources, spells, hocus-pocus . . . Aren't you exaggerating, Merigold? Is this the first child to be brought to the Keep? Geralt didn't find destiny; he found another homeless, orphaned child. We'll teach the girl the sword and let her out into the world like the others. True, I admit we've never trained a girl in Kaer Morhen before. We've had some problems with Ciri, made mistakes, and it's a good thing you've pointed them out to us. But don't let us exaggerate. She is not so remarkable as to make us fall on our knees and raise our eyes to the heavens. Is there a lack of female warriors roaming the world? I assure you, Merigold, Ciri will leave here skilful and healthy, strong and able to face life. And, I warrant, without catatonia or any other epilepsy. Unless you delude her into believing she has some such disease."

"Vesemir," Triss turned in her chair, "tell him to keep quiet, he's getting in the way."

"You think you know it all," said Lambert calmly, "but you don't. Not yet. Look."

He stretched his hand towards the hearth, arranging his fingers together in a strange way. The chimney roared and howled, the flames burst out violently, the glowing embers grew brighter and rained sparks. Geralt, Vesemir and Eskel glanced at Ciri anxiously but the girl paid no attention to the spectacular fireworks.

Triss folded her arms and looked at Lambert defiantly.

"The Sign of Aard," she stated calmly. "Did you think to impress me? With the use of the same sign, strengthened through concentration, will-power and a spell, I can blow the logs from the chimney in a moment and blast them so high you will think they are stars."

"You can," he agreed. "But Ciri can't. She can't form the Sign of Aard. Or any other sign. She has tried hundreds of times, to no effect. And you know our Signs require minimal power. Ciri does not even have that. She is an absolutely normal child. She has not the least magical power – she has, in fact, a comprehensive lack of ability. And here you are telling us she's a Source, trying to threaten us—"

"A Source," she explained coldly, "has no control over their skills, no command over them. They are a medium, something like a transmitter. Unknowingly they get in touch with energy, unknowingly they convert it. And when they try to control it, when they strain trying to form the Signs perhaps, nothing comes of it. And nothing will come of it, not just after hundreds of attempts but after thousands. It is one characteristic of a Source. Then, one day, a moment comes when the Source does not exert itself, does not strain, is daydreaming or thinking about cabbage and sausages, playing dice, enjoying themselves in bed with a partner, picking their nose . . . and suddenly something happens. A house might go up in flames. Or sometimes, half a town goes up."

"You're exaggerating, Merigold."

"Lambert." Geralt released his medallion and rested his hands on the table. "First, stop calling Triss 'Merigold'. She has asked you a number of times not to. Second, Triss is not exaggerating. I saw Ciri's mother, Princess Pavetta, in action with my own eyes. I tell you, it was really something. I don't know if she was a Source or not, but no one suspected she had any power at all until, save by a hair's breadth, she almost reduced the royal castle of Cintra to ashes."

"We should assume, therefore," said Eskel, lighting the candles in yet another candle-stick, "that Ciri could, indeed, be genetically burdened."

"Not only could," said Vesemir, "she *is* so burdened. On the one hand Lambert is right. Ciri is not capable of forming Signs. On the other . . . We have all seen . . ."

He fell silent and looked at Ciri who, with a joyful squeal, acknowledged that she had the upper hand in the game. Triss spied a small smile on Coën's face and was sure he had allowed her to win.

"Precisely," she sneered. "You have all seen. What have you seen? Under what circumstances did you see it?

Don't you think, boys, that the time has come for more truthful confessions? Hell, I repeat, I will keep your secret. You have my word."

Lambert glanced at Geralt; Geralt nodded in assent. The younger witcher stood and took a large rectangular crystal carafe and a smaller phial from a high shelf. He poured the contents of the phial into the carafe, shook it several times and poured the transparent liquid into the chalices on the table.

"Have a drink with us, Triss."

"Is the truth so terrible," she mocked, "that we can't talk about it soberly? Do I have to get drunk in order to hear it?"

"Don't be such a know-all. Take a sip. You will find it easier to understand."

"What is it?"

"White Seagull."

"What?"

"A mild remedy," Eskel smiled, "for pleasant dreams."

"Damn it! A witcher hallucinogenic? That's why your eyes shine like that in the evenings!"

"White Seagull is very gentle. It's Black Seagull that is hallucinogenic."

"If there's magic in this liquid I'm not allowed to take it!"

"Exclusively natural ingredients," Geralt reassured her but he looked, she noticed, disconcerted. He was clearly afraid she would question them about the elixir's ingredients. "And diluted with a great deal of water. We would not offer you anything that could harm you."

The sparkling liquid, with its strange taste, struck her

throat with its chill and then dispersed warmth throughout her body. The magician ran her tongue over her gums and palate. She was unable to recognise any of the ingredients.

"You gave Ciri some of this . . . Seagull to drink," she surmised. "And then—"

"It was an accident," Geralt interrupted quickly. "That first evening, just after we arrived . . . she was thirsty, and the Seagull stood on the table. Before we had time to react, she had drunk it all in one go. And fallen into a trance."

"We had such a fright," Vesemir admitted, and sighed. "Oh, that we did, child. More than we could take."

"She started speaking with another voice," the magician stated calmly, looking at the witchers' eyes gleaming in the candlelight. "She started talking about events and matters of which she could have no knowledge. She started . . . to prophesy. Right? What did she say?"

"Rubbish," said Lambert dryly. "Senseless drivel."

"Then I have no doubt" – she looked straight at him – "that you understood each other perfectly well. Drivel is your speciality – and I am further convinced of it every time you open your mouth. Do me a great favour and don't open it for a while, all right?"

"This once," said Eskel gravely, rubbing the scar across his cheek, "Lambert is right, Triss. After drinking Seagull Ciri really was incomprehensible. That first time it was gibberish. Only after—"

He broke off. Triss shook her head.

"It was only the second time that she started talking sense," she guessed. "So there was a second time, too. Also after she drank a drug because of your carelessness?"

"Triss." Geralt raised his head. "This is not the time for your childish spitefulness. It doesn't amuse us. It worries and upsets us. Yes, there was a second time, too, and a third. Ciri fell, quite by accident, during an exercise. She lost consciousness. When she regained it, she had fallen into another trance. And once again she spoke nonsense. Again it was not her voice. And again it was incomprehensible. But I have heard similar voices before, heard a similar way of speaking. It's how those poor, sick, demented women known as oracles speak. You see what I'm thinking?"

"Clearly. That was the second time, get to the third."

Geralt wiped his brow, suddenly beaded with sweat, on his forearm. "Ciri often wakes up at night," he continued. "Shouting. She has been through a lot. She does not want to talk about it but it is clear that she saw things no child should see in Cintra and Angren. I even fear that . . . that someone harmed her. It comes back to her in dreams. Usually she is easy to reassure and she falls asleep without any problem . . . But once, after waking . . . she was in a trance again. She again spoke with someone else's, unpleasant, menacing voice. She spoke clearly and made sense. She prophesied. Foresaw the future. And what she foretold . . ."

"What? What, Geralt?"

"Death," Vesemir said gently. "Death, child."

Triss glanced at Ciri, who was shrilly accusing Coën of cheating. Coën put his arms around her and burst out laughing. The magician suddenly realised that she had never, up until now, heard any of the witchers laugh.

"For whom?" she asked briefly, still gazing at Coën.

"Him," said Vesemir.

"And me," Geralt added. And smiled.

"When she woke up—"

"She remembered nothing. And we didn't ask her any questions."

"Quite so. As to the prophecy . . . Was it specific? Detailed?"

"No." Geralt looked her straight in the eyes. "Confused. Don't ask about it, Triss. We are not worried by the contents of Ciri's prophecies and ravings but about what happens to her. We're not afraid for ourselves but—"

"Careful," warned Vesemir. "Don't talk about it in front of her."

Coën approached the table carrying the girl piggy-back.

"Wish everybody goodnight, Ciri," he said. "Say goodnight to those night owls. We're going to sleep. It's nearly midnight. In a minute it'll be the end of Midinváerne. As of tomorrow, every day brings spring closer!"

"I'm thirsty." Ciri slipped off his back and reached for Eskel's chalice. Eskel deftly moved the vessel beyond her reach and grabbed a jug of water. Triss stood quickly.

"Here you are." She gave her half-full chalice to the girl while meaningfully squeezing Geralt's arm and looking Vesemir in the eye. "Drink."

"Triss," whispered Eskel, watching Ciri drink greedily, "what are you doing? It's—"

"Not a word, please."

They did not have to wait long for it to take effect. Ciri suddenly grew rigid, cried out, and smiled a broad, happy smile. She squeezed her eyelids shut and stretched out her arms. She laughed, spun a pirouette and danced on tiptoes. Lambert moved the stool away in a flash, leaving Coën standing between the dancing girl and the hearth.

Triss jumped up and tore an amulet from her pouch – a sapphire set in silver on a thin chain. She squeezed it tightly in her hand.

"Child . . ." groaned Vesemir. "What are you doing?"

"I know what I'm doing," she said sharply. "Ciri has fallen into a trance and I am going to contact her psychically. I am going to enter her. I told you, she is something like a magical transmitter – I've got to know what she is transmitting, how, and from where she is drawing the aura, how she is transforming it. It's Midinváerne, a favourable night for such an undertaking . . ."

"I don't like it." Geralt frowned. "I don't like it at all."

"Should either of us suffer an epileptic fit," the magician said ignoring his words, "you know what to do. A stick between our teeth, hold us down, wait for it to pass. Chin up, boys. I've done this before."

Ciri ceased dancing, sank to her knees, extended her arms and rested her head on her lap. Triss pressed the now warm amulet to her temple and murmured the formula of a spell. She closed her eyes, concentrated her willpower and gave out a burst of magic.

The sea roared, waves thundered against the rocky shore and exploded in high geysers amidst the boulders. She flapped her wings, chasing the salty wind. Indescribably happy, she dived, caught up with a flock of her companions, brushed the crests of the waves with her claws, soared into the sky again, shedding water droplets, and glided, tossed by the gale whistling through her pinfeathers. *Force of suggestion*, she thought soberly. *It is only force of suggestion. Seagull!*

Triiiss! Triiss!

Ciri? Where are you?
Triiiss!

The cry of the seagulls ceased. The magician still felt the wet splash of the breakers but the sea was no longer below her. Or it was – but it was a sea of grass, an endless plateau stretching as far as the horizon. Triss, with horror, realised she was looking at the view from the top of Sodden Hill. But it was not the Hill. It could not be the Hill.

The sky suddenly grew dark, shadows swirled around her. She saw a long column of indistinct figures slowly climbing down the mountainside. She heard murmurs superimposed over each other, mingling into an uncanny, incomprehensible chorus.

Ciri was standing nearby with her back turned to her. The wind was blowing her ashen hair about.

The indistinct, hazy figures continued past in a long, unending column. Passing her, they turned their heads. Triss suppressed a cry, watching the listless, peaceful faces and their dead, unseeing eyes. She did not know all of the faces, did not recognise them. But some of them she did know.

Coral. Vanielle. Yoël. Pox-marked Axel . . .

"Why have you brought me here?" she whispered. "Why?"

Ciri turned. She raised her arm and the magician saw a trickle of blood run down her life-line, across her palm and onto her wrist.

"It is the rose," the girl said calmly. "The rose of Shaerrawedd. I pricked myself. It is nothing. It is only blood. The blood of elves . . ."

The sky grew even darker, then, a moment later, flared with the sharp, blinding glare of lightning. Everything froze in the silence and stillness. Triss took a step, wanting to make sure she could. She stopped next to Ciri and saw that both of them stood on the edge of a bottomless chasm where reddish smoke, glowing as though it was lit from behind, was swirling. The flash of another soundless bolt of lightning suddenly revealed a long, marble staircase leading into the depths of the abyss.

"It has to be this way," Ciri said in a shaky voice. "There is no other. Only this. Down the stairs. It has to be this way because . . . Va'esse deireádh aep eigean . . ."

"Speak," whispered the magician. "Speak, child."

"The Child of Elder Blood . . . Feainnewedd . . . Luned aepHenIchaer . . . Deithwen . . . TheWhiteFlame . . . No, no . . . No!"

"Ciri!"

"The black knight . . . with feathers in his helmet . . . What did he do to me? What happened? I was frightened . . . I'm still frightened. It's not ended, it will never end. The lion cub must die . . . Reasons of state . . . No . . . No . . ."

"Ciri!"

"No!" The girl turned rigid and squeezed her eyelids shut. "No, no, I don't want to! Don't touch me!"

Ciri's face suddenly changed, hardened; her voice became metallic, cold and hostile, resounding with threatening, cruel mockery.

"You have come all this way with her, Triss Merigold? All the way here? You have come too far, Fourteenth One. I warned you."

"Who are you?" Triss shuddered but she kept her voice under control.

"You will know when the time comes."

"I will know now!"

The magician raised her arms, extended them abruptly, putting all her strength into a Spell of Identification. The magic curtain burst but behind it was a second . . . A third . . . A fourth . . .

Triss sank to her knees with a groan. But reality continued to burst, more doors opened, a long, endless row leading to nowhere. To emptiness.

"You are wrong, Fourteenth One," the metallic, inhuman voice sneered. "You've mistaken the stars reflected on the surface of the lake at night for the heavens."

"Do not touch— Do not touch that child!"

"She is not a child."

Ciri's lips moved but Triss saw that the girl's eyes were dead, glazed and vacant.

"She is not a child," the voice repeated. "She is the Flame, the White Flame which will set light to the world. She is the Elder Blood, Hen Ichaer. The blood of elves. The seed which will not sprout but burst into flame. The blood which will be defiled . . . When Tedd Deireádh arrives, the Time of End. Va'esse deireádh aep eigean!"

"Are you foretelling death?" shouted Triss. "Is that all you can do, foretell death? For everyone? Them, her . . . Me?"

"You? You are already dead, Fourteenth One. Everything in you has already died."

"By the power of the spheres," moaned the magician, activating what little remained of her strength and drawing her hand through the air, "I throw a spell on you by water, fire, earth and air. I conjure you in thought, in dream and in death, by all that was, by what is and by what will be. I cast my spell on you. Who are you? Speak!"

Ciri turned her head away. The vision of the staircase leading down into the depths of the abyss disappeared, dissolved, and in its place appeared a grey, leaden sea, foaming, crests of waves breaking. And the seagull's cries burst through the silence once more.

"Fly," said the voice, through the girl's lips. "It is time. Go back to where you came from, Fourteenth of the Hill. Fly on the wings of a gull and listen to the cry of other seagulls. Listen carefully!"

"I conjure you—"

"You cannot. Fly, seagull!"

And suddenly the wet salty air was there again, roaring with the gale, and there was the flight, a flight with no beginning and no end. Seagulls cried wildly, cried and commanded.

Triss?

Ciri?

Forget about him! Don't torture him! Forget! Forget, Triss!

Forget!

Triss! Triss! Trisss!

"Triss!"

She opened her eyes, tossed her head on the pillow and moved her numb hands.

"Geralt?"

"I'm here. How are you feeling?"

She cast her eyes around. She was in her chamber, lying on the bed. On the best bed in the whole of Kaer Morhen.

"What is happening to Ciri?"

"She is asleep."

"How long—"

"Too long," he interrupted. He covered her with the duvet and put his arms around her. As he leaned over the wolf's head medallion swayed just above her face. "What you did was not the best of ideas, Triss."

"Everything is all right." She trembled in his embrace. *That's not true*, she thought. *Nothing's all right*. She turned her face so that the medallion didn't touch her. There were many theories about the properties of witcher amulets and none advised magicians to touch them during the Equinox.

"Did . . . Did we say anything during the trance?"

"You, nothing. You were unconscious throughout. Ciri . . . just before she woke up . . . said: 'Va'esse deireádh aep eigean'."

"She knows the Elder Speech?"

"Not enough to say a whole sentence."

"A sentence which means: 'Something is ending'." The magician wiped her face with her hand. "Geralt, this is a serious matter. The girl is an exceptionally powerful medium. I don't know what or who she is contacting, but I think there are no limits to her connection. Something wants to take possession of her. Something which is too powerful for me. I am afraid for her. Another trance could end in mental illness. I have no control over it, don't know how to, can't . . . If it proved necessary, I would not be able to block or suppress her powers; I would not even be capable, if there were no other option, of permanently extinguishing them. You have to get help from another magician. A more gifted one. More experienced. You know who I'm talking about."

"I do." He turned his head away, clenched his lips.

"Don't resist. Don't defend yourself. I can guess why

you turned to me rather than her. Overcome your pride, crush your rancour and obstinacy. There is no point to it, you'll torture yourself to death. And you are risking Ciri's health and life in the process. Another trance is liable to be more dangerous to her than the Trial of Grasses. Ask Yennefer for help, Geralt."

"And you, Triss?"

"What about me?" She swallowed with difficulty. "I'm not important. I let you down. I let you down . . . in everything. I was . . . I was your mistake. Nothing more."

"Mistakes," he said with effort, "are also important to me. I don't cross them out of my life, or memory. And I never blame others for them. You are important to me, Triss, and always will be. You never let me down. Never. Believe me."

She remained silent a long while.

"I will stay until spring," she said finally, struggling against her shaking voice. "I will stay with Ciri . . . I will watch over her. Day and night. I will be with her day and night. And when spring is here . . . when spring is here we will take her to Melitele's Temple in Ellander. The thing that wants to possess her might not be able to reach her in the temple. And then you will ask Yennefer for help."

"All right, Triss. Thank you."

"Geralt?"

"Yes."

"Ciri said something else, didn't she? Something only you heard. Tell me what it was."

"No," he protested and his voice quivered. "No, Triss."

"Please."

"She wasn't speaking to me."

"I know. She was speaking to me. Tell me, please."

"After coming to . . . When I picked her up . . . She whispered: 'Forget about him. Don't torture him.'"

"I won't," she said quietly. "But I can't forget. Forgive me."

"I am the one who ought to be asking for forgiveness. And not only asking you."

"You love her that much," she stated, not asking.

"That much," he admitted in a whisper after a long moment of silence.

"Geralt."

"Yes, Triss?"

"Stay with me tonight."

"Triss . . ."

"Only stay."

"All right."

Not long after Midinváerne the snow stopped falling. The frost came.

Triss stayed with Ciri day and night. She watched over her. She surrounded her with care, visible and invisible.

The girl woke up shouting almost every night. She was delirious, holding her cheek and crying with pain. The magician calmed her with spells and elixirs, put her to sleep, cuddling and rocking her in her arms. And then she herself would be unable to sleep for a long time, thinking about what Ciri had said in her sleep and after she came to. And she felt a mounting fear. Va'esse deireádh aep eigean . . . Something is ending . . .

That is how it was for ten days and nights. And finally it passed. It ended, disappeared without a trace. Ciri calmed, she slept peacefully with no nightmares, and no dreams.

But Triss kept a constant watch. She did not leave the girl for a moment. She surrounded her with care. Visible and invisible.

"Faster, Ciri! Lunge, attack, dodge! Half-pirouette, thrust, dodge! Balance! Balance with your left arm or you'll fall from the comb! And you'll hurt your . . . womanly attributes!"

"What?"

"Nothing. Aren't you tired? We'll take a break, if you like."

"No, Lambert! I can go on. I'm not that weak, you know. Shall I try jumping over every other post?"

"Don't you dare! You might fall and then Merigold will tear my— my head off."

"I won't fall!"

"I've told you once and I'm not going to say it again. Don't show off! Steady on your legs! And breathe, Ciri, breathe! You're panting like a dying mammoth!"

"That's not true!"

"Don't squeal. Practise! Attack, dodge! Parry! Half-pirouette! Parry, full pirouette! Steadier on the posts, damn it! Don't wobble! Lunge, thrust! Faster! Half-pirouette! Jump and cut! That's it! Very good!"

"Really? Was that really very good, Lambert?"

"Who said so?"

"You did! A moment ago!"

"Slip of the tongue. Attack! Half-pirouette! Dodge! And again! Ciri, where was the parry? How many times do I have to tell you? After you dodge you always parry, deliver a blow with the blade to protect your head and shoulders! Always!"

"Even when I'm only fighting one opponent?"

"You never know what you're fighting. You never know what's happening behind you. You always have to cover yourself. Foot and sword work! It's got to be a reflex. Reflex, understand? You mustn't forget that. You forget it in a real fight and you're finished. Again! At last! That's it! See how such a parry lands? You can take any strike from it. You can cut backwards from it, if you have to. Right, show me a pirouette and a thrust backwards."

"Haaa!"

"Very good. You see the point now? Has it got through to you?"

"I'm not stupid!"

"You're a girl. Girls don't have brains."

"Lambert! If Triss heard that!"

"If ifs and ands were pots and pans. All right, that's enough. Come down. We'll take a break."

"I'm not tired!"

"But I am. I said, a break. Come down from the comb."

"Turning a somersault?"

"What do you think? Like a hen off its roost? Go on, jump. Don't be afraid, I'm here for you."

"Haaaa!"

"Nice. Very good – for a girl. You can take off the blindfold now."

"Triss, maybe that's enough for today? What do you think? Maybe we could take the sleigh and ride down the hill? The sun's shining, the snow's sparkling so much it hurts the eyes! The weather's beautiful!"

"Don't lean out or you'll fall from the window."

"Let's go sleighing, Triss!"

"Suggest that again in Elder Speech and we'll end the lesson there. Move away from the window, come back to the table . . . Ciri, how many times do I have to ask you? Stop waving that sword about and put it away."

"It's my new sword! It's real, a witcher's sword! Made of steel which fell from heaven! Really! Geralt said so and he never lies, you know that!"

"Oh, yes. I know that."

"I've got to get used to this sword. Uncle Vesemir had it adjusted just right for my weight, height and arm-length. I've got to get my hand and wrist accustomed to it!"

"Accustom yourself to your heart's content, but outside. Not here! Well, I'm listening. You wanted to suggest we get the sleigh out. In Elder Speech. So — suggest it."

"Hmmm . . . What's 'sleigh'?"

"Sledd as a noun. Aesledde as a verb."

"Aha . . . Vaien aesledde, ell'ea?"

"Don't end a question that way, it's impolite. You form questions using intonation."

"But the children from the Islands—"

"You're not learning the local Skellige jargon but classical Elder Speech."

"And why am I learning the Speech, tell me?"

"So that you know it. It's fitting to learn things you don't know. Anyone who doesn't know other languages is handicapped."

"But people only speak the common tongue anyway!"

"True. But some speak more than just it. I warrant, Ciri, that it is better to count yourself amongst those few than amongst everyone. So, I'm listening. A full sentence: 'The weather today is beautiful, so let's get the sleigh.'"

"Elaine . . . Hmmm . . . Elaine tedd a'taeghane, a va'en aesledde?"

"Very good."

"Ha! So let's get the sleigh."

"We will. But let me finish applying my make-up."

"And who are you putting make-up on for, exactly?"

"Myself. A woman accentuates her beauty for her own self-esteem."

"Hmmm . . . Do you know what? I feel pretty poorly too. Don't laugh, Triss!"

"Come here. Sit on my knee. Put the sword away, I've already asked you! Thank you. Now take that large brush and powder your face. Not so much, girl, not so much! Look in the mirror. See how pretty you are?"

"I can't see any difference. I'll do my eyes, all right? What are you laughing at? You always paint your eyes. I want to too."

"Fine. Here you are, put some shadow on your eyelids with this. Ciri, don't close both your eyes or you won't see anything – you're smudging your whole face. Take a tiny bit and only skim over the eyelids. Skim, I said! Let me, I'll just spread it a little. Close your eyes. Now open them."

"Oooo!"

"See the difference? A tiny bit of shadow won't do any harm, even to such beautiful eyes as yours. The elves knew what they were doing when they invented eye shadow."

"Elves?"

"You didn't know? Make-up is an elvish invention. We've learned a lot of useful things from the Elder People. And we've given bloody little back in return. Now take the pencil and draw a thin line across your upper lids, just above the lashes. Ciri, what are you doing?"

"Don't laugh! My eyelid's trembling! That's why!"

"Part your lips a little and it'll stop trembling. See?"

"Ooooh!"

"Come on, now we'll go and stun the witchers with our beauty. It's hard to find a prettier sight. And then we'll take the sleigh and smudge our make-up in the deep snowdrifts."

"And we'll make ourselves up again!"

"No. We'll tell Lambert to warm the bathroom and we'll take a bath."

"Again? Lambert says we're using up too much fuel with our baths."

"Lambert cáen me a'báeth aep arse."

"What? I didn't understand . . ."

"With time you'll master the idioms, too. We've still got a lot of time for studying before spring. But now . . . Va'en aesledde, me elaine luned!"

"Here, on this engraving . . . No, damn it, not on that one . . . On this one. This is, as you already know, a ghoul. Tell us, Ciri, what you've learned about ghouls . . . Hey, look at me! What the devil have you got on your eyelids?"

"Greater self-esteem!"

"What? Never mind, I'm listening."

"Hmm . . . The ghoul, Uncle Vesemir, is a corpse-devouring monster. It can be seen in cemeteries, in the vicinity of barrows, anywhere the dead are buried. At nec— necropolia. On battlegrounds, on fields of battle . . ."

"So it's only a danger to the dead, is that right?"

"No, not only. A ghoul may also attack the living if it's hungry or falls into a fury. If, for example, there's a battle . . . A lot of people killed . . ."

"What's the matter, Ciri?"

"Nothing . . ."

"Ciri, listen. Forget about that. That will never return."

"I saw . . . In Sodden and in Transriver . . . Entire fields . . . They were lying there, being eaten by wolves and wild dogs. Birds were picking at them . . . I guess there were ghouls there too . . ."

"That's why you're learning about ghouls now, Ciri. When you know about something it stops being a nightmare. When you know how to fight something, it stops being so threatening. So how do you fight a ghoul, Ciri?"

"With a silver sword. The ghoul is sensitive to silver."

"And to what else?"

"Bright light. And fire."

"So you can fight it with light and fire?"

"You can, but it's dangerous. A witcher doesn't use light or fire because it makes it harder to see. Every light creates a shadow and shadows make it harder to get your bearings. One must always fight in darkness, by moon or starlight."

"Quite right. You've remembered it well, clever girl. And now look here, at this engraving."

"Eeeueeeuuueee—"

"Oh well, true enough, it is not a beautiful cu— creature. It's a graveir. A graveir is a type of ghoul. It looks
very much like a ghoul but is considerably larger. He can
also be told apart, as you can see, by these three bony
combs on his skull. The rest is the same as any other
corpse-eater. Take note of the short, blunt claws, adapted
for digging up graves, and churning the earth. Strong teeth
for shattering bones and a long, narrow tongue used to
lick the decaying marrow from them. Such stinking marrow is a delicacy for the graveir . . . What's the matter?"

"Nnnnothing."

"You're completely pale. And green. You don't eat
enough. Did you eat breakfast?"

"Yeeees. I diiiidddddd."

"What was I . . . Aha. I almost forgot. Remember, because this is important. Graveirs, like ghouls and other
monsters in this category, do not have their own ecological niche. They are relicts from the age of the interpen-
etration of spheres. Killing them does not upset the order
and interconnections of nature which prevail in our present sphere. In this sphere these monsters are foreign and
there is no place for them. Do you understand, Ciri?"

"I do, Uncle Vesemir. Geralt explained it to me. I know
all that. An ecological niche is—"

"All right, that's fine. I know what it is. If Geralt has
explained it to you, you don't have to recite it to me. Let
us return to the graveir. Graveirs appear quite rarely,
fortunately, because they're bloody dangerous sons-of-
bitches. The smallest wound inflicted by a graveir will in-
fect you with corpse venom. Which elixir is used to treat
corpse venom poisoning, Ciri?"

" 'Golden Oriole'."

"Correct. But it is better to avoid infection to begin with. That is why, when fighting a graveir, you must never get close to the bastard. You always fight from a distance and strike from a leap."

"Hmm . . . And where's it best to strike one?"

"We're just getting to that. Look . . ."

"Once more, Ciri. We'll go through it slowly so that you can master each move. Now, I'm attacking you with tierce, taking the position as if to thrust . . . Why are you retreating?"

"Because I know it's a feint! You can move into a wide sinistra or strike with upper quarte. And I'll retreat and parry with a counterfeint!"

"Is that so? And if I do this?"

"Auuu! It was supposed to be slow! What did I do wrong, Coën?"

"Nothing. I'm just taller and stronger than you are."

"That's not fair!"

"There's no such thing as a fair fight. You have to make use of every advantage and every opportunity that you get. By retreating you gave me the opportunity to put more force into the strike. Instead of retreating you should have executed a half-pirouette to the left and tried to cut at me from below, with quarte dextra, under the chin, in the cheek or throat."

"As if you'd let me! You'll do a reverse pirouette and get my neck from the left before I can parry! How am I meant to know what you're doing?"

"You have to know. And you do know."

"Oh, sure!"

"Ciri, what we're doing is fighting. I'm your opponent.

I want to and have to defeat you because my life is at stake. I'm taller and stronger than you so I'm going to watch for opportunities to strike in order to avoid or break your parry – as you've just seen. What do I need a pirouette for? I'm already in sinistra, see? What could be simpler than to strike with a seconde, under the arm, on the inside? If I slash your artery, you'll be dead in a couple of minutes. Defend yourself!"

"Haaaa!"

"Very good. A beautiful, quick parry. See how exercising your wrist has come in useful? And now pay attention – a lot of fencers make the mistake of executing a standing parry and freeze for a second, and that's just when you can catch them out, strike – like so!"

"Haa!"

"Beautiful! Now jump away, jump away immediately, pirouette! I could have a dagger in my left hand! Good! Very good! And now, Ciri? What am I going to do now?"

"How am I to know?"

"Watch my feet! How is my body weight distributed? What can I do from this position?"

"Anything!"

"So spin, spin, force me to open up! Defend yourself! Good! And again! Good! And again!"

"Owwww!"

"Not so good."

"Uff . . . What did I do wrong?"

"Nothing. I'm just faster. Take your guards off. We'll sit for a moment, take a break. You must be tired, you've been running the Trail all morning."

"I'm not tired. I'm hungry."

"Bloody hell, so am I. And today's Lambert's turn and he can't cook anything other than noodles . . . If he could only cook those properly . . ."

"Coën?"

"Aha?"

"I'm still not fast enough—"

"You're very fast."

"Will I ever be as fast as you?"

"I doubt it."

"Hmm . . . And are you—? Who's the best fencer in the world?"

"I've no idea."

"You've never known one?"

"I've known many who believed themselves to be the best."

"Oh! What were they? What were their names? What could they do?"

"Hold on, hold on, girl. I haven't got an answer to those questions. Is it all that important?"

"Of course it's important! I'd like to know who these fencers are. And where they are."

"Where they are? I know that."

"Ah! So where?"

"In cemeteries."

"Pay attention, Ciri. We're going to attach a third pendulum now – you can manage two already. You use the same steps as for two only there's one more dodge. Ready?"

"Yes."

"Focus yourself. Relax. Breathe in, breathe out. Attack!"

"Ouch! Owwww . . . Damn it!"

"Don't swear. Did it hit you hard?"

"No, it only brushed me . . . What did I do wrong?"

"You ran in at too even a pace, you sped the second half-pirouette up a bit too much, and your feint was too wide. And as a result you were carried straight under the pendulum."

"But Geralt, there's no room for a dodge and turn there! They're too close to each other!"

"There's plenty of room, I assure you. But the gaps are worked out to force you to make arrhythmic moves. This is a fight, Ciri, not ballet. You can't move rhythmically in a fight. You have to distract the opponent with your moves, confuse his reactions. Ready for another try?"

"Ready. Start those damn logs swinging."

"Don't swear. Relax. Attack!"

"Ha! Ha! Well, how about that? How was that, Geralt? It didn't even brush me!"

"And you didn't even brush the second sack with your sword. So I repeat, this is a fight. Not ballet, not acrobatics— What are you muttering now?"

"Nothing."

"Relax. Adjust the bandage on your wrist. Don't grip the hilt so tightly, it distracts you and upsets your equilibrium. Breathe calmly. Ready?"

"Yes."

"Go!"

"Ouch! May you— Geralt, it's impossible! There's not enough room for a feint and a change of foot. And when I strike from both legs, without a feint . . ."

"I saw what happens when you strike without a feint. Does it hurt?"

"No. Not much . . ."

"Sit down next to me. Take a break."

"I'm not tired. Geralt, I'm not going to be able to jump over that third pendulum even if I rest for ten years. I can't be any faster—"

"And you don't have to be. You're fast enough."

"Tell me how to do it then. Half-pirouette, dodge and hit at the same time?"

"It's very simple; you just weren't paying attention. I told you before you started – an additional dodge is necessary. Displacement. An additional half-pirouette is superfluous. The second time round, you did everything well and passed all the pendulums."

"But I didn't hit the sack because . . . Geralt, without a half-pirouette I can't strike because I lose speed, I don't have the . . . the, what do you call it . . ."

"Impetus. That's true. So gain some impetus and energy. But not through a pirouette and change of foot because there's not enough time for it. Hit the pendulum with your sword."

"The pendulum? I've got to hit the sacks!"

"This is a fight, Ciri. The sacks represent your opponent's sensitive areas, you've got to hit them. The pendulums – which simulate your opponent's weapon – you have to avoid, dodge past. When the pendulum hits you, you're wounded. In a real fight, you might not get up again. The pendulum mustn't touch you. But you can hit the pendulum . . . Why are you screwing your nose up?"

"I'm . . . not going to be able to parry the pendulum with my sword. I'm too weak . . . I'll always be too weak! Because I'm a girl!"

"Come here, girl. Wipe your nose, and listen carefully.

No strongman, mountain-toppling giant or muscle-man
is going to be able to parry a blow aimed at him by a
dracolizard's tail, gigascorpion's pincers or a griffin's
claws. And that's precisely the sort of weapons the pendulum simulates. So don't even try to parry. You're not
deflecting the pendulum, you're deflecting yourself from
it. You're intercepting its energy, which you need in order
to deal a blow. A light, but very swift deflection and in-
stantaneous, equally swift blow from a reverse half-turn
is enough. You're picking impetus up by rebounding. Do
you see?"

"Mhm."

"Speed, Ciri, not strength. Strength is necessary for
a lumberjack axing trees in a forest. That's why, admit-
tedly, girls are rarely lumberjacks. Have you got that?"

"Mhm. Start the pendulums swinging."

"Take a rest first."

"I'm not tired."

"You know how to now? The same steps, feint—"

"I know."

"Attack!"

"Haaa! Ha! Haaaaa! Got you! I got you, you griffin!
Geraaaalt! Did you see that?"

"Don't yell. Control your breathing."

"I did it! I really did it!! I managed it! Praise me,
Geralt!"

"Well done, Ciri. Well done, girl."

In the middle of February, the snow disappeared,
whisked away by a warm wind blowing from the south,
from the pass.

*   *   *

Whatever was happening in the world, the witchers did not want to know.

In the evenings, consistently and determinedly, Triss guided the long conversations held in the dark hall, lit only by the bursts of flames in the great hearth, towards politics. The witchers' reactions were always the same. Geralt, a hand on his forehead, did not say a word. Vesemir nodded, from time to time throwing in comments which amounted to little more than that "in his day" everything had been better, more logical, more honest and healthier. Eskel pretended to be polite, and neither smiled nor made eye contact, and even managed, very occasionally, to be interested in some issue or question of little importance. Coën yawned openly and looked at the ceiling, and Lambert did nothing to hide his disdain.

They did not want to know anything, they cared nothing for dilemmas which drove sleep from kings, wizards, rulers and leaders, or for the problems which made councils, circles and gatherings tremble and buzz. For them, nothing existed beyond the passes drowning in snow or beyond the Gwenllech river carrying ice-floats in its leaden current. For them, only Kaer Morhen existed, lost and lonely amongst the savage mountains.

That evening Triss was irritable and restless – perhaps it was the wind howling along the great castle's walls. And that evening they were all oddly excited – the witchers, apart from Geralt, were unusually talkative. Quite obviously, they only spoke of one thing – spring. About their approaching departure for the Trail. About what the Trail would have in store for them – about vampires, wyverns, leshys, lycanthropes and basilisks.

This time it was Triss who began to yawn and stare at

the ceiling. This time she was the one who remained silent – until Eskel turned to her with a question. A question which she had anticipated.

"And what is it really like in the south, on the Yaruga? Is it worth going there? We wouldn't like to find ourselves in the middle of any trouble."

"What do you mean by trouble?"

"Well, you know . . ." he stammered, "you keep telling us about the possibility of a new war . . . About constant fighting on the borders, about rebellions in the lands invaded by Nilfgaard. You said they're saying the Nilfgaardians might cross the Yaruga again—"

"So what?" said Lambert. "They've been hitting, killing and striking against each other constantly for hundreds of years. It's nothing to worry about. I've already decided – I'm going to the far South, to Sodden, Mahakam and Angren. It's well known that monsters abound wherever armies have passed. The most money is always made in places like that."

"True," Coën acknowledged. "The neighbourhood grows deserted, only women who can't fend for themselves remain in the villages . . . scores of children with no home or care, roaming around . . . Easy prey attracts monsters."

"And the lord barons and village elders," added Eskel, "have their heads full of the war and don't have the time to defend their subjects. They have to hire us. It's true. But from what Triss has been telling us all these evenings, it seems the conflict with Nilfgaard is more serious than that, not just some local little war. Is that right, Triss?"

"Even if it were the case," said the magician spitefully, "surely that suits you? A serious, bloody war will lead to more deserted villages, more widowed women, simply hordes of orphaned children—"

"I can't understand your sarcasm." Geralt took his hand away from his forehead. "I really can't, Triss."

"Nor I, my child." Vesemir raised his head. "What do you mean? Are you thinking about the widows and children? Lambert and Coën speak frivolously, as youngsters do, but it is not the words that are important. After all, they—"

". . . they defend these children," she interrupted crossly. "Yes, I know. From the werewolf who might kill two or three a year, while a Nilfgaardian foray can kill and burn an entire settlement in an hour. Yes, you defend orphans. While I fight that there should be as few of those orphans as possible. I'm fighting the cause, not the effect. That's why I'm on Foltest of Temeria's council and sit with Fercart and Keira Metz. We deliberate on how to stop war from breaking out and, should it come to it, how to defend ourselves. Because war is constantly hovering over us like a vulture. For you it's an adventure. For me, it's a game in which the stakes are survival. I'm involved in this game, and that's why your indifference and frivolity hurt and insult me."

Geralt sat up and looked at her.

"We're witchers, Triss. Can't you understand that?"

"What's there to understand?" The enchantress tossed her chestnut mane back. "Everything's crystal-clear. You've chosen a certain attitude to the world around you. The fact that this world might at any moment fall to pieces has a place in this choice. In mine, it doesn't. That's where we differ."

"I'm not sure it's only there we differ."

"The world is falling to ruins," she repeated. "We can watch it happen and do nothing. Or we can counteract it."

"How?" He smiled derisively. "With our emotions?"

She did not answer, turning her face to the fire roaring in the hearth.

"The world is falling to ruins," repeated Coën, nodding his head in feigned thoughtfulness. "How many times I've heard that."

"Me, too," Lambert grimaced. "And it's not surprising – it's a popular saying of late. It's what kings say when it turns out that a modicum of brains is necessary to rule after all. It's what merchants say when greed and stupidity have led them to bankruptcy. It's what wizards say when they start to lose their influence on politics or income. And the person they're speaking to should expect some sort of proposal straight away. So cut the introduction short, Triss, and present us with your proposition."

"Verbal squabbling has never amused me," the enchantress declared, gauging him with cold eyes, "or displays of eloquence which mock whoever you're talking to. I don't intend to take part in anything like that. You know only too well what I mean. You want to hide your heads in the sand, that's your business. But coming from you, Geralt, it's a great surprise."

"Triss." The white-haired witcher looked her straight in the eyes again. "What do you expect from me? To take an active part in the fight to save a world which is falling to pieces? Am I to enlist in the army and stop Nilfgaard? Should I, if it comes to another battle for Sodden, stand with you on the Hill, shoulder to shoulder, and fight for freedom?"

"I'd be proud," she said quietly, lowering her head. "I'd be proud and happy to fight at your side."

"I believe that. But I'm not gallant enough. Nor valiant enough. I'm not suited to be a soldier or a hero. And having an acute fear of pain, mutilation and death is not the only reason. You can't stop a soldier from being frightened but you can give him motivation to help him overcome that fear. I have no such motivation. I can't have. I'm a witcher: an artificially created mutant. I kill monsters for money. I defend children when their parents pay me to. If Nilfgaardian parents pay me, I'll defend Nilfgaardian children. And even if the world lies in ruin – which does not seem likely to me – I'll carry on killing monsters in the ruins of this world until some monster kills me. That is my fate, my reason, my life and my attitude to the world. And it is not what I chose. It was chosen for me."

"You're embittered," she stated, tugging nervously at a strand of hair. "Or pretending to be. You forget that I know you, so don't play the unfeeling mutant, devoid of a heart, of scruples and of his own free will, in front of me. And the reasons for your bitterness, I can guess and understand. Ciri's prophecy, correct?"

"No, not correct," he answered icily. "I see that you don't know me at all. I'm afraid of death, just like everyone else, but I grew used to the idea of it a very long time ago – I'm not under any illusions. I'm not complaining about fate, Triss – this is plain, cold calculation. Statistics. No witcher has yet died of old age, lying in bed dictating his will. Not a single one. Ciri didn't surprise or frighten me. I know I'm going to die in some cave which stinks of carcases, torn apart by a griffin, lamia or manticore.

But I don't want to die in a war, because they're not my wars."

"I'm surprised at you," she replied sharply. "I'm surprised that you're saying this, surprised by your lack of motivation, as you learnedly chose to describe your supercilious distance and indifference. You were at Sodden, Angren and Transriver. You know what happened to Cintra, know what befell Queen Calanthe and many thousands of people there. You know the hell Ciri went through, know why she cries out at night. And I know, too, because I was also there. I'm afraid of pain and death too, even more so now than I was then – I have good reason. As for motivation, it seems to me that back then I had just as little as you. Why should I, a magician, care about the fates of Sodden, Brugge, Cintra or other kingdoms? The problems of having more or less competent rulers? The interests of merchants and barons? I was a magician. I, too, could have said it wasn't my war, that I could mix elixirs for the Nilfgaardians on the ruins of the world. But I stood on that Hill next to Vilgefortz, next to Artaud Terranova, next to Fercart, next to Enid Findabair and Philippa Eilhart, next to your Yennefer. Next to those who no longer exist – Coral, Yoël, Vanielle . . . There was a moment when out of sheer terror I forgot all my spells except for one – and thanks to that spell I could have teleported myself from that horrific place back home, to my tiny little tower in Maribor. There was a moment, when I threw up from fear, when Yennefer and Coral held me up by the shoulders and hair—"

"Stop. Please, stop."

"No, Geralt. I won't. After all, you want to know what happened there, on the Hill. So listen – there was a din and flames, there were flaming arrows and exploding balls of fire, there were screams and crashes, and I suddenly found myself on the ground on a pile of charred, smoking rags, and I realised that the pile of rags was Yoël and that thing next to her, that awful thing, that trunk with no arms and no legs which was screaming so horrifically was Coral. And I thought the blood in which I was lying was Coral's blood. But it was my own. And then I saw what they had done to me, and I started to howl, howl like a beaten dog, like a battered child— Leave me alone! Don't worry, I'm not going to cry. I'm not a little girl from a tiny tower in Maribor any more. Damn it, I'm Triss Merigold, the Fourteenth One Killed at Sodden. There are fourteen graves at the foot of the obelisk on the Hill, but only thirteen bodies. You're amazed such a mistake could have been made? Most of the corpses were in hard-to-recognise pieces – no one identified them. The living were hard to account for, too. Of those who had known me well, Yennefer was the only one to survive, and Yennefer was blind. Others knew me fleetingly and always recognised me by my beautiful hair. And I, damn it, didn't have it any more!"

Geralt held her closer. She no longer tried to push him away.

"They used the highest magics on us," she continued in a muted voice, "spells, elixirs, amulets and artefacts. Nothing was left wanting for the wounded heroes of the Hill. We were cured, patched up, our former appearances returned to us, our hair and sight restored. You can hardly see the marks. But I will never wear a plunging neckline again, Geralt. Never."

The witchers said nothing. Neither did Ciri, who had

slipped into the hall without a sound and stopped at the threshold, hunching her shoulders and folding her arms.

"So," the magician said after a while, "don't talk to me about motivation. Before we stood on that Hill the Chapter simply told us: 'That is what you have to do.' Whose war was it? What were we defending there? The land? The borders? The people and their cottages? The interests of kings? The wizards' influence and income? Order against Chaos? I don't know! But we defended it because that's what had to be done. And if the need arises, I'll stand on the Hill again. Because if I don't, it will make the sacrifices made the first time futile and unnecessary."

"I'll stand beside you!" shouted Ciri shrilly. "Just wait and see, I'll stand with you! Those Nilfgaardians are going to pay for my grandmother, pay for everything . . . I haven't forgotten!"

"Be quiet," growled Lambert. "Don't butt into grown-ups' conversations—"

"Oh sure!" The girl stamped her foot and in her eyes a green fire kindled. "Why do you think I'm learning to fight with a sword? I want to kill him, that black knight from Cintra with wings on his helmet, for what he did to me, for making me afraid! And I'm going to kill him! That's why I'm learning it!"

"And therefore you'll stop learning," said Geralt in a voice colder than the walls of Kaer Morhen. "Until you understand what a sword is, and what purpose it serves in a witcher's hand, you will not pick one up. You are not learning in order to kill and be killed. You are not learning to kill out of fear and hatred, but in order to save lives. Your own and those of others."

The girl bit her lip, shaking from agitation and anger.

"Understood?"

Ciri raised her head abruptly. "No."

"Then you'll never understand. Get out."

"Geralt, I—"

"Get out."

Ciri spun on her heel and stood still for a moment, undecided, as if waiting – waiting for something that could not happen. Then she ran swiftly up the stairs. They heard the door slam.

"Too severe, Wolf," said Vesemir. "Much too severe. And you shouldn't have done it in Triss's presence. The emotional ties—"

"Don't talk to me about emotions. I've had enough of all this talk about emotions!"

"And why is that?" The magician smiled derisively and coldly. "Why, Geralt? Ciri is normal. She has normal feelings, she accepts emotions naturally, takes them for what they really are. You, obviously, don't understand and are therefore surprised by them. It surprises and irritates you. The fact that someone can experience normal love, normal hatred, normal fear, pain and regret, normal joy and normal sadness. That it is coolness, distance and indifference which are considered abnormal. Oh yes, Geralt, it annoys you, it annoys you so much that you are starting to think about Kaer Morhen's vaults, about the Laboratorium, the dusty demi-johns full of mutagenic poisons—"

"Triss!" called Vesemir, gazing at Geralt's face, suddenly grown pale. But the enchantress refused to be interrupted and spoke faster and faster, louder and louder.

"Who do you want to deceive, Geralt? Me? Her? Or maybe yourself? Maybe you don't want to admit the truth, a truth everyone knows except you? Maybe you don't want to accept the fact that human emotions and feelings weren't killed in you by the elixirs and Grasses! You killed them! You killed them yourself! But don't you dare kill them in the child!"

"Silence!" he shouted, leaping from the chair. "Silence, Merigold!"

He turned away and lowered his arms defencelessly. "Sorry," he said quietly. "Forgive me, Triss." He made for the stairs quickly, but the enchantress was up in a flash and threw herself at him, embracing him.

"You are not leaving here alone," she whispered. "I won't let you be alone. Not right now."

They knew immediately where she had run to. Fine, wet snow had fallen that evening and had covered the forecourt with a thin, impeccably white carpet. In it they saw her footsteps.

Ciri was standing on the very summit of the ruined wall, as motionless as a statue. She was holding the sword above her right shoulder, the cross-guard at eye level. The fingers of her left hand were lightly touching the pommel.

On seeing them, the girl jumped, spun in a pirouette and landed softly in an identical but reverse mirror position.

"Ciri," said the witcher, "come down, please."

It seemed she hadn't heard him. She did not move, not even a muscle. Triss, however, saw the reflection of the moon, thrown across her face by the blade, glisten silver over a stream of tears.

"No one's going to take the sword away from me!" she shouted. "No one! Not even you!"

"Come down," repeated Geralt.

She tossed her head defiantly and the next second leaped once more. A loose brick slipped beneath her foot with a grating sound. Ciri staggered, trying to find her balance. And failed.

The witcher jumped.

Triss raised her hand, opening her mouth to utter a formula for levitation. She knew she couldn't do it in time. She knew that Geralt would not make it. It was impossible.

Geralt did make it.

He was forced down to the ground, thrown on his knees and back. He fell. But he did not let go of Ciri.

The magician approached them slowly. She heard the girl whisper and sniff. Geralt too was whispering. She could not make out the words. But she understood their meaning.

A warm wind howled in the crevices of the wall. The witcher raised his head.

"Spring," he said quietly.

"Yes," she acknowledged, swallowing. "There is still snow in the passes but in the valleys . . . In the valleys, it is already spring. Shall we leave, Geralt? You, Ciri and I?"

"Yes. It is high time."

Upriver we saw their towns, as delicate as if they were woven from the morning mist out of which they loomed. It seemed as if they would disappear a moment later, blown away on the wind which rippled the surface of the water. There were little palaces, white as nenuphar flowers; there were little towers looking as though they were plaited out of ivy; there were bridges as airy as weeping willows. And there were other things for which we could find no word or name. Yet we already had names for everything which our eyes beheld in this new, reborn world. Suddenly, in the far recesses of our memories, we found the words for dragons and griffins, mermaids and nymphs, sylphs and dryads once more. For the white unicorns which drank from the river at dusk, inclining their slender necks towards the water. We named everything. And everything seemed to be close to our hearts, familiar to us, ours.

Apart from them. They, although so resembling us, were alien. So very alien that, for a long time, we could find no word for their strangeness.

Hen Gedymdeith, Elves and Humans

A good elf is a dead elf.

Marshal Milan Raupenneck

CHAPTER FOUR

The misfortune behaved in the eternal manner of misfortunes and hawks – it hung over them for some while waiting for an appropriate moment before it attacked. It chose its moment, when they had passed the few settlements on the Gwenllech and Upper Buina, passed Ard Carraigh and plunged into the forest below, deserted and intersected by gorges. Like a hawk striking, this misfortune's aim was true. It fell accurately upon its victim, and its victim was Triss.

Initially it seemed nasty but not too serious, resembling an ordinary stomach upset. Geralt and Ciri discreetly tried to take no notice of the stops the enchantress's ailment necessitated. Triss, as pale as death, beaded with sweat and painfully contorted, tried to continue riding for several hours longer, but at about midday, and having spent an abnormally long time in the bushes by the road, she was no longer in any condition to sit on a saddle. Ciri tried to help her but to no avail – the enchantress, unable to hold on to the horse's mane, slid down her mount's flank and collapsed to the ground.

They picked her up and laid her on a cloak. Geralt unstrapped the saddle-bags without a word, found a casket containing some magic elixirs, opened it and cursed. All the phials were identical and the mysterious signs on the seals meant nothing to him.

"Which one, Triss?"

"None of them," she moaned, with both hands on her belly. "I can't . . . I can't take them."

"What? Why?"

"I'm sensitised—"

"You? A magician?"

"I'm allergic!" she sobbed with helpless exasperation and despairing anger. "I always have been! I can't tolerate elixirs! I can treat others with them but can only treat myself with amulets."

"Where is the amulet?"

"I don't know." She ground her teeth. "I must have left it in Kaer Morhen. Or lost it—"

"Damn it. What are we going to do? Maybe you should cast a spell on yourself?"

"I've tried. And this is the result. I can't concentrate because of this cramp . . ."

"Don't cry."

"Easy for you to say!"

The witcher got up, pulled his saddle-bags from Roach's back and began rummaging through them. Triss curled up, her face contracted and her lips twisted in a spasm of pain.

"Ciri . . ."

"Yes, Triss?"

"Do you feel all right? No . . . unusual sensations?"

The girl shook her head.

"Maybe it's food poisoning? What did I eat? But we all ate the same thing . . . Geralt! Wash your hands. Make sure Ciri washes her hands . . ."

"Calm down. Drink this."

"What is it?"

"Ordinary soothing herbs. There's next to no magic in them so they shouldn't do you any harm. And they'll relieve the cramps."

"Geralt, the cramps . . . they're nothing. But if I run a fever . . . It could be . . . dysentery. Or paratyphoid."

"Aren't you immune?"

Triss turned her head away without replying, bit her lip and curled up even tighter. The witcher did not pursue the question.

Having allowed her to rest for a while they hauled the enchantress onto Roach's saddle. Geralt sat behind her, supporting her with both hands, while Ciri rode beside them, holding the reins and leading Triss's gelding. They did not even manage a mile. The enchantress kept falling from Geralt's hands; she could not stay in the saddle. Suddenly she started trembling convulsively, and instantly burned with a fever. The gastritis had grown worse. Geralt told himself that it was an allergic reaction to the traces of magic in his witcher's elixir. He told himself that. But he did not believe it.

"Oh, sir," said the sergeant, "you have not come at a good time. Indeed, you could not have arrived at a worse moment."

The sergeant was right. Geralt could neither contest it nor argue.

The fort guarding the bridge, where there would usually be three soldiers, a stable-boy, a toll-collector and – at most – a few passers-by, was swarming with people. The witcher counted over thirty lightly armed soldiers wearing the colours of Kaedwen and a good fifty shield bearers, camping around the low palisade. Most of them were lying by campfires, in keeping with the old soldier's rule which dictates that you sleep when you can and get up when you're woken. Considerable activity could be seen through the thrown-open gates – there were a lot of people and horses inside the fort, too. At the top of the little leaning lookout tower two soldiers were on duty, with their crossbows permanently at the ready. On the worn bridge trampled by horses' hooves, six peasant carts and two merchant wagons were parked. In the enclosure, their heads lowered sadly over the mud and manure, stood umpteen unyoked oxen.

"There was an assault on the fort – last night." The sergeant anticipated his question. "We just got here in time with the relief troops – otherwise we'd have found nothing here but charred earth."

"Who were your attackers? Bandits? Marauders?"

The soldier shook his head, spat and looked at Ciri and Triss, huddled in the saddle.

"Come inside," he said, "your Enchantress is going to fall out of her saddle any minute now. We already have some wounded men there; one more won't make much difference."

In the yard, in an open, roofed shelter, lay several people with their wounds dressed with bloodied bandages. A little further, between the palisade fence and a wooden well with a sweep, Geralt made out six still bodies wrapped in sacking from which only pairs of feet in worn, dirty boots protruded.

"Lay her there, by the wounded men." The soldier indicated the shelter. "Oh sir, it truly is bad luck she's sick. A few of our men were hurt during the battle and we wouldn't turn down a bit of magical assistance. When we pulled the arrow out of one of them its head stuck in his guts. The lad will peter out by the morning, he'll peter out like anything . . . And the enchantress who could have saved him is tossing and turning with a fever and seeking help from us. A bad time, I say, a bad time—"

He broke off, seeing that the witcher could not tear his eyes from the sacking-wrapped bodies.

"Two guards from here, two of our relief troops and two . . . two of the others," he said, pulling up a corner of the stiff material. "Take a look, if you wish."

"Ciri, step away."

"I want to see, too!" The girl leaned out around him, staring at the corpses with her mouth open.

"Step away, please. Take care of Triss."

Ciri huffed, unwilling, but obeyed. Geralt came closer.

"Elves," he noted, not hiding his surprise.

"Elves," the soldier confirmed. "Scoia'tael."

"Who?"

"Scoia'tael," repeated the soldier. "Forest bands."

"Strange name. It means 'Squirrels', if I'm not mistaken?"

"Yes, sir. Squirrels. That's what they call themselves in elvish. Some say it's because sometimes they wear squirrel tails on their fur caps and hats. Others say it's because they live in the woods and eat nuts. They're getting more and more troublesome, I tell you."

Geralt shook his head. The soldier covered the bodies again and wiped his hands on his tunic.

"Come," he said. "There's no point standing here. I'll take you to the commandant. Our corporal will take care of your patient if he can. He knows how to sear and stitch wounds and set bones so maybe he knows how to mix up medicines and what not too. He's a brainy chap, a mountain-man. Come, witcher."

In the dim, smoky toll-collector's hut a lively and noisy discussion was underway. A knight with closely cropped hair wearing a habergeon and yellow surcoat was shouting at two merchants and a greeve, watched by the toll-collector, who had an indifferent, rather gloomy expression, and whose head was wrapped in bandages.

"I said, no!" The knight thumped his fist on the rickety table and stood up straight, adjusting the gorget across his chest. "Until the patrols return, you're not going anywhere! You are not going to roam the highways!"

"I's to be in Daevon in two days!" the greeve yelled, shoving a short notched stick with a symbol branded into it under the knight's nose. "I have a transport to lead! The bailiff's going to have me head if it be late! I'll complain to the voivode!"

"Go ahead and complain," sneered the knight. "But I advise you to line your breeches with straw before you do because the voivode can do a mean bit of arse-kicking. But for the time being I give the orders here – the voivode is far away and your bailiff means no more to me than a heap of dung. Hey, Unist! Who are you bringing here, sergeant? Another merchant?"

"No," answered the sergeant reluctantly. "A witcher, sir. He goes by the name Geralt of Rivia."

To Geralt's astonishment, the knight gave a broad smile, approached and held a hand out in greeting.

"Geralt of Rivia," he repeated, still smiling. "I have heard about you, and not just from gossip and hearsay. What brings you here?"

Geralt explained what brought him there. The knight's smile faded.

"You have not come at a good time. Or to a good place. We are at war here, witcher. A band of Scoia'tael is doing the rounds and there was a skirmish yesterday. I am waiting here for relief forces and then we'll start a counterattack."

"You're fighting elves?"

"Not just elves! Is it possible? Have you, a witcher, not heard of the Squirrels?"

"No. I haven't."

"Where have you been these past two years? Beyond the seas? Here, in Kaedwen, the Scoia'tael have made sure everybody's talking about them, they've seen to it only too well. The first bands appeared just after the war with Nilfgaard broke out. The cursed non-humans took advantage of our difficulties. We were fighting in the south and they began a guerrilla campaign at our rear. They counted on the Nilfgaardians defeating us, started declaring it was the end of human rule and there would be a return to the old order. 'Humans to the sea!' That's their battle cry, as they murder, burn and plunder!"

"It's your own fault and your own problem," the greeve

commented glumly, tapping his thigh with the notched stick, a mark of his position. "Yours, and all the other noblemen and knights. You're the ones who oppressed the non-humans, would not allow them their way of life, so now you pay for it. While we've always moved goods this way and no one stopped us. We didn't need an army."

"What's true is true," said one of the merchants who had been sitting silently on a bench. "The Squirrels are no fiercer than the bandits who used to roam these ways. And who did the elves take in hand first? The bandits!"

"What do I care if it's a bandit or an elf who runs me through with an arrow from behind some bushes?" the toll-collector with the bandaged head said suddenly. "The thatch, if it's set on fire above my head in the night, burns just the same. What difference does it make who lit the fire-brand? You say, sir, that the Scoia'tael are no worse than the bandits? You lie. The bandits wanted loot, but the elves are after human blood. Not everyone has ducats, but we all have blood running through our veins. You say it's the nobility's problem, greeve? That's an even greater folly. What about the lumberjacks shot in the clearing, the tar-makers hacked to pieces at the Beeches, the refugee peasants from the burned down hamlets, did they hurt the non-humans? They lived and worked together, as neighbours, and suddenly they got an arrow in the back . . . And me? Never in my life have I harmed a non-human and look, my head is broken open by a dwarf's cutlass. And if it were not for the soldiers you're snapping at, I would be lying beneath an ell of turf—"

"Exactly!" The knight in the yellow surcoat thumped his fist against the table once again. "We are protecting your mangy skin, greeve, from those, as you call them, oppressed elves, who, according to you, we did not let live. But I will say something different – we have emboldened them too much. We tolerated them, treated them as humans, as equals, and now they are stabbing us in the back. Nilfgaard is paying them for it, I'd stake my life, and the savage elves from the mountains are furnishing them with arms. But their real support comes from those who always lived amongst us – from the elves, half-elves, dwarves, gnomes and halflings. They are the ones who are hiding them, feeding them, supplying them with volunteers—"

"Not all of them," said another merchant, slim, with a delicate and noble face – in no way a typical merchant's features. "The majority of non-humans condemn the Squirrels, sir, and want nothing to do with them. The majority of them are loyal, and sometimes pay a high price for that loyalty. Remember the burgomaster from Ban Ard. He was a half-elf who urged peace and co-operation. He was killed by an assassin's arrow."

"Aimed, no doubt, by a neighbour, some halfling or dwarf who also feigned loyalty," scoffed the knight. "If you ask me, none of them are loyal! Every one of them— Hey there! Who are you?"

Geralt looked around. Ciri stood right behind him casting her huge emerald eyes over everyone. As far as the ability to move noiselessly was concerned, she had clearly made enormous progress.

"She's with me," he explained.

"Hmmm . . ." The knight measured Ciri with his eyes then turned back to the merchant with the noble face, evidently considering him the most serious partner in the discussion. "Yes, sir, do not talk to me about loyal non-humans. They are all our enemies, it's just that some are better than others at pretending otherwise. Halflings, dwarves and gnomes have lived amongst us for centuries – in some sort of harmony, it would seem. But it sufficed for the elves to lift their heads, and all the others grabbed their weapons and took to the woods too. I tell you, it was a mistake to tolerate the free elves and dryads, with their forests and their mountain enclaves. It wasn't enough for them, and now they're yelling: 'It's our world! Begone, strangers!'. By the gods, we'll show them who will be gone, and of which race even the slightest traces will be wiped away. We beat the hides off the Nilfgaardians and now we will do something about these rogue bands."

"It's not easy to catch an elf in the woods," said the witcher. "Nor would I go after a gnome or dwarf in the mountains. How large are these units?"

"Bands," corrected the knight. "They're bands, witcher. They can count up to a hundred heads, sometimes more. They call each pack a 'commando'. It's a word borrowed from the gnomes. And in saying they are hard to catch you speak truly. Evidently you are a professional. Chasing them through the woods and thickets is senseless. The only way is to cut them off from their supplies, isolate them, starve them out. Seize the non-humans who are helping them firmly by the scruff of their necks. Those from the towns and settlements, villages and farms—"

"The problem is," said the merchant with noble features, "that we still don't know which of the non-humans are helping them and which aren't."

"Then we have to seize them all!"

"Ah." The merchant smiled. "I understand. I've heard that somewhere before. Take everyone by the scruff of their neck and throw them down the mines, into enclosed camps, into quarries. Everyone. The innocent, too. Women and children. Is that right?"

The knight raised his head and slammed his hand down on his sword hilt.

"Just so, and no other way!" he said sharply. "You pity the children, yet you're like a child yourself in this world, dear sir. A truce with Nilfgaard is a very fragile thing, like an egg-shell. If not today then the war might start anew tomorrow, and anything can happen in war. If they defeated us, what do you think would happen? I'll tell you what – elven commandos would emerge from the forests, they'd emerge strong and numerous and these 'loyal elements' would instantly join them. Those loyal dwarves of yours, your friendly halflings, do you think they are going to talk of peace, of reconciliation then? No, sir. They'll be tearing our guts out. Nilfgaard is going to deal with us through their hands. And they'll drown us in the sea, just as they promise. No, sir, we must not pussyfoot around them. It's either them or us. There's no third way!"

The door of the hut squeaked and a soldier in a bloodied apron stood in the doorway.

"Forgive me for disturbing you," he hawked. "Which of you, noble sirs, be the one who brought this sick woman here?"

"I did," said the witcher. "What's happened?"

"Come with me, please."

They went out into the courtyard.

"It bodes not well with her, sir," said the soldier, indicating Triss. "Firewater with pepper and saltpetre I gave her – but it be no good. I don't really . . ."

Geralt made no comment because there was nothing to

say. The magician, doubled over, was clear evidence of the fact that firewater with pepper and saltpetre was not something her stomach could tolerate.

"It could be some plague." The soldier frowned. "Or that, what's it called . . . Zintery. If it were to spread to our men—"

"She is a wizard," protested the witcher. "Wizards don't fall sick . . ."

"Just so," the knight who had followed them out threw in cynically. "Yours, as I see, is just emanating good health. Geralt, listen to me. The woman needs help and we cannot offer such. Nor can I risk an epidemic amongst my troops. You understand."

"I understand. I will leave immediately. I have no choice – I have to turn back towards Daevon or Ard Carraigh."

"You won't get far. The patrols have orders to stop everyone. Besides, it is dangerous. The Scoia'tael have gone in exactly that direction."

"I'll manage."

"From what I've heard about you" – the knight's lips twisted – "I have no doubt you would. But bear in mind you are not alone. You have a gravely sick woman on your shoulders and this brat . . ."

Ciri, who was trying to clean her dung-smeared boot on a ladder rung, raised her head. The knight cleared his throat and looked down. Geralt smiled faintly. Over the last two years Ciri had almost forgotten her origins and had almost entirely lost her royal manners and airs, but her glare, when she wanted, was very much like that of her grandmother. So much so that Queen Calanthe would no doubt have been very proud of her granddaughter.

"Yeeessss, what was I . . ." the knight stammered, tugging at his belt with embarrassment. "Geralt, sir, I know what you need to do. Cross beyond the river, south. You will catch up with a caravan which is following the trail. Night is just around the corner and the caravan is certain to stop for a rest. You will reach it by dawn."

"What kind of caravan?"

"I don't know." The knight shrugged. "But it is not a merchant or an ordinary convoy. It's too orderly, the wagons are all the same, all covered . . . A royal bailiff's, no doubt. I allowed them to cross the bridge because they are following the Trail south, probably towards the fords on the Lixela."

"Hmmm . . ." The witcher considered this, looking at Triss. "That would be on my way. But will I find help there?"

"Maybe yes," the knight said coldly. "Maybe no. But you won't find it here, that's for sure."

They did not hear or see him as he approached, engrossed as they were in conversation, sitting around a campfire which, with its yellow light, cadaverously illuminated the canvas of the wagons arranged in a circle. Geralt gently pulled up his mare and forced her to neigh loudly. He wanted to warn the caravan, which had set up camp for the night, wanted to temper the surprise of having visitors and avoid a nervous reaction. He knew from experience that the release mechanisms on crossbows did not like nervous moves.

The campers leaped up and, despite his warning, performed numerous agitated movements. Most of them, he saw at once, were dwarves. This reassured him somewhat

– dwarves, although extremely irascible, usually asked questions first in situations such as these and only then aimed their crossbows.

"Who's that?" shouted one of the dwarves hoarsely and with a swift, energetic move, prised an axe from a stump by the campfire. "Who goes there?"

"A friend." The witcher dismounted.

"I wonder whose," growled the dwarf. "Come closer. Hold your hands out so we can see them."

Geralt approached, holding his hands out so they could be seen even by someone afflicted with conjunctivitis or night blindness.

"Closer."

He obeyed. The dwarf lowered his axe and tilted his head a little.

"Either my eyes deceive me," he said, "or it's the witcher Geralt of Rivia. Or someone who looks damn like him."

The fire suddenly shot up into flames, bursting into a golden brightness which drew faces and figures from the dark.

"Yarpen Zigrin," declared Geralt, astonished. "None other than Yarpen Zigrin in person, complete with beard!"

"Ha!" The dwarf waved his axe as if it were an osier twig. The blade whirred in the air and cut into a stump with a dull thud. "Call the alarm off! This truly is a friend!"

The rest of the gathering visibly relaxed and Geralt thought he heard deep sighs of relief. The dwarf walked up to him, holding out his hand. His grip could easily rival a pair of iron pincers.

"Welcome, you warlock," he said. "Wherever you've

come from and wherever you're going, welcome. Boys! Over here! You remember my boys, witcher? This is Yannick Brass, this one's Xavier Moran and here's Paulie Dahlberg and his brother Regan."

Geralt didn't remember any of them, and besides they all looked alike, bearded, stocky, practically square in their thick quilted jerkins.

"There were six of you," one by one he squeezed the hard, gnarled hands offered him, "if I remember correctly."

"You've a good memory," laughed Yarpen Zigrin. "There were six of us, indeed. But Lucas Corto got married, settled down in Mahakam and dropped out of the company, the stupid oaf. Somehow we haven't managed to find anybody worthy of his place yet. Pity, six is just right, not too many, not too few. To eat a calf, knock back a barrel, there's nothing like six—"

"As I see," with a nod Geralt indicated the rest of the group standing undecided by the wagons, "there are enough of you here to manage three calves, not to mention a quantity of poultry. What's this gang of fellows you're commanding, Yarpen?"

"I'm not the one in command. Allow me to introduce you. Forgive me, Wenck, for not doing so straight away but me and my boys have known Geralt of Rivia for a long time – we've a fair number of shared memories behind us. Geralt, this is Commissar Vilfrid Wenck, in the service of King Henselt of Ard Carraigh, the merciful ruler of Kaedwen."

Vilfrid Wenck was tall, taller than Geralt and near twice the dwarf's height. He wore an ordinary, simple outfit like that worn by greeves, bailiffs or mounted messengers, but there was a sharpness in his movements, a stiffness and sureness which the witcher knew and could faultlessly recognise, even at night, even in the meagre light of the campfire. That was how men accustomed to wearing hauberks and belts weighed down with weapons moved. Wenck was a professional soldier. Geralt was prepared to wager any sum on it. He shook the proffered hand and gave a little bow.

"Let's sit down." Yarpen indicated the stump where his mighty axe was still embedded. "Tell us what you're doing in this neighbourhood, Geralt."

"Looking for help. I'm journeying in a threesome with a woman and youngster. The woman is sick. Seriously sick. I caught up with you to ask for help."

"Damn it, we don't have a medic here." The dwarf spat at the flaming logs. "Where have you left them?"

"Half a furlong from here, by the roadside."

"You lead the way. Hey, you there! Three to the horses, saddle the spare mounts! Geralt, will your sick woman hold up in the saddle?"

"Not really. That's why I had to leave her there."

"Get the sheepskin, canvas sheet and two poles from the wagon! Quick!"

Vilfrid Wenck, crossing his arms, hawked loudly.

"We're on the trail," Yarpen Zigrin said sharply, without looking at him. "You don't refuse help on the Trail."

"Damn it." Yarpen removed his palm from Triss's forehead. "She's as hot as a furnace. I don't like it. What if it's typhoid or dysentery?"

"It can't be typhoid or dysentery," Geralt lied with conviction, wrapping the horse blankets around the sick woman. "Wizards are immune to those diseases. It's food poisoning, nothing contagious."

"Hmm . . . Well, all right. I'll rummage through the bags. I used to have some good medicine for the runs, maybe there's still a little left."

"Ciri," muttered the witcher, passing her a sheepskin unstrapped from the horse, "go to sleep, you're barely on your feet. No, not in the wagon. We'll put Triss in the wagon. You lie down next to the fire."

"No," she protested quietly, watching the dwarf walk away. "I'm going to lie down next to her. When they see you keeping me away from her, they won't believe you. They'll think it's contagious and chase us away, like the soldiers in the fort."

"Geralt?" the enchantress moaned suddenly. "Where . . . are we?"

"Amongst friends."

"I'm here," said Ciri, stroking her chestnut hair. "I'm at your side. Don't be afraid. You feel how warm it is here? A campfire's burning and a dwarf is just going to bring some medicine for . . . For your stomach."

"Geralt," sobbed Triss, trying to disentangle herself from the blankets. "No . . . no magic elixirs, remember . . ."

"I remember. Lie peacefully."

"I've got to . . . Oooh . . ."

The witcher leaned over without a word, picked up the enchantress together with her cocoon of caparisons and blankets, and marched to the woods, into the darkness. Ciri sighed.

She turned, hearing heavy panting. Behind the wagon appeared the dwarf, hefting a considerable bundle under his arm. The campfire flame gleamed on the blade of the axe behind his belt; the rivets on his heavy leather jerkin also glistened.

"Where's the sick one?" he snarled. "Flown away on a broomstick?"

Ciri pointed to the darkness.

"Right." The dwarf nodded. "I know the pain and I've known the same nasty complaint. When I was younger I used to eat everything I managed to find or catch or cut down, so I got food poisoning many a time. Who is she, this Enchantress?"

"Triss Merigold."

"I don't know her, never heard of her. I rarely have anything to do with the Brotherhood anyway. Well, but it's polite to introduce oneself. I'm called Yarpen Zigrin. And what are you called, little goose?"

"Something other than Little Goose," snarled Ciri with a gleam in her eyes.

The dwarf chuckled and bared his teeth.

"Ah." He bowed with exaggeration. "I beg your forgiveness. I didn't recognise you in the darkness. This isn't a goose but a noble young lady. I fall at your feet. What is the young lady's name, if it's no secret?"

"It's no secret. I'm Ciri."

"Ciri. Aha. And who is the young lady?"

"That," Ciri turned her nose up proudly, "is a secret."

Yarpen snorted again.

"The young lady's little tongue is as sharp as a wasp. If the young lady will deign to forgive me, I've brought the medicine and a little food. Will the young lady accept it or will she send the old boor, Yarpen Zigrin, away?"

"I'm sorry . . ." Ciri had second thoughts and lowered

her head. "Triss really does need help, Master . . . Zigrin. She's very sick. Thank you for the medicine."

"It's nothing." The dwarf bared his teeth again and patted her shoulder amicably. "Come on, Ciri, you help me. The medicine has to be prepared. We'll roll some pellets according to my grandmother's recipe. No disease sitting in the guts will resist these kernels."

He unwrapped the bundle, extracted something shaped like a piece of turf and a small clay vessel. Ciri approached, curious.

"You should know, Ciri," said Yarpen, "that my grandmother knew her medicine like nobody's business. Unfortunately, she believed that the source of most disease is idleness, and idleness is best cured through the application of a stick. As far as my siblings and I were concerned, she chiefly used this cure preventively. She beat us for anything and for nothing. She was a rare old hag. And once when, out of the blue, she gave me a chunk of bread with dripping and sugar, it was such a surprise that I dropped it in astonishment, dripping down. So my gran gave me a thrashing, the nasty old bitch. And then she gave me another chunk of bread, only without the sugar."

"My grandmother," Ciri nodded in understanding, "thrashed me once, too. With a switch."

"A switch?" The dwarf laughed. "Mine whacked me once with a pickaxe handle. But that's enough reminiscing, we have to roll the pellets. Here, tear this up and mould it into little balls."

"What is it? It's sticky and messy . . . Eeeuuggh . . . What a stink!"

"It's mouldy oil-meal bread. Excellent medicine. Roll

it into little balls. Smaller, smaller, they're for a magician, not a cow. Give me one. Good. Now we're going to roll the ball in medicine."

"Eeeeuuuugggghh!"

"Stinks?" The dwarf brought his upturned nose closer to the clay pot. "Impossible. Crushed garlic and bitter salt has no right to stink, even if it's a hundred years old."

"It's foul, uugghh. Triss won't eat that!"

"We'll use my grandmother's method. You squeeze her nose and I'll shove the pellets in."

"Yarpen," Geralt hissed, emerging abruptly from the darkness with the magician in his arms. "Watch out or I'll shove something down you."

"It's medicine!" The dwarf took offence. "It helps! Mould, garlic . . ."

"Yes," moaned Triss weakly from the depths of her cocoon. "It's true . . . Geralt, it really ought to help . . ."

"See?" Yarpen nudged Geralt with his elbow, turning his beard up proudly and pointing to Triss, who swallowed the pellets with a martyred expression. "A wise magician. Knows what's good for her."

"What are you saying, Triss?" The witcher leaned over. "Ah, I see. Yarpen, do you have any angelica? Or saffron?"

"I'll have a look, and ask around. I've brought you some water and a little food—"

"Thank you. But they both need rest above all. Ciri, lie down."

"I'll just make up a compress for Triss—"

"I'll do it myself. Yarpen, I'd like to talk to you."

"Come to the fire. We'll broach a barrel—"

"I want to talk to *you*. I don't need an audience. Quite the contrary."

"Of course. I'm listening."

"What sort of convoy is this?"

The dwarf raised his small, piercing eyes at him.

"The king's service," he said slowly and emphatically.

"That's what I thought." The witcher held the gaze. "Yarpen, I'm not asking out of any inappropriate curiosity."

"I know. And I also know what you mean. But this convoy is . . . hmm . . . special."

"So what are you transporting?"

"Salt fish," said Yarpen casually, and proceeded to embellish his lie without batting an eyelid. "Fodder, tools, harnesses, various odds and ends for the army. Wenck is a quartermaster to the king's army."

"If he's quartermaster then I'm a druid," smiled Geralt. "But that's your affair – I'm not in the habit of poking my nose into other people's secrets. But you can see the state Triss is in. Let us join you, Yarpen, let us put her in one of the wagons. Just for a few days. I'm not asking where you're going because this trail goes straight to the south without forking until past the Lixela and it's a ten-day journey to the Lixela. By that time the fever will have subsided and Triss will be able to ride a horse. And even if she isn't then I'll stop in a town beyond the river. Ten days in a wagon, well covered, hot food . . . Please."

"I don't give the orders here. Wenck does."

"I don't believe you lack influence over him. Not in a convoy primarily made up of dwarves. Of course he has to bear you in mind."

"Who is this Triss to you?"

"What difference does it make in this situation?"

"In this situation – none. I asked out of an inappropriate curiosity born of the desire to start new rumours going around the inns. But be that as it may, you're mighty attracted to this enchantress, Geralt."

The witcher smiled sadly.

"And the girl?" Yarpen indicated Ciri with his head as she wriggled under the sheepskin. "Yours?"

"Mine," he replied without thinking. "Mine, Zigrin."

The dawn was grey, wet, and smelled of night rain and morning mist. Ciri felt she had slept no more than a few minutes, as though she had been woken up the very minute she laid her head down on the sacks heaped on the wagon.

Geralt was just settling Triss down next to her, having brought her in from another enforced expedition into the woods. The rugs cocooning the enchantress sparkled with dew. Geralt had dark circles under his eyes. Ciri knew he had not closed them for an instant – Triss had run a fever through the night and suffered greatly.

"Did I wake you? Sorry. Sleep, Ciri. It's still early."

"What's happening with Triss? How is she?"

"Better," moaned the magician. "Better, but . . . Listen, Geralt . . . I'd like to—"

"Yes?" The witcher leaned over but Triss was already asleep. He straightened himself, stretched.

"Geralt," whispered Ciri, "are they going to let us travel on the wagon?"

"We'll see." He bit his lip. "Sleep while you can. Rest."

He jumped down off the wagon. Ciri heard the sound

of the camp packing up – horses stamping, harnesses ringing, poles squeaking, swingle-trees grating, and talking
and cursing. And then, nearby, Yarpen Zigrin's hoarse
voice and the calm voice of the tall man called Wenck.
And the cold voice of Geralt. She raised herself and carefully peered out from behind the canvas.

"I have no categorical interdictions on this matter," declared Wenck.

"Excellent." The dwarf brightened. "So the matter's
settled?"

The commissar raised his hand a little, indicating that
he had not yet finished. He was silent for a while, and
Geralt and Yarpin waited patiently.

"Nevertheless," Wenck said finally, "when it comes to
the safe arrival of this caravan, it's my head on the line."

Again he said nothing. This time no one interrupted.
There was no question about it – one had to get used to
long intervals between sentences when speaking to the
commissar.

"For its safe arrival," he continued after a moment.
"And for its timely arrival. Caring for this sick woman
might slow down the march."

"We're ahead of schedule on the route," Yarpen assured him, after a significant pause. "We're ahead of
time, Wenck, sir, we won't miss the deadline. And as for
safety . . . I don't think the witcher's company will harm
that. The Trail leads through the woods right up to the
Lixela, and to the right and left there's a wild forest. And
rumour has it all sorts of evil creatures roam the forest."

"Indeed," the commissar agreed. Looking the witcher
straight in the eye, he seemed to be weighing out every
single word. "One can come across certain evil creatures

in Kaedwen forests, lately incited by other evil creatures. They could jeopardise our safety. King Henselt, knowing this, empowered me to recruit volunteers to join our armed escort. Geralt? That would solve your problem."

The witcher's silence lasted a long while, longer than Wenck's entire speech, interspersed though it had been with regular pauses.

"No," he said finally. "No, Wenck. Let us put this clearly. I am prepared to repay the help given Lady Merigold, but not in this manner. I can groom the horses, carry water and firewood, even cook. But I will not enter the king's service as a soldier. Please don't count on my sword. I have no intention of killing those, as you call them, evil creatures on the order of other creatures whom I do not consider to be any better."

Ciri heard Yarpen Zigrin hiss loudly and cough into his rolled-up sleeve. Wenck stared at the witcher calmly.

"I see," he stated dryly. "I like clear situations. All right then. Zigrin, see to it that the speed of our progress does not slow. As for you, Geralt . . . I know you will prove to be useful and helpful in a way you deem fit. It would be an affront to both of us if I were to treat your good stead as payment for aid offered to a suffering woman. Is she feeling better today?"

The witcher gave a nod which seemed, to Ciri, to be somewhat deeper and politer than usual. Wenck's expression did not change.

"That pleases me," he said after a normal pause. "In taking Lady Merigold aboard a wagon in my convoy I take on the responsibility for her health, comfort and safety. Zigrin, give the command to march out."

"Wenck."

"Yes, Geralt?"

"Thank you."

The commissar bowed his head, a bit more deeply and politely, it seemed to Ciri, than the usual, perfunctory politeness required.

Yarpen Zigrin ran the length of the column, giving orders and instructions loudly, after which he clambered onto the coachman's box, shouted and whipped the horses with the reins. The wagon jolted and rattled along the forest trail. The bump woke Triss up but Ciri reassured her and changed the compress on her forehead. The rattling had a soporific effect and the magician was soon asleep; Ciri, too, fell to dozing.

When she woke the sun was already high. She peered out between the barrels and packages. The wagon she was in was at the vanguard of the convoy. The one following them was being driven by a dwarf with a red kerchief tied around his neck. From conversations between the dwarves, she had gathered that his name was Paulie Dahlberg. Next to him sat his brother Regan. She also saw Wenck riding a horse, in the company of two bailiffs.

Roach, Geralt's mare, tethered to the wagon, greeted her with a quiet neigh. She couldn't see her chestnut anywhere or Triss's dun. No doubt they were at the rear, with the convoy's spare horses.

Geralt was sitting on the coachman's box next to Yarpen. They were talking quietly, drinking beer from a barrel perched between them. Ciri pricked up her ears but soon grew bored – the discussion concerned politics and was mainly about King Henselt's intentions and plans, and some special service or missions to do with secretly aiding his neighbour, King Demawend of Aedirn, who was being threatened by war. Geralt expressed interest about how five wagons of salted fish could help Aedirn's defence. Yarpen, ignoring the gibe in Geralt's voice, explained that some species of fish were so valuable that a few wagon-loads would suffice to pay an armoured company for a year, and each new armoured company was a considerable help. Geralt was surprised that the aid had to be quite so secretive, to which the dwarf replied that was why the secret was a secret.

Triss tossed in her sleep, shook the compress off and talked indistinctly to herself. She demanded that someone called Kevyn kept his hands to himself, and immediately after that declared that destiny cannot be avoided. Finally, having stated that everyone, absolutely everyone, is a mutant to a certain degree, she fell into a peaceful sleep.

Ciri also felt sleepy but was brought to her senses by Yarpen's chuckle, as he reminded Geralt of their past adventures. This one concerned a hunt for a golden dragon who instead of allowing itself to be hunted down had counted the hunters' bones and then eaten a cobbler called Goatmuncher. Ciri began to listen with greater interest.

Geralt asked about what had happened to the Slashers but Yarpen didn't know. Yarpen, in turn, was curious about a woman called Yennefer, at which Geralt grew oddly uncommunicative. The dwarf drank more beer and started to complain that Yennefer still bore him a grudge although a good few years had gone by since those days.

"I came across her at the market in Gors Velen," he recounted. "She barely noticed me – she spat like a she-cat and insulted my deceased mother horribly. I fled for all I was worth, but she shouted after me that she'd catch up with me one day and make grass grow out of my arse."

Ciri giggled, imagining Yarpen with the grass. Geralt grunted something about women and their impulsive natures – which the dwarf considered far too mild a description for maliciousness, obstinacy and vindictiveness. Geralt did not take up the subject and Ciri fell into dozing once more.

This time she was woken by raised voices. Yarpen's voice to be exact – he was yelling.

"Oh yes! So you know! That's what I've decided!"

"Quieter," said the witcher calmly. "There's a sick woman in the wagon. Understand, I'm not criticising your decisions or your resolutions . . ."

"No, of course not," the dwarf interrupted sarcastically. "You're just smiling knowingly about them."

"Yarpen, I'm warning you, as one friend to another: both sides despise those who sit on the fence, or at best they treat them with suspicion."

"I'm not sitting. I'm unambiguously declaring myself to be on one side."

"But you'll always remain a dwarf for that side. Someone who's different. An outsider. While for the other side . . ."

He broke off.

"Well!" growled Yarpen, turning away. "Well, go on, what are you waiting for? Call me a traitor and a dog on a human leash who for a handful of silver and a bowl of lousy food, is prepared to be set against his rebelling kinsmen who are fighting for freedom. Well, go on, spit it out. I don't like insinuations."

"No, Yarpen," said Geralt quietly. "No. I'm not going to spit anything out."

"Ah, you're not?" The dwarf whipped the horses.

"You don't feel like it? You prefer to stare and smile? Not a word to me, eh? But you could say it to Wenck! 'Please don't count on my sword.' Oh, so haughtily, nobly and proudly said! Shove your haughtiness up a dog's arse, and your bloody pride with it!"

"I just wanted to be honest. I don't want to get mixed up in this conflict. I want to remain neutral."

"It's impossible!" yelled Yarpen. "It's impossible to remain neutral, don't you understand that? No, you don't understand anything. Oh, get off my wagon, get on your horse, and get out of my sight, with your arrogant neutrality. You get on my nerves."

Geralt turned away. Ciri held her breath in anticipation. But the witcher didn't say a word. He stood and jumped from the wagon, swiftly, softly and nimbly. Yarpen waited for him to untether his mare from the ladder, then whipped his horses once again, growling something incomprehensible, sounding terrifying under his breath.

She stood up to jump down too, and find her chestnut. The dwarf turned and measured her with a reluctant eye.

"And you're just a nuisance, too, little madam," he snorted angrily. "All we need are ladies and girls, damn it. I can't even take a piss from the box – I have to stop the cart and go into the bushes!"

Ciri put her hands on her hips, shook her ashen fringe and turned up her nose.

"Is that so?" she shrilled, enraged. "Drink less beer, Zigrin, and then you won't have to!"

"My beer's none of your shitin' business, you chit!"

"Don't yell, Triss has just fallen asleep!"

"It's my wagon! I'll yell if I want to!"

"Stumpy!"

"What? You impertinent brat!"

"Stump!"

"I'll show you stump . . . Oh, damn it! Pprrr!"

The dwarf leaned far back, pulling at the reins at the very last moment, just as the two horses were on the point of stepping over a log blocking their way. Yarpen stood up in the box and, swearing in both human and dwarvish, whistling and roaring, brought the cart to a halt. Dwarves and humans alike, leaping from their wagons, ran up and helped lead the horses to the clear path, tugging them on by their halters and harnesses.

"Dozing off, eh Yarpen?" growled Paulie Dahlberg as he approached. "Bloody hell, if you'd ridden over that the axle would be done for, and the wheels shattered to hell. Damn it, what were you—"

"Piss off, Paulie!" roared Yarpen Zigrin and furiously lashed the horses' hindquarters with the reins.

"You were lucky," said Ciri, ever so sweetly, squeezing onto the box next to the dwarf. "As you can see, it's better to have a witcher-girl on your wagon than to travel alone. I warned you just in time. But if you'd been in the middle of pissing from the box and ridden onto that log, well, well. It's scary to think what might have happened—"

"Are you going to be quiet?"

"I'm not saying any more. Not a word."

She lasted less than a minute.

"Zigrin, sir?"

"I'm not a sir." The dwarf nudged her with his elbow and bared his teeth. "I'm Yarpen. Is that clear? We'll lead the horses together, right?"

"Right. Can I hold the reins?"

"If you must. Wait, not like that. Pass them over your

index finger and hold them down with your thumb, like this. The same with the left. Don't tug them, don't pull too hard."

"Is that right?"

"Right."

"Yarpen?"

"Huh?"

"What does it mean, 'remain neutral'?"

"To be indifferent," he muttered reluctantly. "Don't let the reins hang down. Pull the left one closer to yourself!"

"What's indifferent? Indifferent to what?"

The dwarf leaned far out and spat under the wagon.

"If the Scoia'tael attack us, your Geralt intends to stand by and look calmly on as they cut our throats. You'll probably stand next to him, because it'll be a demonstration class. Today's subject: the witcher's behaviour in the face of conflict between intelligent races."

"I don't understand."

"That doesn't surprise me in the least."

"Is that why you quarrelled with him and were angry? Who are these Scoia'tael anyway? These . . . Squirrels?"

"Ciri," Yarpen tussled his beard violently, "these aren't matters for the minds of little girls."

"Aha, now you're angry at me. I'm not little at all. I heard what the soldiers in the fort said about the Squirrels. I saw . . . I saw two dead elves. And the knight said they also kill. And that it's not just elves amongst them. There are dwarves too."

"I know," said Yarpen sourly.

"And you're a dwarf."

"There's no doubt about that."

"So why are you afraid of the Squirrels? It seems they only fight humans."

"It's not so simple as that." He grew solemn. "Unfortunately."

Ciri stayed silent for a long time, biting her lower lip and wrinkling her nose.

"Now I know," she said suddenly. "The Squirrels are fighting for freedom. And although you're a dwarf, you're King Henselt's special secret servant on a human leash."

Yarpen snorted, wiped his nose on his sleeve and leaned out of the box to check that Wenck had not ridden up too close. But the commissar was far away, engaged in conversation with Geralt.

"You've got pretty good hearing, girl, like a marmot." He grinned broadly. "You're also a bit too bright for someone destined to give birth, cook and spin. You think you know everything, don't you? That's because you're a brat. Don't pull silly faces. Faces like that don't make you look any older, just uglier than usual. You've grasped the nature of the Scoia'taels quickly, you like the slogans. You know why you understand them so well? Because the Scoia'taels are brats too. They're little snotheads who don't understand that they're being egged on, that someone's taking advantage of their childish stupidity by feeding them slogans about freedom."

"But they really are fighting for freedom." Ciri raised her head and gazed at the dwarf with wide-open green eyes. "Like the dryads in the Brokilon woods. They kill people because people . . . some people are harming them. Because this used to be your country, the dwarves' and the elves' and those . . . halflings', gnomes' and other . . . And now there are people here so the elves—"

"Elves!" snorted Yarpen. "They – to be accurate – happen to be strangers just as much as you humans, although they arrived in their white ships a good thousand years before you. Now they're competing with each other to offer us friendship, suddenly we're all brothers, now they're grinning and saying: 'we, kinsmen', 'we, the Elder Races'. But before, shi— Hm, hm . . . Before, their arrows used to whistle past our ears when we—"

"So the first on earth were dwarves?"

"Gnomes, to be honest. As far as this part of the world is concerned – because the world is unimaginably huge, Ciri."

"I know. I saw a map—"

"You couldn't have. No one's drawn a map like that, and I doubt they will in the near future. No one knows what exists beyond the Mountains of Fire and the Great Sea. Even elves, although they claim they know everything. They know shit all, I tell you."

"Hmm . . . But now . . . There are far more people than . . . Than there are you."

"Because you multiply like rabbits." The dwarf ground his teeth. "You'd do nothing but screw day in day out, without discrimination, with just anyone and anywhere. And it's enough for your women to just sit on a man's trousers and it makes their bellies swell . . . Why have you gone so red, crimson as a poppy? You wanted to know, didn't you? So you've got the honest truth and faithful history of a world where he who shatters the skulls of others most efficiently and swells women's bellies fastest, reigns. And it's just as hard to compete with you people in murdering as it is in screwing—"

"Yarpen," said Geralt coldly, riding up on Roach. "Restrain yourself a little, if you please, with your choice of words. And Ciri, stop playing at being a coachwoman and have a care for Triss, check if she's awake and needs anything."

"I've been awake for a long time," the magician said weakly from the depths of the wagon. "But I didn't want to . . . interrupt this interesting conversation. Don't disturb them, Geralt. I'd like . . . to learn more about the role of screwing in the evolution of society."

"Can I heat some water? Triss wants to wash."

"Go ahead," agreed Yarpen Zigrin. "Xavier, take the spit off the fire, our hare's had enough. Hand me the cauldron, Ciri. Oh, look at you, it's full to the brim! Did you lug this great weight from the stream by yourself?"

"I'm strong."

The elder of the Dahlberg brothers burst out laughing.

"Don't judge her by appearances, Paulie," said Yarpen seriously as he skilfully divided the roasted grey hare into portions. "There's nothing to laugh at here. She's skinny but I can see she's a robust and resilient lass. She's like a leather belt: thin, but it can't be torn apart in your hands. And if you were to hang yourself on it, it would bear your weight, too."

No one laughed. Ciri squatted next to the dwarves sprawled around the fire. This time Yarpen Zigrin and his four "boys" had lit their own fire at the camp because they did not intend to share the hare which Xavier Moran had shot. For them alone there was just enough for one, at most two, mouthfuls each.

"Add some wood to the fire," said Yarpen, licking his fingers. "The water will heat quicker."

"That water's a stupid idea," stated Regan Dahlberg, spitting out a bone. "Washing can only harm you when you're sick. When you're healthy, too, come to that. You remember old Schrader? His wife once told him to wash, and Schrader went and died soon afterwards."

"Because a rabid dog bit him."

"If he hadn't washed, the dog wouldn't have bitten him."

"I think," said Ciri, checking the temperature of the water in the cauldron with her finger, "it's excessive to wash every day too. But Triss asked for it – she even started crying once . . . So Geralt and I—"

"We know." The elder Dahlberg nodded. "But that a witcher should . . . I'm constantly amazed. Hey, Zigrin, if you had a woman would you wash her and comb her hair? Would you carry her into the bushes if she had to—"

"Shut up, Paulie." Yarpen cut him short. "Don't say anything against that witcher, because he's a good fellow."

"Am I saying anything? I'm only surprised—"

"Triss," Ciri butted in cheekily, "is *not* his woman."

"I'm all the more surprised."

"You're all the more a blockhead, you mean," Yarpen summed up. "Ciri, pour a bit of water in to boil. We'll infuse some more saffron and poppy seeds for the magician. She felt better today, eh?"

"Probably did," murmured Yannick Brass. "We only had to stop the convoy six times for her. I know it wouldn't do to deny aid on the trail, and he's a prick who thinks otherwise. And he who denies it would be an arch-prick and base son-of-a-bitch. But we've been in these woods too long, far too long, I tell you. We're tempting fate, damn it, we're tempting fate too much, boys. It's not safe here. The Scoia'tael—"

"Spit that word out, Yannick."

"Ptoo, ptoo. Yarpen, fighting doesn't frighten me, and a bit of blood's nothing new but . . . If it comes to fighting our own . . . Damn it! Why did this happen to us? This friggin' load ought to be transported by a hundred friggin' cavalrymen, not us! The devil take those know-alls from Ard Carraigh, may they—"

"Shut up, I said. And pass me the pot of kasha. The hare was a snack, damn it, now we have to eat something. Ciri, will you eat with us?"

"Of course."

For a long while all that could be heard was the smacking of lips, munching, and the crunch of wooden spoons hitting the pot.

"Pox on it," said Paulie Dahlberg and gave a long burp. "I could still eat some more."

"Me, too," declared Ciri and burped too, delighted by the dwarves' unpretentious manners.

"As long as it's not kasha," said Xavier Moran. "I can't stomach those milled oats any more. I've gone off salted meat, too."

"So gorge yourself on grass, if you've got such delicate taste-buds."

"Or rip the bark off the birch with your teeth. Beavers do it and survive."

"A beaver – now that's something I could eat."

"As for me, a fish." Paulie lost himself in dreams as he crunched on a husk pulled from his beard. "I've a fancy for a fish, I can tell you."

"So let's catch some fish."

"Where?" growled Yannick Brass. "In the bushes?"

"In the stream."

"Some stream. You can piss to the other side. What sort of fish could be in there?"

"There are fish." Ciri licked her spoon clean and slipped it into the top of her boot. "I saw them when I went to get the water. But they're sick or something, those fish. They've got a rash. Black and red spots—"

"Trout!" roared Paulie, spitting crumbs of husk. "Well, boys, to the stream double-quick! Regan! Get your breeches down! We'll turn them into a fishing-trap."

"Why mine?"

"Pull them off, at the double, or I'll wallop you, snot-head! Didn't mother say you have to listen to me?"

"Hurry up if you want to go fishing because dusk is just round the corner," said Yarpen. "Ciri, is the water hot yet? Leave it, leave it, you'll burn yourself and get dirty from the cauldron. I know you're strong but let me – I'll carry it."

Geralt was already waiting for them; they could see his white hair through the gap in the canvas covering the wagon from afar. The dwarf poured the water into the bucket.

"Need any help, witcher?"

"No, thank you, Yarpen. Ciri will help."

Triss was no longer running a high temperature but she was extremely weak. Geralt and Ciri were, by now, efficient at undressing and washing her. They had also learned to temper her ambitious but, at present, unrealistic attempts to manage on her own. They coped exceptionally well – he supported the enchantress in his arms, Ciri washed and dried her. Only one thing had started to surprise and annoy Ciri – Triss, in her opinion, snuggled up to Geralt too tightly. This time she was even trying to kiss him.

Geralt indicated the magician's saddle-bags with his head. Ciri understood immediately because this, too, was part of the ritual – Triss always demanded to have her hair combed. She found the comb and knelt down beside her. Triss, lowering her head towards her, put her arms around the witcher. In Ciri's opinion, definitely a little too tightly.

"Oh, Geralt," she sobbed. "I so regret . . . I so regret that what was between us—"

"Triss, please."

". . . it should have happened . . . now. When I'm better . . . It would be entirely different . . . I could . . . I could even—"

"Triss."

"I envy Yennefer . . . I envy her you—"

"Ciri, step out."

"But—"

"Go, please."

She jumped out of the wagon and straight onto Yarpen who was waiting, leaning against a wheel and pensively chewing a blade of grass. The dwarf put his arm around her. He did not need to lean over in order to do so, as Geralt did. He was no taller than her.

"Never make the same mistake, little witcher-girl," he murmured, indicating the wagon with his eyes. "If someone shows you compassion, sympathy and dedication, if they surprise you with integrity of character, value it but don't mistake it for . . . something else."

"It's not nice to eavesdrop."

"I know. And it's dangerous. I only just managed to jump aside when you threw out the suds from the bucket. Come on, let's go and see how many trout have jumped into Regan's breeches."

"Yarpen?"

"Huh?"

"I like you."

"And I like you, kid."

"But you're a dwarf. And I'm not."

"And what diff— Ah, the Scoia'tael. You're thinking about the Squirrels, aren't you? It's not giving you any peace, is it?"

Ciri freed herself from his heavy arm.

"Nor you," she said. "Nor any of the others. I can plainly see that."

The dwarf said nothing.

"Yarpen?"

"Yes?"

"Who's right? The Squirrels or you? Geralt wants to be . . . neutral. You serve King Henselt even though you're a dwarf. And the knight in the fort shouted that everybody's our enemy and that everyone's got to be . . . Everyone. Even the children. Why, Yarpen? Who's right?"

"I don't know," said the dwarf with some effort. "I'm not omniscient. I'm doing what I think right. The Squirrels have taken up their weapons and gone into the woods. 'Humans to the sea,' they're shouting, not realising that their catchy slogan was fed them by Nilfgaardian emissaries. Not understanding that the slogan is not aimed at them but plainly at humans, that it's meant to ignite human hatred, not fire young elves to battle. I understood – that's why I consider the Scoia'tael's actions criminally stupid. What to do? Maybe in a few years time I'll be called a traitor who sold out and they'll be heroes . . . Our history, the history of our world, has seen events turn out like that."

He fell silent, ruffled his beard. Ciri also remained silent.

"Elirena . . ." he muttered suddenly. "If Elirena was a hero, if what she did is heroism, then that's just too bad. Let them call me a traitor and a coward. Because I, Yarpen Zigrin, coward, traitor and renegade, state that we should not kill each other. I state that we ought to live. Live in such a way that we don't, later, have to ask anyone for forgiveness. The heroic Elirena . . . She had to ask. Forgive me, she begged, forgive me. To hell with that! It's better to die than to live in the knowledge that you've done something that needs forgiveness."

Again he fell quiet. Ciri did not ask the questions pressing to her lips. She instinctively felt she should not.

"We have to live next to each other," Yarpen continued. "We and you, humans. Because we simply don't have any other option. We've known this for two hundred years and we've been working towards it for over a hundred. You want to know why I entered King Henselt's service, why I made such a decision? I can't allow all that work to go to waste. For over a hundred years we've been trying to come to terms with the humans. The halflings, gnomes, us, even the elves – I'm not talking about rusalkas, nymphs and sylphs, they've always been savages, even when you weren't here. Damn it all, it took a hundred years but, somehow or other, we managed to live a common life, next to each other, together. We man-

aged to partially convince humans that we're not so very
different—"

"We're not different at all, Yarpen."

The dwarf turned abruptly.

"We're not different at all," repeated Ciri. "After all,
you think and feel like Geralt. And like . . . like I do. We
eat the same things, from the same pot. You help Triss
and so do I. You had a grandmother and I had a grandmother . . . My grandmother was killed by the Nilfgaardians. In Cintra."

"And mine by the humans," the dwarf said with some
effort. "In Brugge. During the pogrom."

"Riders!" shouted one of Wenck's advance guards.
"Riders ahead!"

The commissar trotted up to Yarpen's wagon and Geralt approached from the other side.

"Get in the back, Ciri," he said brusquely. "Get off the
box and get in the back! Stay with Triss."

"I can't see anything from there!"

"Don't argue!" growled Yarpen. "Scuttle back there
and be quick about it! And hand me the martel. It's under
the sheepskin."

"This?" Ciri held up a heavy, nasty-looking object, like
a hammer with a sharp, slightly curved hook at its head.

"That's it," confirmed the dwarf. He slipped the handle
into the top of his boot and laid the axe on his knees.
Wenck, seeming calm, watched the highway while shel-
tering his eyes with his hand.

"Light cavalry from Ban Gleán," he surmised after
a while. "The so-called Dun Banner – I recognise them
by their cloaks and beaver hats. Remain calm. And stay

sharp. Cloaks and beaver hats can be pretty quick to change owners."

The riders approached swiftly. There were about ten of them. Ciri saw Paulie Dahlberg, in the wagon behind her, place two readied crossbows on his knee and Regan covered them with a cloak. Ciri crept stealthily out from under the canvas, hiding behind Yarpen's broad back. Triss tried to raise herself, swore and collapsed against her bedding.

"Halt!" shouted the first of the riders, no doubt their leader. "Who are you? From whence and to where do you ride?"

"Who asks?" Wenck calmly pulled himself upright in the saddle. "And on whose authority?"

"King Henselt's army, inquisitive sir! Lance-corporal Zyvik asks, and he is unused to asking twice! So answer at the double! Who are you?"

"Quartermaster's service of the King's army."

"Anyone could claim that! I see no one here bearing the King's colours!"

"Come closer, lance-corporal, and examine this ring."

"Why flash a ring at me?" The soldier grimaced. "Am I supposed to know every ring, or something? Anyone could have a ring like that. Some significant sign!"

Yarpen Zigrin stood up in the box, raised his axe and with a swift move pushed it under the soldier's nose.

"And this sign," he snarled. "You know it? Smell it and remember how it smells."

The lance-corporal yanked the reins and turned his horse.

"Threaten me, do you?" he roared. "Me? I'm in the king's service!"

"And so are we," said Wenck quietly. "And have been for longer than you at that, I'm sure. I warn you, trooper, don't overdo it."

"I'm on guard here! How am I to know who you are?"

"You saw the ring," drawled the commissar. "And if you didn't recognise the sign on the jewel then I wonder who *you* are. The colours of your unit bear the same emblem so you ought to know it."

The soldier clearly restrained himself, influenced, no doubt, equally by Wenck's calm words and the serious, determined faces peering from the escort's carts.

"Hmm . . ." he said, shifting his fur-hat towards his left ear. "Fine. But if you truly are who you claim to be, you will not, I trust, have anything against my having a look to see what you carry in the wagons."

"We will indeed." Wenck frowned. "And very much, at that. Our load is not your business, lance-corporal. Besides, I do not understand what you think you may find there."

"You do not understand." The soldier nodded, lowering his hand towards the hilt of his sword. "So I shall tell you, sir. Human trafficking is forbidden and there is no lack of scoundrels selling slaves to the Nilfgaardians. If I find humans in stocks in your wagons, you will not convince me that you are in the king's service. Even if you were to show me a dozen rings."

"Fine," said Wenck dryly. "If it is slaves you are looking for, then look. You have my permission."

The soldier cantered to the wagon in the middle, leaned over from the saddle and raised the canvas.

"What's in those barrels?"

"What do you expect? Prisoners?" sneered Yannick Brass, sprawled in the coachman's box.

"I am asking you what's in them, so answer me!"

"Salt fish."

"And in those trunks there?" The warrior rode up to the next wagon and kicked the side.

"Hooves," snapped Paulie Dahlberg. "And there, in the back, are buffalo skins."

"So I see." The lance-corporal waved his hand, smacked his lips at his horse, rode up to the vanguard and peered into Yarpen's wagon.

"And who is that woman lying there?"

Triss Merigold smiled weakly, raised herself to her elbow and traced a short, complicated sign with her hand.

"Who am I?" she asked in a quiet voice. "But you can't see me at all."

The soldier winked nervously, shuddered slightly.

"Salt fish," he said, convinced, lowering the canvas. "All is in order. And this child?"

"Dried mushrooms," said Ciri, looking at him impudently. The soldier fell silent, frozen with his mouth open.

"What's that?" he asked after a while, frowning. "What?"

"Have you concluded your inspection, warrior?" Wenck showed cool interest as he rode up on the other side of the cart. The soldier could barely look away from Ciri's green eyes.

"I have concluded it. Drive on, and may the gods guide you. But be on your guard. Two days ago, the Scoia'tael wiped out an entire mounted patrol up by Badger Ravine.

It was a strong, large command. It's true that Badger Ravine is far from here but elves travel through the forest faster than the wind. We were ordered to round them up, but how do you catch an elf? It's like trying to catch the wind—"

"Good, enough, we're not interested," the commissar interrupted him brusquely. "Time presses and we still have a long journey ahead of us."

"Fare you well then. Hey, follow me!"

"You heard, Geralt?" snarled Yarpen Zigrin, watching the patrol ride away. "There are bloody Squirrels in the vicinity. I felt it. I've got this tingling feeling in my back all the time as if some archer was already aiming at me. No, damn it, we can't travel blindly as we've been doing until now, whistling away, dozing and sleepily farting. We have to know what lies ahead of us. Listen, I've an idea."

Ciri pulled her chestnut up sharply, and then launched into a gallop, leaning low in the saddle. Geralt, engrossed in conversation with Wenck, suddenly sat up straight.

"Don't run wild!" he called. "No madness, girl! Do you want to break your neck? And don't go too far—"

She heard no more – she had torn ahead too fiercely. She had done it on purpose, not wanting to listen to the daily cautions. Not too quickly, not too fiercely, Ciri! *Pah-pah*. Don't go too far! *Pah-pah-pah*. Be careful! *Pah-pah! Exactly as if I were a child*, she thought. *And I'm almost thirteen and have a swift chestnut beneath me and a sharp sword across my back. And I'm not afraid of anything! And it's spring!*

"Hey, careful, you'll burn your backside!"

Yarpen Zigrin. Another know-it-all. *Pah-pah!*

Further, further, at a gallop, along the bumpy path, through the green, green grasses and bushes, through the silver puddles, through the damp golden sand, through the feathery ferns. A frightened fallow deer disappeared into the woods, flashing the black and white lantern of its tail and rump as it skipped away. Birds soared up from the trees – colourful jays and bee-eaters, screaming black magpies with their funny tails. Water splashed beneath her horse's hooves in the puddles and the clefts.

Further, even further! The horse, which had been trudging sluggishly behind the wagon for too long, carried her joyously and briskly; happy to be allowed speed, it ran fluidly, muscles playing between her thighs, damp mane thrashing her face. The horse extended its neck as Ciri gave it free rein. *Further, dear horse, don't feel the bit, further, at the gallop, at the gallop, sharp, sharp! Spring!*

She slowed and glanced back. There, alone at last. Far away at last. No one was going to tell her off any more, remind her of something, demand her attention, threaten that this would be the end of such rides. Alone at last, free, at ease and independent.

Slower. A light trot. After all, this wasn't just a fun ride, she also had responsibilities. Ciri was, after all, a mounted foray now, a patrol, an advance guard. *Ha,* she thought, looking around, *the safety of the entire convoy depends on me now. They're all waiting impatiently for me to return and report: the way is clear and passable, I didn't see anyone – there are no traces of wheels or hooves. I'll report it, and thin Master Wenck with his cold,*

blue eyes will nod his head gravely, Yarpen Zigrin will
bare his yellow, horse teeth, Paulie Dahlberg will shout:
"Well done, little one!', and Geralt will smile faintly. He'll
smile, although he very rarely smiles recently.

Ciri looked around and took a mental note. Two felled
birches – no problem. A heap of branches – nothing the
wagons couldn't pass. A cleft washed out by the rain – a
small obstacle, the wheels of the first wagon will run over
it, the others will follow in the ruts. A huge clearing – a
good place for a rest . . .

Traces? What traces can there be here? There's no one
here. There's the forest. There are birds screeching amidst
fresh, green leaves. A red fox runs leisurely across the
path . . . And everything smells of spring.

The track broke off halfway up the hill, disappeared in
the sandy ravine, wound through the crooked pines which
clung to the slopes. Ciri abandoned the path and, wanting to scrutinise the area from a height, climbed the steep
slope. And so she could touch the wet, sweet-smelling
leaves . . .

She dismounted, threw the reins over a snag in a tree
and slowly strolled among the junipers which covered the
hill. On the other side of the hill was an open space, gaping in the thick of the forest like a hole bitten out of the
trees – left, no doubt, after a fire which had raged here a
very long time ago, for there was no sign of blackened or
charred remains, everywhere was green with low birches
and little fir trees. The trail, as far as the eye could see,
seemed clear and passable.

And safe.

What are they afraid of? she thought. *The Scoia'tael?*

But what was there to be afraid of? I'm not frightened of elves. I haven't done anything to them.

Elves. The Squirrels. Scoia'tael.

Before Geralt had ordered her to leave, Ciri had managed to take a look at the corpses in the fort. She remembered one in particular – his face covered by hair stuck together with darkened blood, his neck unnaturally twisted and bent. Pulled back in a ghastly, set grimace, his upper lip revealed teeth, very white and very tiny, non-human. She remembered the elf's boots, ruined and reaching up to the knees, laced at the bottom and fastened at the top with many wrought buckles.

Elves who kill humans and die in battles themselves. Geralt says you have to remain neutral . . . And Yarpen says you have to behave in such a way that you don't have to ask for forgiveness . . .

She kicked a molehill and, lost in thought, dug her heel into the sand.

Who and whom, whom and what should one forgive?

The Squirrels kill humans. And Nilfgaard pays them for it. Uses them. Incites them. Nilfgaard.

Ciri had not forgotten – although she very much wanted to forget – what had happened in Cintra. The wandering, the despair, the fear, the hunger and the pain. The apathy and torpor, which came later, much later when the druids from Transriver had found her and taken her in. She remembered it all as though through a mist, and she wanted to stop remembering it.

But it came back. Came back in her thoughts, into her dreams. Cintra. The thundering of horses and the savage cries, corpses, flames . . . And the black knight in his winged helmet . . . And later . . . Cottages in Transriver . . . A flame-blackened chimney amongst charred ruins . . . Next to it, by an unscathed well, a black cat licking a terrible burn on its side. A well . . . A sweep . . . A bucket . . .

A bucket full of blood.

Ciri wiped her face, looked down at her hand, taken aback. Her palm was wet. The girl sniffed and wiped the tears with her sleeve.

Neutrality? Indifference? She wanted to scream. *A witcher looking on indifferently? No! A witcher has to defend people. From the leshy, the vampire, the werewolf. And not only from them. He has to defend people from every evil. And in Transriver I saw what evil is.*

A witcher has to defend and save. To defend men so that they aren't hung on trees by their hands, aren't impaled and left to die. To defend fair girls from being spread-eagled between stakes rammed into the ground. Defend children so they aren't slaughtered and thrown into a well. Even a cat burned alive in a torched barn deserves to be defended. That's why I'm going to become a witcher, that's why I've got a sword, to defend people like those in Sodden and Transriver – because they don't have swords, don't know the steps, half-turns, dodges and pirouettes. No one has taught them how to fight, they are defenceless and helpless in face of the werewolf and the Nilfgaardian marauder. They're teaching me to fight so that I can defend the helpless. And that's what I'm going to do. Never will I be neutral. Never will I be indifferent.

Never!

She didn't know what warned her – whether it was the sudden silence which fell over the forest like a cold shadow, or a movement caught out of the corner of her eye. But she reacted in a flash, instinctively – with a re-action she had learnt in the woods of Transriver when, escaping from Cintra, she had raced against death. She fell to the ground, crawled under a juniper bush and froze, motionless. *Just let the horse not neigh*, she thought.

On the other side of the ravine something moved again; she saw a silhouette show faintly, hazily amidst the leaves. An elf peered cautiously from the thicket. Having thrown the hood from his head, he looked around for a moment, pricked up his ears and then, noiselessly and swiftly, moved along the ridge. After him, two more leaned out. And then others moved. Many of them. In single file. About half were on horseback – these rode slowly, straight in their saddles, focused and alert. For a moment she saw them all clearly and precisely as, in utter silence, they flowed across a bright breach in the wall of trees, framed against the background of the sky – before they disappeared, dissolved in the shimmering shadows of the wild forest. They vanished without a rustle or a sound, like ghosts. No horse tapped its hoof or snorted, no branch cracked under foot or hoof. The weapons slung across them did not clang.

They disappeared but Ciri did not move. She lay flat on the ground under the juniper bush, trying to breathe as quietly as possible. She knew that a frightened bird or animal could give her away, and a bird or animal could be frightened by any sound or movement – even the slight-est, the most careful. She got up only when the woods had grown perfectly calm and the magpies chattered again among the trees where the elves had disappeared.

She rose only to find herself in a strong grip. A black,

leather glove fell across her mouth, muffled the scream of fear.

"Be quiet."

"Geralt?"

"Quiet, I said."

"You saw them?"

"I did."

"It's them . . ." she whispered. "The Scoia'tael. Isn't it?"

"Yes. Quick back to the horses. Watch your feet."

They rode carefully and silently down the slope without returning to the trail; they remained in the thicket. Geralt looked around, alert. He did not allow her to ride independently; he did not give her the chestnut's reins; he led the horse himself.

"Ciri," he said suddenly. "Not a word about what we saw. Not to Yarpen, not to Wenck. Not to anybody. Understand?"

"No," she grunted, lowering her head. "I don't understand. Why shouldn't I say anything? They have to be warned. Whose side are we on, Geralt? Whose side are we against? Who's our friend and who's our enemy?"

"We'll part with the convoy tomorrow," he said after a moment's silence. "Triss is almost recovered. We'll say goodbye and go our own way. We have problems of our own, our own worries and our own difficulties. Then, I hope, you'll finally stop dividing the inhabitants of this world into friends and enemies."

"We're to be . . . neutral? Indifferent, is that right? And if they attack . . ."

"They won't."

"And if—"

"Listen to me." He turned to her. "Why do you think that such a vital load of gold and silver, King Henselt's secret aid for Aedirn, is being escorted by dwarves and not humans? I saw an elf watching us from a tree yesterday. I heard them pass by our camp during the night. The Scoia'tael will not attack the dwarves, Ciri."

"But they're here," she muttered. "They are. They're moving around, surrounding us . . ."

"I know why they're here. I'll show you."

He turned the horse abruptly and threw the reins to her. She kicked the chestnut with her heels and moved away faster, but he motioned for her to stay behind him. They cut across the trail and reentered the wild forest. The witcher led, Ciri following in his tracks. Neither said anything. Not for a long time.

"Look." Geralt held back his horse. "Look, Ciri."

"What is it?" she sighed.

"Shaerrawedd."

In front of them, as far as the woods allowed them to see, rose smoothly hewn blocks of granite and marble with blunt corners, worn away by the winds, decorated with patterns long leached out by the rains, cracked and shattered by frost, split by tree roots. Amongst the trunks broken columns flashed white, arcades, the remains of ornamental friezes entwined with ivy, and wrapped in a thick layer of green moss.

"This was . . . a castle?"

"A palace. The elves didn't build castles. Dismount, the horses won't manage in the rubble."

"Who destroyed it all? Humans?"

"No, they did. Before they left."

"Why?"

"They knew they wouldn't be coming back. It happened following their second clash with the humans, more than two hundred years ago. Before that, they used to leave towns untouched when they retreated. Humans used to build on the foundations left by the elves. That's how Novigrad, Oxenfurt, Wyzima, Tretogor, Maribor and Cidaris were built. And Cintra."

"Cintra?"

He confirmed it with a nod of the head, not taking his eyes off the ruins.

"They left," whispered Ciri, "but now they're coming back. Why?"

"To have a look."

"At what?"

Without a word he laid his hand on her shoulder and pushed her gently before him. They jumped down the marble stairs, climbing down holding on to the springy hazel, clusters of which had burst through every gap, every crevice in the moss-covered, cracked plates.

"This was the centre of the palace, its heart. A fountain."

"Here?" she asked, surprised, gazing at the dense thicket of alders and white birch trunks amongst the misshapen blocks and slabs. "Here? But there's nothing there."

"Come."

The stream feeding the fountain must have changed its course many times, patiently and constantly washing the marble blocks and alabaster plates which had sunk or fallen to form dams, once again changing the course of the current. As a result the whole area was divided up by shallow gullies. Here and there the water cascaded over the remains of the building, washing it clean of leaves, sand and litter. In these places, the marble, terracotta and mosaics were still as vibrant with colour, as fresh as if they had been lying there for three days, not two centuries.

Geralt leapt across the stream and went in amongst what remained of the columns. Ciri followed. They jumped off the ruined stairs and, lowering their heads, walked beneath the untouched arch of the arcade, half buried beneath a mound of earth. The witcher stopped and indicated with his hand. Ciri sighed loudly.

From rubble colourful with smashed terracotta grew an enormous rose bush covered with beautiful white-lilied flowers. Drops of dew as bright as silver glistened on the petals. The bush wove its shoots around a large slab of white stone and from it a sad, pretty face looked out at them; the downpours and snows had not yet managed to blur or wash away its delicate and noble features. It was a face which the chisels of plunderers digging out golden ornaments, mosaics and precious stones from the relief sculpture had not managed to disfigure.

"Aelirenn," said Geralt after a long silence.

"She's beautiful," whispered Ciri, grabbing him by the hand. The witcher didn't seem to notice. He stared at the sculpture and was far away, far away in a different world and time.

"Aelirenn," he repeated after a while. "Known as Eli-rena by dwarves and humans. She led them into battle two hundred years ago. The elders of the elves were against it, they knew they had no chance. That they would not be able to pick themselves up after the defeat. They wanted to save their people, wanted to survive. They decided to destroy their towns and retreat to the inaccessible, wild mountains . . . and to wait. Elves live a long time, Ciri. By our time scale they are almost eternal. They thought humans were something that would pass, like a drought, like a heavy winter, or a plague of locust, after which comes rain, spring, a new harvest. They wanted to sit it out. Survive. They decided to destroy their towns and palaces, amongst them their pride – the beautiful Shaer-rawedd. They wanted to weather out the storm, but Eli-rena . . . Elirena stirred up the young. They took up arms and followed her into their last desperate battle. And they were massacred. Mercilessly massacred."

Ciri did not say anything, staring at the beautiful, still face.

"They died with her name on their lips," the witcher continued quietly. "Repeating her challenge, her cry, they died for Shaerrawedd. Because Shaerrawedd was a symbol. They died for this stone and marble . . . and for Ae-lirenn. Just as she promised them, they died with dignity, heroically and honourably. They saved their honour but they brought nothing but ruin as a result, condemned their own race to annihilation. Their own people. You remember what Yarpen told you? Those who rule the world and those who die out? He explained it to you coarsely but truly. Elves live for a long time, but only their young-sters are fertile, only the young can have offspring. And practically all the elven youngsters had followed Elirena. They followed Aelirenn, the White Rose of Shaerrawedd. We are standing in the ruins of her palace, by the foun-tain whose waters she listened to in the evenings. And these . . . these were her flowers."

Ciri was silent. Geralt drew her to himself, put his arm around her.

"Do you know now why the Scoia'tael were here, do you see what they wanted to look at? And do you understand why the elven and dwarven young must not be allowed to be massacred once again? Do you understand why neither you nor I are permitted to have a hand in this massacre? These roses flower all year round. They ought to have grown wild by now, but they are more beautiful than any rose in a tended garden. Elves continue to come to Shaerrawedd, Ciri. A variety of elves. The impetuous and the foolish ones for whom the cracked stone is a symbol as well as the sensible ones for whom these immortal, forever reborn flowers are a symbol. Elves who understand that if this bush is torn from the ground and the earth burned out, the roses of Shaerrawedd will never flower again. Do you understand?"

She nodded.

"Do you understand what this neutrality is, which stirs you so? To be neutral does not mean to be indifferent or insensitive. You don't have to kill your feelings. It's enough to kill hatred within yourself. Do you understand?"

"Yes," she whispered. "I understand. Geralt, I . . . I'd like to take one . . . One of these roses. To remind me. May I?"

"Do," he said after some hesitation. "Do, in order to remember. Let's go now. Let's return to the convoy."

Ciri pinned the rose under the lacing of her jerkin. Suddenly she cried out quietly, lifted her hand. A trickle of blood ran from her finger down her palm.

"Did you prick yourself?"

"Yarpen . . ." whispered the girl, looking at the blood filling her life-line. "Wenck . . . Paulie . . ."

"What?"

"Triss!" she shouted with a piercing voice which was not hers, shuddered fiercely and wiped her face with her arm. "Quick, Geralt! We've got to help! To the horses, Geralt!"

"Ciri! What's happening?"

"They're dying!"

She galloped with her ear almost touching the horse's neck and spurred her mount on, kicking with her heels and shouting. The sand of the forest path flew beneath the hooves. She heard screaming in the distance, and smelt smoke.

Coming straight at them, blocking the path, raced two horses dragging a harness, reins and a broken shaft behind them. Ciri did not hold her chestnut back and shot past them at full speed, flakes of froth skimming across her face. Behind her she heard Roach neigh and Geralt's curses as he was forced to a halt.

She tore around a bend in the path in to a large glade.

The convoy was in flames. From thickets, flaming arrows flew towards the wagons like fire birds, perforating the canvas and digging into the boards. The Scoia'tael attacked with war-cries and yells.

Ciri, ignoring Geralt's shouts from behind her, directed her horse straight at the first two wagons brought to the fore. One was lying on its side and Yarpen Zigrin, axe in one hand, crossbow in the other, stood next to it. At his feet, motionless, with her blue dress hitched halfway up her thighs, lay . . .

"Triiiiiisss!" Ciri straightened in the saddle, thumping her horse with her heels. The Scoia'tael turned towards

her and arrows whistled past the girl's ears. She shook her
head without slowing her gallop. She heard Geralt shout,
ordering her to flee into the woods. She did not intend to
obey. She leaned down and bolted straight towards the
archers shooting at her. Suddenly she smelt the overpowering scent of the white rose pinned to her jerkin.

"Triiiiisss!"

The elves leaped out of the way of the speeding horses.
Ciri caught one lightly with her stirrup. She heard a sharp
buzz, her steed struggled, whinnied and threw itself to
the side. Ciri saw an arrow dug deep, just below the with-
ers, right by her thigh. She tore her feet from the stirrups,
jumped up, squatted in the saddle, bounced off strongly
and leaped.

She fell softly on the body of the overturned wagon,
used her hands to balance herself and jumped again, landing with bent knees next to Yarpen who was roaring and
brandishing his axe. Next to them, on the second wagon,
Paulie Dahlberg was fighting while Regan, leaning back
and bracing his legs against the board, was struggling to
hold on to the harnessed horses. They neighed wildly,
stamped their hooves and yanked at the shaft in fear of the
fire devouring the canvas.

She rushed to Triss, who lay amongst the scattered barrels and chests, grabbed her by her clothes and started to
drag her towards the overturned wagon. The enchantress
moaned, holding her head just above the ear. Right by
Ciri's side, hooves suddenly clattered and horses snorted
– two elves, brandishing their swords, were pressing the
madly fighting Yarpen hard. The dwarf spun like a top
and agilely deflected the blows directed against him with

his axe. Ciri heard curses, grunts and the whining clang of metal.

Another span of horses detached itself from the flaming convoy and rushed towards them, dragging smoke and flames behind it and scattering burning rags. The wagon-man hung inertly from the box and Yannick Brass stood next to him, barely keeping his balance. With one hand he wielded the reins, with the other he was cutting himself away from two elves galloping one at each side of the wagon. A third Scoia'tael, keeping up with the harnessed horses, was shooting arrow after arrow into their sides.

"Jump!" yelled Yarpen, shouting over the noise. "Jump, Yannick!"

Ciri saw Geralt catch up with the speeding wagon and with a short, spare slash of his sword swipe one of the elves from his saddle while Wenck, riding up on the opposite side, hewed at the other, the elf shooting the horses. Yannick threw the reins down and jumped off – straight under the third Scoia'tael's horse. The elf stood in his stirrups and slashed at him with his sword. The dwarf fell. At that moment the flaming wagon crashed into those still fighting, parting and scattering them. Ciri barely managed to pull Triss out from beneath the crazed horses' hooves at the last moment. The swingle-tree tore away with a crack, the wagon leaped into the air, lost a wheel and overturned, scattering its load and smouldering boards everywhere.

Ciri dragged the enchantress under Yarpen's overturned wagon. Paulie Dahlberg, who suddenly found himself next to her, helped, while Geralt covered them both, shoving Roach between them and the charging Scoia'tael. All around the wagon, battle seethed: Ciri heard shouting, blades clashing, horses snorting, hooves clattering. Yarpen, Wenck and Geralt, surrounded on all sides by the elves, fought like raging demons.

The fighters were suddenly parted by Regan's span as he struggled in the coachman's box with a halfling wearing a lynx fur hat. The halfling was sitting on Regan trying to jab him with a long knife.

Yarpen deftly leaped onto the wagon, caught the halfling by the neck and kicked him overboard. Regan gave a piercing yell, grabbed the reins and lashed the horses. The span jerked, the wagon rolled and gathered speed in a flash.

"Circle, Regan!" roared Yarpen. "Circle! Go round!"

The wagon turned and descended on the elves again, parting them. One of them sprang up, grabbed the right lead-horse by the halter but couldn't stop him; the impetus threw him under the hooves and wheels. Ciri heard an excruciating scream.

Another elf, galloping next to them, gave a backhanded swipe with his sword. Yarpen ducked, the blade rang against the hoop supporting the canvas and the momentum carried the elf forward. The dwarf hunched abruptly and vigorously swung his arm. The Scoia'tael yelled, stiffened in the saddle and tumbled to the ground. A martel protruded between his shoulder blades.

"Come on then, you whoresons!" Yarpen roared, whirling his axe. "Who else? Chase a circle, Regan! Go round!"

Regan, tossing his bloodied mane of hair, hunched in the box amidst the whizzing of arrows, howled like the damned, and mercilessly lashed the horses on. The span dashed in a tight circle, creating a moving barricade

belching flames and smoke around the overturned wagon
beneath which Ciri had dragged the semi-conscious, battered magician.

Not far from them danced Wenck's horse, a mouse-
coloured stallion. Wenck was hunched over; Ciri saw the
white feathers of an arrow sticking out of his side. Despite the wound, he was skilfully hacking his way past
two elves on foot, attacking him from both sides. As Ciri
watched another arrow struck him in the back. The commissar collapsed forward onto his horse's neck but remained in the saddle. Paulie Dahlberg rushed to his aid.

Ciri was left alone.

She reached for her sword. The blade which throughout her training had leaped out from her back in a flash
would not let itself be drawn for anything; it resisted her,
stuck in its scabbard as if glued in tar. Amongst the whirl
seething around her, amongst moves so swift that they
blurred in front of her eyes, her sword seemed strangely,
unnaturally slow; it seemed ages would pass before it
could be fully drawn. The ground trembled and shook.
Ciri suddenly realised that it was not the ground. It was
her knees.

Paulie Dahlberg, keeping the elf charging at him at
bay with his axe, dragged the wounded Wenck along the
ground. Roach flitted past, beside the wagon, and Geralt
threw himself at the elf. He had lost his headband and
his hair streamed out behind him with his speed. Swords
clashed.

Another Scoia'tael, on foot, leaped out from behind
the wagon. Paulie abandoned Wenck, pulled himself upright and brandished his axe. Then froze.

In front of him stood a dwarf wearing a hat adorned

with a squirrel's tail, his black beard braided into two plaits. Paulie hesitated.

The black-beard did not hesitate for a second. He struck with both arms. The blade of the axe whirred and fell, slicing into the collar-bone with a hideous crunch. Paulie fell instantly, without a moan; it looked as if the force of the blow had broken both his knees.

Ciri screamed.

Yarpen Zigrin leaped from the wagon. The black-bearded dwarf spun and cut. Yarpen avoided the blow with an agile half-turn dodge, grunted and struck ferociously, chopping in to black-beard – throat, jaw and face, right up to the nose. The Scoia'tael bent back and collapsed, bleeding, pounding his hands against the ground and tearing at the earth with his heels.

"Geraaaalllltttt!" screamed Ciri, feeling something move behind her. Sensing death behind her.

There was only a hazy shape, caught in a turn, a move and a flash but the girl – like lightning – reacted with a diagonal parry and feint taught her in Kaer Morhen. She caught the blow but had not been standing firmly enough, had been leaning too far to the side to receive the full force. The strength of the strike threw her against the body of the wagon. Her sword slipped from her hand.

The beautiful, long-legged elf wearing high boots standing in front of her grimaced fiercely and, tossing her hair free of her lowered hood, raised her sword. The sword flashed blindingly, the bracelets on the Squirrel's wrists glittered.

Ciri was in no state to move.

But the sword did not fall, did not strike. Because the

elf was not looking at Ciri but at the white rose pinned to her jerkin.

"Aelirenn!" shouted the Squirrel loudly as if wanting to shatter her hesitation with the cry. But she was too late. Geralt, shoving Ciri away, slashed her broadly across the chest with his sword. Blood spurted over the girl's face and clothes, red drops spattered on the white petals of the rose.

"Aelirenn . . ." moaned the elf shrilly, collapsing to her knees. Before she fell on her face, she managed to shout one more time. Loudly, lengthily, despairingly:

"Shaerraweeeeedd!"

Reality returned just as suddenly as it had disappeared. Through the monotonous, dull hum which filled her ears, Ciri began to hear voices. Through the flickering, wet curtain of tears, she began to see the living and the dead.

"Ciri," whispered Geralt who was kneeling next to her. "Wake up."

"A battle . . ." she moaned, sitting up. "Geralt, what—"

"It's all over. Thanks to the troops from Ban Gleán which came to our aid."

"You weren't . . ." she whispered, closing her eyes, "you weren't neutral . . ."

"No, I wasn't. But you're alive. Triss is alive."

"How is she?"

"She hit her head falling out of the wagon when Yarpen tried to rescue it. But she's fine now. Treating the wounded."

Ciri cast her eyes around. Amidst the smoke from the last wagons, burning out, silhouettes of armed men flickered. And all around lay chests and barrels. Some of were shattered and the contents scattered. They had contained ordinary, grey field stones. She stared at them, astounded.

"Aid for Demawend from Aedirn." Yarpen Zigrin, standing nearby, ground his teeth. "Secret and exceptionally important aid. A convoy of special significance!"

"It was a trap?"

The dwarf turned, looked at her, at Geralt. Then he looked back at the stones pouring from the barrels and spat.

"Yes," he confirmed. "A trap."

"For the Squirrels?"

"No."

The dead were arranged in a neat row. They lay next to each other, not divided – elves, humans and dwarves. Yannick Brass was amongst them. The dark-haired elf in the high boots was there. And the dwarf with his black, plaited beard, glistening with dried blood. And next to them . . .

"Paulie!" sobbed Regan Dahlberg, holding his brother's head on his knees. "Paulie! Why?"

No one said anything. No one. Even those who knew why. Regan turned his contorted face, wet with tears, towards them.

"What will I tell our mother?" he wailed. "What am I going to say to her?"

No one said anything.

Not far away, surrounded by soldiers in the black and gold of Kaedwen, lay Wenck. He was breathing with difficulty and every breath forced bubbles of blood to his lips. Triss knelt next to him and a knight in shining armour stood over them both.

"Well?" asked the knight. "Lady enchantress? Will he live?"

"I've done everything I can." Triss got to her feet, pinched her lips. "But . . ."

"What?"

"They used this." She showed him an arrow with a strange head to it and struck it against a barrel standing by them. The tip of the arrow fell apart, split into four barbed, hook-like needles. The knight cursed.

"Fredegard . . ." Wenck uttered with difficulty. "Fredegard, listen—"

"You mustn't speak!" said Triss severely. "Or move! The spell is barely holding!"

"Fredegard," the commissar repeated. A bubble of blood burst on his lips and another immediately appeared in its place. "We were wrong . . . Everyone was wrong. It's not Yarpen . . . We suspected him wrongly . . . I vouch for him. Yarpen did not betray . . . Did not betr—"

"Silence!" shouted the knight. "Silence, Vilfrid! Hey, quick now, bring the stretcher! Stretcher!"

"No need," the magician said hollowly, gazing at Wenck's lips where no more bubbles appeared. Ciri turned away and pressed her face to Geralt's side.

Fredegard drew himself up. Yarpen Zigrin did not look at him. He was looking at the dead. At Regan Dahlberg still kneeling over his brother.

"It was necessary, Zigrin," said the knight. "This is war. There was an order. We had to be sure . . ."

Yarpen did not say anything. The knight lowered his eyes.

"Forgive us," he whispered.

The dwarf slowly turned his head, looked at him. At Geralt. At Ciri. At them all. The humans.

"What have you done to us?" he asked bitterly. "What have you done to us? What have you made of us?"

No one answered him.

The eyes of the long-legged elf were glassy and dull. Her contorted lips were frozen in a soundless cry.

Geralt put his arms around Ciri. Slowly, he unpinned the white rose, spattered with dark stains, from her jerkin and, without a word, threw it on the Squirrel's body.

"Farewell," whispered Ciri. "Farewell, Rose of Shaerrawedd. Farewell and . . ."

"And forgive us," added the witcher.

They roam the land, importunate and insolent, nominating themselves the stalkers of evil, vanquishers of werewolves and exterminators of spectres, extorting payment from the gullible and, on receipt of their ignoble earnings, moving on to dispense the same deceit in the near vicinity. The easiest access they find at cottages of honest, simple and unwitting peasants who readily ascribe all misfortune and ill events to spells, unnatural creatures and monsters, the doings of windsprites or evil spirits. Instead of praying to the gods, instead of bearing rich offerings to the temple, such a simpleton is ready to give his last penny to the base witcher, believing the witcher, the godless changeling, will turn around his fate and save him from misfortune.

Anonymous, *Monstrum*, or *Description of the Witcher*

I have nothing against witchers. Let them hunt vampires. As long as they pay taxes.

Radovid III the Bold, King of Redania

If you thirst for justice, hire a witcher.

Graffitti on the wall of the Faculty of Law, University of Oxenfurt

CHAPTER FIVE

"Did you say something?"

The boy sniffed and pushed his over-sized velvet hat, a pheasant's feather hanging rakishly to the side, back from his forehead.

"Are you a knight?" he repeated, gazing at Geralt with wide eyes as blue as the sky.

"No," replied the witcher, surprised that he felt like answering. "I'm not."

"But you've got a sword! My daddy's one of King Foltest's knights. He's got a sword, too. Bigger than yours!"

Geralt leaned his elbows on the railing and spat into the water eddying at the barge's wake.

"You carry it on your back," the little snot persisted. The hat slipped down over his eyes again.

"What?"

"The sword. On your back. Why have you got the sword on your back?"

"Because someone stole my oar."

The little snot opened his mouth, demanding that the impressive gaps left by milk teeth be admired.

"Move away from the side," said the witcher. "And shut your mouth or flies will get in."

The boy opened his mouth even wider.

"Grey-haired yet stupid!" snarled the little snot's mother, a richly attired noblewoman, pulling her offspring away by the beaver collar of his cloak. "Come here, Everett! I've told you so many times not to be familiar with the passing rabble!"

Geralt sighed, gazing at the outline of islands and islets looming through the morning mist. The barge, as ungainly as a tortoise, trudged along at an appropriate speed – that being the speed of a tortoise – dictated by the lazy Delta current. The passengers, mostly merchants and peasants, were dozing on their baggage. The witcher unfurled the scroll once more and returned to Ciri's letter.

. . . I sleep in a large hall called a Dormitorium and my bed is terribly big, I tell you. I'm with the Intermediary Girls. There are twelve of us but I'm most friendly with Eurneid, Katye and Iola the Second. Whereas today I Ate Broth and the worst is that sometimes we have to Fast and get up very early at Dawn. Earlier than in Kaer Morhen. I will write the rest tomorrow for we shall presently be having Prayers. No one ever prayed in Kaer Morhen, I wonder why we have to here. No doubt because this is a Temple.

Geralt. Mother Nenneke has read and said I must not write Silly Things and write clearly without mistakes. And about what I'm studying and that I feel

*well and healthy. I feel well and am healthy if unfor-
tunately Hungry, but Soone be Dinner. And Mother
Nenneke also said write that prayer has never
harmed anybody yet, neither me nor, certainly, you.*

*Geralt, I have some free time again, I will write
therefore that I am studying. To read and write correct Runes. History. Nature. Poetry and Prose. To
express myself well in the Common Speech and in
the Elder Speech. I am best at the Elder Speech, I
can also write Elder Runes. I will write something
for you and you will see for yourself. Elaine blath,
Feainnéwedd. That meant: Beautiful flower, child of
the Sun. You see for yourself that I can. And also—*

*Now I can write again for I have found a new
quill for the old one broke. Mother Nenneke read
this and praised me that it was correct. That I am
obedient, she told me to write, and that you should
not worry. Don't worry, Geralt.*

*Again I have some time so I will write what hap-
pened. When we were feeding the turkey hens, I, Iola
and Katye, One Enormous Turkey attacked us, a red
neck it had and was Terrible Horrible. First it attacked Iola and then it wanted to attack me but I was
not afraid because it was smaller and slower than
the Pendulum anyway. I dodged and did a pirouette
and walloped it twice with a switch until it Made
Off. Mother Nenneke does not allow me to carry My
Sword here, a pity, for I would have shown that Turkey what I learned in Kaer Morhen. I already know
that in the Elder Runes it would be written Caer
a'Muirehen and that it means Keep of the Elder
Sea. So no doubt that is why there are Shells and*

Snails there as well as Fish imprinted on the stones.
And Cintra is correctly written Xin'trea. Whereas
my name comes from Zireael for that means Swal-
low and that means that . . .

"Are you busy reading?"

He raised his head.

"I am. So? Has anything happened? Someone noticed something?"

"No, nothing," replied the skipper, wiping his hands on his leather jerkin. "There's calm on the water. But there's a mist and we're already near Crane Islet—"

"I know. It's the sixth time I've sailed this way, Boat-bug, not counting the return journeys. I've come to know the trail. My eyes are open, don't worry."

The skipper nodded and walked away to the prow, stepping over travellers' packages and bundles stacked everywhere. Squeezed in amidships, the horses snorted and pounded their hooves on the deck-boards. They were in the middle of the current, in dense fog. The prow of the barge ploughed the surface of water lilies, parting their clumps. Geralt turned back to his reading.

. . . that means I have an elven name. But I am not,
after all, an elf, Geralt, there is also talk about the
Squirrels here. Sometimes even the Soldiers come
and ask questions and say that we must not treat
wounded elves. I have not squealed a word to any-
one about what happened in spring, don't worry.
And I also remember to practise, don't think other-
wise. I go to the park and train when I have time. But
not always, for I also have to work in the kitchen or

*in the orchard like all the girls. And we also have a
terrible amount of studying to do. But never mind,
I will study. After all, you too studied in the Temple,
Mother Nenneke told me. And she also told me that
just any idiot can brandish a sword but a witcher-
girl must be wise.*

Geralt, you promised to come. Come.
Your Ciri

PS Come, come.
*PS II. Mother Nenneke told me to end with Praise
be to Great Melitele, may her blessing and favour
always go with you. And may nothing happen to
you.*

Ciri

I'd like to go to Ellander, he thought, putting away the
letter. *But it's dangerous. I might lead them to— These
letters have got to end. Nenneke makes use of temple
mail but still . . . Damn it, it's too risky.*

"Hmmm . . . Hmm . . ."

"What now, Boatbug? We've passed Crane Islet."

"And without incident, thank the gods," sighed the
skipper. "Ha, Geralt, I see this is going to be another
peaceful trip. Any moment now the mist is going to clear
and when the sun peeps through, the fear is over. The
monster won't show itself in the sunlight."

"That won't worry me in the least."

"So I should think." Boatbug smiled wryly. "The company pays you by the trip. Regardless whether something
happens or not a penny falls into your pouch, doesn't
it?"

"You ask as if you didn't know. What is this – envy talking? That I earn money standing leaning against the side, watching the lapwings? And what do you get paid for? The same thing. For being on board. When everything is going smoothly you haven't got anything to do. You stroll from prow to stern, grinning at the women or trying to entice merchants to have a drink. I've been hired to be on board too. Just in case. The transport is safe because a witcher is on board. The cost of the witcher is included in the price of the trip, right?"

"Well, that certainly is true," sighed the skipper. "The company won't lose out. I know them well. This is the fifth year I sail the Delta for them from Foam to Novigrad, from Novigrad to Foam. Well, to work, witcher, sir. You go on leaning against the side and I'll go for a stroll from prow to stern."

The mist thinned a little. Geralt extracted another letter from his bag, one he had recently received from a strange courier. He had already read it about thirty times.

Dear friend . . .

The witcher swore quietly, looking at the sharp, angular, even runes drawn with energetic sweeps of the pen, faultlessly reflecting the author's mood. He felt once again the desire to try to bite his own backside in fury. When he was writing to the enchantress a month ago he had spent two nights in a row contemplating how best to begin. Finally, he had decided on "Dear friend." Now he had his just deserts.

Dear friend, your unexpected letter – which I received not quite three years after we last saw each other – has given me much joy. My joy is all the greater as various rumours have been circulating about your sudden and violent death. It is a good thing that you have decided to disclaim them by writing to me; it is a good thing, too, that you are doing so so soon. From your letter it appears that you have lived a peaceful, wonderfully boring life, devoid of all sensation. These days such a life is a real privilege, dear friend, and I am happy that you have managed to achieve it.

I was touched by the sudden concern which you deigned to show as to my health, dear friend. I hasten with the news that, yes, I now feel well; the period of indisposition is behind me, I have dealt with the difficulties, the description of which I shall not bore you with.

It worries and troubles me very much that the unexpected present you received from Fate brings you worries. Your supposition that this requires professional help is absolutely correct. Although your description of the difficulty – quite understandably – is enigmatic, I am sure I know the Source of the problem. And I agree with your opinion that the help of yet another magician is absolutely necessary. I feel honoured to be the second to whom you turn. What have I done to deserve to be so high on your list?

Rest assured, my dear friend; and if you had the intention of supplicating the help of additional magicians, abandon it because there is no need. I leave without delay, and go to the place which you

*indicated in an oblique yet, to me, understandable
way. It goes without saying that I leave in absolute
secrecy and with great caution. I will surmise the
nature of the trouble on the spot and will do all
that is in my power to calm the gushing source. I
shall try, in so doing, not to appear any worse than
other ladies to whom you have turned, are turning
or usually turn with your supplications. I am, after
all, your dear friend. Your valuable friendship is too
important to me to disappoint you, dear friend.*

*Should you, in the next few years, wish to write
to me, do not hesitate for a moment. Your letters in-
variably give me boundless pleasure.*

Your friend Yennefer

The letter smelled of lilac and gooseberries.

Geralt cursed.

He was torn from his reverie by the movement on deck
and a rocking of the barge that indicated they were changing course. Some of the passengers crowded starboard.
Skipper Boatbug was yelling orders from the bow; the
barge was slowly and laboriously turning towards the
Temerian shore, leaving the fairway and ceding right of
way to two ships looming through the mist. The witcher
watched with curiosity.

The first was an enormous three-masted galliass at least
a hundred and forty yards long, carrying an amaranth flag
with a silver eagle. Behind it, its forty oars rhythmically
hard at work, glided a smaller, slim galley adorned with a
black ensign with gold-red chevron.

"Ooohh, what huge dragons," said Boatbug standing

next to the witcher. "They're pushing a heck of a wave, the way they're ploughing the river."

"Interesting," muttered Geralt. "The galliass is sailing under the Redanian flag but the galley is from Aedirn."

"From Aedirn, very much so," confirmed the skipper. "And it carries the Governor of Hagge's pennon. But note, both ships have sharp keels, near on four yards' draught. That means they're not sailing to Hagge itself – they wouldn't cross the rapids and shallows up the river. They're heading to Foam or White Bridge. And look, there are swarms of soldiers on the decks. These aren't merchants. They're war ships, Geralt."

"Someone important is on that galliass. They've set up a tent on deck."

"That's right, that's how the nobles travel." Boatbug nodded, picking his teeth with a splinter peeled from the barge's side. "It's safer by river. Elven commandos are roaming the forests. There's no knowing which tree an arrow's going to come flying from. But on the water there's no fear. Elves, like cats, don't like water. They prefer dwelling in brushwood . . ."

"It's got to be someone really important. The tent is rich."

"That's right, could be. Who knows, maybe King Vizimir himself is favouring the river with his presence? All sorts of people are travelling this way now . . . And while we're at it, in Foam you asked me to keep my ears open in case anyone was interested in you, asking about you. Well, that weakling there, you see him?"

"Don't point, Boatbug. Who is he?"

"How should I know? Ask him yourself, he's coming over. Just look at his stagger! And the water's as still as a mirror, pox on it; if it were to swell just a little he'd probably be on all fours, the oaf."

The "oaf" turned out to be a short, thin man of uncertain age, dressed in a large, woollen and none-too-clean cloak pinned in place with a circular brass brooch. Its pin, clearly lost, had been replaced by a crooked nail with a flattened head. The man approached, cleared his throat and squinted with his myopic eyes.

"Hmm . . . Do I have the pleasure of speaking to Geralt of Rivia, the witcher?"

"Yes, sir. You do."

"Allow me to introduce myself. I am Linus Pitt, Master Tutor and Lecturer in Natural History at the Oxenfurt Academy."

"My very great pleasure."

"Hmm . . . I've been told that you, sir, are on commission from the Malatius and Grock Company to protect this transport. Apparently from the danger of some monster attack. I wonder what this 'monster' could be."

"I wonder myself." The witcher leaned against the ship's side, gazing at the dark outline of the marshy meadows on the Temerian river bank looming in the mist. "And have come to the conclusion that I have most likely been hired as a precaution against an attack from a Scoia'tael commando force said to be roaming the vicinity. This is my sixth journey between Foam and Novigrad and no aeschna has shown itself—"

"Aeschna? That's some kind of common name. I would rather you used the scientific terminology. Hmm . . . aeschna . . . I truly do not know which species you have in mind—"

"I'm thinking of a bumpy and rough-skinned monster

four yards in length resembling a stump overgrown with algae and with ten paws and jaws like cut-saws."

"The description leaves a lot to be desired as regards scientific precision. Could it be one of the species of the *Hyphydridae* family?"

"I don't exclude the possibility," sighed Geralt. "The aeschna, as far as I know, belongs to an exceptionally nasty family for which no name can be abusive. The thing is, Master Tutor, that apparently a member of this unsympathetic clan attacked the Company's barge two weeks ago. Here, on the Delta, not far from where we are."

"He who says this" – Linus Pitt gave a screeching laugh – "is either an ignoramus or a liar. Nothing like that could have happened. I know the fauna of the Delta very well. The family *Hyphydridae* does not appear here at all. Nor do any other quite so dangerous predatory species. The considerable salinity and atypical chemical composition of the water, especially during high tide—"

"During high tide," interrupted Geralt, "when the incoming tide wave passes the Novigrad canals, there is no water – to use the word precisely – in the Delta at all. There is a liquid made up of excrement, soapsuds, oil and dead rats."

"Unfortunately, unfortunately." The Master Tutor grew sad. "Degradation of the environment . . . You may not believe it, but of more than two thousand species of fish living in this river only fifty years ago, not more than nine hundred remain. It is truly sad."

They both leaned against the railing and stared into the murky green depths. The tide must have already been coming in because the stench of the water was growing stronger. The first dead rats appeared.

"The white-finned bullhead has died off completely." Linus Pitt broke the silence. "The mullet has died, as have the snakehead, the kithara, the striped loach, the redbelly dace, the long-barbel gudgeon, the king pickerel . . ."

At a distance of about twenty yards from the ship's side, the water surged. For a moment, both men saw a twenty-pound or more specimen of the king pickerel swallowing a dead rat and disappearing into the depths, having gracefully flashed its tail fin.

"What was that?" The Master Tutor shuddered.

"I don't know." Geralt looked at the sky. "A penguin maybe?"

The scholar glanced at him and bit his lips.

"In all certainty it was not, however, your mythical aeschna! I have been told that witchers possess considerable knowledge about some rare species. But you, you not only repeat rumours and tales, you are also mocking me in a most crude manner . . . Are you listening to me at all?"

"The mist isn't going to lift," said Geralt quietly.

"Huh?"

"The wind is still weak. When we sail into the arm of the river, between the islets, it will be even weaker. It is going to be misty right up to Novigrad."

"I'm not going to Novigrad. I get off at Oxenfurt," declared Pitt dryly. "And the mist? It is surely not so thick as to render navigation impossible; what do you think?"

The little boy in the feathered hat ran past them and leaned far out, trying, with his stick, to fish out a rat bouncing against the boat. Geralt approached and tore the stick from him.

"Scram. Don't get near the side!"

"Muuuummyyyy!"

"Everett! Come here immediately!"

The Master Tutor pulled himself up and glared at the witcher with piercing eyes.

"It seems you really do believe we are in some danger?"

"Master Pitt," said Geralt as calmly as he could, "two weeks ago something pulled two people off the deck of one of the Company's barges. In the mist. I don't know what it was. Maybe it was your hyphydra or whatever its name is. Maybe it was a long-barbel gudgeon. But I think it was an aeschna."

The scholar pouted. "Conjecture," he declared, "should always be based on solid scientific foundations, not on rumours and gossip. I told you, the hyphydra, which you persist in calling an aeschna, does not appear in the waters of the Delta. It was wiped out a good half-century ago, due – incidentally – to the activity of individuals such as yourself who are prepared to kill anything that does not instantly look right, without forethought, tests, observation or considering its ecological niche."

For a moment, Geralt felt a sincere desire to tell the scholar where he could put the aeschna and its niche, but he changed his mind.

"Master Tutor," he said calmly, "one of those pulled from the deck was a young pregnant girl. She wanted to cool her swollen feet in the water. Theoretically, her child could, one day, have become chancellor of your college. What do you have to say to such an approach to ecology?"

"It is unscientific; it is emotional and subjective. Nature is governed by its own rules and although these rules are cruel and ruthless, they should not be amended. It is a struggle for survival!" The Master Tutor leaned over the railing and spat into the water. "And nothing can justify the extermination of a species, even a predatory one. What do you say to that?"

"I say that it's dangerous to lean out like that. There might be an aeschna in the vicinity. Do you want to try out the aeschna's struggle for survival on your own skin?"

Linus Pitt let go of the railing and abruptly jumped away. He turned a little pale but immediately regained his self-assurance and pursed his lips again.

"No doubt you know a great deal about these fantastical aeschna, witcher?"

"Certainly less than you. So maybe we should make use of the opportunity? Enlighten me, Master Tutor, expound a little upon your knowledge of aquatic predators. I'll willingly listen, and the journey won't seem so long."

"Are you making fun of me?"

"Not at all. I would honestly like to fill in the gaps in my education."

"Hmmm . . . If you really . . . Why not? Listen then to me. The *Hyphydridae* family, belonging to the *Amphipoda* order, includes four species known to science. Two live exclusively in tropical waters. In our climate, on the other hand, one can come across – though very rarely now – the not-so-large *Hyphydra longicauda* and the somewhat larger *Hyphydra marginata*. The biotope of both species is stagnant water or water which flows very slowly. The species are, indeed, predatory, preferring to feed on warm-blooded creatures . . . . Have you anything to add?"

"Not right now. I'm listening with bated breath."

"Yes, hmm . . . Mention can also be found, in the great books, of the subspecies *Pseudohyphydra*, which lives in the marshy waters of Angren. However, the learned Bumbler of Aldersberg recently proved that this is an entirely different species, one from the *Mordidae* family. It feeds exclusively on fish and small amphibians. It has been named *Ichthyovorax bumbleri*."

"The monster's lucky," smiled the witcher. "That's the third time he was named."

"How come?"

"The creature you're talking about is an ilyocoris, called a cinerea in Elder Speech. And if the learned Bumbler states that it feeds exclusively on fish then I assume he has never bathed in a lake with an ilyocoris. But Bumbler is right on one account: the aeschna has as much in common with a cinerea as I do with a fox. We both like to eat duck."

"What cinerea?" The Master Tutor bridled. "The cinerea is a mythical creature! Indeed, your lack of knowledge disappoints me. Truly, I am amazed—"

"I know," interrupted Geralt. "I lose a great deal of my charm when one gets to know me better. Nevertheless I will permit myself to correct your theories a little further, Master Pitt. So, aeschnae have always lived in the Delta and continue to do so. Indeed, there was a time when it seemed that they had become extinct. For they lived off those small seals—"

"River porpoises," corrected the Master Tutor. "Don't be an ignoramus. Don't mistake seals for—"

"—they lived off porpoises and the porpoises were killed off because they looked like seals. They provided seal-like skins and fat. Then, later, canals were dug out in the upper reaches of the river, dams and barriers built. The current grew weaker; the Delta got silted up and overgrown. And the aeschna underwent mutation. It adapted."

"Huh?"

"Humans have rebuilt its food chain. They supplied warm-blooded creatures in the place of porpoises. Sheep, cattle, swine began to be transported across the Delta. The aeschnae learned in a flash that every barge, raft or barque on the Delta was, in fact, a large platter of food."

"And the mutation? You spoke of mutation!"

"This liquid manure" – Geralt indicated the green water – "seems to suit the aeschna. It enhances its growth. The damn thing can become so large, apparently, that it can drag a cow off a raft with no effort whatsoever. Pulling a human off a deck is nothing. Especially the deck of one of these scows the Company uses to transport passengers. You can see for yourselves how low it sits in the water."

The Master Tutor quickly backed away from the ship's side, as far as the carts and baggage allowed.

"I heard a splash!" he gasped, staring at the mist between the islets. "Witcher! I heard—"

"Calm down. Apart from the splashing you can also hear oars squeaking in rowlocks. It's the customs officers from the Redanian shore. You'll see them in a moment and they'll cause more of a commotion than three, or even four, aeschnae."

Boatbug ran past. He cursed obscenely as the little boy in the feathered hat got under his feet. The passengers and messengers, all extremely nervous, were going through their possessions trying to hide any smuggled goods.

After a little while, a large boat hit the side of the barge and four lively, angry and very noisy individuals jumped on board. They surrounded the skipper, bawled threateningly in an effort to make themselves and their positions seem important, then threw themselves enthusiastically at the baggage and belongings of the travellers.

"They check even before we land!" complained Boatbug, coming up to the witcher and the ·Master Tutor. "That's illegal, isn't it? After all, we're not on Redanian soil yet. Redania is on the right bank, half a mile from here!"

"No," contradicted the Master Tutor. "The boundary between Redania and Temeria runs through the centre of the Pontar current."

"And how the shit do you measure a current? This is the Delta! Islets, shoals and skerries are constantly changing its layout – the Fairway is different every day! It's a real curse! Hey! You little snot! Leave that boathook alone or I'll tan your arse black and blue! Honourable lady! Watch your child! A real curse!"

"Everett! Leave that alone or you'll get dirty!"

"What's in that chest?" shouted the customs officers. "Hey, untie that bundle! Whose is that cart? Any currency? Is there any currency, I say? Temerian or Nilfgaardian money?"

"That's what a customs war looks like," Linus Pitt commented on the chaos with a wise expression on his face. "Vizimir forced Novigrad to introduce the *ius stapulae*. Foltest of Temeria retaliated with a retortive, absolute *ius stapulae* in Wyzima and Gors Velen. That was a great blow for Redanian merchants so Vizimir increased the tax on Temerian products. He is defending the Redanian economy. Temeria is flooded with cheap goods coming from Nilfgaardian manufactories. That's why the customs officers are so keen. If too many Nilfgaardian goods were to cross the border, the Redanian economy would collapse. Redania has practically no manufactories and the craftsmen wouldn't be able to cope with competition."

"In a nutshell," smiled Geralt, "Nilfgaard is slowly taking over with its goods and gold that which it couldn't take with arms. Isn't Temeria defending itself? Hasn't Foltest blocked his southern borders?"

"How? The goods are coming through Mahakam, Brugge, Verden and the ports in Cidaris. Profit is all the merchants are interested in, not politics. If King Foltest were to block his borders, the merchants' guilds would raise a terrible outcry—"

"Any currency?" snarled an approaching customs officer with bloodshot eyes. "Anything to declare?"

"I'm a scholar!"

"Be a prince if you like! I'm asking what you're bringing in?"

"Leave them, Boratek," said the leader of the group, a tall, broad-shouldered customs officer with a long, black moustache. "Don't you recognise the witcher? Greetings, Geralt. Do you know him? Is he a scholar? So you're going to Oxenfurt, are you, sir? With no luggage?"

"Quite so. To Oxenfurt. With no luggage."

The customs officer pulled out an enormous handkerchief and wiped his forehead, moustache and neck.

"And how's it going today, Geralt?" he asked. "The monster show itself?"

"No. And you, Olsen, seen anything?"

"I haven't got time to look around. I'm working."

"My daddy," declared Everett, creeping up without a sound, "is one of King Foltest's knights! And he's got an even bigger moustache than you!"

"Scram, kid," said Olsen, then sighed heavily. "Got any vodka, Geralt?"

"No."

"But I do." The learned man from the Academy, pulling a flat skin from his bag, surprised them all.

"And I've got a snack," boasted Boatbug looming up as if from nowhere. "Smoked burbot!"

"And my daddy—"

"Scarper, little snot."

They sat on coils of rope in the shade of the carts parked amidships, sipping from the skin and devouring the burbot in turn. Olsen had to leave them momentarily when an argument broke out. A dwarven merchant from Mahakam was demanding a lower tax and trying to convince the customs officers that the furs he was bringing in were not silver fox but exceptionally large cats. The mother of the nosey and meddlesome Everett, on the other hand, did not want to undergo an inspection at all, shrilly evoking her husband's rank and the privileges of nobility.

The ship, trailing braids of gathered nenuphars, water lilies and pond-weed at its sides, slowly glided along the wide strait amongst shrub-covered islets. Bumble bees buzzed menacingly amongst the reeds, and tortoises whistled from time to time. Cranes, standing on one leg, gazed at the water with stoical calm, knowing there was no point in getting worked up – sooner or later a fish would swim up of its own accord.

"And what do you think, Geralt?" Boatbug uttered,

licking the burbot's skin clean. "Another quiet voyage? You know what I'd say? That monster's no fool. It knows you're lying in ambush. Hearken to this – at home in our village, there was a river and in that river lived an otter which would creep into the yard and strangle hens. It was so crafty that it never crept in when Father was home, or me and my brothers. It only showed up when Grandpa was left by himself. And our grandpa, hearken, was a bit feeble in the head and paralysis had taken his legs. It was as if the otter, that son-of-a-bitch, knew. Well then, one day our pa—"

"Ten per cent *ad valorem*!" yelled the dwarven merchant from amidships, waving the fox skin about. "That's how much I owe you and I'm not going to pay a copper more!"

"Then I'll confiscate the lot!" roared Olsen angrily. "And I'll let the Novigrad guards know so you'll go to the clink together with your 'Valorem'! Boratek, charge him to the penny! Hey, have you left anything for me? Have you guzzled it down to the dregs?"

"Sit down, Olsen." Geralt made room for him on the ropes. "Stressful job you've got, I see."

"Ah, I've had it up to my ears," sighed the customs officer, then took a swig from the skin and wiped his moustache. "I'm throwing it in, I'm going back to Aedirn. I'm an honest Vengerberger who followed his sister and brother-in-law to Redania but now I'm going back. You know what, Geralt? I'm set on enlisting in the army. They say King Demawend is recruiting for special troops. Half a year's training in a camp and then it's a soldier's pay, three times what I get here, bribes included. This burbot's too salty."

"I've heard about this special army," confirmed Boat-bug. "It's getting ready for the Squirrels because the regular army can't deal with the elven commandos. They particularly want half-elves to enlist, I hear. But that camp where they teach them to fight is real hell apparently. They leave fifty-fifty, some to get soldier's pay, some to the burial ground, feet first."

"And so it should be," said the customs officer. "The special army, skipper, isn't just any old unit. It's not some shitty shield-bearers who just need to be shown which end of the javelin pricks. A special army has to know how to fight like nobody's business!"

"So you're such a fierce warrior, are you, Olsen? And the Squirrels, aren't you afraid of them? That they'll spike your arse with arrows?"

"Big deal! I know how to draw a bow too. I've already fought Nilfgaard, so elves are nothing to me."

"They say," Boatbug said with a shudder, "if someone falls into their hands alive, the Scoia'taels' . . . It's better they hadn't been born. They'll be tortured horrifically."

"Ah, do yourself a favour and shut your face, skipper. You're babbling like a woman. War is war. You whack the enemy in the backside, and they whack you back. Captured elves aren't pampered by our men either, don't you worry."

"The tactic of terror." Linus Pitt threw the burbot's head and backbone overboard. "Violence breeds violence. Hatred has grown into hearts . . . and has poisoned kindred blood . . ."

"What?" Olsen grimaced. "Use a human language!"

"Hard times are upon us."

"So they are, true," agreed Boatbug. "There's sure to

be a great war. Every day the sky is thick with ravens, they smell the carrion already. And the seeress Ithlin foretold the end of the world. White Light will come to be, the White Chill will then follow. Or the other way round, I've forgotten how it goes. And people are saying signs were also visible in the sky—"

"You keep an eye on the fairway, skipper, 'stead of the sky, or this skiff of yours is going to end up in the shallows. Ah, we're already level with Oxenfurt. Just look, you can see the Cask!"

The mist was clearly less dense now so that they could see the hillocks and marshy meadows of the right bank and, rising above them, a part of the aqueduct.

"That, gentlemen, is the experimental sewage purification plant," boasted the Master Tutor, refusing his turn to drink. "A great success for science, a great achievement for the Academy. We repaired the old elven aqueduct, canals and sediment trap and we're already neutralising the sewers of the university, town and surrounding villages and farms. What you call the Cask is a sediment trap. A great success for science—"

"Heads down, heads down!" warned Olsen, ducking behind the rail. "Last year, when that thing exploded, the shit flew as far as Crane Islet."

The barge sailed in between islands and the squat tower of the sediment trap and the aqueduct disappeared in the mist. Everyone sighed with relief.

"Aren't you sailing straight by way of the Oxenfurt arm, Boatbug?" asked Olsen.

"I'm putting in at Acorn Bay first. To collect fish traders and merchants from the Temerian side."

"Hmm . . ." The customs officer scratched his neck.

"At the Bay . . . Listen, Geralt, you aren't in any conflict with the Temerians by any chance, are you?"

"Why? Was someone asking about me?"

"You've guessed it. As you see, I remember you asked me to keep an eye out for anyone interested in you. Well, just imagine, the Temerian Guards have been enquiring about you. The customs officers there, with whom I have a good understanding, told me. Something smells funny here, Geralt."

"The water?" Linus Pitt was afraid, glancing nervously at the aqueduct and the great scientific success.

"That little snotrag?" Boatbug pointed to Everett who was still milling around nearby.

"I'm not talking about that." The customs officer winced. "Listen, Geralt, the Temerian customs men said these Guards were asking strange questions. They know you sail with the Malatius and Grock barges. They asked . . . if you sail alone. If you have— Bloody hell, just don't laugh! They were going on about some underage girl who has been seen in your company, apparently."

Boatbug chuckled. Linus Pitt looked at the witcher with eyes filled with the distaste which befitted someone looking at a white-haired man who has drawn the attention of the law on account of his preference for underage girls.

"That's why," Olsen hawked, "the Temerian customs officers thought it might be some private matters being settled, into which the Guards had been drawn. Like . . . Well, the girl's family or her betrothed. So the officers cautiously asked who was behind all this. And they found out. Well, apparently it's a nobleman with a tongue ready as a chancellor's, neither poor nor miserly, who calls himself . . . Rience, or something like that. He's got a red mark on his left cheek as if from a burn. Do you know anyone like that?"

Geralt got up.

"Boatbug," he said. "I'm disembarking in Acorn Bay."

"How's that? And what about the monster?"

"That's your problem."

"Speaking of problems," interrupted Olsen, "just look starboard, Geralt. Speak of the devil."

From behind an island, from the swiftly lifting mist, loomed a lighter. A black burgee dotted with silver lilies fluttered lazily from its mast. The crew consisted of several men wearing the pointed hats of Temerian Guards.

Geralt quickly reached into his bag and pulled out both letters – the one from Ciri and the one from Yennefer. He swiftly tore them into tiny shreds and threw them into the river. The customs officer watched him in silence.

"Whatever are you doing, may I ask?"

"No. Boatbug, take care of my horse."

"You want to . . ." Olsen frowned. "You intend to—"

"What I intend is my business. Don't get mixed up in this or there'll be an incident. They're sailing under the Temerian flag."

"Bugger their flag." The customs officer moved his cutlass to a more accessible place on his belt and wiped his enamelled gorget, an eagle on a red background, with his sleeve. "If I'm on board carrying out an inspection, then this is Redania. I will not allow—"

"Olsen," the witcher interrupted, grabbing him by the sleeve, "don't interfere, please. The man with a burned face isn't on the lighter. And I have to know who he is and what he wants. I've got to see him face to face."

"You're going to let them put you in the stocks? Don't be a fool! If this is a private settling of scores, privately commissioned revenge, then as soon as you get past the islet, on the Whirl, you'll fly overboard with an anchor round your neck. You'll be face to face all right, but it'll be with crabs at the bottom of the river!"

"They're Temerian Guards, not bandits."

"Is that so? Then just look at their mugs! Besides, I'll know instantly who they really are. You'll see."

The lighter, approaching rapidly, reached the barge. One of the Guards threw the rope over while another attached the boathook to the railing.

"I be the skipper!" Boatbug blocked the way as three men leaped on deck. "This is a ship belonging to the Malatius and Grock Company! What . . ."

One of the men, stocky and bald, pushed him brusquely aside with his arm, thick as the branch of an oak.

"A certain Gerald, called Gerald of Rivia!" he thundered, measuring the skipper with his eyes. "Is such a one on board?"

"No."

"I am he." The witcher stepped over the bundles and packages and drew near. "I am Geralt, and called Geralt. What is this about?"

"I arrest you in the name of the law." The bald man's eyes skimmed over the passengers. "Where's the girl?"

"I'm alone."

"You lie!"

"Hold it, hold it." Olsen emerged from behind the witcher's back and put his hand on his shoulder. "Keep

calm, no shouting. You're too late, Temerians. He has
already been arrested and in the name of the law at that. I
caught him. For smuggling. I'm taking him to the guardhouse in Oxenfurt according to orders."

"What's that?" The bald man frowned. "And the
girl?"

"There is no girl here, nor has there been."

The Guards looked at each other in uncertain silence. Olsen grinned broadly and turned up his black
moustache.

"You know what we'll do?" he snorted. "Sail with us
to Oxenfurt, Temerians. We and you are simple folk, how
are we to know the ins and outs of law? The commandant
of the Oxenfurt guardhouse is a wise and worldly man,
he'll judge the matter. You know our commandant, don't
you? Because he knows yours, the one from the Bay, very
well. You'll present your case to him . . . Show him your
orders and seals . . . You do have a warrant with all the
necessary seals, don't you, eh?"

The bald man just stared grimly at the customs
officer.

"I don't have the time or the inclination to go to Oxenfurt!" he suddenly bawled. "I'm taking the rogue to our
shore and that's that! Stran, Vitek! Get on with it, search
the barge! Find me the girl, quick as a flash!"

"One minute, slow down." Olsen was not perturbed by
the yelling and drew out his words slowly and distinctly.
"You're on the Redanian side of the Delta, Temerians.
You don't have anything to declare, by any chance, do
you? Or any contraband? We'll have a look presently.
We'll do a search. And if we do find something then you
will have to take the trouble to go to Oxenfurt for a while,

after all. And we, if we wish to, we can always find something. Boys! Come here!"

"My daddy," squeaked Everett all of a sudden, appearing at the bald man's side as if from nowhere, "is a knight! He's got an even bigger blade than you!"

In a flash, the bald man caught the boy by his beaver collar and snatched him up from the deck, knocking his feathered hat off. Wrapping his arm around the boy's waist he put the cutlass to his throat.

"Move back!" he roared. "Move back or I'll slash the brat's neck!"

"Evereeeeett!" howled the noblewoman.

"Curious methods," said the witcher slowly, "you Temerian Guards use. Indeed, so curious that it makes it hard to believe you're Guards."

"Shut your face!" yelled the bald one, shaking Everett, who was squealing like a piglet. "Stran, Vitek, get him! Fetter him and take him to the lighter! And you, move back! Where's the girl, I'm asking you? Give her to me or I'll slaughter this little snot!"

"Slaughter him then," drawled Olsen giving a sign to his men and pulling out his cutlass. "Is he mine or something? And when you've slaughtered him, we can talk."

"Don't interfere!" Geralt threw his sword on the deck and, with a gesture, held back the customs officers and Boatbug's sailors. "I'm yours, liar-guard, sir. Let the boy go."

"To the lighter!" The bald man retreated to the side of the barge without letting Everett go, and grabbed a rope. "Vitek, tie him up! And all of you, to the stern! If any of you move, the kid dies!"

"Have you lost your mind, Geralt?" growled Olsen.

"Don't interfere!"

"Evereeeett!"

The Temerian lighter suddenly rocked and bounced away from the barge. The water exploded with a splash and two long green, coarse paws bristling with spikes like the limbs of a praying mantis, shot out. The paws grabbed the Guard holding the boathook and, in the wink of an eye, dragged him under water. The bald Guard howled savagely, released Everett, and clung onto the ropes which dangled from the lighter's side. Everett plopped into the already-reddening water. Everybody – those on the barge and those on the lighter – started to scream as if possessed.

Geralt tore himself away from the two men trying to bind him. He thumped one in the chin then threw him overboard. The other took a swing at the witcher with an iron hook, but faltered and drooped into Olsen's hands with a cutlass buried to the hilt in his ribs.

The witcher leaped over the low railing. Before the water – thick with algae – closed in over his head, he heard Linus Pitt, the Lecturer of Natural History at the Academy of Oxenfurt, shout, "What is that? What species? No such animal exists!"

He emerged just by the Temerian lighter, miraculously avoiding the fishing spear which one of baldy's men was jabbing at him. The Guard didn't have time to strike him again before he splashed into the water with an arrow in his throat. Geralt, catching hold of the dropped spear, rebounded with his legs against the side of the boat, dived into the seething whirlpool and forcefully jabbed at something, hoping it was not Everett.

"It's impossible!" he heard the Master Tutor's cries. "Such an animal can't exist! At least, it shouldn't!"

I agree with that last statement entirely, thought the witcher, jabbing the aeschna's armour, bristling with its hard bumps. The corpse of the Temerian Guard was bouncing up and down inertly in the sickle-shaped jaws of the monster, trailing blood. The aeschna swung its flat tail violently and dived to the bottom, raising clouds of silt.

He heard a thin cry. Everett, stirring the water like a little dog, had caught hold of baldy's legs as he was trying to climb on to the lighter by the ropes hanging down the side. The ropes gave way and both the Guard and the boy disappeared with a gurgle under the surface of the water. Geralt threw himself in their direction and dived. The fact that he almost immediately came across the little boy's beaver collar was nothing but luck. He tore Everett from the entangled algae, swam out on his back and, kicking with his legs, reached the barge.

"Here, Geralt! Here!" He heard cries and shouts, each louder than the other: "Give him here!", "The rope! Catch hold of the rope!", "Pooooox!", "The rope! Geraaalt!", "With the boathook, with the boathook!", "My booyyyy!".

Someone tore the boy from his arms and dragged him upwards. At the same moment, someone else caught Geralt from behind, struck him in the back of the head, covered him over with his bulk and pushed him under the water. Geralt let go of the fishing spear, turned and caught his assailant by the belt. With his other hand he tried to grab him by the hair but in vain. It was baldy.

Both men emerged, but only for an instant. The Temerian lighter had already moved a little from the barge and both Geralt and baldy, locked in an embrace, were in between them. Baldy caught Geralt by the throat; the witcher dug a thumb in his eye. The Guard yelled, let go and swam away. Geralt could not swim – something was holding him by the leg and dragging him into the depths. Next to him, half a body bounced to the surface like a cork. And then he knew what was holding him; the information Linus Pitt yelled from the barge deck was unnecessary.

"It's an anthropod! Order *Amphipoda*! Group Mandibulatissimae!"

Geralt violently thrashed his arms in the water, trying to yank his leg from the aeschna's claws as they pulled him towards the rhythmical snap of its jaws. The Master Tutor was correct once again. The jaws were anything but small.

"Grab hold of the rope!" yelled Olsen. "The rope, grab it!"

A fishing spear whistled past the witcher's ear and plunged with a smack into the monster's algae-ridden armour as it surfaced. Geralt caught hold of the shaft, pressed down on it, bounced forcefully away, brought his free leg in and kicked the aeschna violently. He tore himself away from the spiked paws, leaving his boot, a fair part of his trousers and a good deal of skin behind. More fishing spears and harpoons whizzed through the air, most of them missing their mark. The aeschna drew in its paws, swished its tail and gracefully dived into the green depths.

Geralt seized the rope which fell straight onto his face. The boathook, catching him painfully in the side, caught him by the belt. He felt a tug, rode upwards and, taken up by many hands, rolled over the railing and tumbled on deck dripping with water, slime, weeds and blood. The passengers, barge crew and customs officers crowded around him. Leaning over the railings, the dwarf with the fox furs and Olsen were firing their bows. Everett, wet and green with algae, his teeth clattering, sobbed in his mother's arms explaining to everybody that he hadn't meant to do it.

"Geralt!" Boatbug yelled at his ear, "are you dead?"

"Damn it . . ." The witcher spat out seaweed. "I'm too old for this sort of thing . . . Too old . . ."

Nearby, the dwarf released his bowstring and Olsen roared joyously.

"Right in the belly! Ooh-ha-ha! Great shot, my furry friend! Hey, Boratek, give him back his money! He deserves a tax reduction for that shot!"

"Stop . . ." wheezed the witcher, attempting in vain to stand up. "Don't kill them all, damn it! I need one of them alive!"

"We've left one," the customs officer assured him. "The bald one who was bickering with me. We've shot the rest. But baldy is over there, swimming away. I'll fish him out right away. Give us the boathooks!"

"Discovery! A great discovery!" shouted Linus Pitt, jumping up and down by the barge side. "An entirely new species unknown to science! Absolutely unique! Oh, I'm so grateful to you, witcher! As of today, this species is going to appear in books as . . . As *Geraltia maxiliosa pitti*!"

"Master Tutor," Geralt groaned, "if you really want

to show me your gratitude, let that damn thing be called *Everetia.*"

"Just as beautiful," consented the scholar. "Oh, what a discovery! What a unique, magnificent specimen! No doubt the only one alive in the Delta—"

"No," uttered Boatbug suddenly and grimly. "Not the only one. Look!"

The carpet of water lilies adhering to the nearby islet trembled and rocked violently. They saw a wave and then an enormous, long body resembling a rotting log, swiftly paddling its many limbs and snapping its jaws. The bald man looked back, howled horrifically and swam away, stirring up the water with his arms and legs.

"What a specimen, what a specimen," Pitt quickly noted, thrilled no end. "Prehensile cephalic limbs, four pairs of chelae . . . Strong tail-fan . . . Sharp claws . . ."

The bald man looked back again and howled even more horribly. And the *Everetia maxiliosa pitti* extended its prehensile cephalic limbs and swung its tail-fan vigorously. The bald man surged the water in a desperate, hopeless attempt to escape.

"May the water be light to him," said Olsen. But he did not remove his hat.

"My daddy," rattled Everett with his teeth, "can swim faster than that man!"

"Take the child away," growled the witcher.

The monster spread its claws, snapped its jaws. Linus Pitt grew pale and turned away.

Baldy shrieked briefly, choked and disappeared below the surface. The water throbbed dark red.

"Pox." Geralt sat down heavily on the deck. "I'm too old for this sort of thing . . . Far, far too old . . ."

*   *   *

What can be said? Dandilion simply adored the town of Oxenfurt.

The university grounds were surrounded by a wall and around this wall was another ring – that of the huge, loud, breathless, busy and noisy townlet. The wooden, colourful town of Oxenfurt with its narrow streets and pointed roofs. The town of Oxenfurt which lived off the Academy, off its students, lecturers, scholars, researchers and their guests, who lived off science and knowledge, off what accompanies the process of learning. In the town of Oxenfurt, from the by-products and chippings of theory, practice, business and profit were born.

The poet rode slowly along a muddy, crowded street, passing workshops, studios, stalls, shops small and large where, thanks to the Academy, tens of thousands of articles and wonderful things were produced and sold which were unattainable in other corners of the world where their production was considered impossible, or pointless. He passed inns, taverns, stands, huts, counters and portable grills from which floated the appetising aromas of elaborate dishes unknown elsewhere in the world, seasoned in ways not known elsewhere, with garnishes and spices neither known of nor used anywhere else. This was Oxenfurt, the colourful, joyful, noisy and sweet-smelling town of miracles into which shrewd people, full of initiative, had turned dry and useless theories drawn little by little from the university. It was also a town of amusements, constant festivities, permanent holidays and incessant revelry. Night and day the streets resounded with music, song, and the clinking of chalices and tankards, for it is well known that nothing is such thirsty work as the acquisition of knowledge. Although the chancellor's orders forbade students and tutors to drink and play before dusk, drinking and playing took place around the clock in Oxenfurt, for it is well known that if there is anything that makes men thirstier than the acquisition of knowledge it is the full or partial prohibition of drinking.

Dandilion smacked his lips at his bay gelding and rode on, making his way through the crowds roaming the streets. Vendors, stall-holders and travelling charlatans advertised their wares and services loudly, adding to the confusion which reigned all around them.

"Squid! Roast squid!"

"Ointment for all spots'n'boils! Only sold here! Reliable, miraculous ointment!"

"Cats, mouse-catching, magic cats! Just listen, my good people, how they miaow!"

"Amulets! Elixirs! Philtres, love potions, guaranteed aphrodisiacs! One pinch and even a corpse will regain its vigour! Who'll buy, who'll buy?"

"Teeth extracted! Almost painless! Cheap, very cheap!"

"What do you mean by cheap?" Dandilion was curious as he bit into a stick-skewered squid as tough as a boot.

"Two farthings an hour!"

The poet shuddered and spurred his gelding on. He looked back surreptitiously. Two people who had been following in his tracks since the town hall stopped at the barber-shop pretending to ponder over the price of the barber's services displayed on a chalkboard. Dandilion did not let himself be deceived. He knew what really interested them.

He rode on. He passed the enormous building of the

bawdy-house The Rosebud, where he knew refined services either unknown or simply unpopular in other corners of the world were offered. For some time his rational mind struggled against his character and that desire to enter for an hour. Reason triumphed. Dandilion sighed and rode on towards the university trying not to look in the direction of the taprooms from which issued the sounds of merriment.

Yes, what more can be said – the troubadour loved the town of Oxenfurt.

He looked around once more. The two individuals had not made use of the barber's services, although they most certainly should have. At present they were standing outside a musical instrument shop, pretending to ponder over the clay ocarinas. The shopkeeper was falling over himself praising his goods and counting on making some money. Dandilion knew there was nothing to count on.

He directed his horse towards the Philosophers' Gate, the main gate to the Academy. He dealt swiftly with the formalities, which consisted of signing into a guest book and someone taking his gelding to the stables.

Beyond the Philosophers' Gate a different world greeted him. The college land was excluded from the ordinary infrastructure of town buildings; unlike the town it was not a place of dogged struggle for every square yard of space. Everything here was practically as the elves had left it. Wide lanes – laid with colourful gravel – between neat, eye-pleasing little palaces, open-work fences, walls, hedges, canals, bridges, flower-beds and green parks had been crushed in only a few places by some huge, crude mansion constructed in later, post-elven times. Everything was clean, peaceful and dignified – any kind of trade or paid service was forbidden here, not to mention entertainment or carnal pleasures.

Students, absorbed in large books and parchments, strolled along the lanes. Others, sitting on benches, lawns and in flower-beds, repeated their homework to each other, discussed or discreetly played at evens or odds, leapfrog, pile-up or other games demanding intelligence. Professors engrossed in conversation or debate also strolled here with dignity and decorum. Younger tutors milled around with their eyes glued to the backsides of female students. Dandilion ascertained with joy that, since his day, nothing had changed in the Academy.

A breeze swept in from the Delta carrying the faint scent of the sea and the somewhat stronger stink of hydrogen sulphide from the direction of the grand edifice of the Department of Alchemy which towered above the canal. Grey and yellow linnets warbled amongst the shrubs in the park adjacent to the students' dormitories, while an orang-utan sat in the poplar having, no doubt, escaped from the zoological gardens in the Department of Natural History.

Not wasting any time, the poet marched briskly through the labyrinth of lanes and hedges. He knew the University grounds like the back of his hand – and no wonder, considering he had studied there for four years, then had lectured for a year in the Faculty of Trouvereship and Poetry. The post of lecturer had been offered to him when he had passed his final exams with full marks, to the astonishment of professors with whom he had earned the reputation of lazybones, rake and idiot during his studies. Then, when, after several years of roaming around the country with his lute, his fame as a minstrel had spread far and wide, the Academy had taken great pains to have him visit and give guest lectures. Dandilion yielded to their requests only sporadically, for his love of wandering was constantly at odds with his predilection for comfort, luxury and a regular income. And also, of course, with his liking for the town of Oxenfurt.

He looked back. The two individuals, not having purchased any ocarinas, pipes or violins, strode behind him at a distance, paying great attention to the treetops and façades.

Whistling lightheartedly the poet changed direction and made towards the mansion which housed the Faculty of Medicine and Herbology. The lane leading to the faculty swarmed with female students wearing characteristic pale green cloaks. Dandilion searched intently for familiar faces.

"Shani!"

A young medical student with dark red hair cropped just below her ears raised her head from a volume on anatomy and got up from her bench.

"Dandilion!" She smiled, squinting her happy, hazel eyes. "I haven't seen you for years! Come on, I'll introduce you to my friends. They adore your poems—"

"Later," muttered the bard. "Look discreetly over there, Shani. See those two?"

"Snoops." The medical student wrinkled her upturned nose and snorted, amazing Dandilion – not for the first time – with how easily students could recognise secret agents, spies and informers. Students' aversion to the secret service was legendary, if not very rational. The university grounds were extraterritorial and sacred, and students and lecturers were untouchable while there – and the service, although it snooped, did not dare to bother or annoy academics.

"They've been following me since the market place," said Dandilion, pretending to embrace and flirt with the medical student. "Will you do something for me, Shani?"

"Depends what." The girl tossed her shapely neck like a frightened deer. "If you've got yourself into something stupid again . . ."

"No, no," he quickly reassured her. "I only want to pass on some information and can't do it myself with these shits stuck to my heels—"

"Shall I call the lads? I've only got to shout and you'll have those snoops off your back."

"Oh, come on. You want a riot to break out? The row over the bench ghetto for non-humans has just about ended and you can't wait for more trouble? Besides, I loathe violence. I'll manage the snoops. However, if you could . . ."

He brought his lips closer to the girl's hair and took a while to whisper something. Shani's eyes opened wide.

"A witcher? A real witcher?"

"Quiet, for the love of gods. Will you do that, Shani?"

"Of course." The medical student smiled readily. "Just out of curiosity to see, close up, the famous—"

"Quieter, I asked you. Only remember: not a word to anyone."

"A physician's secret." Shani smiled even more beautifully and Dandilion was once more filled with the desire to finally compose a ballad about girls like her – not too pretty but nonetheless beautiful, girls of whom one dreams at night when those of classical beauty are forgotten after five minutes.

"Thank you, Shani."

"It's nothing, Dandilion. See you later. Take care."

Duly kissing each other's cheeks, the bard and the medical student briskly moved off in opposite directions – she towards the faculty, he towards Thinkers' Park.

He passed the modern, gloomy Faculty of Technology building, dubbed the "Deus ex machina" by the students, and turned on to Guildenstern Bridge. He did not get far. Two people lurked around a corner in the lane, by the flowerbed with a bronze bust of the first chancellor of the Academy, Nicodemus de Boot. As was the habit of all snoops in the world, they avoided meeting others' eyes and, like all snoops in the world, they had coarse, pale faces. These they tried very hard to furnish with an intelligent expression, thanks to which they resembled demented monkeys.

"Greetings from Dijkstra," said one of the spies. "We're off."

"Likewise," the bard replied impudently. "Off you go."

The spies looked at each other then, rooted to the spot, fixed their eyes on an obscene word which someone had scribbled in charcoal on the plinth supporting the chancellor's bust. Dandilion sighed.

"Just as I thought," he said, adjusting the lute on his shoulder. "So am I going to be irrevocably forced to accompany you somewhere, gentlemen? Too bad. Let's go then. You go first, I'll follow. In this particular instance, age may go before beauty."

* * *

Dijkstra, head of King Vizimir of Redania's secret service, did not resemble a spy. He was far from the stereotype which dictated that a spy should be short, thin, rat-like, and have piercing eyes forever casting furtive glances from beneath a black hood. Dijkstra, as Dandilion knew, never wore hoods and had a decided preference for bright coloured clothing. He was almost seven foot tall and probably only weighed a little under two quintals. When he crossed his arms over his chest – which he did with habitual pleasure – it looked as if two cachalots had prostrated themselves over a whale. As far as his features, hair colour and complexion were concerned, he looked like a freshly scrubbed pig. Dandilion knew very few people whose appearance was as deceptive as Dijkstra's – because this porky giant who gave the impression of being a sleepy, sluggish moron, possessed an exceptionally keen mind. And considerable authority. A popular saying at King Vizimir's court held that if Dijkstra states it is noon yet darkness reigns all around, it is time to start worrying about the fate of the sun.

At present, however, the poet had other reasons to worry.

"Dandilion," said Dijkstra sleepily, crossing the cachalots over the whale, "you thick-headed halfwit. You unmitigated dunce. Do you have to spoil everything you touch? Couldn't you, just once in your life, do something right? I know you can't think for yourself. I know you're almost forty, look almost thirty, think you're just over twenty and act as though you're barely ten. And being aware of this, I usually furnish you with precise instructions. I tell you what you have to do, when you have to do it and how you're to go about it. And I regularly get the impression that I'm talking to a stone wall."

"I, on the other hand," retorted the poet, feigning insolence, "regularly have the impression that you talk simply to exercise your lips and tongue. So get to the point, and eliminate the figures of speech and fruitless rhetoric. What are you getting at this time?"

They were sitting at a large oak table amongst bookshelves crammed with volumes and piled with rolls of parchment, on the top floor of the vice-chancellor's offices, in leased quarters which Dijkstra had amusingly named the Faculty of Most Contemporary History and Dandilion called the Faculty of Comparative Spying and Applied Sabotage. There were, including the poet, four present – apart from Dijkstra, two other people took part in the conversation. One of these was, as usual, Ori Reuven, the aged and eternally sniffing secretary to the chief of Redanian spies. The other was no ordinary person.

"You know very well what I'm getting at," Dijkstra replied coldly. "However, since you clearly enjoy playing the idiot I won't spoil your game and will explain using simple words. Or maybe you'd like to make use of this privilege, Philippa?"

Dandilion glanced at the fourth person present at the meeting, who until then had remained silent. Philippa Eilhart must have only recently arrived in Oxenfurt, or was perhaps intending to leave at once, since she wore neither a dress nor her favourite black agate jewellery nor any sharp makeup. She was wearing a man's short jacket, leggings and high boots – a "field" outfit as the poet called it. The enchantress's dark hair, usually loose and worn in a picturesque mess, was brushed smooth and tied back at the nape of her neck.

"Let's not waste time," she said, raising her even eyebrows. "Dandilion's right. We can spare ourselves the rhetoric and slick eloquence which leads nowhere when the matter at hand is so simple and trivial."

"Ah, even so." Dijkstra smiled. "Trivial. A dangerous Nilfgaardian agent, who could now be trivially locked away in my deepest dungeon in Tretogor, has trivially escaped, trivially warned and frightened away by the trivial stupidity of two gentlemen known as Dandilion and Geralt. I've seen people wander to the scaffolds over lesser trivialities. Why didn't you inform me about your ambush, Dandilion? Did I not instruct you to keep me informed about all the witcher's intentions?"

"I didn't know anything about Geralt's plans," Dandilion lied with conviction. "I told you that he went to Temeria and Sodden to hunt down this Rience. I also told you that he had returned. I was convinced he had given up. Rience had literally dissolved into thin air, the witcher didn't find the slightest trail, and this – if you remember – I also told you—"

"You lied," stated the spy coldly. "The witcher did find Rience's trail. In the form of corpses. That's when he decided to change his tactics. Instead of chasing Rience, he decided to wait for Rience to find *him*. He signed up to the Malatius and Grock Company barges as an escort. He did so intentionally. He knew that the Company would advertise it far and wide, that Rience would hear of it and then venture to try something. And so Rience did. The strange, elusive Master Rience. The insolent, self-assured Master Rience who does not even bother to use aliases or false names. Master Rience who, from a mile off, smells of Nilfgaardian chimney smoke. And of being a renegade sorcerer. Isn't that right, Philippa?"

The magician neither affirmed nor denied it. She remained silent, watching Dandilion closely and intently. The poet lowered his eyes and hawked hesitantly. He did not like such gazes.

Dandilion divided women – including magicians – into very likeable, likeable, unlikeable and very unlikeable. The very likeable reacted to the proposition of being bedded with joyful acquiescence, the likeable with a happy smile. The unlikeable reacted unpredictably. The very unlikeable were counted by the troubadour to be those to whom the very thought of presenting such a proposition made his back go strangely cold and his knees shake.

Philippa Eilhart, although very attractive, was decidedly very unlikeable.

Apart from that, Philippa Eilhart was an important figure in the Council of Wizards, and King Vizimir's trusted court magician. She was a very talented enchantress. Word had it that she was one of the few to have mastered the art of polymorphy. She looked thirty. In truth she was probably no less than three hundred years old.

Dijkstra, locking his chubby fingers together over his belly, twiddled his thumbs. Philippa remained silent. Ori Reuven coughed, sniffed and wriggled, constantly adjusting his generous toga. His toga resembled a professor's but did not look as if it had been presented by a senate. It looked more as if it had been found on a rubbish heap.

"Your witcher, however," suddenly snarled the spy, "underestimated Master Rience. He set a trap but – demonstrating a complete lack of common sense – banked on Rience troubling himself to come in person. Rience, according to the witcher's plan, was to feel safe. Rience wasn't to smell a trap anywhere, wasn't to spy Master Dijkstra's subordinates lying in wait for him. Because, on the witcher's instructions, Master Dandilion had not squealed to Master Dijkstra about the planned ambush. But according to the instructions received, Master Dandilion was duty bound to do so. Master Dandilion had clear, explicit instructions in this matter which he deigned to ignore."

"I am not one of your subordinates." The poet puffed up with pride. "And I don't have to comply with your instructions and orders. I help you sometimes but I do so out of my own free will, from patriotic duty, so as not to stand by idly in face of the approaching changes—"

"You spy for anyone who pays you," Dijkstra interrupted coldly. "You inform on anyone who has something on you. And I've got a few pretty good things on you, Dandilion. So don't be saucy."

"I won't give in to blackmail!"

"Shall we bet on it?"

"Gentlemen." Philippa Eilhart raised her hand. "Let's be serious, if you please. Let's not be diverted from the matter in hand."

"Quite right." The spy sprawled out in the armchair. "Listen, poet. What's done is done. Rience has been warned and won't be duped a second time. But I can't let anything like this happen in the future. That's why I want to see the witcher. Bring him to me. Stop wandering around town trying to lose my agents. Go straight to Geralt and bring him here, to the faculty. I have to talk to him. Personally, and without witnesses. Without the noise and publicity which would arise if I were to arrest the witcher. Bring him to me, Dandilion. That's all I require of you at present."

"Geralt has left," the bard lied calmly. Dijkstra glanced at the magician. Dandilion, expecting an impulse to sound out his mind, tensed but he did not feel anything. Philippa was watching him, her eyes narrowed, but nothing indicated that she was using spells to verify his truthfulness.

"Then I'll wait until he's back," sighed Dijkstra, pretending to believe him. "The matter I want to see him about is important so I'll make some changes to my schedule and wait for the witcher. When he's back, bring him here. The sooner the better. Better for many people."

"There might be a few difficulties," Dandilion grimaced, "in convincing Geralt to come here. He – just imagine it – harbours an inexplicable aversion to spies. Although to all intents and purposes he seems to understand it is a job like any other, he feels repulsion for those who execute it. Patriotic reasons, he's wont to say, are one thing, but the spying profession attracts only out-and-out scoundrels and the lowest—"

"Enough, enough." Dijkstra waved his hand carelessly. "No platitudes, please, platitudes bore me. They're so crude."

"I think so, too," snorted the troubadour. "But the witcher's a simple soul, a straightforward honest simpleton in his judgement, nothing like us men-of-the-world. He simply despises spies and won't want to talk to you for anything in the world, and as for helping the secret services, there's no question about it. And you haven't got anything on him."

"You're mistaken," said the spy. "I do. More than one

thing. But for the time being that brawl on the barge near Acorn Bay is enough. You know who those men who came on board were? They weren't Rience's men."

"That's not news to me," said the poet casually. "I'm sure they were a few scoundrels of the likes of which there is no shortage in the Temerian Guards. Rience has been asking about the witcher and no doubt offering a nice sum for any news about him. It's obvious that the witcher is very important to him. So a few crafty dogs tried to grab Geralt, bury him in some cave and then sell him to Rience, dictating their conditions and trying to bargain as much out of him as possible. Because they would have got very little, if anything at all, for mere information."

"My congratulations on such perspicacity. The witcher's, of course, not yours – it would never have occurred to you. But the matter is more complex than you think. My colleagues, men belonging to King Foltest's secret service, are also, as it turns out, interested in Master Rience. They saw through the plan of those – as you called them – crafty dogs. It is they who boarded the barge, they who wanted to grab the witcher. Perhaps as bait for Rience, perhaps for a different end. At Acorn Bay, Dandilion, the witcher killed Temerian agents. Their chief is very, very angry. You say Geralt has left? I hope he hasn't gone to Temeria. He might never return."

"And that's what you have on him?"

"Indeed. That's what I have. I can pacify the Temerians. But not for nothing. Where has the witcher gone, Dandilion?"

"Novigrad," the troubadour lied without thinking. "He went to look for Rience there."

"A mistake, a mistake," smiled the spy, pretending not

to have caught the lie. "You see what a shame it is he didn't overcome his repulsion and get in touch with me. I'd have saved him the effort. Rience isn't in Novigrad. Whereas there's no end of Temerian agents there. Probably all waiting for the witcher. They've caught on to something I've known for a long time. Namely, that Geralt, the witcher from Rivia, can answer all kinds of questions if he's asked in the right manner. Questions which the secret services of each of the Four Kingdoms are beginning to ask themselves. The arrangement is simple: the witcher comes here, to the department, and gives me the answers to these questions. And he'll be left in peace. I'll calm the Temerians and guarantee his safety."

"What questions are you talking about? Maybe I can answer them?"

"Don't make me laugh, Dandilion."

"Yet," Philippa Eilhart said suddenly, "perhaps he can? Maybe he can save us time? Don't forget, Dijkstra, our poet is mixed up to his ears in this affair and we've got him here but we haven't got the witcher. Where is the child seen with Geralt in Kaedwen? The girl with ashen hair and green eyes? The one Rience asked you about back in Temeria when he caught and tortured you? Eh, Dandilion? What do you know about the girl? Where has the witcher hidden her? Where did Yennefer go when she received Geralt's letter? Where is Triss Merigold hiding, and why is she hiding?"

Dijkstra did not stir, but his swift glance at the magician showed Dandilion that the spy was taken aback. The questions Philippa had raised had clearly been asked too soon. And directed to the wrong person. The questions appeared rash and careless. The trouble was that Philippa

Eilhart could be accused of anything but rashness and carelessness.

"I'm very sorry," he said slowly, "but I don't know the answer to any of the questions. I'd help you if I could. But I can't."

Philippa looked him straight in the eyes.

"Dandilion," she drawled. "If you know where that girl is, tell us. I assure you that all that I and Dijkstra care about is her safety. Safety which is being threatened."

"I have no doubt," lied the poet, "that's all you care about. But I really don't know what you're talking about. I've never seen the child you're so interested in. And Geralt—"

"Geralt," interrupted Dijkstra, "never confided in you, never said a word even though, no doubt, you inundated him with questions. Why do you think that might be, Dandilion? Could it be that this simple soul, this simpleton who despises spies, sensed who you really are? Leave him alone, Philippa, it's a waste of time. He knows shit-all, don't be taken in by his cocksure expressions and ambiguous smirks. He can help us in only one way. When the witcher emerges from his hide-out, he'll get in touch with him, no one else. Just imagine, he considers him to be a friend."

Dandilion slowly raised his head.

"Indeed," he confirmed. "He considers me to be such. And just imagine, Dijkstra, that it's not without reason. Finally accept the fact and draw your conclusions. Have you drawn them? Right, so now you can try blackmail."

"Well, well," smiled the spy. "How touchy you are on that point. But don't sulk, poet. I was joking. Blackmail between us comrades? Out of the question. And believe me, I don't wish that witcher of yours any ill nor am I thinking of harming him. Who knows – maybe I'll even come to some understanding with him, to the advantage of us both? But in order for that to happen I've got to see him. When he appears, bring him to me. I ask you sincerely, Dandilion, very sincerely. Have you understood how sincerely?"

The troubadour snorted. "I've understood how sincerely."

"I'd like to believe that's true. Well, go now. Ori, show our troubadour to the door."

"Take care." Dandilion got to his feet. "I wish you luck in your work and your personal life. My regards, Philippa. Oh, and Dijkstra! Those agents traipsing after me. Call them off."

"Of course," lied the spy. "I'll call them off. Is it possible you don't believe me?"

"Nothing of the kind," lied the poet. "I believe you."

Dandilion stayed on the Academy premises until evening. He kept looking around attentively but didn't spot any snoops following him. And that was precisely what worried him most.

At the Faculty of Trouvereship he listened to a lecture on classical poetry. Then he slept sweetly through a seminar on modern poetry. He was woken up by some tutors he knew and together they went to the Department of Philosophy to take part in a long-enduring stormy dispute on "The essence and origins of life." Before it had even grown dark, half of the participants were outright drunk while the rest were preparing for blows, out-shouting each other and creating a hullabaloo hard to describe. All this proved handy for the poet.

He slipped unseen into the garret, clambered out by the window vent, slid down by way of the gutter onto the roof of the library, and – nearly breaking his leg – jumped across onto the roof of the dissecting theatre. From there he got into the garden adjacent to the wall. Amidst the dense gooseberry bushes he found a hole which he himself had made bigger when a student. Beyond the hole lay the town of Oxenfurt.

He merged into the crowd, then quickly sneaked down the backstreets, dodging like a hare chased by hounds. When he reached the coach house he waited a good half hour, hidden in the shadows. Not spotting anything suspicious, he climbed the ladder to the thatch and leaped onto the roof of the house belonging to Wolfgang Amadeus Goatbeard, a brewer he knew. Gripping the moss-covered roof tiles, he finally arrived at the window of the attic he was aiming for. An oil lamp was burning inside the little room. Perched precariously on the guttering, Dandilion knocked on the lead frames. The window was not locked and gave way at the slightest push.

"Geralt! Hey, Geralt!"

"Dandilion? Wait . . . Don't come in, please . . ."

"What's that, don't come in? What do you mean, don't come in?" The poet pushed the window. "You're not alone or what? Are you bedding someone right now?"

Neither receiving nor waiting for an answer he clambered onto the sill, knocking over the apples and onions lying on it.

"Geralt . . ." he panted and immediately fell silent. Then cursed under his breath, staring at the light green robes of a medical student strewn across the floor. He opened his mouth in astonishment and cursed once more. He could have expected anything. But not this.

"Shani." He shook his head. "May the—"

"No comments, thank you very much." The witcher sat down on the bed. And Shani covered herself, yanking the sheet right up to her upturned nose.

"Well, come in then." Geralt reached for his trousers. "Since you're coming by way of the window, this must be important. Because if it isn't I'm going to throw you straight back out through it."

Dandilion clambered off the sill, knocking down the rest of the onions. He sat down, pulling the high-backed, wooden chair closer with his foot. The witcher gathered Shani's clothes and his own from the floor. He looked abashed and dressed in silence. The medical student, hiding behind him, was struggling with her shirt. The poet watched her insolently, searching in his mind for similes and rhymes for the golden colour of her skin in the light of the oil lamp and the curves of her small breasts.

"What's this about, Dandilion?" The witcher fastened the buckles on his boots. "Go on."

"Pack your bags," he replied dryly. "Your departure is imminent."

"How imminent?"

"Exceptionally."

"Shani . . ." Geralt cleared his throat. "Shani told me about the snoops following you. You lost them, I understand?"

"You don't understand anything."

"Rience?"

"Worse."

"In that case I really don't understand . . . Wait. The Redanians? Tretogor? Dijkstra?"

"You've guessed."

"That's still no reason—"

"It's reason enough," interrupted Dandilion. "They're not concerned about Rience any more, Geralt. They're after the girl and Yennefer. Dijkstra wants to know where they are. He's going to force you to disclose it to him. Do you understand now?"

"I do now. And so we're fleeing. Does it have to be through the window?"

"Absolutely. Shani? Will you manage?"

The student of medicine smoothed down her robe.

"It won't be my first window."

"I was sure of that." The poet scrutinised her intently, counting on seeing a blush worthy of rhyme and metaphor. He miscalculated. Mirth in her hazel eyes and an impudent smile were all he saw.

A big grey owl glided down to the sill without a sound. Shani cried out quietly. Geralt reached for his sword.

"Don't be silly, Philippa," said Dandilion.

The owl disappeared and Philippa Eilhart appeared in its place, squatting awkwardly. The magician immediately jumped into the room, smoothing down her hair and clothes.

"Good evening," she said coldly. "Introduce me, Dandilion."

"Geralt of Rivia. Shani of Medicine. And that owl which so craftily flew in my tracks is no owl. This is Philippa Eilhart from the Council of Wizards, at present in King Vizimir's service and pride of the Tretogor court. It's a shame we've only got one chair in here."

"It's quite enough." The enchantress made herself comfortable in the high-backed chair vacated by Dandilion, and cast a smouldering glance over those present, fixing her eyes somewhat longer on Shani. The medical student, to Dandilion's surprise, suddenly blushed.

"In principle, what I've come about is the sole concern of Geralt of Rivia," Philippa began after a short pause. "I'm aware, however, that to ask anybody to leave would be tactless, and so . . ."

"I can leave," said Shani hesitantly.

"You can't," muttered Geralt. "No one can until the situation's made clear. Isn't that so, my lady?"

"Philippa to you," smiled the enchantress. "Let's throw formalities aside. And no one has to go – no one's presence bothers me. Astonishes me, at most, but what to do? – life is an endless train of surprises . . . as one of my friends says . . . As our mutual friend says, Geralt. You're studying medicine, are you, Shani? What year?"

"Third," grunted the girl.

"Ah," Philippa Eilhart was looking not at her but at the witcher, "seventeen, what a beautiful age. Yennefer would give a lot to be that age again. What do you reckon, Geralt? Because I'll ask her when I get the chance."

The witcher smiled nastily.

"I've no doubt you will ask. I've no doubt you'll follow the question with a commentary. I've no doubt it'll amuse you no end. Now come to the point, please."

"Quite right." The magician nodded, growing serious. "It's high time. And you haven't got much time. Dandilion has, no doubt, already informed you that Dijkstra has suddenly acquired the wish to see and talk to you to establish the location of a certain girl. Dijkstra has orders from King Vizimir in this matter and so I think he will be very insistent that you reveal this place to him."

"Of course. Thank you for the warning. Only one thing puzzles me a little. You say Dijkstra received instructions from the king. And you didn't receive any? After all, you hold a prominent seat in Vizimir's council."

"Indeed." The magician was not perturbed by the gibe. "I do. I take my responsibilities seriously, and they consist of warning the king against making mistakes. Sometimes – as in this particular instance – I am not allowed to tell the king outright that he is committing a mistake, or to dissuade him from a hasty action. I simply have to render it impossible for him to make a mistake. You understand what I'm saying?"

The witcher confirmed with a nod. Dandilion wondered whether he really did understand, because he knew that Philippa was lying through her teeth.

"So I see," said Geralt slowly, proving that he understood perfectly well, "that the Council of Wizards is also interested in my ward. The wizards wish to find out where my ward is. And they want to get to her before Vizimir or anybody else does. Why, Philippa? What is it about my ward? What makes her so very interesting?"

The magician's eyes narrowed. "Don't you know?" she hissed. "Do you know so little about her? I wouldn't like to draw any hasty conclusions but such a lack of knowledge would indicate that your qualifications as her guardian amount to nothing. In truth, I'm surprised that being so unaware and so lacking in information, you decided to look after her. And not only that – you decided to deny the right to look after her to others, others who have both the qualifications and the right. And, on top of that, you ask why? Careful, Geralt, or your arrogance will be the end of you. Watch out. And guard that child, damn it! Guard that girl as though she's the apple of your eye! And if you can't do so yourself, ask others to!"

For a moment Dandilion thought the witcher was going to mention the role undertaken by Yennefer. He would not be risking anything, and would flatten Philippa's arguments. But Geralt said nothing. The poet guessed why. Philippa knew everything. Philippa was warning him. And the witcher understood her warning.

He concentrated on observing their eyes and faces, wondering whether by any chance something in the past had tied the two together. Dandilion knew that similar duels of words and allusions – demonstrating a mutual fascination – waged between the witcher and enchantresses very often ended in bed. But observation, as usual, gave him nothing. There was only one way to find out whether something had tied the witcher to anyone – one had to enter through the window at the appropriate moment.

"To look after someone," the enchantress continued after a while, "means to take upon oneself the responsibility for the safety of a person unable to assure that safety for herself. If you expose your ward . . . If she comes to any misfortune, the responsibility falls on you, Geralt. Only you."

"I know."

"I'm afraid you still know too little."

"So enlighten me. What makes so many people suddenly want to free me from the burden of that responsibility, want to take on my duties and care for my ward? What does the Council of Wizards want from Ciri? What do Dijkstra and King Vizimir want from her? What do the Temerians want from her? What does a certain Rience, who has already murdered three people in Sodden and Temeria who were in touch with me and the girl two years ago, want from her? Who almost murdered Dandilion trying to extract information about her? Who is this Rience, Philippa?"

"I don't know," said the magician. "I don't know who Rience is. But, like you, I'd very much like to find out."

"Does this Rience –" Shani unexpectedly – "have a third-degree burn on his face? If so, then I know who he is. And I know where he is."

In the silence which fell the first drops of rain knocked on the gutter outside the window.

Murder is always murder, regardless of motive or circumstance. Thus those who murder or who prepare to murder are malefactors and criminals, regardless of who they may be: kings, princes, marshals or judges. None who contemplates and commits violence has the right to consider himself better than an ordinary criminal. Because it is in the nature of all violence to lead inevitably to crime.

Nicodemus de Boot, *Meditations on Life, Happiness and Prosperity*

CHAPTER SIX

"Let us not commit a mistake," said Vizimir, King of Redania, sliding his ringed fingers through the hair at his temples. "We can't afford to make a blunder or mistake now."

Those assembled said nothing. Demawend, ruler of Aedirn, sprawled in his armchair staring at the tankard of beer resting on his belly. Foltest, the Lord of Temeria, Pontar, Mahakam and Sodden, and recently Senior Protector of Brugge, presented his noble profile to everyone by turning his head towards the window. At the opposite side of the table sat Henselt, King of Kaedwen, running his small, piercing eyes – glistening from a face as bearded as a brigand's – over the other participants of the council. Meve, Queen of Lyria, toyed pensively with the enormous rubies in her necklace, occasionally twisting her beautiful full lips into an ambiguous grimace.

"Let us not commit a mistake," repeated Vizimir, "because a mistake could cost us too much. Let us make use of the experience of others. When our ancestors landed on the beaches five hundred years ago the elves also hid their heads in the sand. We tore the country away from them piece by piece, and they retreated, thinking all the while that *this* would be the last border, that we would encroach no further. Let us be wiser! Because now it is our turn. Now we are the elves. Nilfgaard is at the Yaruga and I hear: 'So, let them stay there'. I hear: 'They won't come any further'. But they will, you'll see. So I repeat, let us not make the same mistake as the elves!"

Raindrops knocked against the window panes and the wind howled eerily. Queen Meve raised her head. She thought she heard the croaking of ravens and crows, but it was only the wind. The wind and rain.

"Do not compare us to the elves," said Henselt of Kaedwen. "You dishonour us with such a comparison. The elves did not know how to fight – they retreated before our ancestors and hid in the mountains and forests. The elves did not treat our ancestors to a Sodden. But we showed the Nilfgaardians what it means to pick a quarrel with us. Do not threaten us with Nilfgaard, Vizimir, don't sow the seeds of propaganda. Nilfgaard, you say, is at the Yaruga? I say that Nilfgaard is sitting as quiet as a church mouse beyond the river. Because we broke their spine at Sodden. We broke them militarily, and above all we broke their morale. I don't know whether it is true that Emhyr var Emreis was, at the time, against aggression on such a scale, that the attack on Cintra was the work of some party hostile to him – I take it that if they had defeated us, he would be applauding, and distributing privileges and endowments amongst them. But after Sodden it suddenly turns out he was against it, and that everything which occurred was due to his marshals' insubordination.

And heads fell. The scaffolds flowed with blood. These are certain facts, not rumours. Eight solemn executions, and many more modest ones. Several apparently natural yet mysterious deaths, a good many cases of people suddenly choosing to retire. I tell you, Emhyr fell into a rage and practically finished off his own commanders. So who will lead their army now? The sergeants?"

"No, not the sergeants," said Demawend of Aedirn coldly. "It will be young and gifted officers who have long waited for such an opportunity and have been trained by Emhyr for an equally long time. Those whom the older marshals stopped from taking command, prevented from being promoted. The young, gifted commanders about whom we already hear. Those who crushed the uprisings in Metinna and Nazair, who rapidly broke up the rebels in Ebbing. Commanders who appreciate the roles of outflanking manoeuvres, of far-reaching cavalry raids, of swift infantry marches and of landing operations from the sea. They use the tactics of crushing assaults in specific directions, they use the newest siege techniques instead of relying on the uncertainties of magic. They must not be underestimated. They are itching to cross the Yaruga and prove that they have learned from the mistakes of their old marshals."

"If they have truly learned anything," Henselt shrugged, "they will not cross the Yaruga. The river estuary on the border between Cintra and Verden is still controlled by Ervyll and his three strongholds: Nastrog, Rozrog and Bodrog. They cannot be seized just like that – no new technology is going to help them there. Our flank is defended by Ethain of Cidaris's fleet, and thanks to it we control the shore. And also thanks to the pirates of Skellige. Jarl Crach an Craite, if you remember, didn't sign a truce with Nilfgaard, and regularly bites them, attacking and setting fire to their maritime settlements and forts in the Provinces. The Nilfgaardians have nicknamed him Tirth ys Muire, Sea Boar. They frighten children with him!"

"Frightening Nilfgaardian children," smiled Vizimir wryly, "will not ensure our safety."

"No," agreed Henselt. "Something else will. Without control of the estuary or the shore and with a flank exposed, Emhyr var Emreis will be in no position to ensure provisions reach any detachments he might care to send across the Yaruga. What swift marches, what cavalry raids? Ridiculous. The army will come to a standstill within three days of crossing the river. Half will lay siege to the stronghold and the rest will be slowly dispersed to plunder the region in search of fodder and food. And when their famed cavalry has eaten most of its own horses, we'll give them another Sodden. Damn it, I'd like them to cross the river! But don't worry, they won't."

"Let us say," Meve of Lyria said suddenly, "that they do not cross the Yaruga. Let us say that Nilfgaard will simply wait. Now let us consider: who would that suit, them or us? Who can let themselves wait and do nothing and who can't?"

"Exactly!" picked up Vizimir. "Meve, as usual, does not say much but she hits the nail on the head. Emhyr has time on his hands, gentlemen, but we don't. Can't you see what is happening? Three years ago, Nilfgaard disturbed a small stone on the mountainside and now they are calmly waiting for an avalanche. They can simply wait while new stones keep pouring down the slope. Because, to some, that first small stone looked like a boulder which would be impossible to move. And since it turned out that a mere touch sufficed to set it rolling, others appeared for whom an avalanche would prove convenient. From the Grey Mountains to Bremervoord, elven commandos rove the forests – this is no longer a small group of guerrilla fighters, this is war. Just wait and we'll see the free elves of Dol Blathanna rising to fight. In Mahakam the dwarves are rebelling, the dryads of Brokilon are growing bolder and bolder. This is war, war on a grand scale. Civil war. Domestic. Our own. While Nilfgaard waits . . . Whose side you think time is on? The Scoia'tael commandos have thirty- or forty-year old elves fighting for them. And they live for three hundred years! They have time, we don't!"

"The Scoia'tael," admitted Henselt, "have become a real thorn in the backside. They're paralysing my trade and transport, terrorising the farmers . . . we have to put an end to this!"

"If the non-humans want war, they will get it," threw in Foltest of Temeria. "I have always been an advocate of mutual agreement and co-existence but if they prefer a test of strength then we will see who is the stronger. I am ready. I undertake to put an end to the Squirrels in Temeria and Sodden within six months. Those lands have already run with elven blood once, shed by our ancestors. I consider the blood-letting a tragedy, but I do not see an alternative – the tragedy will be repeated. The elves have to be pacified."

"Your army will march against the elves if you give the order," nodded Demawend. "But will it march against humans? Against the peasantry from which you muster your infantry? Against the guilds? Against the free towns? Speaking of the Scoia'tael, Vizimir described only one stone in the avalanche. Yes, yes, gentlemen, do not gape at me like that! Word is already going round the villages and towns that on the lands already taken by the Nilfgaard, peasants, farmers and craftsmen are having an easier life, freer and richer, and that merchants' guilds have more privileges . . . We are inundated with goods from Nilfgaardian manufactories. In Brugge and Verden their coin is ousting local currency. If we sit and do nothing we will be finished, at odds with our neighbours, embroiled in conflict, tangled up in trying to quell rebellions and riots, and slowly subdued by the economic strength of the Nilfgaardians. We will be finished, suffocating in our own stuffy parochial corner because – understand this – Nilfgaard is cutting off our route to the South and we have to develop, we have to be expansive, otherwise there won't be enough room here for our grandchildren!"

Those gathered said nothing. Vizimir of Redania sighed deeply, grabbed one of the chalices standing on the table and took a long draught. Rain battered against the windows throughout the prolonged silence, and the wind howled and pounded against the shutters.

"All the worries of which we talk," said Henselt finally, "are the work of Nilfgaard. It is Emhyr's emissaries who are inciting the non-humans, spreading propaganda and calling for riots. It is they who are throwing gold around and promising privileges to corporations and guilds, assuring barons and dukes they will receive high positions in the provinces they plan to create in place of our kingdoms. I don't know what it's like in your countries, but in Kaedwen we've been inundated with clerics, preachers, fortune-tellers and other shitty mystics all appearing out of the blue, all preaching the end of the world . . ."

"It's the same in my country," agreed Foltest. "Damn it, for so many years there was peace. Ever since my grandfather showed the clerics their place and decimated their ranks, those who remained stuck to useful tasks. They studied books and instilled knowledge in children, treated the sick, took care of the poor, the handicapped and the homeless. They didn't get mixed up in politics. And now all of a sudden they've woken up and are yelling nonsense to the rabble – and the rabble is listening and believes they know, at last, why their lives are so hard. I put up with it because I'm less impetuous than my grandfather and less sensitive about my royal authority and dignity than he was. What sort of dignity or authority would it be, anyway, if it could be undermined by the squealings of some deranged fanatic? But my patience is coming to an end. Recently the main topic of preaching has been of a Saviour who will come from the south. From the south! From beyond the Yaruga!"

"The White Flame," muttered Demawend. "White Chill will come to be, and after it the White Light. And then the world will be reborn through the White Flame and the White Queen . . . I've heard it, too. It's a travesty of the prophecy of Ithlinne aep Aevenien, the elven seeress. I gave orders to catch one cleric who was going on about it in the Vengerberg market place and the torturer asked him politely and at length how much gold the prophet had received from Emhyr for doing it . . . But the preacher only prattled on about the White Flame and the White Queen . . . the same thing, to the very end."

"Careful, Demawend," grimaced Vizimir. "Don't

make any martyrs. That's exactly what Emhyr is after. Catch all the Nilfgaardian agents you please, but do not lay hands on clerics, the consequences are too unpredictable. They still are held in regard and have an important influence on people. We have too much trouble with the Squirrels to risk riots in our towns or war against our own peasants."

"Damn it!" snorted Foltest, "let's not do this, let's not risk that, we mustn't this, we mustn't that . . . Have we gathered here to talk about all we can't do? Is that why you dragged us all to Hagge, Demawend, to cry our hearts out and bemoan our weakness and helplessness? Let us finally do something! Something must be done! What is happening has to be stopped!"

"I've been saying that from the start." Vizimir pulled himself up. "I propose action."

"What sort of action?"

"What can we do?"

Silence fell again. The wind blustered, the shutters banged against the castle wall.

"Why," said Meve suddenly, "are you all looking at me?"

"We're admiring your beauty," Henselt mumbled from the depths of his tankard.

"That too," seconded Vizimir. "Meve, we all know you can find a solution to everything. You have a woman's intuition, you're a wise wo—"

"Stop flattering me." The Queen of Lyria clasped her hands in her lap and fixed her gaze on the darkened tapestries with their depictions of hunting scenes. Hounds, extended in a leap, were turning their muzzles up towards the flanks of a fleeing white unicorn. *I've never seen a live unicorn*, thought Meve. *Never. And I probably never will.*

"The situation in which we find ourselves," she said after a while, tearing her eyes away from the tapestry, "reminds me of long, winter evenings in Rivian Castle. Something always hung in the air. My husband would be contemplating how to get his hands on yet another maid-of-honour. The marshal would be working out how to start a war which would make him famous. The wizard would imagine he was king. The servants wouldn't feel like serving, the jester would be sad, gloomy and excruciatingly dull, the dogs would howl with melancholy and the cats sleep, careless of any mice that might be scuttling around on the table. Everybody was waiting for something. Everyone was scowling at me. And I . . . then I . . . I showed them. I showed them all what I was capable of, in a way that made the very walls shake and the local grizzly bears wake in their winter lairs. And any silly thoughts disappeared from their heads in a trice. Suddenly everyone knew who ruled."

No one uttered a word. The wind howled a little louder. The guards on the buttresses outside hailed each other casually. The patter of drops on the panes in the lead window frames grew to a frenzied staccato.

"Nilfgaard is watching and waiting," continued Meve slowly, toying with her necklace. "Nilfgaard is observing us. Something is hanging in the air, silly thoughts are springing up in many heads. So let us show them what we are capable of. Let us show them who is really king here. Let us shake the walls of this great castle plunged into a winter torpor!"

"Eradicate the Squirrels," said Henselt quickly. "Start

a huge joint military operation. Treat the non-humans to a blood bath. Let the Pontar, Gwenllech and Buina flow with elven blood from source to estuary!"

"Send a penal expedition to smother the free elves of Dol Blathanna," added Demawend, frowning. "March an interventionary force into Mahakam. Allow Ervyll of Verden a chance, at last, to get at the dryads in Brokilon. Yes, a blood bath! And any survivors – to the reservations!"

"Set Crach an Craite at the Nilfgaardian shores," picked up Vizimir. "Support him with Ethain of Cidaris's fleet, let them go ravaging from the Yaruga to Ebbing! A show of strength—"

"Not enough." Foltest shook his head. "All of that is still not enough. We need . . . I know what we need."

"So tell us!"

"Cintra."

"What?"

"To take Cintra back from the Nilfgaardians. Let us cross the Yaruga, be the first to attack. Now, while they don't expect it. Let us throw them out, back beyond the Marnadal."

"How? We've just said that it's impossible for an army to cross the Yaruga—"

"Impossible for Nilfgaard. But we have control of the river. We hold the estuary in our grasp, and the supply routes, and our flank is protected by Skellige, Cidaris and the strongholds in Verden. For Nilfgaard, getting forty or fifty thousand men across the river is a considerable effort. We can get far more across to the left bank. Don't gape, Vizimir. You wanted something to put an end to the waiting? Something spectacular? Something which will make us true kings again? That something is Cintra. Cintra will bind us and our rule together because Cintra is a symbol. Remember Sodden! If it were not for the massacre of that town and Calanthe's martyrdom, there would not have been such a victory then. The forces were equal – no one counted on our crushing them like that. But our armies threw themselves at their throats like wolves, like rabid dogs, to avenge the Lioness of Cintra. And there are those whose fury was not quelled by the blood spilt on the field of Sodden. Remember Crach an Craite, the Wild Boar of the Sea!"

"That is true," nodded Demawend. "Crach swore bloody vengeance on Nilfgaard. For Eist Tuirseach, killed at Marnadal. And for Calanthe. If we were to strike at the left bank, Crach would back us up with all the strength of Skellige. By the gods, this has a chance at success! I back Foltest! Let us not wait, let us strike first, let us liberate Cintra and chase those sons-of-bitches beyond the Amell pass!"

"Slow down," snarled Henselt. "Don't be in such a hurry to tug the lion's whiskers, because this lion is not dead yet. That is for starters. Secondly, if we are the first to strike, we will put ourselves in the position of aggressors. We will be breaking the truce to which we all put our seals. We will not be backed by Niedamir and his League, we will not be backed by Esterad Thyssen. I don't know how Ethain of Cidaris will react. An aggressive war will also be opposed by our guilds, merchants, nobles . . . And above all, the wizards. Do not forget the wizards!"

"The wizards won't back an assault on the left bank," confirmed Vizimir. "The peace agreement was the work of Vilgefortz of Roggeveen. It is well known that his plan was for the armistice to gradually turn into permanent peace. Vilgefortz will not back a war. And the Chapter, believe me, will do whatever Vilgefortz wishes. After Sodden he has become the most important person in the Chapter – let other magicians say what they will, Vilgefortz plays first fiddle there."

"Vilgefortz, Vilgefortz," bridled Foltest. "He has grown too large for us, that magician. Taking into account Vilgefortz's and the Chapter's plans – plans which I am not acquainted with anyway, and which I do not understand at that – is beginning to annoy me. But there is a way around that, too, gentlemen. What if it were Nilfgaard who was the aggressor? At Dol Angra for example? Against Aedirn and Lyria? We could arrange that somehow . . . could stage some tiny provocation . . . A border incident caused by them? An attack on a border fort, let us say? We will, of course, be prepared – we will react decisively and forcefully, with everybody's full acceptance, including that of Vilgefortz and the entire Chapter of Wizards. And when Emhyr var Emreis turns his eyes from Sodden and Transriver, the Cintrians will demand their country back – all those the emigrants and refugees who are gathering themselves in Brugge under Vissegerd's leadership. Nearly eight thousand of them are armed. Could there be a better spearhead? They live in the hope of regaining the country they were forced to flee. They are burning to fight. They are ready to strike the left bank. They await only the battle cry."

"The battle cry," bore out Meve, "and the promise that we will back them up. Because Emhyr can command eight thousand men at his border garrison; with that strength he won't even have to send for relief troops. Vissegerd knows this very well and won't move until he has the assurance that your armies, Foltest, reinforced by Redanian corps, will disembark on the left bank at his heels. But above all Vissegerd is waiting for the Lion Cub of Cintra. Apparently the queen's granddaughter survived the slaughter. Allegedly, she was seen amongst the refugees, but the child mysteriously disappeared. The emigrants persist in their search for her . . . Because they need someone of royal blood to sit on their regained throne. Someone of Calanthe's blood."

"Nonsense," said Foltest coldly. "More than two years have passed. If the child has not been found by now, she's dead. We can forget that myth. Calanthe is no more and there is no Lion Cub, no royal blood to whom the throne belongs. Cintra . . . will never again be what it was during the Lioness's lifetime. Obviously, we cannot say that to Vissegerd's emigrants."

"So you are going to send Cintrian guerrillas to their deaths?" Meve narrowed her eyes. "In the line of attack? Not telling them that Cintra can only be reborn as a vassal country under your protectorship? You are proposing, to all of us, an attack on Cintra for your own gain? You have suborned Sodden and Brugge for yourself, are sharpening your teeth on Verden and now you have caught a whiff of Cintra, is that right?"

"Admit it, Foltest," snapped Henselt. "Is Meve right? Is that why you are inciting us to this affair?"

"Come on, leave it." The ruler of Temeria furrowed his noble brow and bristled angrily. "Don't make me out as some conqueror dreaming of an empire. What are you talking about? Sodden and Brugge? Ekkehard of Sodden was my mother's half-brother. Are you surprised that following his death the Free States brought the crown to me, his relative? Blood not water! And yes Venzlav of Brugge paid me homage as a vassal – but without coercion! He did it to protect his country because, on a fine day, he can see Nilfgaardian lances flashing on the left bank of the Yaruga!"

"And we are talking about the left bank," drawled out the Queen of Lyria. "The bank we are to strike. And the left bank is Cintra. Destroyed, burned out, ruined, decimated and occupied . . . but still Cintra. The Cintrians won't bring you their crown, Foltest, nor will they pay you homage. Cintra will not agree to be a vassal state. Blood, not water!"

"Cintra, if we . . . When we liberate it, it should become our joint protectorate," said Demawend of Aedirn. "Cintra is at the mouth of the Yaruga, in too important a strategic position to allow ourselves to lose control over it."

"It has to be a free country," objected Vizimir. "Free, independent and strong. A country which will be an iron gateway, a bulwark to the north, and not a strip of burned ground over which the Nilfgaardian cavalry will be able to gather speed!"

"Is it possible to rebuild such a Cintra? Without Calanthe?"

"Don't get all worked up, Foltest," pouted Meve. "I've already told you, the Cintrians will never accept a protectorate or foreign blood on their throne. If you try to force yourself on them as their lord the tables will be turned. Vissegerd will again prepare his troops for battle, but this time under Emhyr's wings. And one day those detachments are going to assail us in the vanguard of a Nilfgaardian onslaught. As the spear point, as you just vividly described it."

"Foltest knows that," snorted Vizimir. "That's why he's searching so hard for this Lion Cub, for Calanthe's granddaughter. Don't you understand? Blood not water, the crown through marriage. It's enough for him to find the girl and force her to marry—"

"Are you out of your mind?" choked out the King of Temeria. "The Lion Cub is dead! I'm not looking for the girl at all, but if I were . . . It has not even occurred to me to force her to do such a thing—"

"You wouldn't have to force her," interrupted Meve, smiling charmingly. "You are still a strapping, handsome man, cousin. And Calanthe's blood runs through the Lion Cub. Very hot blood. I knew Cali when she was young. When she saw a fellow she liked, she leaped up and down so fast that if you put dry twigs beneath her feet they would have caught real fire. Her daughter, Pavetta, the Lion Cub's mother, was exactly the same. So, no doubt, the Lion Cub has not fallen far from the apple tree. A bit of effort, Foltest, and the girl would not be long in resisting. That is what you are counting on, admit it."

"Of course he's counting on it," chuckled Demawend. "Our king has thought up a cunning little plan for himself! We assail the left bank and before we realise it our Foltest will have found the girl, won her heart and have a young wife whom he will place on the throne of Cintra while her people cry for joy and pee in their knickers for happiness. For they will have their queen, blood of the blood and flesh of the flesh of Calanthe. They will have a queen . . . albeit one who comes with a king. King Foltest."

"What rubbish!" yelled Foltest, turning red then white in turn. "What's got into you? There's not a grain of sense in your prattling!"

"There is a whole lot of sense," said Vizimir dryly. "Because I know that someone is searching for the child very earnestly. Who, Foltest?"

"It's obvious! Vissegerd and the Cintrians!"

"No, it's not them. At least, not just them. Someone else is, too. Someone who is leaving a trail of corpses behind them. Someone who does not shrink from black-mail, bribery or torture . . . While we are on the subject, is a gentleman by the name of Rience in any of your ser-vices? Ah, I see from your expressions that either he isn't or you won't admit it – which comes to the same thing. I repeat: they are searching for Calanthe's granddaughter, and searching in such a way as to make you think twice about their intentions. Who is looking for her, I ask?"

"Hell!" Foltest thumped his fist on the table. "It's not me! It never occurred to me to marry some child for some throne! After all, I—"

"After all, you have been secretly sleeping with the Baroness La Valette for the past four years." Meve smiled again. "You love each other like two turtle doves and just wait for the old baron to finally kick the bucket. What are you staring at? We all know about it. What do you think we pay our spies for? But for the throne of Cintra, cousin, many a king would be prepared to sacrifice his personal happiness—"

"Hold on." Henselt scratched his beard with a rasp. "Many a king, you say. Then leave Foltest in peace for a moment. There are others. In her time, Calanthe wanted to give her granddaughter's hand to Ervyll of Verden's son. Ervyll, too, might have caught a whiff of Cintra. And not just him . . ."

"Hmm . . ." muttered Vizimir. "True. Ervyll has three sons . . . And what about those present here who also have male descendants? Huh? Meve? Are you not, by any chance, pulling wool over our eyes?"

"You can count me out." The Queen of Lyria smiled even more charmingly. "It is true, two of my offspring are roaming the world – the fruits of delightful abandon – if they have not been brought to the gallows yet. I doubt that either of them would suddenly desire to be king. They were neither predisposed nor inclined that way. Both were even stupider than their father, may he rest in peace. Whoever knew my deceased husband will understand what I mean."

"That's a fact," agreed the King of Redania. "I knew him. Are your sons really more stupid? Damn it, I thought it wasn't possible to get any more stupid . . . Forgive me, Meve . . ."

"It's nothing, Vizimir."

"Who else has sons?"

"You do, Henselt."

"My son is married!"

"And what is poison for? For the throne of Cintra, as someone here so wisely said, many would sacrifice their personal happiness. It would be worth it!"

"I will not permit such insinuations! And leave me alone! Others have sons, too!"

"Niedamir of Hengfors has two. And is a widower

himself. And he isn't old. And don't forget Esterad Thyssen of Kovir."

"I would count those out." Vizimir shook his head. "The Hengfors League and Kovir are planning a dynastic union with each other. They are not interested in Cintra or the south. Hmm . . . But Ervyll of Verden . . . It's not so far from him."

"There is someone else who is just as near," remarked Demawend suddenly.

"Who?"

"Emhyr var Emreis. He is not married. And he is younger than you, Foltest."

"Bloody hell." The King of Redania frowned. "If that were true . . . Emhyr would bugger us without grease! It's obvious that the people and nobility of Cintra will follow Calanthe's blood. Imagine what would happen if Emhyr were to get his hands on the Lion Cub? Damn it, that's all we need! Queen of Cintra, and Empress of Nilfgaard!"

"Empress!" snorted Henselt. "You exaggerate, Vizimir. What does Emhyr need the girl for, what the hell does he need to get married for? The throne of Cintra? Emhyr already has Cintra! He conquered the country and made it a province of Nilfgaard! He's got his whole butt on the throne and still has enough room to wriggle about!"

"Firstly," noted Foltest, "Emhyr grips Cintra by law, or rather by an aggressor's lawlessness. If he had the girl and married her, he could rule legally. You understand? Nilfgaard bound in marriage to Calanthe's blood is no longer Nilfgaard the invader, at which the entire north bares its teeth. It is Nilfgaard the neighbour whom one has to take into account. How would you want to force such a Nilfgaard beyond Marnadal, beyond the Amell

passes? Attacking a kingdom whose throne is legally occupied by the Lion Cub, granddaughter of the Lioness of
Cintra? Pox! I don't know who's looking for that child.
I'm not looking for her. But I declare that now I'm going
to start to. I still believe the girl is dead, but we can't take
the risk. It looks as if she is too important. If she survived
then we must find her!"

"And shall we decide now who she will marry when
we find her?" Henselt grimaced. "Such matters should
not be left to chance. We could, for that matter, hand her
over to Vissegerd's guerrillas as a battle standard, tied to
a long pole – they could carry her before the front line
as they attack the left bank. But if the recaptured Cintra
is to be useful to us all . . . Surely you see what I mean?
If we attack Nilfgaard and retrieve Cintra, the Lion Cub
can be put on the throne. But the Lion Cub can have only
one husband. One who will look after our interests at the
mouth of the Yaruga. Who of those present is going to
volunteer?"

"Not me," joked Meve. "I waive the privilege."

"I wouldn't exclude those who aren't present here,"
said Demawend seriously. "Neither Ervyll, nor Niedamir,
nor the Thyssens. And bear in mind that Vissegerd could
surprise you and put the standard attached to a long pole
to unexpected use. You've heard about morganatic mar-
riages? Vissegerd is old and as ugly as cow's dung but
with enough decoctions of absinthe and damiana down
her throat, the Lion Cub might unexpectedly fall in love
with him! Is King Vissegerd included in our plans?"

"No," muttered Foltest, "not in mine."

"Hmm . . ." Vizimir hesitated. "Nor in mine. Vissegerd is a tool, not a partner, that's the role he is to play in

our plans for attacking Nilfgaard – that and no other. Besides, if the one who is so earnestly seeking the Lion Cub is indeed Emhyr var Emreis, we cannot take the risk."

"Absolutely not," seconded Foltest. "The Lion Cub cannot fall into Emhyr's hands. She cannot fall into anybody's— Into the wrong hands . . . Alive."

"Infanticide?" Meve grimaced. "An ugly solution, my kings. Unworthy. And surely unnecessarily drastic. First of all, let us find the girl – because we still don't have her. And when we have found her, give her to me. I'll keep her in some castle in the mountains for a couple of years, and marry her off to one of my knights. When you see her again, she will already have two children and a belly out to here."

"Leading to, if I count correctly, at least three future eventual pretenders and usurpers?" Vizimir nodded. "No, Meve. It is ugly, indeed, but the Lion Cub, if she has survived, must now die. For reasons of state. Gentlemen?"

The rain hammered against the windows. The gale howled among the towers of Hagge castle.

The kings grew silent.

"Vizimir, Foltest, Demawend, Henselt and Meve," repeated the marshal. "They met in a secret council in Hagge Castle on the Pontar. They conferred in privacy."

"How symbolic," said the slender, black-haired man wearing an elk tunic marked with the imprints of armour and rust stains, without looking round. "After all, it was at Hagge, not forty years ago, that Virfuril defeated Medell's armies, strengthened his control over the Pontar Valley and established today's borders between Aedirn and

Temeria. And today Demawend, Virfuril's son, invites Foltest, Medell's son, to Hagge, summoning Vizimir of Tretogor, Henselt of Ard Carraigh and the merry widow Meve of Lyria to complete the set. They are meeting now and holding council in secrecy. Can you guess what they are discussing, Coehoorn?"

"I can," the marshal replied succinctly. He did not say a word more. He knew that the man with his back turned hated anyone to display any eloquence or comment on obvious facts in his presence.

"They did not invite Ethain of Cidaris." The man in the elk tunic turned away from the window, clasped his hands behind his back and strolled slowly from the window to the table and then back again. "Nor Ervyll of Verden. They did not invite Esterad Thyssen or Niedamir. Which means they are either very sure of themselves, or very unsure. They did not invite anyone from the Chapter of Wizards. Which is interesting, and significant. Coehoorn, try to see to it that the wizards learn of this council. Let them know that their monarchs do not treat them as equals. It seems to me that the wizards of the Chapter have had some doubts in this respect. Disperse them."

"It's an order."

"Any news from Rience?"

"None."

The man paused at the window and stood there for a long while gazing at the hills drenched in rain. Coehoorn waited, restlessly clenching and unclenching his fist around the pommel of his sword. He was afraid he would be forced to listen to a long monologue. The marshal knew that the man standing at the window considered his monologues a conversation, and viewed conversation as a privilege and proof of trust. He knew this, but still didn't like listening to the monologues.

"How do you find the country, Governor? Have you grown to like your new province?"

He shuddered, taken unawares. He did not expect the question. But he did not ponder the answer for long. Insincerity and indecisiveness could cost him a great deal.

"No, your Highness. I haven't. That country is so . . . gloomy."

"It was different once," the man replied without looking round. "And it will be different again. You will see. You will still see a beautiful, happy Cintra, Coehoorn. I promise you. But don't be saddened, I shan't keep you here long. Someone else will take over the governorship of the province. I'll be needing you in Dol Angra. You'll leave immediately once the rebellion is quashed. I need someone responsible in Dol Angra. Someone who will not allow himself to be provoked. The merry widow of Lyria or Demawend . . . will want to provoke us. You'll take the young officers in hand. Cool their hot heads. You will let yourselves be provoked only when I give the order. No sooner."

"Yes, sir!"

The clatter of arms and spurs and the sound of raised voices came from the antechamber. Someone knocked on the door. The man in the elk tunic turned away from the window and nodded his head in consent. The marshal bowed a little and left.

The man returned to the table, sat down and lowered his head over some maps. He studied them for a long time then finally rested his brow on his interlocked hands. The enormous diamond in his ring sparkled in the candlelight as if a thousand flames.

"Your Highness?" The door squeaked faintly.

The man did not change his position. But the marshal noticed that his hands twitched. He spotted it by the flash of the diamond. He closed the door carefully and quietly behind him.

"News, Coehoorn? From Rience maybe?"

"No, your Highness. But good news. The rebellion in the province has been quelled. We have broken up the rebels. Only a few managed to escape to Verden. And we've caught their leader, Duke Windhalm of Attre."

"Good," said the man after a while, still not raising his head from his hands. "Windhalm of Attre . . . Order him to be beheaded. No . . . Not beheaded. Executed in some other way. Spectacularly, lengthily and cruelly. And publicly, it goes without saying. A terrifying example is necessary. Something that will frighten others. Only please, Coehoorn, spare me the details. You don't have to bother with a vivid description in your report. I take no pleasure from it."

The marshal nodded, then swallowed hard. He too found no pleasure in it. No pleasure whatsoever. He intended to leave the preparation and performance of the execution to the specialists, and he did not have the least intention of asking those specialists for details. And, above all, he did not intend to be there.

"You will be present at the execution." The man raised his head, picked a letter up from the table and broke the seal. "Officially. As the Governor of the Province of Cintra. You will stand in for me. I don't intend to watch it. That's an order, Coehoorn."

"Yes, sir!" The marshal did not even try to hide his embarrassment and discomfort. The man who had given the order did not allow anything to be kept from him. And rarely did anyone succeed in doing so.

The man glanced at the open letter and almost immediately threw it into the fire, into the hearth.

"Coehoorn."

"Yes, your Highness?"

"I am not going to wait for Rience's report. Set the magicians to work and have them prepare a telecommunication link with their point of contact in Redania. Let them pass on my verbal orders, which must immediately be sent to Rience. The order is to run as follows: Rience is to stop pussyfooting around, and to stop playing with the witcher. Else it could end badly. No one toys with the witcher. I know him, Coehoorn. He is too clever to lead Rience to the Trail. I repeat, Rience is to organise the assassination immediately, to take the witcher out of the game at once. He's to kill him, and then disappear, bide his time and await my orders. If he comes across the enchantress's trail before that he is to leave her alone. Not a hair on Yennefer's head is to be harmed. Have you remembered that, Coehoorn?"

"Yes, sir."

"The communiqué is to be coded and firmly secured against any magical deciphering. Forewarn the wizards about this. If they bungle it, if any undesirables learn of my order, I will hold them responsible."

"Yes, sir." The marshal hawked and pulled himself up straight.

"What else, Coehoorn?"

"The count . . . He is here already, your Highness. He came at your command."

"Already?" He smiled. "Such speed is worthy of admiration. I hope he didn't exhaust that black horse of his everyone envies so much. Have him come in."

"Am I to be present during the conversation, your Highness?"

"Of course, Governor of Cintra."

Summoned from the antechambers, the knight entered the chamber with an energetic, strong and noisy stride, his black armour grating. He stopped short, drew himself up proudly, threw his wet, muddy black cloak back from his shoulder, and laid his hand on the hilt of his mighty sword. He leaned his black helmet, adorned with wings of a bird of prey, on his hip. Coehoorn looked at the knight's face. He saw there the hard pride of a warrior, and impudence. He did not see any of the things that should have been visible in the face of one who had spent the past two years incarcerated in a place from which – as everything had indicated – he would only leave for the scaffold. A faint smile touched the marshal's lips. He knew that the disdain for death and crazy courage of youngsters stemmed from a lack of imagination. He knew that perfectly well. He had once been such a youngster himself.

The man sitting at the table rested his chin on his interlaced fingers and looked at the knight intently. The youngster pulled himself up taut as a string.

"In order for everything to be perfectly clear," the man behind the table addressed him, "you should understand that the mistake you made in this town two years ago has not been forgiven. You are getting one more chance. You are getting one more order. My decision as to your ultimate fate depends on the way in which you carry it out."

The young knight's face did not twitch, and nor did a single feather on the wings adorning the helmet at his hip.

"I never deceive anyone, I never give anyone false illusions," continued the man. "So let it be known that, naturally, the prospect of saving your neck from the executioner's axe exists only if you do not make a mistake this time. Your chances of a full pardon are small. Your chances of my forgiving and forgetting are . . . non-existent."

The young knight in the black armour did not flinch this time either, but Coehoorn detected the flash in his eyes. *He doesn't believe him*, he thought. *He doesn't believe him and is deluding himself. He is making a great mistake.*

"I command your full attention," continued the man behind the table. "Yours, too, Coehoorn, because the orders I am about to give concern you too. They come in a moment, for I have to give some thought to their substance and delivery."

Marshal Menno Coehoorn, Governor of the Province of Cintra and future Commander-in-Chief of the Dol Angra army, lifted his head and stood to attention, his hand on the pommel of his sword. The same attitude was assumed by the knight in black armour with the bird-of-prey-winged helmet. They both waited. In silence. Patiently. The way one should wait for orders, the substance and presentation of which were being pondered by the Emperor of Nilfgaard, Emhyr var Emreis, Deithwen

Addan yn Carn aep Morvudd, the White Flame Dancing on the Grave-Mounds of Enemies.

Ciri woke.

She was lying, or rather half-sitting, with her head resting high on several pillows. The compresses on her forehead had grown warm and only slightly damp. She threw them off, unable to bear their unpleasant weight and their stinging against her skin. She found it hard to breathe. Her throat was dry and her nose almost completely blocked with clots of blood. But the elixirs and spells had worked – the pain which had exploded within her skull and dimmed her sight a few hours ago had disappeared and given way to a dull throbbing and a sensation of pressure on her temples.

Carefully she touched her nose with the back of her hand. It was no longer bleeding.

What a strange dream I had, she thought. *The first dream for many days. The first where I wasn't afraid. The first which wasn't about me. I was an . . . observer. I saw everything as if from above, from high up . . . As if I were a bird . . . A night bird . . .*

A dream in which I saw Geralt.

In the dream it was night. And the rain, which furrowed the surface of the canal, spattered on the shingle roofs and thatches of sheds, glistened on the planks of foot-bridges and the decks of boats and barges . . . And Geralt was there. Not alone. There was a man with him in a funny hat with a feather, limp from the damp. And a slim girl in a green cloak with a hood . . . All three were walking slowly and carefully along a wet foot-bridge . . . *And I saw them from above. As if I were a bird. A night bird . . .*

Geralt had stopped short. "Is it still far?" he had asked. "No," the slim girl had answered, shaking the water off her green cloak. "We're almost there . . . Hey, Dandilion, don't lag behind or you'll get lost in these cul-de-sacs . . . And where the hell is Philippa? I saw her a moment ago, she was flying alongside the canal . . . What foul weather . . . Let's go. Lead on, Shani. And between you and me, where do you know this charlatan from? What have you got to do with him?"

"I sometimes sell him medicaments looted from the college workshop. What are you staring at me like that for? My stepfather can barely pay for my tuition . . . I sometimes need a little money . . . And the charlatan, having real medicaments, treats people . . . Or at least he doesn't poison them . . . Well, let's get going."

Strange dream, thought Ciri. *Shame I woke up. I'd like to have seen what was going to happen . . . I'd like to know what they were doing there. Where they were going . . .*

From the chamber next door came the sound of voices, the voices which had woken her. Mother Nenneke was speaking quickly, clearly worked up, agitated and angry. "You betrayed my trust," she was saying. "I shouldn't have allowed it. I might have guessed that your dislike of her would lead to disaster. I shouldn't have allowed you to— Because, after all, I know you. You're ruthless, you're cruel, and to make matters worse, it turns out you're also irresponsible and careless. You're torturing that child mercilessly, forcing her to try things which she can't possibly do. You've no heart.

"You really have no heart, Yennefer."

Ciri pricked up her ears, wanting to hear the enchantress's reply, her cold, hard and melodious voice. Wanting to hear how she reacted, how she sneered at the high priestess, how she ridiculed her over-protectiveness. She wanted to hear her say what she usually said – that using magic is no joke, that it isn't an occupation for young ladies made of porcelain, for dolls blown from thin glass. But Yennefer answered quietly, so quietly that the girl could neither understand nor even make out the individual words.

I'll fall asleep, she thought, carefully and delicately feeling her nose which was still tender, painful and blocked with clotted blood. *I'll go back to my dream. I'll see what Geralt is doing there, in the night, in the rain, by the canal* . . .

Yennefer was holding her by the hand. They were both walking down a long, dark corridor, between stone columns or, perhaps, statues. Ciri could not make out their forms in the thick darkness. But there was someone there, in that darkness, someone hiding and observing them as they walked. She heard whispers, quiet as the rustle of the wind.

Yennefer was holding her by the hand, walking briskly and assuredly, full of decisiveness, so much so that Ciri could barely keep up with her. Doors opened before them in succession, one after another. An infinite number of doors with gigantic, heavy leaves opened up before them noiselessly.

The darkness thickened. Ciri saw yet another great door in front of her. Yennefer did not slow her stride but Ciri suddenly knew that this door would not open of its own accord. And she suddenly had an overwhelming certainty that this door must not be opened. That she must not go through it. That, behind this door, something was waiting for her . . .

She stopped short, tried to pull away, but Yennefer's hand was strong and unyielding and unrelentingly dragged her forward. And Ciri finally understood that she had been betrayed, deceived, sold out. That, ever since the first meeting, from the very beginning, from the first day, she had been no more than a marionette, a puppet on a string. She tugged harder, tore herself away from that grip. The darkness undulated like smoke and the whispering in the dark, all of a sudden, died away. The magician took a step forward, stopped, turned round and looked at her.

If you're afraid, turn back.

That door mustn't be opened. You know that.

I do.

But you're still leading me there.

If you're afraid, turn back. You still have time to turn back. It's not too late.

And you?

For me, it is.

Ciri looked around. Despite the omnipresent darkness she saw the door which they had passed through – and a long, distant vista. And there, from a distance, from the darkness, she heard . . .

The clatter of hooves. The grating of black armour. And the flutter of the wings of a bird of prey. And the voice. That quiet voice, boring into her skull . . .

You have made a mistake. You mistook the stars reflected in the surface of the lake at night for the heavens.

She woke and lifted her head abruptly, displacing the compress, fresh because it was still cool and wet. She was drenched in sweat; the dull pain was ringing and throbbing in her temples again. Yennefer was sitting beside on the bed. Her head was turned away so that Ciri did not see her face. She saw only the tempest of black hair.

"I had a dream . . ." whispered Ciri. "In the dream . . ."

"I know," the magician said in a strange voice not her own. "That's why I'm here. I'm beside you."

Beyond the window, in the darkness, the rain rustled in the leaves of the trees.

"Damn it," snarled Dandilion, shaking water from the brim of his hat, soggy from the rain. "It's a veritable fortress, not a house. What's that fraud frightened of, fortifying himself like that?"

Boats and barges moored to the bank rocked lazily on water furrowed by the rain, bumping against each other, creaking and rattling their chains.

"It's the port," explained Shani. "There's no shortage of thugs and scum, both local and just passing through. Quite a few people visit Myhrman, bringing money . . . Everybody knows that. And that he lives alone. So he's secured himself. Are you surprised?"

"Not in the least." Geralt looked at the mansion built on stakes dug into the bottom of the canal some ten yards from the shore. "I'm trying to work out how to get to that islet, to that waterside cottage. We'll probably have to borrow one of those boats on the quiet—"

"No need," said the student of medicine. "There's a drawbridge."

"And how are you going to persuade that charlatan to

lower it? Besides, there's also the door, and we didn't bring a battering ram with us—"

"Leave it to me."

An enormous grey owl landed soundlessly on the deck's railing, fluttered its wings, ruffled its feathers and turned into Philippa Eilhart, equally ruffled and wet.

"What am I doing here?" the magician mumbled angrily. "What am I doing here with you, damn it? Balancing on a wet bar . . . And on the edge of betraying the state. If Dijkstra finds out I was helping you . . . And on top of it all, this endless drizzle! I hate flying in the rain. Is this it? This is Myhrman's house?"

"Yes," confirmed Geralt. "Listen, Shani, we'll try . . ."

They bunched together and started whispering, concealed in the dark under the eaves of a hut's reed roof. A strip of light fell on the water from the tavern on the opposite side of the canal. Singing, laughter and yelling resounded. Three bargemen rolled out on to the shore. Two were arguing, tugging, shoving each other and repeatedly swearing the same curses to the point of boredom. The third, leaning against a stake, was peeing into the canal and whistling. He was out of tune.

Dong, metallically reverberated the iron sheet tied by a strap to a pole by the deck. *Dong.*

The charlatan Myhrman opened a tiny window and peered out. The lantern in his hand only blinded him, so he set it aside.

"Who the devil is ringing at this time of the night?" he bawled furiously. "Whack yourself on that empty head of yours, you shit, you lame dick, when you get the urge to knock! Get out, get lost, you old soaks, right now! I've got my crossbow at the ready here! Does one of you want six inches of crossbow bolt in their arse?"

"Master Myhrman! It's me, Shani!"

"Eh?" The charlatan leaned out further. "Miss Shani? Now, in the night? How come?"

"Lower the bridge, Master Myhrman! I've brought you what you asked for!"

"Right now, in the dark? Couldn't you do it during the day, miss?"

"Too many eyes here, during the day." A slim outline in a green cloak loomed on the deck. "If word gets out about what I'm bringing you they'll throw me out of the Academy. Lower the bridge, I'm not going to stand around in the rain, I'm soaked!"

"You're not alone, miss," the charlatan noted suspiciously. "You usually come alone. Who's there with you?"

"A friend, a student like me. Was I supposed to come alone, at night, to this forsaken neighbourhood of yours? What, you think I don't value my maidenhood or something? Let me in, damn it!"

Muttering under his breath, Myhrman released the stopper on the winch and the bridge creaked down, hitting the planks of the deck. The old fraud minced to the door and pulled back the bolts and locks. Without putting his crossbow aside, he carefully peered out.

He didn't notice the fist clad in a black silver-studded glove as it flew towards the side of his head. But although the night was dark, the moon was new and the sky overcast, he suddenly saw ten thousand dazzlingly bright stars.

*   *   *

Toublanc Michelet drew the whetstone over the blade of his sword once more, looking totally engrossed in this activity.

"So we are to kill one man for you." He set the stone aside, wiped the blade with a piece of greased rabbit skin and closely examined the blade. "An ordinary fellow who walks around the streets of Oxenfurt by himself, without a guard, an escort or bodyguards. Doesn't even have any knaves hanging about. We won't have to clamber into any castles, town halls, mansion houses or garrisons to get at him . . . Is that right, honourable Rience? Have I understood you correctly?"

The man with a face disfigured by a burn nodded, narrowing his moist eyes with their unpleasant expression a little.

"On top of that," Toublanc continued, "after killing this fellow we won't be forced to remain hidden somewhere for the next six months because no one is going to chase or follow us. No one is going to set a posse or reward seekers on us. We won't get drawn into any blood feuds or vendettas. In other words, Master Rience, we're to finish off an ordinary, common fool of no importance to you?"

The man with the scar did not reply. Toublanc looked at his brothers sitting motionless and stiff on the bench. Rizzi, Flavius and Lodovico, as usual, said nothing. In the team they formed, it was they who killed, Toublanc who talked. Because only Toublanc had attended the Temple school. He was as efficient at killing as his brothers but he could also read and write. And talk.

"And in order to kill such an ordinary dunce, Master Rience, you're hiring not just any old thug from the port but us, the Michelet brothers? For a hundred Novigrad crowns?"

"That is your usual rate," drawled the man with the scar, "correct?"

"Incorrect," contradicted Toublanc coldly. "Because we're not for the killing of ordinary fools. But if we do . . . Master Rience, this fool you want to see made a corpse is going to cost you two hundred. Two hundred untrimmed, shining crowns with the stamp of the Novigrad mint on them. Do you know why? Because there's a catch here, honourable sir. You don't have to tell us what it is, we can manage without that. But you will pay for it. Two hundred, I say. You shake on that price and you can consider that no-friend of yours dead. You don't want to agree, find someone else for the job."

Silence fell in the cellar reeking of mustiness and soured wine. A cockroach, briskly moving its limbs, scudded along the dirt floor. Flavius Michelet, moving his leg in a flash, flattened it with a crunch – hardly changing his position and not changing his expression in the least.

"Agreed," said Rience. "You get two hundred. Let's go."

Toublanc Michelet, professional killer from the age of fourteen, did not betray his surprise with so much as the flicker of an eyelid. He had not counted on being able to bargain for more than a hundred and twenty, a hundred and fifty at the most. Suddenly he was sure that he had named too low a price for the snag hidden in his latest job.

Charlatan Myhrman came to on the floor of his own room. He was lying on his back, trussed up like a sheep.

The back of his head was excruciatingly painful and he recalled that, in falling, he had thumped his head on the door-frame. The temple, where he had been struck, also hurt. He could not move because his chest was being heavily and mercilessly crushed by a high boot fastened with buckles. The old fraud, squinting and wrinkling up his face, looked up. The boot belonged to a tall man with hair as white as milk. Myhrman could not see his face – it was hidden in a darkness not dispersed by the lantern standing on the table.

"Spare my life . . ." he groaned. "Spare me, I swear by the gods . . . I'll hand you my money . . . Hand you everything . . . I'll show you where it's hidden . . ."

"Where's Rience, Myhrman?"

The charlatan shook at the sound of the voice. He was not a fearful man; there were not many things of which he was afraid. But the voice of the white-haired man contained them all. And a few others in addition.

With a superhuman effort of the will, he overcame the fear crawling in his viscera like some foul insect.

"Huh?" He feigned astonishment. "What? Who? What did you say?"

The man bent over and Myhrman saw his face. He saw his eyes. And the sight made his stomach slip right down to his rectum.

"Don't beat about the bush, Myhrman, don't twist up your tail." The familiar voice of Shani, the medical student, came from the shadows. "When I was here three days ago, here, in this high-backed chair, at this table, sat a gentleman in a cloak lined with musk-rat. He was drinking wine, and you never entertain anybody – only the best of friends. He flirted with me, brazenly urged me to go dancing at the Three Little Bells. I even had to slap his hand because he was starting to fondle me, remember? And you said: 'Leave her alone, Master Rience, don't frighten her, I needs must be on good terms with the little academics and do business'. And you both chuckled, you and your Master Rience with the burned face. So don't start playing dumb now because you're not dealing with someone dumber than yourself. Talk while you're still being asked politely."

Oh, you cocksure little student, thought the charlatan. *You treacherous creep, you red-haired hussy, I'm going to find you and pay you back . . . Just let me get myself out of this.*

"What Rience?" he yelped, writhing, trying in vain to free himself from the heel pressing down on his breastbone. "And how am I to know who he is and where he is? All sorts come here, what am I—?"

The white-haired man leaned over further, slowly pulling the dagger from his other boot while pressing down harder on the charlatan's chest with his first.

"Myrhman," he said quietly, "believe me or don't – as you like. But if you don't immediately tell me where Rience is . . . If you don't immediately reveal how you contact him . . . Then I will feed you, piece by piece, to the eels in the canal. Starting with your ears."

There was something in the white-haired man's voice which made the charlatan believe his every word. He stared at the stiletto blade and knew that it was sharper than the knives with which he punctured ulcers and boils. He started to shake so hard that the boot resting on his chest bounced nervously. But he did not say anything. He could not say anything. Not for the time being. Because if

Rience were to return and ask why he had betrayed him,
Myhrman would have to be able to show him why. *One
ear*, he thought, *one ear I have to endure. Then I'll tell
him . . .*

"Why waste time and mess about with blood?" A
woman's soft alto suddenly resounded from the semi-
darkness. "Why risk him twisting the truth and lying?
Allow me to take care of him my way. He'll talk so fast
he'll bite his own tongue. Hold him down."

The charlatan howled and struggled against his fetters
but the white-haired man crushed him to the floor with
his knee, grabbed him by the hair and twisted his head.
Someone knelt down next to them. He smelled perfume
and wet bird feathers, felt the touch of fingers on his temple. He wanted to scream but terror choked him – all he
managed was a croak.

"You want to scream already?" The soft alto right
next to his ear purred like a cat. "Too soon, Myhrman,
too soon. I haven't started yet. But I will in a moment. If
evolution has traced any groove at all in your brain then
I'm going to plough it somewhat deeper. And then you'll
see what a scream can really be."

"And so," said Vilgefortz, having heard the report, "our
kings have started to think independently. They have
started to plan independently, in an amazingly short
time evolving from thinking on a tactical level to a strategic one? Interesting. Not so long ago – at Sodden – all
they could do was gallop around with savage cries and
swords raised at the van of their company without even
looking around to check their company hadn't by chance
been left behind, or wasn't galloping in an entirely dif-

ferent direction. And today, there they are – in Hagge Castle – deciding the fate of the world. Interesting. But to be honest, I expected as much."

"We know," confirmed Artaud Terranova. "And we remember, you warned us about it. That's why we're telling you about it."

"Thank you for remembering," smiled the wizard, and Tissaia de Vries was suddenly sure that he had already been aware of each of the facts just presented to him, and had been for a long time. She did not say a word. Sitting upright in her armchair, she evened up her lace cuffs as the left fell a little differently from the right. She felt Terranova's unfavourable gaze and Vilgefortz's amused eyes on her. She knew that her legendary pedantry either annoyed or amused everybody. But she did not care in the least.

"What does the Chapter say to all this?"

"First of all," retorted Terranova, "we would like to hear your opinion, Vilgefortz."

"First of all," smiled the wizard, "let us have something to eat and drink. We have enough time – allow me to prove myself a good host. I can see you are frozen through and tired from your journeys. How many changes of portals, if I may ask?"

"Three." Tissaia de Vries shrugged.

"It was nearer for me," added Artaud. "Two proved enough. But still complicated, I must admit."

"Such foul weather everywhere?"

"Everywhere."

"So let us fortify ourselves with good fare and an old red wine from Cidaris. Lydia, would you be so kind?"

Lydia van Bredevoort, Vilgefortz's assistant and personal secretary, appeared from behind the curtain like an ethereal phantom and smiled with her eyes at Tissaia de Vries. Tissaia, controlling her face, replied with a pleasant smile and bow of her head. Artaud Terranova stood up and bowed with reverence. He, too, controlled his expression very well. He knew Lydia.

Two servants, bustling around and rustling their skirts, swiftly laid out the tableware, plates and platters. Lydia van Bredevoort, delicately conjuring up a tiny flame between her thumb and index finger, lit the candles in the candelabras. Tissaia saw traces of oil paint on her hand. She filed it in her memory so later, after supper, she could ask the young enchantress to show her her latest work. Lydia was a talented artist.

They supped in silence. Artaud Terranova did not stint himself and reached without embarrassment for the platters and – probably a little too frequently, and without his host's encouragement – clanged the silver top of the carafe of red wine. Tissaia de Vries ate slowly, devoting more attention to arranging her plates, cutlery and napkins symmetrically – although, in her opinion, they still lay irregularly and hurt her predilection for order and her aesthetic sensibility – than to the fare. She drank sparingly. Vilgefortz ate and drank even more sparingly. Lydia, of course, did not drink or eat at all.

The candle flames undulated in long red and golden whiskers of fire. Drops of rain tinkled against the stained glass of the windows.

"Well, Vilgefortz," said Terranova finally, rummaging in a platter with his fork in search of an adequately fatty piece of game. "What is your position regarding our monarchs' behaviour? Hen Gedymdeith and Francesca sent us here because they want to know your opinion. Tissaia and I are also interested. The Chapter wants to assume a unanimous stand in this matter. And, should it come to action, we also want to act unanimously. So what do you advise?"

"It flatters me greatly" – with a gesture, Vilgefortz thanked Lydia, who was offering to put more broccoli on his plate – "that my opinion in this matter should be decisive for the Chapter."

"No one said that." Artaud poured himself some more wine. "We're going to make a collective decision anyway, when the Chapter meets. But we wish to let everybody have the opportunity to express themselves beforehand so we can have an idea of all the various views. We're listening, therefore."

If we've finished supping, let us go through into the workshop, Lydia proposed telepathically, smiling with her eyes. Terranova looked at her smile and quickly downed what he had in his chalice. To the dregs.

"Good idea." Vilgefortz wiped his fingers on a napkin. "We'll be more comfortable there. My protection against magical eavesdropping is stronger there, too. Let us go. You can bring the carafe, Artaud."

"I won't say no. It's my favourite vintage."

They went through to the workshop. Tissaia could not stop herself from casting an eye over the workbench weighed down with retorts, crucibles, test-tubes, crystals and numerous magical utensils. All were enveloped in a screening spell, but Tissaia de Vries was an Archmage – there was no screen she could not penetrate. And she was a little curious as to what the mage had been doing of late. She worked out the configuration of the recently used apparatus in a flash. It served for the detection of persons who had disappeared while enabling a psychic vision by means of the "crystal, metal, stone" method. The wizard was either searching for someone or resolving a theoretical, logistical problem. Vilgefortz of Roggeveen was well known for his love of solving such problems.

They sat down in carved ebony armchairs. Lydia glanced at Vilgefortz, caught the sign transmitted by his eye and immediately left. Tissaia sighed imperceptibly.

Everyone knew that Lydia van Bredevoort was in love with Vilgefortz of Roggeveen, that she had loved him for years with a silent, relentless and stubborn love. The wizard, it is to be understood, also knew about this but pretended not to. Lydia made it easier for him by never betraying her feelings to him – she never took the slightest step or made the slightest gesture, transmitted no sign by thought and, even if she could speak, would never have said a word. She was too proud. Vilgefortz, too, did nothing because he did not love Lydia. He could, of course, simply have made her his lover, tied her to him even more strongly and, who knows, maybe even made her happy. There were those who advised him to do so. But Vilgefortz did not. He was too proud and too much a man of principle. The situation, therefore, was hopeless but stable, and this patently satisfied them both.

"So." The young wizard broke the silence. "The Chapter are racking their brains about what to do about the initiatives and plans of our kings? Quite unnecessarily. Their plans must simply be ignored."

"I beg your pardon?" Artaud Terranova froze with the chalice in his left hand, the carafe in his right. "Did I understand you correctly? We are to do nothing? We're to let—"

"We already have," interrupted Vilgefortz. "Because no one asked us for our permission. And no one will. I repeat, we ought to pretend that we know nothing. That is the only rational thing to do."

"The things they have thought up threaten war, and on a grand scale at that."

"The things they have thought up have been made known to us thanks to enigmatic and incomplete information, which comes from a mysterious and highly dubious source. So dubious that the word 'disinformation' stubbornly comes to mind. And even if it were true, their designs are still at the planning stage and will remain so for a long while yet. And if they move beyond that stage . . . Well, then we will act accordingly."

"You mean to say," Terranova screwed up his face, "we will dance to the tune they play?"

"Yes, Artaud." Vilgefortz looked at him and his eyes flashed. "You will dance to the tune they play. Or you will take leave of the dance-floor. Because the orchestra's podium is too high for you to climb up there and tell the musicians to play some other tune. Realise that at last. If you think another solution is possible, you are making a mistake. You mistake the stars reflected in the surface of the lake at night for the heavens."

The Chapter will do as he says, disguising his order as advice, thought Tissaia de Vries. *We are all pawns on his chess board. He's moved up, grown, obscured us with his brightness, subordinated us to him. We're pawns in his game. A game the rules of which we do not know.*

Her left cuff had once again arranged itself differently from the right. The enchantress adjusted it with care.

"The kings' plans are already at the stage of practical realisation," she said slowly. "In Kaedwen and Aedirn an offensive against the Scoia'tael has begun. The blood of young elves is flowing. It is reaching the point of persecution and pogroms against non-humans. There is talk of an attack on the free elves of Dol Blathanna and the Grey Mountains. This is mass murder. Are we to say to Gedymdeith and Enid Findabair that you advise us to stand idly by, to watch and do nothing? Pretending we can't see anything?"

Vilgefortz turned his head towards her. *Now you're going to change tactics*, thought Tissaia. *You're a player, you can hear which way the dice roll on the table. You're going to change tactics. You're going to strike a different note.*

Vilgefortz did not lower his eyes from hers.

"You are right," he said curtly. "You are right, Tissaia. War with Nilfgaard is one thing but we must not look on idly at the massacre of non-humans and do nothing. I suggest we call a convention, a general convention of everyone up to and including Masters of the Third Degree, including those who have been sitting on royal councils since Sodden. At the convention we will make them see reason and order them to keep their monarchs in check."

"I second this proposition," said Terranova. "Let us call a convention and remind them to whom they owe first loyalty. Note that even some members of our Council now advise kings. The kings are served by Carduin, Philippa Eilhart, Fercart, Radcliffe, Yennefer—"

At the last name Vilgefortz twitched internally. But

Tissaia de Vries was an Archmage. Tissaia sensed the
thought, the impulse leaping from the workbench and
magical apparatus to the two volumes lying on the table.
Both books were invisible, enveloped in magic. The magician focused herself and penetrated the screen.

Aen Ithlinnespeath, the prophecy foretold by Ithlinne
Aegli aep Aevenien, the elven seeress. The prophecy
of the end of civilisation, the prophecy of annihilation,
destruction and the return of barbarianism which are to
come with the masses of ice pressing down from the borders of the eternal freeze. And the other book . . . Very
old . . . Falling apart . . . *Aen Hen Ichaer* . . . The Elder
Blood . . . The Blood of Elves?

"Tissaia? And what do you think?"

"I second it." The enchantress adjusted her ring which
had turned the wrong way round. "I second Vilgefortz's
plan. Let us call a convention. As soon as possible."

Metal, stone, crystal, she thought. *Are you looking
for Yennefer? Why? And what does she have to do with
Ithlin's prophecy? Or with the Elder Blood of the Elves?
What are you brewing, Vilgefortz?*

I'm sorry, said Lydia van Bredevoort telepathically,
coming in without a sound. The wizard stood up.

"Forgive me," he said, "but this is urgent. I've been
waiting for this letter since yesterday. It will only take a
minute."

Artaud yawned, muffled a belch and reached for the
carafe. Tissaia looked at Lydia. Lydia smiled. With her
eyes. She could not do so any other way.

The lower half of Lydia van Bredevoort's face was an
illusion.

Four years ago, on Vilgefortz's – her master's – recommendation, Lydia had taken part in experiments concerning the properties of an artefact found amongst the excavations of an ancient necropolis. The artefact turned out to be cursed. It activated only once. Of the five wizards taking part in the experiment, three died on the spot. The fourth lost his eyes, both hands and went mad. Lydia escaped with burns, a mangled jaw and a mutation of the larynx and throat which, to this day, effectively resisted all efforts at regeneration. A powerful illusion was therefore drawn so that people did not faint at the sight of Lydia's face. It was a very strong, very efficiently placed illusion, difficult for even the Chosen Ones to penetrate.

"Hmm . . ." Vilgefortz put the letter aside. "Thank you, Lydia."

Lydia smiled. *The messenger is waiting for a reply*, she said.

"There will be no reply."

I understand. I have given orders to prepare chambers for your guests.

"Thank you. Tissaia, Artaud, I apologise for the short delay. Let us continue. Where were we?"

Nowhere, thought Tissaia de Vries. *But I'm listening carefully to you. Because at some stage you'll finally mention the thing which really interests you.*

"Ah," began Vilgefortz slowly. "Now I know what I wanted to say. I'm thinking about those members of the Council who have had the least experience. Fercart and Yennefer. Fercart, as far as I know, is tied to Foltest of Temeria and sits on the king's council with Triss Merigold. But who is Yennefer tied to? You said, Artaud, that she is one of those who are serving kings."

"Artaud exaggerated," said Tissaia calmly. "Yennefer is living in Vengerberg so Demawend sometimes turns to her for help, but they do not work together all the time. It cannot be said for certain that she is serving Demawend."

"How is her sight? Everything is all right, I hope?"

"Yes. Everything's all right."

"Good. Very good. I was worried . . . You know, I wanted to contact her but it turned out she had left. No one knew where for."

Stone, metal, crystal, thought Tissaia de Vries. "Everything that Yennefer wears is active and cannot be detected using psychic visions. You won't find her that way, my dear. If Yennefer does not wish anyone to know where she is, no one will find out.

"Write to her," she said calmly, straightening out her cuffs. "And send the letter in the ordinary way. It will get there without fail. And Yennefer, wherever she is, will reply. She always does."

"Yennefer," threw in Artaud, "frequently disappears, sometimes for entire months. The reasons tend to be quite trivial . . ."

Tissaia looked at him, pursing her lips. The wizard fell silent. Vilgefortz smiled faintly.

"Precisely," he said. "That is just what I thought. At one time she was closely tied to . . . a certain witcher. Geralt, if I'm not mistaken. It seems it wasn't just an ordinary passing affair. It appeared Yennefer was quite strongly involved . . ."

Tissaia de Vries sat up straight and gripped the armrests of her chair.

"Why are you asking about that? They're personal matters. It is none of our business."

"Of course." Vilgefortz glanced at the letter lying discarded on the pulpit. "It is none of our business. But I'm not being guided by unhealthy curiosity but concern about the emotional state of a member of the Council. I am wondering about Yennefer's reaction to the news of . . . of Geralt's death. I presume she would get over it, come to terms with it, without falling into a depression or exaggerated mourning?"

"No doubt, she would," said Tissaia coldly. "Especially as such news has been reaching her every now and again – and always proving to be a rumour."

"That's right," confirmed Terranova. "This Geralt, or whatever he's called, knows how to fend for himself. And why be surprised? He is a mutant, a murdering machine, programmed to kill and not let himself be killed. And as for Yennefer, let us not exaggerate her alleged emotions. We know her. She does not give in to emotions. She toyed with the witcher, that's all. She was fascinated with death, which this character constantly courts. And when he finally brings it onto himself, that will be the end of it."

"For the time being," remarked Tissaia de Vries dryly, "the witcher is alive."

Vilgefortz smiled and once more glanced at the letter lying in front of him.

"Is that so?" he said. "I don't think so."

Geralt flinched a little and swallowed hard. The initial shock of drinking the elixir had passed and the second stage was beginning to take effect, as indicated by a faint but unpleasant dizziness which accompanied the adaptation of his sight to darkness.

The adaptation progressed quickly. The deep darkness

of the night paled; everything around him started to take
on shades of grey, shades which were at first hazy and unclear then increasingly contrasting, distinct and sharp. In
the little street leading to the canal bank which, a moment
ago, had been as dark as the inside of a tar barrel, Geralt
could now make out the rats roaming through the gutters,
and sniffing at puddles and gaps in the walls.

His hearing, too, had been heightened by the witchers' decoction. The deserted tangle of lanes where, only
a moment ago, there had been the sound of rain against
guttering, began to come to life, to throb with sounds. He
heard the cries of cats fighting, dogs barking on the other
side of the canal, laughter and shouting from the taprooms
and inns of Oxenfurt, yelling and singing from the bargemen's tavern, and the distant, quiet warble of a flute playing a jaunty tune. The dark, sleepy houses came to life as
well – Geralt could make out the snoring of slumbering
people, the thuds of oxen in enclosures, the snorting of
horses in stables. From one of the houses in the depths of
the street came the stifled, spasmodic moans of a woman
in the throes of lovemaking.

The sounds increased, grew louder. He now made out
the obscene lyrics of the carousing songs, learned the
name of the moaning woman's lover. From Myhrman's
homestead on the canal came the broken, uncoordinated
gibberish of the charlatan who had been put, by Philippa
Eilhart's treatment, into a state of complete and, no doubt,
permanent idiocy.

Dawn was approaching. It had finally stopped raining,
a wind started up which blew the clouds away. The sky in
the east was clearly paling.

The rats in the lane suddenly grew uneasy, scattered in all directions and hid amongst the crates and rubbish.

The witcher heard footsteps. Four or five men; he could not as yet say exactly how many. He looked up but did not see Philippa.

Immediately he changed tactics. If Rience was amongst those approaching he had little chance of grabbing him. He would first have to fight his escort and he did not want to do so. Firstly, as he was under the influence of the elixir, those men would have to die. Secondly, Rience would then have the opportunity to flee.

The footsteps grew nearer. Geralt emerged from the shadows.

Rience loomed out of the lane. The witcher recognised the sorcerer instantly and instinctively, although he had never seen him before. The burn, a gift from Yennefer, was masked by the shadow of his hood.

He was alone. His escort did not reveal themselves, remaining hidden in the little street. Geralt immediately understood why. Rience knew who was waiting for him by the charlatan's house. Rience had suspected an ambush, yet he had still come. The witcher realised why. And that was even before he had heard the quiet grating of swords being drawn from their scabbards. *Fine*, he thought. *If that's what you want, fine*.

"It is a pleasure hunting for you," said Rience quietly. "You appear where you're wanted of your own accord."

"The same can be said of you," calmly retorted the witcher. "You appeared here. I wanted you here and here you are."

"You must have pushed Myhrman hard to tell you about the amulet, to show you where it is hidden. And how to activate it to send out a message. But Myhrman didn't know that the amulet informs and warns at the same time, and so he could not have told you even if roasted on red coals. I have distributed a good many of these amulets. I knew that sooner or later you would come across one of them."

Four men emerged from around a corner of the little street. They moved slowly, deftly and noiselessly. They still kept to the areas of darkness and wielded their drawn swords in such a way as not to be betrayed by a flash of blades. The witcher, obviously, saw them clearly. But he did not reveal the fact. *Fine, murderers*, he thought. *If that's what you want, that's what you'll get.*

"I waited," continued Rience without moving from the spot, "and here you are. I intend to finally rid the earth of your burden, you foul changeling."

"You intend? You overrate yourself. You are nothing but a tool. A thug hired by others to deal with their dirty work. Who hired you, stooge?"

"You want to know too much, mutant. You call me a stooge? And do you know what you are? A heap of dung on the road which has to be removed because someone prefers not to soil their boots. No, I am not going to disclose who that person is to you, although I could. But I will tell you something else so you have something to think about on your way to hell. I already know where to find the little bastard you were looking after. And I know where to find that witch of yours, Yennefer. My patrons don't care about her but I bear the whore a personal grudge. As soon as I've finished with you, I'm going after her. I'll see to it that she regrets her tricks with fire. Oh, yes, she is going to regret them. For a very long time."

"You shouldn't have said that." The witcher smiled nastily, feeling the euphoria of battle aroused by the elixir, reacting with adrenalin. "Before you said that, you still had a chance to live. Now you don't."

A powerful oscillation of his witcher's medallion warned him of a sudden assault. He jumped aside and, drawing his sword in a flash, deflected and annihilated the violent, paralysing wave of magical energy directed at him with his rune-covered blade. Rience backed away, raised his arm to make a move but at the last moment took fright. Not attempting a second spell, he swiftly retreated down the lane. The witcher could not run after him – the four men who thought they were concealed in the shadows threw themselves at him. Swords flashed.

They were professionals. All four of them. Experienced, skilled professionals working as a team. They came at him in pairs, two on the left, two on the right. In pairs – so that one always covered the other's back. The witcher chose those on the left. On top of the euphoria produced by the elixir came fury.

The first thug attacked with a feint from dextra only to jump aside and allow the man behind him to execute a deceptive thrust. Geralt spun in a pirouette, evaded and passed by them and with the very tip of his sword slashed the other one from behind across the occiput, shoulders and back. He was angry and hit hard. A fountain of blood spurted on the wall.

The first man backed away with lightning speed, making room for the next pair. These separated for the attack, slashing their swords from two directions in such a way that only one blow could be parried, the other having to meet its aim. Geralt did not parry and, whirling in a pirou-

ette, came between them. In order not to collide, they both
had to break their teamed rhythm, their rehearsed steps.
One of them managed to turn in a soft, feline feint and
leaped away dextrously. The other did not have time. He
lost his balance and stumbled backwards. The witcher,
turning in a reverse pirouette, used his momentum to
slash him across the lower back. He was angry. He felt
his sharp witcher's blade sever the spine. A terrifying
howl echoed down the streets. The two remaining men
immediately attacked him, showering him with blows
which he parried with the greatest of difficulties. He went
into a pirouette and tore himself from beneath the flashing
blades. But instead of leaning his back against the wall
and defending himself, he attacked.

They were not expecting it, did not have time to leap
away and apart. One of them countered but the witcher
evaded the counter-attack, spun, slashed from behind
– blindly – counting on the rush of air. He was angry.
He aimed low, at the belly. And hit his mark. He heard a
stifled cry but did not have time to look back. The last of
the thugs was already at his side, already striking a nasty
sinistra with a quarte. Geralt parried at the last moment,
statically, without a turn, with a quarte from dextra. The
thug, making use of the impetus of the parry, unwound
like a spring and slashed from a half-turn, wide and hard.
Too hard. Geralt was already spinning. The killer's blade,
considerably heavier than the witcher's, cut the air and
the thug had to follow the blow. The impetus caused him
to turn. Geralt slipped out of the half-turn just beside him,
very close. He saw his contorted face, his horrified eyes.
He was angry. He struck. Short but powerful. And sure.
Right in the eyes.

He heard Shani's terrified scream as she tried to pull herself free of Dandilion on the bridge leading to the charlatan's house.

Rience retreated into the depths of the lane, raising and spreading both arms in front of him, a magical light already beginning to exude from them. Geralt grasped his sword with both hands and without second thoughts ran towards him. The sorcerer's nerves could not take it. Without completing his spell, he began to run away, yelling incomprehensibly. But Geralt understood. He knew that Rience was calling for help. Begging for help.

And help arrived. The little street blazed with a bright light and on the dilapidated, sullied walls of a house, flared the fiery oval of a portal. Rience threw himself towards it. Geralt jumped. He was furious.

Toublanc Michelet groaned and curled up, clutching his riven belly. He felt the blood draining from him, flowing rapidly through his fingers. Not far from him lay Flavius. He had still been twitching a moment ago, but now he lay motionless. Toublanc squeezed his eyelids shut, then opened them. But the owl sitting next to Flavius was clearly not a hallucination – it did not disappear. He groaned again and turned his head away.

Some wench, a young one judging by her voice, was screaming hysterically.

"Let me go! There are wounded there! I've got to . . . I'm a medical student, Dandilion! Let me go, do you hear?"

"You can't help them," replied Dandilion in a dull voice. "Not after a witcher's sword . . . Don't even go there. Don't look . . . I beg you, Shani, don't look."

Toublanc felt someone kneel next to him. He detected the scent of perfume and wet feathers. He heard a quiet, gentle, soothing voice. It was hard to make out the words, the annoying screams and sobs of the young wench interfered. Of that . . . medical student. But if it was the medical student who was yelling then who was kneeling next to him? Toublanc groaned.

". . . be all right. Everything will be all right."

"The son . . . of . . . a . . . bitch," he grunted. "Rience . . . He told us . . . An ordinary fool . . . But it . . . was a witcher . . . Caa . . . tch . . . Heee . . . elp . . . My . . . guts . . ."

"Quiet, quiet, my son. Keep calm. It's all right. It doesn't hurt any more. Isn't that right, it doesn't hurt? Tell me who called you up here? Who introduced you to Rience? Who recommended him? Who got you into this? Tell me, please, my son. And then everything will be all right. You'll see, it'll be all right. Tell me, please."

Toublanc tasted blood in his mouth. But he did not have the strength to spit it out. His cheek pressing into the wet earth, he opened his mouth and blood poured out.

He no longer felt anything.

"Tell me," the gentle voice kept repeating. "Tell me, my son."

Toublanc Michelet, professional murderer since the age of fourteen, closed his eyes and smiled a bloodied smile. And whispered what he knew.

And when he opened his eyes, he saw a stiletto with a narrow blade and a tiny golden hilt.

"Don't be frightened," said the gentle voice as the point of the stiletto touched his temple. "This won't hurt."

Indeed, it did not hurt.

*   *   *

He caught up with the sorcerer at the last moment, just in front of the portal. Having already thrown his sword aside, his hands were free and his fingers, extended in a leap, dug into the edge of Rience's cloak. Rience lost his balance; the tug had bent him backwards, forcing him to totter back. He struggled furiously, violently ripped the cloak from clasp to clasp and freed himself. Too late.

Geralt spun him round by hitting him in the shoulder with his right hand, then immediately struck him in the neck under the ear with his left. Rience reeled but did not fall. The witcher, jumping softly, caught up with him and forcefully dug his fist under his ribs. The sorcerer moaned and drooped over the fist. Geralt grabbed him by the front of his doublet, spun him and threw him to the ground. Pressed down by the witcher's knee, Rience extended his arm and opened his mouth to cast a spell. Geralt clenched his fist and thumped him from above. Straight in the mouth. His lips split like blackcurrants.

"You've already received a present from Yennefer," he uttered in a hoarse voice. "Now you're getting one from me."

He struck once more. The sorcerer's head bounced up; blood spurted onto the witcher's forehead and cheeks. Geralt was slightly surprised – he had not felt any pain but had, no doubt, been injured in the fight. It was his blood. He did not bother nor did he have time to look for the wound and take care of it. He unclenched his fist and walloped Rience once more. He was angry.

"Who sent you? Who hired you?"

Rience spat blood at him. The witcher struck him yet again.

"Who?"

The fiery oval of the portal flared more strongly; the light emanating from it flooded the entire lane. The witcher felt the power throbbing from the oval, had felt it even before his medallion had begun to oscillate violently, in warning.

Rience also felt the energy streaming from the portal, sensed help approaching. He yelled, struggling like an enormous fish. Geralt buried his knees in the sorcerer's chest, raised his arm, forming the Sign of Aard with his fingers, and aimed at the flaming portal. It was a mistake.

No one emerged from the portal. Only power radiated from it and Rience had taken the power.

From the sorcerer's outstretched fingers grew six-inch steel spikes. They dug into Geralt's chest and shoulder with an audible crack. Energy exploded from the spikes. The witcher threw himself backwards in a convulsive leap. The shock was such that he felt and heard his teeth, clenched in pain, crunch and break. At least two of them.

Rience attempted to rise but immediately collapsed to his knees again and began to struggle to the portal on all fours. Geralt, catching his breath with difficulty, drew a stiletto from his boot. The sorcerer looked back, sprang up and reeled. The witcher was also reeling but he was quicker. Rience looked back again and screamed. Geralt gripped the knife. He was angry. Very angry.

Something grabbed him from behind, overpowered him, immobilised him. The medallion on his neck pulsated acutely; the pain in his wounded shoulder throbbed spasmodically.

Some ten paces behind him stood Philippa Eilhart.

From her raised arms emanated a dull light – two streaks, two rays. Both were touching his back, squeezing his arms with luminous pliers. He struggled, in vain. He could not move from the spot. He could only watch as Rience staggered up to the portal, which pulsated with a milky glow.

Rience, in no hurry, slowly stepped into the light of the portal, sank into it like a diver, blurred and disappeared. A second later, the oval went out, for a moment plunging the little street into impenetrable, dense, velvety blackness.

Somewhere in the lanes fighting cats yowled. Geralt looked at the blade of the sword he had picked up on his way towards the magician.

"Why, Philippa? Why did you do it?"

The magician took a step back. She was still holding the knife which a moment earlier had penetrated Toublanc Michelet's skull.

"Why are you asking? You know perfectly well."

"Yes," he agreed. "Now I know."

"You're wounded, Geralt. You can't feel the pain because you're intoxicated with the witchers' elixir but look how you're bleeding. Have you calmed down sufficiently for me to safely approach and take a look at you? Bloody hell, don't look at me like that! And don't come near me. One more step and I'll be forced to . . . Don't come near me! Please! I don't want to hurt you but if you come near—"

"Philippa!" shouted Dandilion, still holding the weeping Shani. "Have you gone mad?"

"No," said the witcher with some effort. "She's quite sane. And knows perfectly well what she's doing. She knew all along what she was doing. She took advantage of us. Betrayed us. Deceived—"

"Calm down," repeated Philippa Eilhart. "You won't understand and you don't have to understand. I did what I had to do. And don't call me a traitor. Because I did this precisely so as not to betray a cause which is greater than you can imagine. A great and important cause, so important that minor matters have to be sacrificed for it without second thoughts, if faced with such a choice. Geralt, damn it, we're nattering and you're standing in a pool of blood. Calm down and let Shani and me take care of you."

"She's right!" shouted Dandilion, "you're wounded, damn it! Your wound has to be dressed and we've got to get out of here! You can argue later!"

"You and your great cause . . ." The witcher, ignoring the troubadour, staggered forward. "Your great cause, Philippa, and your choice, is a wounded man, stabbed in cold blood once he told you what you wanted to know, but what I wasn't to find out. Your great cause is Rience, whom you allowed to escape so that he wouldn't by any chance reveal the name of his patron. So that he can go on murdering. Your great cause is those corpses which did not have to be. Sorry, I express myself poorly. They're not corpses, they're minor matters!"

"I knew you wouldn't understand."

"Indeed, I don't. I never will. But I do know what it's about. Your great causes, your wars, your struggle to save the world . . . Your end which justifies the means . . . Prick up your ears, Philippa. Can you hear those voices, that yowling? Those are cats fighting for a great cause. For indivisible mastery over a heap of rubbish. It's no joking matter – blood is being spilled and clumps of fur are flying. It's war. But I care incredibly little about either of these wars, the cats' or yours."

"That's only what you imagine," hissed the magician. "All this is going to start concerning you – and sooner than you think. You're standing before necessity and choice. You've got yourself mixed up in destiny, my dear, far more than you've bargained for. You thought you were taking a child, a little girl, into your care. You were wrong. You've taken in a flame which could at any moment set the world alight. Our world. Yours, mine, that of the others. And you will have to choose. Like I did. Like Triss Merigold. Choose, as your Yennefer had to. Because Yennefer has already chosen. Your destiny is in her hands, witcher. You placed it in those hands yourself."

The witcher staggered. Shani yelled and tore herself away from Dandilion. Geralt held her back with a gesture, stood upright and looked straight into the dark eyes of Philippa Eilhart.

"My destiny," he said with effort. "My choice . . . I'll tell you, Philippa, what I've chosen. I won't allow you to involve Ciri in your dirty machinations. I am warning you. Whoever dares harm Ciri will end up like those four lying there. I won't swear an oath. I have nothing by which to swear. I simply warn you. You accused me of being a bad guardian, that I don't know how to protect the child. I will protect her. As best I can. I will kill. I will kill mercilessly . . ."

"I believe you," said the magician with a smile. "I believe you will. But not today, Geralt. Not now. Because in a minute you're going to faint from loss of blood. Shani, are you ready?"

No one is born a wizard. We still know too little about genetics and the mechanisms of heredity. We sacrifice too little time and means on research. Unfortunately, we constantly try to pass on inherited magical abilities in, so to say, a natural way. Results of these pseudo-experiments can be seen all too often in town gutters and within temple walls. We see too many of them, and too frequently come across morons and women in a catatonic state, dribbling seers who soil themselves, seeresses, village oracles and miracle-workers, cretins whose minds are degenerate due to the inherited, uncontrolled Force.

These morons and cretins can also have offspring, can pass on abilities and thus degenerate further. Is anyone in a position to foresee or describe how the last link in such a chain will look?

Most of us wizards lose the ability to procreate due to somatic changes and dysfunction of the pituitary gland. Some wizards – usually women – attune to magic while still maintaining efficiency of the gonads. They can conceive and give birth – and have the audacity to consider this happiness and a blessing. But I repeat: no one is born a wizard. And no one should be born one! Conscious of the gravity of what I write, I answer the question posed at the Congress in Cidaris. I answer most emphatically: each one of us must decide what she wants to be – a wizard or a mother.

I demand all apprentices be sterilised. Without exception.

Tissaia de Vries, *The Poisoned Source*

CHAPTER SEVEN

"I'm going to tell you something," said Iola the Second suddenly, resting the basket of grain on her hip. "There's going to be a war. That's what the duke's greeve who came to fetch the cheeses said."

"A war?" Ciri shoved her hair back from her forehead. "With who? Nilfgaard?"

"I didn't hear," the novice admitted. "But the greeve said our duke had received orders from King Foltest himself. He's sending out a call to arms and all the roads are swarming with soldiers. Oh dear! What's going to happen?"

"If there's going to be a war," said Eurneid, "then it'll most certainly be with Nilfgaard. Who else? Again! Oh gods, that's terrible!"

"Aren't you exaggerating a bit with this war, Iola?" Ciri scattered some grains for the chickens and guinea-hens crowding around them in a busy, noisy whirl. "Maybe it's only another raid on the Scoia'tael?"

"Mother Nenneke asked the greeve the same thing,"

declared Iola the Second. "And the greeve said that no, this time it wasn't about the Squirrels. Castles and citadels have apparently been ordered to store supplies in case of a siege. But elves attack in forests, they don't lay siege to castles! The greeve asked whether the Temple could give more cheese and other things. For the castle stores. And he demanded goose feathers. They need a lot of goose feathers, he said. For arrows. To shoot from bows, understand? Oh, gods! We're going to have masses of work! You'll see! We'll be up to our ears in work!"

"Not all of us," said Eurneid scathingly. "Some aren't going to get their little hands dirty. Some of us only work two days a week. They don't have any time for work because they are, apparently, studying witchery. But in actual fact they're probably only idling or skipping around the park thrashing weeds with a stick. You know who I'm talking about, Ciri, don't you?"

"Ciri will leave for the war no doubt," giggled Iola the Second. "After all, she is apparently the daughter of a knight! And herself a great warrior with a terrible sword! At last she'll be able to cut real heads off instead of nettles!"

"No, she is a powerful wizard!" Eurneid wrinkled her little nose. "She's going to change all our enemies into field mice. Ciri! Show us some amazing magic. Make yourself invisible or make the carrots ripen quicker. Or do something so that the chickens can feed themselves. Well, go on, don't make us ask! Cast a spell!"

"Magic isn't for show," said Ciri angrily. "Magic is not some street market trick."

"But of course, of course," laughed the novice. "Not

for show. Eh, Iola? It's exactly as if I were hearing that hag Yennefer talk!"

"Ciri is getting more and more like her," appraised Iola, sniffing ostentatiously. "She even smells like her. Huh, no doubt some magical scent made of mandrake or ambergris. Do you use magical scents, Ciri?"

"No! I use soap! Something you rarely use!"

"Oh ho." Eurneid twisted her lips. "What sarcasm, what spite! And what airs!"

"She never used to be like this," Iola the Second puffed up. "She became like this when she started spending time with that witch. She sleeps with her, eats with her, doesn't leave her side. She's practically stopped attending lessons at the Temple and no longer has a moment to spare for us!"

"And we have to do all the work for her! Both in the kitchen and in the garden! Look at her little hands, Iola! Like a princess!"

"That's the way it is!" squeaked Ciri. "Some have brains, so they get a book! Others are feather-brained, so they get a broom!"

"And you only use a broom for flying, don't you? Pathetic wizard!"

"You're stupid!"

"Stupid yourself!"

"No, I'm not!"

"Yes, you are! Come on, Iola, don't pay any attention to her. Sorceresses are not our sort of company."

"Of course they aren't!" yelled Ciri and threw the basket of grain on the ground. "Chickens are your sort of company!"

The novices turned up their noses and left, passing through the horde of cackling fowl.

Ciri cursed loudly, repeating a favourite saying of Vesemir's which she did not entirely understand. Then she added a few words she had heard Yarpen Zigrin use, the meanings of which were a total mystery to her. With a kick, she dispersed the chickens swarming towards the scattered grain, picked up the basket, turned it upside down, then twirled in a witcher's pirouette and threw the basket like a discus over the reed roof of the henhouse. She turned on her heel and set off through the Temple park at a run.

She ran lightly, skilfully controlling her breath. At every other tree she passed, she made an agile half-turn leap, marking slashes with an imaginary sword and immediately following them with dodges and feints she had learned. She jumped deftly over the fence, landing surely and softly on bent knees.

"Jarre!" she shouted, turning her head up towards a window gaping in the stone wall of the tower. "Jarre, are you there? Hey! It's me!"

"Ciri?" The boy leaned out. "What are you doing here?"

"Can I come up and see you?"

"Now? Hmm . . . Well, all right then . . . Please do."

She flew up the stairs like a hurricane, catching the novice unexpectedly just as, with his back turned, he was quickly adjusting his clothes and hiding some parchments on the table under other parchments. Jarre ran his fingers through his hair, cleared his throat and bowed awkwardly. Ciri slipped her thumbs into her belt and tossed her ashen fringe.

"What's this war everybody's talking about?" she fired. "I want to know!"

"Please, have a seat."

She cast her eyes around the chamber. There were four large tables piled with large books and scrolls. There was only one chair. Also piled high.

"War?" mumbled Jarre. "Yes, I've heard those rumours . . . Are you interested in it? You, a g—? No, don't sit on the table, please, I've only just got all the documents in order . . . Sit on the chair. Just a moment, wait, I'll take those books . . . Does Lady Yennefer know you're here?"

"No."

"Hmm . . . Or Mother Nenneke?"

Ciri pulled a face. She knew what he meant. The sixteen-year-old Jarre was the high priestess's ward, being prepared by her to be a cleric and chronicler. He lived in Ellander where he worked as a scribe at the municipal tribunal, but he spent more time in Melitele's sanctuary than in the town, studying, copying and illuminating volumes in the Temple library for whole days and sometimes even nights. Ciri had never heard it from Nenneke's lips but it was well known that the high priestess absolutely did not want Jarre to hang around her young novices. And vice-versa. But the novices, however, did sneak keen glances at the boy and chatted freely, discussing the various possibilities presented by the presence on the Temple grounds of something which wore trousers. Ciri was amazed because Jarre was the exact opposite of everything which, in her eyes, should represent an attractive male. In Cintra, as she remembered, an attractive man was one whose head reached the ceiling, whose shoulders were as broad as a doorway, who swore like a dwarf, roared like a buffalo and stank at thirty paces of horses, sweat and beer, regardless of what time of day or night it was. Men who did not correspond to this description were not recognised by Queen Calanthe's chambermaids as worthy of sighs and gossip. Ciri had also seen a number of different men – the wise and gentle druids of Angren, the tall and gloomy settlers of Sodden, the witchers of Kaer Morhen. Jarre was different. He was as skinny as a stick-insect, ungainly, wore clothes which were too large and smelled of ink and dust, always had greasy hair and on his chin, instead of stubble, there were seven or eight long hairs, about half of which sprang from a large wart. Truly, Ciri did not understand why she was so drawn to Jarre's tower. She enjoyed talking to him, the boy knew a great deal and she could learn much from him. But recently, when he looked at her, his eyes had a strange, dazed and cloying expression.

"Well." She grew impatient. "Are you going to tell me or not?"

"There's nothing to say. There isn't going to be any war. It's all gossip."

"Aha," she snorted. "And so the duke is sending out a call to arms just for fun? The army is marching the highways out of boredom? Don't twist things, Jarre. You visit the town and castle, you must know something!"

"Why don't you ask Lady Yennefer about it?"

"Lady Yennefer has more important things to worry about!" Ciri spat, but then immediately had second thoughts, smiled pleasantly and fluttered her eyelashes. "Oh, Jarre, tell me, please! You're so clever! You can talk so beautifully and learnedly, I could listen to you for hours! Please, Jarre!"

The boy turned red and his eyes grew unfocused and bleary. Ciri sighed surreptitiously.

"Hmm . . ." Jarre shuffled from foot to foot and moved his arms undecidedly, evidently not knowing what to do with them. "What can I tell you? It's true, people are gossiping in town, all excited by the events in Dol Angra . . . But there isn't going to be a war. That's for sure. You can believe me."

"Of course, I can," she snorted. "But I'd rather know what you base this certainty on. You don't sit on the duke's council, as far as I know. And if you were made a voivode yesterday, then do tell me about it. I'll congratulate you."

"I study historical treatises," Jarre turned crimson, "and one can learn more from them than sitting on a council. I've read *The History of War* by Marshal Pelligram, Duke de Ruyter's *Strategy*, Bronibor's *The Victorious Deeds of Redania's Gallant Cavalrymen* . . . And I know enough about the present political situation to be able to draw conclusions through analogy. Do you know what an analogy is?"

"Of course," lied Ciri, picking a blade of grass from the buckle of her shoe.

"If the history of past wars" – the boy stared at the ceiling – "were to be laid over present political geography, it is easy to gauge that minor border incidents, such as the one in Dol Angra, are fortuitous and insignificant. You, as a student of magic, must, no doubt, be acquainted with the present political geography?"

Ciri did not reply. Lost in thought, she skimmed

through the parchments lying on the table and turned a few pages of the huge leather-bound volume.

"Leave that alone. Don't touch it." Jarre was worried. "It's an exceptionally valuable and unique work."

"I'm not going to eat it."

"Your hands are dirty."

"They're cleaner than yours. Listen, do you have any maps here?"

"I do, but they're hidden in the chest," said the boy quickly, but seeing Ciri pull a face, he sighed, pushed the scrolls of parchment off the chest, lifted the lid and started to rummage through the contents. Ciri, wriggling in the chair and swinging her legs, carried on flicking through the book. From between the pages suddenly slipped a loose page with a picture of a woman, completely naked with her hair curled into ringlets, entangled in an embrace with a completely naked bearded man. Her tongue sticking out, the girl spent a long time turning the etching around, unable to make out which way up it should be. She finally spotted the most important detail in the picture and giggled. Jarre, walking up with an enormous scroll under his arm, blushed violently, took the etching from her without a word and hid it under the papers strewn across the table.

"An exceptionally valuable and unique work," she gibed. "Are those the analogies you're studying? Are there any more pictures like that in there? Interesting, the book is called *Healing and Curing*. I'd like to know what diseases are cured that way."

"You can read the First Runes?" The boy was surprised and cleared his throat with embarrassment. "I didn't know . . ."

"There's still a lot you don't know." She turned up her nose. "And what do you think? I'm not just some novice feeding hens for eggs. I am . . . a wizard. Well, go on. Show me that map!"

They both knelt on the floor, holding down the stiff sheet, which was stubbornly trying to roll up again, with their hands and knees. Ciri finally weighed down one corner with a chair leg and Jarre pressed another down with a hefty book entitled *The Life and Deeds of Great King Radovid*.

"Hmm . . . This map is so unclear! I can't make head or tail of it . . . Where are we? Where is Ellander?"

"Here." He pointed. "Here is Temeria, this space. Here is Wyzima, our King Foltest's capital. Here, in Pontar Valley, lies the duchy of Ellander. And here . . . Yes, here is our Temple."

"And what's this lake? There aren't any lakes around here."

"That isn't a lake. It's an ink blot . . ."

"Ah. And here . . . This is Cintra. Is that right?"

"Yes. South of Transriver and Sodden. This way, here, flows the River Yaruga, flowing into the sea right at Cintra. That country, I don't know if you know, is now dominated by the Nilfgaardians—"

"I do know," she cut him short, clenching her fist. "I know very well. And where is this Nilfgaard? I can't see a country like that here. Doesn't it fit on this map of yours, or what? Get me a bigger one!"

"Hmm . . ." Jarre scratched the wart on his chin. "I don't have any maps like that . . . But I do know that Nilfgaard is somewhere further towards the south . . . There, more or less there. I think."

"So far?" Ciri was surprised, her eyes fixed on the place on the floor which he indicated. "They've come all the way from there? And on the way conquered those other countries?"

"Yes, that's true. They conquered Metinna, Maecht, Nazair, Ebbing, all the kingdoms south of the Amell Mountains. Those kingdoms, like Cintra and Upper Sodden, the Nilfgaardians now call the Provinces. But they didn't manage to dominate Lower Sodden, Verden and Brugge. Here, on the Yaruga, the armies of the Four Kingdoms held them back, defeating them in battle—"

"I know, I studied history." Ciri slapped the map with her open palm. "Well, Jarre, tell me about the war. We're kneeling on political geography. Draw conclusions through analogy and through anything you like. I'm all ears."

The boy blushed, then started to explain, pointing to the appropriate regions on the map with the tip of a quill.

"At present, the border between us and the South – dominated by Nilfgaard – is demarcated, as you can see, by the Yaruga River. It constitutes an obstacle which is practically insurmountable. It hardly ever freezes over, and during the rainy season it can carry so much water that its bed is almost a mile wide. For a long stretch, here, it flows between precipitous, inaccessible banks, between the rocks of Mahakam . . ."

"The land of dwarves and gnomes?"

"Yes. And so the Yaruga can only be crossed here, in its lower reaches, in Sodden, and here, in its middle reaches, in the valley of Dol Angra . . ."

"And it was exactly in Dol Angra, that inci— Incident?"

"Wait. I'm just explaining to you that, at the moment, no army could cross the Yaruga River. Both accessible valleys, those along which armies have marched for centuries, are very heavily manned and defended, both by us and by Nilfgaard. Look at the map. Look how many strongholds there are. See, here is Verden, here is Brugge, here the Isles of Skellige . . ."

"And this, what is this? This huge white mark?"

Jarre moved closer; she felt the warmth of his knee.

"Brokilon Forest," he said, "is forbidden territory. The kingdom of forest dryads. Brokilon also defends our flank. The dryads won't let anyone pass. The Nilfgaardians either . . ."

"Hmm . . ." Ciri leaned over the map. "Here is Aedirn . . . And the town of Vengerberg . . . Jarre! Stop that immediately!"

The boy abruptly pulled his lips away from her hair and went as red as a beetroot.

"I do not wish you to do that to me!"

"Ciri, I—"

"I came to you with a serious matter, as a wizard to a scholar," she said icily and with dignity, in a tone of voice which exactly copied that of Yennefer. "So behave!"

The "scholar" blushed an even deeper shade and had such a stupid expression on his face that the "wizard" could barely keep herself from laughing. He leaned over the map once more.

"All this geography of yours," she continued, "hasn't led to anything yet. You're telling me about the Yaruga River but the Nilfgaardians have, after all, already crossed to the other side once. What's stopping them now?"

"That time," hawked Jarre, wiping the sweat which

had all of a sudden appeared on his brow, "they only had Brugge, Sodden and Temeria against them. Now, we're united in an alliance. Like at the battle of Sodden. The Four Kingdoms. Temeria, Redania, Aedirn and Kaedwen . . ."

"Kaedwen," said Ciri proudly. "Yes, I know what that alliance is based on. King Henselt of Kaedwen offers special, secret aid to King Demawend of Aedirn. That aid is transported in barrels. And when King Demawend suspects someone of being a traitor, he puts stones in the barrels. Sets a trap—"

She broke off, recalling that Geralt had forbidden her to mention the events in Kaedwen. Jarre stared at her suspiciously.

"Is that so? And how can you know all that?"

"I read about it in a book written by Marshal Pelican," she snorted. "And in other analogies. Tell me what happened in Dol Angra or whatever it's called. But first, show me where it is."

"Here. Dol Angra is a wide valley, a route leading from the south to the kingdoms of Lyria and Rivia, to Aedirn, and further to Dol Blathanna and Kaedwen . . . And through Pontar Valley to us, to Temeria."

"And what happened there?"

"There was fighting. Apparently. I don't know much about it, but that's what they're saying at the castle."

"If there was fighting," frowned Ciri, "there's a war already! So what are you talking about?"

"It's not the first time there's been fighting," clarified Jarre, but the girl saw that he was less and less sure of himself. "Incidents at the border are very frequent. But they're insignificant."

"And how come?"

"The forces are balanced. Neither we nor the Nilf-gaardians can do anything. And neither of the sides can give their opponent a *casus belli*—"

"Give what?"

"A reason for war. Understand? That's why the armed incidents in Dol Angra are most certainly fortuitous matters, probably attacks by brigands or skirmishes with smugglers . . . In no way can they be the work of regular armies, neither ours nor those of Nilfgaard . . . Because that would be precisely a *casus belli* . . ."

"Aha. Jarre, tell me—"

She broke off. She raised her head abruptly, quickly touched her temples with her fingers and frowned.

"I've got to go," she said. "Lady Yennefer is calling me."

"You can hear her?" The boy was intrigued. "At a distance? How . . ."

"I've got to go," she repeated, getting to her feet and brushing the dust off her knees. "Listen, Jarre. I'm leaving with Lady Yennefer, on some very important matters. I don't know when we'll be back. I warn you they are secret matters which concern only wizards, so don't ask any questions."

Jarre also stood up. He adjusted his clothing but still did not know what to do with his hands. His eyes glazed over sickeningly.

"Ciri . . ."

"What?"

"I . . . I . . ."

"I don't know what you're talking about," she said

impatiently, glaring at him with her huge, emerald eyes. "Nor do you, obviously. I'm off. Take care, Jarre."

"Goodbye . . . Ciri. Have a safe journey. I'll . . . I'll be thinking of you . . ."

Ciri sighed.

"I'm here, Lady Yennefer!"

She flew into the chamber like a shot from a catapult and the door thumped open, slamming against the wall. She could have broken her legs on the stool standing in her way but Ciri jumped over it deftly, gracefully executed a half-pirouette feigning the slash of a sword, and joyfully laughed at her successful trick. Despite running briskly, she did not pant but breathed evenly and calmly. She had mastered breath control to perfection.

"I'm here!" she repeated.

"At last. Get undressed, and into the tub. Quick."

The enchantress did not look round, did not turn away from the table, looked at Ciri in the mirror. Slowly. She combed her damp, black curls which straightened under the pressure of the comb only to spring back a moment later into shiny waves.

The girl unbuckled her boots in a flash, kicked them off, freed herself of her clothes and with a splash landed in the tub. Grabbing the soap, she started to energetically scrub her forearms.

Yennefer sat motionless, staring at the window and toying with her comb. Ciri snorted, spluttered and spat because soap had got into her mouth. She tossed her head wondering whether a spell existed which could make washing possible without water, soap and wasting time.

The magician put the comb aside but, lost in thought,

kept gazing through the window at the swarms of ravens and crows croaking horrifically as they flew east. On the table, next to the mirror and an impressive array of bottled cosmetics, lay several letters. Ciri knew that Yennefer had been waiting for them a long time and that the day on which they were to leave the Temple depended on her receiving these letters. In spite of what she had told Jarre, the girl had no idea where and why they were leaving. But in those letters . . .

Splashing with her left hand so as to mislead, she arranged the fingers of her right in a gesture, concentrated on a formula, fixed her eyes on the letters and sent out an impulse.

"Don't you even dare," said Yennefer, without turning around.

"I thought . . ." She cleared her throat. "I thought one of them might be from Geralt . . ."

"If it was, I'd have given it to you." The magician turned in her chair and sat facing her. "Are you going to be long washing?"

"I've finished."

"Get up, please."

Ciri obeyed. Yennefer smiled faintly.

"Yes," she said, "you've finished with childhood. You've rounded out where necessary. Lower your hands. I'm not interested in your elbows. Well, well, don't blush, no false shyness. It's your body, the most natural thing in the world. And the fact that you're developing is just as natural. If your fate had turned out differently . . . If it weren't for the war, you'd have long been the wife of some duke or prince. You realise that, don't you? We've discussed matters concerning your gender often enough and in enough detail for you to know that you're already a woman. Physiologically, that is to say. Surely you've not forgotten what we talked about?"

"No. I haven't."

"When you visit Jarre I hope there aren't any problems with your memory either?"

Ciri lowered her eyes, but only momentarily. Yennefer did not smile.

"Dry yourself and come here," she said coolly. "No splashing, please."

Wrapped in a towel, Ciri sat down on the small chair at the magician's knees. Yennefer brushed the girl's hair, every now and again snipping off a disobedient wisp with a pair of scissors.

"Are you angry with me?" asked the girl reluctantly. "For, for . . . going to the tower?"

"No. But Nenneke doesn't like it. You know that."

"But I haven't . . . I don't care about Jarre in the least." Ciri blushed a little. "I only . . ."

"Exactly," muttered the enchantress. "You only. Don't play the child because you're not one any more, let me remind you. That boy slobbers and stammers at the sight of you. Can't you see that?"

"That's not my fault! What am I supposed to do?"

Yennefer stopped combing Ciri's hair and measured her with a deep, violet gaze.

"Don't toy with him. It's base."

"But I'm not toying with him! I'm only talking to him!"

"I'd like to believe," the enchantress said as she snipped her scissors, cutting yet another wisp of hair which would not allow itself to be styled for anything in the world, "that during these conversations, you remember what I asked you."

"I remember, I remember!"

"He's an intelligent and bright boy. One or two inadvertent words could lead him on the right track, to matters he should know nothing about. No one, absolutely no one must find out who you are."

"I remember," repeated Ciri. "I haven't squealed a word to anyone, you can be sure of that. Tell me, is that why we have to leave so suddenly? Are you afraid that someone's going to find out I'm here? Is that why?"

"No. There are other reasons."

"Is it because . . . there might be a war? Everybody's talking about another war! Everybody's talking about it, Lady Yennefer."

"Indeed," the magician confirmed coolly, snipping her scissors just above Ciri's ear. "It's a subject which belongs to the so-called interminable category. There's been talk about wars in the past, there is talk now and there always will be. And not without reason – there have been wars and there will be wars. Lower your head."

"Jarre said . . . that there's not going to be a war with Nilfgaard. He spoke of some sort of analogies . . . Showed me a map. I don't know what to think myself any more. I don't know what these analogies are, probably something terribly clever . . . Jarre reads various learned books and knows it all, but I think . . ."

"It interests me, what you think, Ciri."

"In Cintra . . . That time . . . Lady Yennefer, my grandmother was much cleverer than Jarre. King Eist was clever, too. He sailed the seas, saw everything, even a narwhal and sea serpent, and I bet he also saw many an analogy. And so what? Suddenly they appeared, the Nilfgaardians . . ."

Ciri raised her head and her voice stuck in her throat. Yennefer put her arms around her and hugged her tightly.

"Unfortunately," she said quietly, "unfortunately, you're right, my ugly one. If the ability to make use of experience and draw conclusions decided, we would have forgotten what war is a long time ago. But those whose goal is war have never been held back, nor will be, by experience or analogy."

"So . . . It's true, after all. There is going to be a war. Is that why we have to leave?"

"Let's not talk about it. Let's not worry too soon."

Ciri sniffed.

"I've already seen a war," she whispered. "I don't want to see another. Never. I don't want to be alone again. I don't want to be frightened. I don't want to lose everything again, like that time. I don't want to lose Geralt . . . or you, Lady Yennefer. I don't want to lose you. I want to stay with you. And him. Always."

"You will." The magician's voice trembled a little. "And I'm going to be with you, Ciri. Always. I promise you."

Ciri sniffed again. Yennefer coughed quietly, put down the scissors and comb, got to her feet and crossed over to the window. The ravens were still croaking in their flight towards the mountains.

"When I arrived here," the lady magician suddenly said in her usual, melodious, slightly mocking voice. "When we first met . . . You didn't like me."

Ciri did not say anything. *Our first meeting*, she

thought. *I remember. I was in the Grotto with the other girls. Hrosvitha was showing us plants and herbs. Then Iola the First came in and whispered something in Hrosvitha's ear. The priestess grimaced with animosity. And Iola the First came up to me with a strange expression on her face.* "Get yourself together, Ciri," *she said*, "and go the refectory, quick. Mother Nenneke is summoning you. Someone has arrived."

Strange, meaningful glances, excitement in their eyes. And whispers. Yennefer. "Magician Yennefer. Quick, Ciri, hurry up. Mother Nenneke is waiting. And she is waiting."

I knew immediately, thought Ciri, *that it was her. Because I'd seen her. I'd seen her the night before. In my dream.*

Her.

I didn't know her name then. She didn't say anything in my dream. She only looked at me and behind her, in the darkness, I saw a closed door . . .

Ciri sighed. Yennefer turned and the obsidian star on her neck glittered with a thousand reflections.

"You're right," admitted the girl seriously, looking straight into the magician's violet eyes. "I didn't like you."

"Ciri," said Nenneke, "come closer. This is Lady Yennefer from Vengerberg, Mistress of Wizardry. Don't be frightened. Lady Yennefer knows who you are. You can trust her."

The girl bowed, interlocking her palms in a gesture of full respect. The enchantress, rustling her long, black dress, approached, took Ciri by the chin and quite offhandedly lifted her head, turning it right and left. The girl felt anger and rebellion rising within her – she was not used to being treated this way. And at the same time, she experienced a burning envy. Yennefer was very beautiful. Compared to the delicate, pale and rather common comeliness of the priestesses and novices who Ciri saw every day, the magician glowed with a conscious, even demonstrative loveliness, emphasised and accentuated in every detail. Her raven-black locks cascading down her shoulders shone, reflected the light like the feathers of a peacock, curling and undulating with every move. Ciri suddenly felt ashamed, ashamed of her grazed elbows, chapped hands, broken nails, her ashen, stringy hair. All of a sudden, she had an overwhelming desire to possess what Yennefer had – a beautiful, exposed neck and on it a lovely black velvet ribbon with a lovely glittering star. Regular eyebrows, accentuated with charcoal, and long eyelashes. Proud lips. And those two mounds which rose with every breath, hugged by black cloth and white lace . . .

"So this is the famous Surprise." The magician twisted her lips a little. "Look me in the eyes, girl."

Ciri shuddered and hunched her shoulders. No, she did not envy Yennefer that one thing – did not desire to have it or even look at it. Those eyes, violet, deep as a fathomless lake, strangely bright, dispassionate and malefic. Terrifying.

The magician turned towards the stout high priestess. The star on her neck flamed with reflections of the sun beaming through the window into the refectory.

"Yes, Nenneke," she said. "There can be no doubt. One just has to look into those green eyes to know that there is something in her. High forehead, regular arch of the brows, eyes set attractively apart. Narrow nose. Long fingers. Rare hair pigment. Obvious elven blood, although there is not much of it in her. An elven great-grandfather or great-grandmother. Have I guessed correctly?"

"I don't know her family tree," the high priestess replied calmly. "It didn't interest me."

"Tall for her age," continued the magician, still appraising Ciri with her eyes. The girl was boiling over with fury and annoyance, struggling with an overpowering desire to scream defiantly, scream her lungs out, stamp her feet and run off to the park, on the way knocking over the vase on the table and slamming the door so as to make the plaster crumble from the ceiling.

"Not badly developed." Yennefer did not take her eyes off her. "Has she suffered any infectious diseases in childhood? Ha, no doubt you didn't ask her about that either. Has she been ill since she's been here?"

"No."

"Any migraines? Fainting? Inclination to catch cold? Painful periods?"

"No. Only those dreams."

"I know." Yennefer gathered the hair from her cheek. "He wrote about that. It appears from his letter that in Kaer Morhen they didn't try out any of their . . . experiments on her. I would like to believe that's true."

"It is. They gave her only natural stimulants."

"Stimulants are never natural!" The magician raised her voice. "Never! It is precisely the stimulants which may have aggravated her symptoms in . . . Damn it, I never suspected him of such irresponsibility!"

"Calm down." Nenneke looked at her coldly and, all

of a sudden, somehow oddly without respect. "I said they were natural and absolutely safe. Forgive me, dear, but in this respect I am a greater authority than you. I know it is exceedingly difficult for you to accept someone else's authority but in this case I am forced to inflict it on you. And let there be no more talk about it."

"As you wish." Yennefer pursed her lips. "Well, come on, girl. We don't have much time. It would be a sin to waste it."

Ciri could barely keep her hands from shaking; she swallowed hard and looked inquiringly at Nenneke. The high priestess was serious, as if sad, and the smile with which she answered the unspoken question was unpleasantly false.

"You're going with Lady Yennefer now," she said. "Lady Yennefer is going to be looking after you for a while."

Ciri bowed her head and clenched her teeth.

"You are no doubt baffled," continued Nenneke, "that a Mistress of Wizardry is suddenly taking you into her care. But you are a reasonable girl, Ciri. You can guess why. You have inherited certain . . . attributes from your ancestors. You know what I am talking about. You used to come to me, after those dreams, after the nocturnal disturbances in the dormitory. I couldn't help you. But Lady Yennefer—"

"Lady Yennefer," interrupted the magician, "will do what is necessary. Let us go, girl."

"Go," nodded Nenneke, trying, in vain, to make her smile at least appear natural. "Go, child. Remember it is a great privilege to have someone like Lady Yennefer look after you. Don't bring shame on the Temple and us, your mentors. And be obedient."

I'll escape tonight, Ciri made up her mind. *Back to Kaer Morhen. I'll steal a horse from the stables and that's the last they'll see of me. I'll run away!*

"Indeed you will," said the magician under her breath.

"I beg your pardon?" the priestess raised her head. "What did you say?"

"Nothing, nothing," smiled Yennefer. "You just thought I did. Or maybe I thought I did? Just look at this ward of yours, Nenneke. Furious as a cat. Sparks in her eyes; just wait and she'll hiss. And if she could flatten her ears, she would. A witcher-girl! I'll have to take her firmly in hand, file her claws."

"Be more understanding." The high priestess's features visibly hardened. "Please, be kind-hearted and understanding. She really is not who you take her to be."

"What do you mean by that?"

"She's not your rival, Yennefer."

For a moment they measured each other with their eyes, the enchantress and the priestess, and Ciri felt the air quiver, a strange, terrible force between them growing in strength. This lasted no more than a fraction of a second after which the force disappeared and Yennefer burst out laughing, lightheartedly and sweetly.

"I forgot," she said. "Always on his side, aren't you, Nenneke? Always worrying about him. Like the mother he never had."

"And you're always against him," smiled the priestess. "Bestowing him with strong feelings, as usual. And defending yourself as hard as you can not to call the feelings by their rightful name."

Once again, Ciri felt fury rise up somewhere in the pit of her stomach, and her temples throbbed with spite and rebellion. She remembered how many times and under what circumstances she had heard that name. Yennefer. A name which caused unease, a name which was the symbol of some sinister secret. She guessed what that secret was.

They're talking quite openly in front of me, without any restraint, she thought, feeling her hands start to shake with anger once more. *They're not bothered about me at all. Ignoring me completely. As if I were a child. They're talking about Geralt in front of me, in my presence, but they can't because I . . . I am . . .*

Who?

"You, on the other hand, Nenneke," retorted the magician, "are amusing yourself, as usual, analysing other people's emotions, and on top of that interpreting them to suit yourself!"

"And putting my nose into other people's business?"

"I didn't want to say that." Yennefer tossed her black locks, which gleamed and writhed like snakes. "Thank you for doing so for me. And now let us change the subject, please, because the one we were discussing is exceptionally silly – disgraceful in front of our young pupil. And as for being understanding, as you ask . . . I will be. But kind-hearted – with that, there might be a problem because, after all, it is widely thought I don't possess any such organ. But we'll manage somehow. Isn't that right, Surprise?"

She smiled at Ciri and, despite herself, despite her anger and annoyance, Ciri had to respond with a smile.

Because the enchantress's smile was unexpectedly pleasant, friendly and sincere. And very, very beautiful.

She listened to Yennefer's speech with her back ostentatiously turned, pretending to bestow her full attention on the bumble bee buzzing in the flower of one of the hollyhocks growing by the temple wall.

"No one asked me about it," she mumbled.

"What didn't anybody ask you about?"

Ciri turned in a half-pirouette and furiously whacked the hollyhock with her fist. The bumble bee flew away, buzzing angrily and ominously.

"No one asked me whether I wanted you to teach me!"

Yennefer rested her fists on her hips; her eyes flashed.

"What a coincidence," she hissed. "Imagine that – no one asked me whether I wanted to teach you either. Besides, wanting has got nothing to do with it. I don't apprentice just anybody and you, despite appearances, might still turn out to be a nobody. I was asked to check how things stand with you. To examine what is inside you and how that could endanger you. And I, though not unreluctantly, agreed."

"But I haven't agreed yet!"

The magician raised her arm and moved her hand. Ciri experienced a throbbing in her temples and a buzzing in her ears, as if she were swallowing but much louder. She felt drowsy, and an overpowering weakness, tiredness stiffened her neck and softened her knees.

Yennefer lowered her hand and the sensation instantly passed.

"Listen to me carefully, Surprise," she said. "I can easily cast a spell on you, hypnotise you, or put you in a trance. I can paralyse you, force you to drink an elixir, strip you naked, lay you out on the table and examine you for hours, taking breaks for meals while you lie there, looking at the ceiling, unable to move even your eyeballs. That is what I would do with just any snotty kid. I do not want to do that to you because one can see, at first glance, that you are an intelligent and proud girl, that you have character. I don't want to put you or myself to shame. Not in front of Geralt. Because he is the one who asked me to take care of your abilities. To help you deal with them."

"He asked you? Why? He never said anything to me! He never asked me—"

"You keep going back to that," cut in the magician. "No one asked for your opinion, no one took the trouble to check what you want or don't want. Could you have given cause for someone to consider you a contrary, stubborn, snotty kid, whom it is not worth asking questions like that? But I'm going to take the risk and am going to ask something no one has ever asked you. Will you allow yourself to be examined?"

"And what will it involve? What are these tests? And why . . ."

"I have already explained. If you haven't understood, that's too bad. I have no intention of polishing your perception or working on your intelligence. I can examine a sensible girl just as well as a stupid one."

"I'm not stupid! And I understood everything!"

"All the better."

"But I'm not cut out to be a magician! I haven't got any abilities! I'm never going to be a magician nor want to be one! I'm destined for Geralt . . . I'm destined to be a

witcher! I've only come here for a short period! I'm going
back to Kaer Morhen soon . . ."

"You are persistently staring at my neckline," said
Yennefer icily, narrowing her violet eyes a little. "Do you
see anything unusual there or is it just plain jealousy?"

"That star . . ." muttered Ciri. "What's it made of?
Those stones move and shine so strangely . . ."

"They pulsate," smiled the magician. "They are active
diamonds, sunken in obsidian. Do you want to see them
close up? Touch them?"

"Yes . . . No!" Ciri backed away and angrily tossed her
head, trying to dispel the faint scent of lilac and gooseberries emanating from Yennefer. "I don't. Why should I?
I'm not interested! Not a bit! I'm a witcher! I haven't got
any magical abilities! I'm not cut out to be a magician,
surely that's clear because I'm . . . And anyway . . ."

The magician sat on the stone bench under the wall
and concentrated on examining her fingernails.

". . . and anyway," concluded Ciri, "I've got to think
about it."

"Come here. Sit next to me."

She obeyed.

"I've got to have time to think about it," she said
hesitantly.

"Quite right." Yennefer nodded, still gazing at her
nails. "It is a serious matter. It needs to be thought over."

Both said nothing for a while. The novices strolling
through the park glanced at them with curiosity, whispered, giggled.

"Well?"

"Well what?"

"Have you thought about it?"

Ciri leaped to her feet, snorted and stamped.

"I . . . I . . ." she panted, unable to catch her breath from anger. "Are you making fun of me? I need time! I need to think about it! For longer! For a whole day . . . And night!"

Yennefer looked her in the eyes and Ciri shrivelled under the gaze.

"The saying goes," said the magician slowly, "that the night brings solutions. But in your case, Surprise, the only thing night can bring is yet another nightmare. You will wake up again, screaming and in pain, drenched in sweat. You will be frightened again, frightened of what you saw, frightened of what you won't be able to remember. And there will be no more sleep that night. There will be fear. Until dawn."

The girl shuddered, lowered her head.

"Surprise." Yennefer's voice changed imperceptibly. "Trust me."

The enchantress's shoulder was warm. The black velvet of her dress asked to be touched. The scent of lilac and gooseberries intoxicated delightfully. Her embrace calmed and soothed, relaxed, tempered excitement, stilled anger and rebellion.

"You'll submit to the tests, Surprise."

"I will," she answered, understanding that she did not really have to reply. Because it was not a question.

"I don't understand anything any more," said Ciri. "First you say I've got abilities because I've got those dreams. But you want to do tests and check . . . So how is it? Do I have abilities or don't I?"

"That question will be answered by the tests."

"Tests, tests." She pulled a face. "I haven't got any abilities, I tell you. I'd know if I had them, wouldn't I? Well, but . . . If, by some sheer chance, I had abilities, what then?"

"There are two possibilities," the magician informed her with indifference as she opened the window. "Your abilities will either have to be extinguished or you will have to learn how to control them. If you are gifted and want to, I can try to instil in you some elementary knowledge of magic."

"What does 'elementary' mean?"

"Basic."

They were alone in the large chamber next to the library in an unoccupied side wing of the building, which Nenneke had allocated to the lady magician. Ciri knew that this chamber was used by guests. She knew that Geralt, whenever he visited the Temple, stayed right here.

"Are you going to want to teach me?" She sat on the bed and skimmed her hand over the damask eiderdown. "Are you going to want to take me away from here? I'm never going to leave with you!"

"So I'll leave alone," said Yennefer coldly, untying the straps of her saddle-bags. "And I assure you, I'm not going to miss you. I did tell you that I'll educate you only if you decide you want to. And I can do so here, on the spot."

"How long are you going to edu— Teach me for?"

"As long as you want." The magician leaned over, opened the chest of drawers, pulled out an old leather bag, a belt, two boots trimmed with fur and a clay demijohn in a wicker basket. Ciri heard her curse under her breath while smiling, and saw her hide the finds back in the drawers. She guessed whose they were. Who had left them there.

"What does that mean, as long as I want?" she asked. "If I get bored or don't like the work—"

"We'll put an end to it. It's enough that you tell me. Or show me."

"Show you? How?"

"Should we decide on educating you, I will demand absolute obedience. I repeat: absolute. If, on the other hand, you get tired of it, it will suffice for you to disobey. Then the lessons will instantly cease. Is that clear?"

Ciri nodded and cast a fleeting glance of her green eyes at the magician.

"Secondly," continued Yennefer, unpacking her saddle-bags, "I will demand absolute sincerity. You will not be allowed to hide anything from me. Anything. So if you feel you have had enough, it will suffice for you to lie, pretend, feign or close in on yourself. If I ask you something and you do not answer sincerely, that will also indicate an instant end to our lessons. Have you understood?"

"Yes," muttered Ciri. "And that . . . sincerity . . . Does that work both ways? Will I be able to . . . ask you questions?"

Yennefer looked at her and her lips twisted strangely.

"Of course," she answered after a while. "That goes without saying. That will be the basis of the learning and protection I aim to give you. Sincerity works both ways. You are to ask me questions. At any time. And I will answer. Sincerely."

"Any question?"

"Any question."

"As of now?"

"Yes. As of now."

"What is there between you and Geralt, Lady Yennefer?"

Ciri almost fainted, horrified at her own impertinence, chilled by the silence which followed the question.

The enchantress slowly approached her, placed her hands on her shoulders, looked her in the eyes from up close – and deeply.

"Longing," she answered gravely. "Regret. Hope. And fear. Yes, I don't think I have omitted anything. Well, now we can get on with the tests, you little green-eyed viper. We will see if you're cut out for this. Although after your question I would be very surprised if it turned out you aren't. Let's go, my ugly one."

Ciri bridled.

"Why do you call me that?"

Yennefer smiled with the corners of her lips.

"I promised to be sincere."

Ciri, annoyed, pulled herself up straight and wriggled in her hard chair which, after many hours of sitting, hurt her backside.

"Nothing's going to come of it!" she snarled, wiping her charcoal-smeared fingers on the table. "After all this, nothing . . . Nothing works out for me! I'm not cut out to be a magician! I knew that right from the start but you didn't want to listen to me! You didn't pay any attention!"

Yennefer raised her eyebrows.

"I didn't want to listen to you, you say? That's interesting. I usually devote my attention to every sentence uttered in my presence and note it in my memory. The one condition being that there be at least a little sense in the sentence."

"You're always mocking me." Ciri grated her teeth. "And I just wanted to tell you . . . Well, about these abilities. You see in Kaer Morhen, in the mountains . . . I couldn't form a single witcher Sign. Not one!"

"I know."

"You know?"

"I know. But that doesn't mean anything."

"How's that? Well . . . But that's not all!"

"I'm listening in suspense."

"I'm not cut out for it. Can't you understand that? I'm . . . I'm too young."

"I was younger than you when I started."

"But I'm sure you weren't . . ."

"What do you mean, girl? Stop stuttering! At least one full sentence, please."

"Because . . ." Ciri lowered her head and blushed. "Because Iola, Myrrha, Eurneid and Katye – when we were having dinner – laughed at me and said that witch-craft doesn't have access to me and that I'm not going to perform any magic because . . . Because I'm . . . a virgin, that means—"

"I know what it means, believe it or not," interrupted the magician. "No doubt you'll see this as another spiteful piece of mockery but I hate to tell you that you are talking a lot of rubbish. Let us get back to the test."

"I'm a virgin!" repeated Ciri aggressively. "Why the tests? Virgins can't do magic!"

"I can't see a solution," Yennefer leaned back in her chair. "So go out and lose your virginity if it gets in your way so much. But be quick about it if you please."

"Are you making fun of me?"

"You've noticed?" The magician smiled faintly. "Congratulations. You've passed the preliminary test in perspicacity. And now for the real test. Concentrate, please. Look: there are four pine trees in this picture. Each one has a different number of branches. Draw a fifth to fit in with the other four and to fit in this space here."

"Pine trees are silly," decreed Ciri, sticking out her tongue and drawing a slightly crooked tree with her charcoal. "And boring! I can't understand what pine trees have to do with magic? What? Lady Yennefer! You promised to answer my questions!"

"Unfortunately," sighed the magician, picking up the sheet of paper and critically appraising the drawing, "I think I'm going to regret that promise. What do pine trees have in common with magic? Nothing. But you've drawn it correctly, and on time. In truth, excellent for a virgin."

"Are you laughing at me?"

"No. I rarely laugh. I really need to have a good reason to laugh. Concentrate on the next page, Surprise. There are rows of stars, circles, crosses and triangles drawn on it, a different number of each shape in each row. Think and answer: how many stars should there be in the last row?"

"Stars are silly!"

"How many?"

"Three!"

Yennefer did not say anything for a long time. She stared at a detail on the carved wardrobe door known only to her. The mischievous smile on Ciri's lips started slowly to disappear until finally it disappeared altogether, without a trace.

"No doubt you were curious to learn," said the magician very slowly, not ceasing to admire the wardrobe, "what would happen if you gave me a senseless and stupid reply. You thought perhaps that I might not notice because I am not in the least interested in your answers? You thought wrongly. You believed, perhaps, that I would simply accept that you are stupid? You were wrong. But if you are bored of being tested and wanted, for a change, to test me . . . Well, that has clearly worked, hasn't it? Either way, this test is concluded. Return the paper."

"I'm sorry, Lady Yennefer." The girl lowered her head. "There should, of course, be . . . one star there. I'm very sorry. Please don't be angry with me."

"Look at me, Ciri."

The girl raised her eyes, astonished. Because for the first time the magician had called her by her name.

"Ciri," said Yennefer. "Know that, despite appearances, I get angry just as rarely as I laugh. You haven't made me angry. But in apologising you have proved I wasn't wrong about you. And now take the next sheet of paper. As you can see there are five houses on it. Draw the sixth . . ."

"Again? I really can't understand why—"

". . . the sixth house." The lady magician's voice changed dangerously and her eyes flashed with a violet glow. "Here, in this space. Don't make me repeat myself, please."

After apples, pine trees, stars, fishes and houses, came the turn of labyrinths through which she had to quickly find a path, wavy lines, blots which looked like squashed cockroaches, and mosaics which made her go cross-eyed and set her head spinning. Then there was a shining ball on a piece of string at which she had to stare for a long time. Staring at it was as dull as dish-water and Ciri kept falling asleep. Yennefer, surprisingly, did not care even though a few days earlier she had scolded her grimly for napping over one of the cockroach blots.

Poring over the tests had made her neck and back ache and day by day they grew more painful. She missed movement and fresh air and, obliged to be sincere, she immediately told Yennefer. The magician took it easily, as if she had been expecting this for a long time.

For the next two days they both ran through the park, jumped over ditches and fences under the amused or pitying eyes of the priestesses and novices. They exercised and practised their balance walking along the top of the wall which encircled the orchard and farm buildings. Unlike the training in Kaer Morhen, though, the exercises with Yennefer were always accompanied by theory. The magician taught Ciri how to breathe, guiding the movement of her chest and diaphragm with strong pressure from her hand. She explained the rules of movement, how muscles and bones work, and demonstrated how to rest, release tension and relax.

During one such session of relaxation, stretched out on the grass and gazing at the sky, Ciri asked a question which was bothering her. "Lady Yennefer? When are we finally going to finish the tests?"

"Do they bore you so much?"

"No . . . But I'd like to know whether I'm cut out to be a magician."

"You are."

"You know that already?"

"I knew from the start. Few people can detect the activity of my star. Very few. You noticed it straight away."

"And the tests?"

"Concluded. I already know what I wanted to about you."

"But some of the tasks . . . They didn't work out very well. You said yourself that . . . Are you really sure? You're not mistaken? You're sure I have the ability?"

"I'm sure."

"But—"

"Ciri." The enchantress looked both amused and impatient. "From the moment we lay down in the meadow, I have been talking to you without using my voice. It's called telepathy, remember that. And as you no doubt noticed, it has not made our talking together any more difficult."

"Magic" – Yennefer, her eyes fixed on the sky above the hills, rested her hands on the pommel of her saddle – "is, in some people's opinion, the embodiment of Chaos. It is a key capable of opening the forbidden door. The door behind which lurk nightmares, fear and unimaginable horrors, behind which enemies hide and wait, destructive powers, the forces of pure Evil capable of annihilating not only the one who opens the door but with them the entire world. And since there is no lack of those who try to open the door, someone, at some point, is going to make a mistake and then the destruction of the world will be forejudged and inevitable. Magic is, therefore, the revenge and the weapon of Chaos. The fact that, following the Conjunction of the Spheres, people have learned to use magic, is the curse and undoing of the world. The undoing of mankind. And that's how it is, Ciri. Those who believe that magic is Chaos are not mistaken."

Spurred on by its mistress's heels, the magician's black stallion neighed lengthily and slowly made his way into the heather. Ciri hastened her horse, followed in Yennefer's tracks and caught up with her. The heather reached to their stirrups.

"Magic," Yennefer continued after a while, "is, in some people's opinion, art. Great, elitist art, capable of creating beautiful and extraordinary things. Magic is a talent granted to only a chosen few. Others, deprived of talent, can only look at the results of the artists' works with admiration and envy, can admire the finished work while feeling that without these creations and without this talent the world would be a poorer place. The fact that, following the Conjunction of the Spheres, some chosen few discovered talent and magic within themselves, the fact that they found Art within themselves, is the blessing of beauty. And that's how it is. Those who believe that magic is art are also right."

On the long bare hill which protruded from the heath like the back of some lurking predator lay an enormous boulder supported by a few smaller stones. The magician guided her horse in its direction without pausing her lecture.

"There are also those according to whom magic is a science. In order to master it, talent and innate ability alone are not enough. Years of keen study and arduous work are essential; endurance and self-discipline are necessary. Magic acquired like this is knowledge, learning, the limits of which are constantly stretched by enlightened and vigorous minds, by experience, experiments and practice. Magic acquired in such a way is progress. It is the plough, the loom, the watermill, the smelting furnace, the winch and the pulley. It is progress, evolution, change. It is constant movement. Upwards. Towards improvement. Towards the stars. The fact that following the Conjunction of the Spheres we discovered magic will, one day, allow us to reach the stars. Dismount, Ciri."

Yennefer approached the monolith, placed her palm on the coarse surface of the stone and carefully brushed away the dust and dry leaves.

"Those who consider magic to be a science," she continued, "are also right. Remember that, Ciri. And now come here, to me."

The girl swallowed and came closer. The enchantress put her arm around her.

"Remember," she repeated, "magic is Chaos, Art and Science. It is a curse, a blessing and progress. It all depends on who uses magic, how they use it, and to what purpose. And magic is everywhere. All around us. Easily accessible. It is enough to stretch out one's hand. See? I'm stretching out my hand."

The cromlech trembled perceptibly. Ciri heard a dull, distant noise and a rumble coming from within the earth. The heather undulated, flattened by the gale which suddenly gusted across the hill. The sky abruptly turned dark, covered with clouds scudding across it at incredible speed. The girl felt drops of rain on her face. She narrowed her eyes against the flash of lightning which suddenly flared across the horizon. She automatically huddled up to the enchantress, against her black hair smelling of lilac and gooseberries.

"The earth which we tread. The fire which does not go out within it. The water from which all life is born and without which life is not possible. The air we breathe. It is enough to stretch out one's hand to master them, to subjugate them. Magic is everywhere. It is in air, in water, in earth and in fire. And it is behind the door which the Conjunction of the Spheres has closed on us. From there, from behind the closed door, magic sometimes extends its hand to us. For us. You know that, don't you? You have already felt the touch of that magic, the touch of the hand from behind that door. That touch filled you with fear. Such a touch fills everyone with fear. Because there is Chaos and Order, Good and Evil in all of us. But it is possible and necessary to control it. This has to be learnt. And you will learn it, Ciri. That is why I brought you here, to this stone which, from time immemorial, has stood at the crossing of veins of power pulsating with force. Touch it."

The boulder shook, vibrated, and with it the entire hill vibrated and shook.

"Magic is extending its hand towards you, Ciri. To you, strange girl, Surprise, Child of the Elder Blood, the Blood of Elves. Strange girl, woven into Movement and Change, into Annihilation and Rebirth. Destined and destiny. Magic extends its hand towards you from behind the closed door, towards you, a tiny grain of sand in the workings of the Clock of Fate. Chaos extends its talons towards you, still uncertain if you will be its tool or an obstacle in its design. That which Chaos shows you in your dreams is this very uncertainty. Chaos is afraid of you, Child of Destiny. But it wants you to be the one who feels fear."

There was a flash of lightning and a long rumble of thunder. Ciri trembled with cold and dread.

"Chaos cannot show you what it really is. So it is showing you the future, showing you what is going to happen. It wants you to be afraid of the coming days, so that fear of what is going to happen to you and those closest to you will start to guide you, take you over completely. That is why Chaos is sending you those dreams. Now, you are going to show me what you see in your dreams. And you are going to be frightened. And then you will forget and master your fear. Look at my star, Ciri. Don't take your eyes from it!"

A flash. A rumble of thunder.

"Speak! I command you!"

Blood. Yennefer's lips, cut and crushed, move silently, flow with blood. White rocks flitter past, seen from a gallop. A horse neighs. A leap. Valley, abyss. Screaming. Flight, an endless flight. Abyss . . .

In the depth of the abyss, smoke. Stairs leading down.

Va'esse deireádh aep eigean . . . Something is coming to an end . . . What?

Elaine blath, Feainnewedd . . . Child of the Elder Blood? Yennefer's voice seems to come from somewhere afar, is dull, awakens echoes amidst the stone walls dripping with damp. Elaine blath—

"Speak!"

The violet eyes shine, burn in the emaciated, shrivelled face, blackened with suffering, veiled with a tempest of dishevelled, dirty black hair. Darkness. Damp. Stench. The excruciating cold of stone walls. The cold of iron on wrists, on ankles . . .

Abyss. Smoke. Stairs leading down. Stairs down

which she must go. Must because . . . Because something is coming to an end. Because Tedd Deireádh, the Time of End, the Time of the Wolf's Blizzard is approaching. The Time of the White Chill and White Light . . .

The Lion Cub must die! For reasons of state!

"Let's go," says Geralt. "Down the stairs. We must. It must be so. There is no other way. Only the stairs. Down!"

His lips are not moving. They are blue. Blood, blood everywhere . . . The whole stairs in blood . . . Mustn't slip . . . Because the witcher trips just once . . . The flash of a blade. Screams. Death. Down. Down the stairs.

Smoke. Fire. Frantic galloping, hooves thundering. Flames all around. "Hold on! Hold on, Lion Cub of Cintra!"

The black horse neighs, rears. "Hold on!"

The black horse dances. In the slit of the helmet adorned with the wings of a bird of prey shine and burn merciless eyes.

A broad sword, reflecting the glow of the fire, falls with a hiss. Dodge, Ciri! Feign! Pirouette, parry! Dodge! Dodge! Too sloooowwww!

The blow blinds her with its flash, shakes her whole body, the pain paralyses her for a moment, dulls, deadens, and then suddenly explodes with a terrible strength, sinks its cruel, sharp fangs into her cheek, yanks, penetrates right through, radiates into the neck, the shoulders, chest, lungs . . .

"Ciri!"

She felt the coarse, unpleasant, still coolness of stone on her back and head. She did not remember sitting down. Yennefer was kneeling next to her. Gently, but decisively, she straightened her fingers, pulled her hand away from her cheek. The cheek throbbed, pulsated with pain.

"Mama . . ." groaned Ciri. "Mama . . . How it hurts! Mama . . ."

The magician touched her face. Her hand was as cold as ice. The pain stopped instantly.

"I saw . . ." the girl whispered, closing her eyes, "the things I saw in the dreams . . . A black knight . . . Geralt . . . And also . . . You . . . I saw you, Lady Yennefer!"

"I know."

"I saw you . . . I saw how—"

"Never more. You will never see that again. You won't dream about it any more. I will give you the force to push those nightmares away. That is why I have brought you here, Ciri – to show you that force. Tomorrow, I am going to start giving it to you."

Long, arduous days followed, days of intensive study and exhausting work. Yennefer was firm, frequently stern, sometimes masterfully formidable. But she was never boring. Previously, Ciri could barely keep her eyes open in the Temple school and would sometimes even doze off during a lesson, lulled by the monotonous, gentle voice of Nenneke, Iola the First, Hrosvitha or some other teacher. With Yennefer, it was impossible. And not only because of the timbre of the lady magician's voice and the short, sharply accentuated sentences she used. The most important element was the subject of her studies. The study of magic. Fascinating, exciting and absorbing study.

Ciri spent most of the day with Yennefer. She returned to the dormitory late at night, collapsed into bed like a log and fell asleep immediately. The novices complained that she snored very loudly and tried to wake her. In vain.

Ciri slept deeply.

With no dreams.

"Oh, gods." Yennefer sighed in resignation and, ruffling her black hair with both hands, lowered her head. "But it's so simple! If you can't master this move, what will happen with the harder ones?"

Ciri turned away, mumbled something in a raspy voice and massaged her stiff hand. The magician sighed once more.

"Take another look at the etching. See how your fingers should be spread. Pay attention to the explanatory arrows and runes describing how the move should be performed."

"I've already looked at the drawing a thousand times! I understand the runes! Vort, cáelme. Ys, veloë. Away from oneself, slowly. Down, quickly. The hand . . . like this?"

"And the little finger?"

"It's impossible to position it like that without bending the ring finger at the same time!"

"Give me your hand."

"Ouuuch!"

"Not so loud, Ciri, otherwise Nenneke will come running again, thinking that I'm skinning you alive or frying you in oil. Don't change the position of your fingers. And now perform the gesture. Turn, turn the wrist! Good. Now shake the hand, relax the fingers. And repeat. No, no! Do you know what you did? If you were to cast a real spell like that, you'd be wearing your hand in splints for a month! Are your hands made of wood?"

"My hand's trained to hold a sword! That's why!"

"Nonsense. Geralt has been brandishing his sword for his whole life and his fingers are agile and . . . mm-mm . . . very gentle. Continue, my ugly one, try again. See? It's enough to want to. It's enough to try. Once more. Good. Shake your hand. And once again. Good. Are you tired?"

"A little . . ."

"Let me massage your hand and arm. Ciri, why aren't you using the ointment I gave you? Your hands are as rough as crocodile skin . . . But what's this? A mark left by a ring, am I right? Was I imagining it or did I forbid you to wear any jewellery?"

"But I won the ring from Myrrha playing spinning tops! And I only wore it for half a day—"

"That's half a day too long. Don't wear it any more, please."

"I don't understand, why aren't I allowed—"

"You don't have to understand," the magician said cutting her short, but there was no anger in her voice. "I'm asking you not to wear any ornaments like that. Pin a flower in your hair if you want to. Weave a wreath for your hair. But no metal, no crystals, no stones. It's important, Ciri. When the time comes, I will explain why. For the time being, trust me and do as I ask."

"You wear your star, earrings and rings! And I'm not allowed? Is that because I'm . . . a virgin?"

"Ugly one," Yennefer smiled and stroked her on the head, "are you still obsessed with that? I have already explained to you that it doesn't matter whether you are or not. Not in the least. Wash your hair tomorrow; it needs it, I see."

"Lady Yennefer?"

"Yes."

"May I . . . As part of the sincerity you promised . . . May I ask you something?"

"You may. But, by all the gods, not about virginity, please."

Ciri bit her lip and did not say anything for a long time.

"Too bad," sighed Yennefer. "Let it be. Ask away."

"Because, you see . . ." Ciri blushed and licked her lips, "the girls in the dormitory are always gossiping and telling all sorts of stories . . . About Belleteyn's feast and others like that . . . And they say I'm a snotty kid, a child because it's time . . . Lady Yennefer, how does it really work? How can one know that the time has come . . ."

". . . to go to bed with a man?"

Ciri blushed a deep shade of crimson. She said nothing for a while then raised her eyes and nodded.

"It's easy to tell," said Yennefer, naturally. "If you are beginning to think about it then it's a sign the time has come."

"But I don't want to!"

"It's not compulsory. You don't want to, then you don't."

"Ah." Ciri bit her lip again. "And that . . . Well . . . Man . . . How can you tell it's the right one to . . ."

". . . go to bed with?"

"Mmmh."

"If you have any choice at all," the enchantress twisted

her lips in a smile, "but don't have much experience, you first appraise the bed."

Ciri's emerald eyes turned the shape and size of saucers.

"How's that . . . The bed?"

"Precisely that. Those who don't have a bed at all, you eliminate on the spot. From those who remain, you eliminate the owners of any dirty or slovenly beds. And when only those who have clean and tidy beds remain, you choose the one you find most attractive. Unfortunately, the method is not a hundred per cent foolproof. You can make a terrible mistake."

"You're joking?"

"No. I'm not joking, Ciri. As of tomorrow, you are going to sleep here with me. Bring your things. From what I hear, too much time is wasted in the novices' dormitory on gabbling, time which would be better spent resting and sleeping."

After mastering the basic positions of the hands, the moves and gestures, Ciri began to learn spells and their formulae. The formulae were easier. Written in Elder Speech, which the girl already knew to perfection, they sank easily into her memory. Nor did she have any problems enunciating the frequently complicated intonations. Yennefer was clearly pleased and, from day to day, was becoming more pleasant and sympathetic. More and more frequently, taking breaks in the studies, both gossiped and joked about any old thing; both even began to amuse themselves by delicately poking fun at Nenneke who often "visited" their lectures and exercises – bristling and puffed up like a brooding hen

– ready to take Ciri under her protective wing, to protect and save her from the magician's imagined severity and the "inhuman tortures" of her education.

Obeying instructions, Ciri moved to Yennefer's chamber. Now they were together not only by day but also by night. Sometimes, their studies would take place during the night – certain moves, formulae and spells could not be performed in daylight.

The magician, pleased with the girl's progress, slowed the speed of her education. They had more free time. They spent their evenings reading books, together or separately. Ciri waded through Stammelford's *Dialogues on the Nature of Magic*, Giambattista's *Forces of the Elements* and Richert and Monck's *Natural Magic*. She also flicked through – because she did not manage to read them in their entirety – such works as Jan Bekker's *The Invisible World* and Agnes of Glanville's *The Secret of Secrets*. She dipped into the ancient, yellowed *Codex of Mirthe, Ard Aercane*, and even the famous, terrible *Dhu Dwimmermorc*, full of menacing etchings.

She also reached for other books which had nothing to do with magic. She read *The History of the World* and *A Treatise on Life*. Nor did she leave out lighter works from the Temple library. Blushing, she devoured Marquis La Creahme's *Gambols* and Anna Tiller's *The King's Ladies*. She read *The Adversities of Loving* and *Time of the Moon*, collections of poems by the famous troubadour Dandilion. She shed tears over the ballads of Essi Daven, subtle, infused with mystery, and collected in a small, beautifully bound volume entitled *The Blue Pearl*.

She made frequent use of her privilege to ask questions. And she received answers. More and more fre-

quently, however, she was the one being questioned. In
the beginning it had seemed that Yennefer was not at all
interested in her lot, in her childhood in Cintra or the later
events of war. But in time her questions became more and
more concrete. Ciri had to reply and did so very unwillingly because every question the magician asked opened
a door in her memory which she had promised herself
never to open, which she wanted to keep forever locked.
Ever since she had met Geralt in Sodden, she had believed
she had begun "another life," that the other life – the one
in Cintra – had been irrevocably wiped out. The witchers in Kaer Morhen never asked her about anything and,
before coming to the temple, Geralt had even prevailed
upon her not to say a word to anyone about who she was.
Nenneke, who, of course knew about everything, saw to it
that to the other priestesses and the novices Ciri was exceptionally ordinary, an illegitimate daughter of a knight
and a peasant woman, a child for whom there had been no
place either in her father's castle or her mother's cottage.
Half of the novices in Melitele's Temple were just such
children.

And Yennefer too knew the secret. She was the one
who "could be trusted." Yennefer asked. About it. About
Cintra.

"How did you get out of the town, Ciri? How did you
slip past the Nilfgaardians?"

Ciri did not remember. Everything broke off, was lost
in obscurity and smoke. She remembered the siege, saying goodbye to Queen Calanthe, her grandmother; she
remembered the barons and knights forcibly dragging her
away from the bed where the wounded, dying Lioness of
Cintra lay. She remembered the frantic escape through

flaming streets, bloody battle and the horse falling. She remembered the black rider in a helmet adorned with the wings of a bird of prey.

And nothing more.

"I don't remember. I really don't remember, Lady Yennefer."

Yennefer did not insist. She asked different questions. She did so gently and tactfully and Ciri grew more and more at ease. Finally, she started to speak herself. Without waiting to be asked, she recounted her years as a child in Cintra and on the Isles of Skellige. About how she learned about the Law of Surprise and that fate had decreed her to be the destiny of Geralt of Rivia, the white-haired witcher. She recalled the war, her exile in the forests of Transriver, her time among the druids of Angren and the time spent in the country. How Geralt had found her there and taken her to Kaer Morhen, the Witchers' Keep, thus opening a new chapter in her short life.

One evening, of her own initiative, unasked, casually, joyfully and embellishing a great deal, she told the enchantress about her first meeting with the witcher in Brokilon Forest, amongst the dryads who had abducted her and wanted to force her to stay and become one of them.

"Oh!" said Yennefer on listening to the story, "I'd give a lot to see that – Geralt, I mean. I'm trying to imagine the expression on his face in Brokilon, when he saw what sort of Surprise destiny had concocted for him! Because he must have had a wonderful expression when he found out who you were?"

Ciri giggled and her emerald eyes lit up devilishly.

"Oh, yes!" she snorted. "What an expression! Do you want to see? I'll show you. Look at me!"

Yennefer burst out laughing.

That laughter, thought Ciri watching swarms of black birds flying eastwards, *that laughter, shared and sincere, really brought us together, her and me. We understood – both she and I – that we can laugh and talk together about him. About Geralt. Suddenly we became close, although I knew perfectly well that Geralt both brought us together and separated us, and that that's how it would always be.*

Our laughter together brought us closer to each other.

As did the events two days later. In the forest, on the hills. She was showing me how to find . . .

"I don't understand why I have to look for these . . . I've forgotten what they're called again . . ."

"Intersections," prompted Yennefer, picking off the burrs which had attached themselves to her sleeve as they crossed the scrubs. "I am showing you how to find them because they're places from which you can draw the force."

"But I know how to draw the force already! And you taught me yourself that the force is everywhere. So why are we roaming around in the bushes? After all, there's a great deal of force in the Temple!"

"Yes, indeed, there is a fair amount there. That's exactly why the Temple was built there and not somewhere else. And that's why, on Temple grounds, drawing it seems so easy to you."

"My legs hurt! Can we sit down for a while?"

"All right, my ugly one."

"Lady Yennefer?"

"Yes?"

"Why do we always draw the force from water veins? Magical energy, after all, is everywhere. It's in the earth, isn't it? In air, in fire?"

"True."

"And earth . . . Here, there's plenty of earth around here. Under our feet. And air is everywhere! And should we want fire, it's enough to light a bonfire and . . ."

"You are still too weak to draw energy from the earth. You still don't know enough to succeed in drawing anything from air. And as for fire, I absolutely forbid you to play with it. I've already told you, under no circumstances are you allowed to touch the energy of fire!"

"Don't shout. I remember."

They sat in silence on a fallen dry tree trunk, listening to the wind rustling in the tree tops, listening to a woodpecker hammering away somewhere close by. Ciri was hungry and her saliva was thick from thirst, but she knew that complaining would not get her anywhere. In the past, a month ago, Yennefer had reacted to such complaints with a dry lecture on how to control such primitive instincts; later, she had ignored them in contemptuous silence. Protesting was just as useless and produced as few results as sulking over being called "ugly one."

The magician plucked the last burr from her sleeve. *She's going to ask me something in a moment*, thought Ciri, *I can hear her thinking about it. She's going to ask about something I don't remember again. Or something I don't want to remember. No, it's senseless. I'm not going*

to answer. All of that is in the past, and there's no return-
ing to the past. She once said so herself.

"Tell me about your parents, Ciri."

"I can't remember them, Lady Yennefer."

"Please try to."

"I really don't remember my papa . . ." she said in a quiet
voice, succumbing to the command. "Except . . . Practically nothing. My mama . . . My mama, I do. She had
long hair, like this . . . And she was always sad . . . I remember . . . No, I don't remember anything . . ."

"Try to remember, please."

"I can't!"

"Look at my star."

Seagulls screamed, diving down between the fishing
boats where they caught scourings and tiny fish emp-
tied from the crates. The wind gently fluttered the lowered sails of the drakkars, and smoke, quelled by drizzle,
floated above the landing-stage. Triremes from Cintra
were sailing into the port, golden lions glistening on blue
flags. Uncle Crach, who was standing next to her with his
hand – as large as the paw of a grizzly bear – on her shoulder, suddenly fell to one knee. Warriors, standing in rows,
rhythmically struck their shields with their swords.

Along the gang-plank towards them came Queen
Calanthe. Her grandmother. She who was officially called
Ard Rhena, the Highest Queen, on the Isles of Skellige.
But Uncle Crach an Craite, the Earl of Skellige, still
kneeling with bowed head, greeted the Lioness of Cintra
with a title which was less official but considered by the
islanders to be more venerable.

"Hail, Modron."

"Princess," said Calanthe in a cold and authoritative

voice, without so much as a glance at the earl, "come here. Come here to me, Ciri."

Her grandmother's hand was as strong and hard as a man's, her rings cold as ice.

"Where is Eist?"

"The King . . ." stammered Crach. "Is at sea, Modron. He is looking for the remains . . . And the bodies. Since yesterday . . ."

"Why did he let them?" shouted the queen. "How could he allow it? How could you allow it, Crach? You're the Earl of Skellige! No drakkar is allowed to go out to sea without your permission! Why did you allow it, Crach?"

Uncle Crach bowed his head even lower.

"Horses!" said Calanthe. "We're going to the fort. And tomorrow, at dawn, I am setting sail. I am taking the princess to Cintra. I will never allow her to return here. And you . . . You have a huge debt to repay me, Crach. One day I will demand repayment."

"I know, Modron."

"If I do not claim it, she will do so." Calanthe looked at Ciri. "You will repay the debt to her, Earl. You know how."

Crach an Craite got to his feet, straightened himself and the features of his weatherbeaten face hardened. With a swift move, he drew from its sheath a simple, steel sword devoid of ornaments and pulled up the sleeve on his left arm, marked with thickened white scars.

"Without the dramatic gestures," snorted the queen. "Save your blood. I said: one day. Remember!"

"Aen me Gláeddyv, zvaere a'Bloedgeas, Ard Rhena, Lionors aep Xintra!" Crach an Craite, the Earl of the Isles of Skellige, raised his arms and shook his sword. The warriors roared hoarsely and beat their weapons against their shields.

"I accept your oath. Lead the way to the fort, Earl."

Ciri remembered King Eist's return, his stony, pale face. And the queen's silence. She remembered the gloomy, horrible feast at which the wild, bearded sea wolves of Skellige slowly got drunk in terrifying silence. She remembered the whispers. "Geas Muire . . . Geas Muire!"

She remembered the trickles of dark beer poured onto the floor, the horns smashed against the stone walls of the hall in bursts of desperate, helpless, senseless anger. "Geas Muire! Pavetta!"

Pavetta, the Princess of Cintra, and her husband, Prince Duny. Ciri's parents. Perished. Killed. Geas Muire, the Curse of the Sea, had killed them. They had been swallowed up by a tempest which no one had foreseen. A tempest which should not have broken out . . .

Ciri turned her head away so that Yennefer would not see the tears swelling in her eyes. *Why all this,* she thought. *Why these questions, these recollections? There's no returning to the past. There's no one there for me any more. Not my papa, nor my mama, nor my grandmother, the one who was Ard Rhena, the Lioness of Cintra. Uncle Crach an Craite, no doubt, is also dead. I haven't got anybody any more and am someone else. There's no returning . . .*

The magician remained silent, lost in thought.

"Is that when your dreams began?" she asked suddenly.

"No," Ciri reflected. "No, not then. Not until later."

"When?"

The girl wrinkled her nose.

"In the summer . . . The one before . . . Because the following summer there was the war already . . ."

"Aha. That means the dreams started after you met Geralt in Brokilon?"

She nodded. *I'm not going to answer the next question*, she decided. But Yennefer did not ask anything. She quickly got to her feet and looked at the sun.

"Well, that's enough of this sitting around, my ugly one. It's getting late. Let's carry on looking. Keep your hand held loosely in front of you, and don't tense your fingers. Forward."

"Where am I to go? Which direction?"

"It's all the same."

"The veins are everywhere?"

"Almost. You're going to learn how to discover them, to find them in the open and recognise such spots. They are marked by trees which have dried up, gnarled plants, places avoided by all animals. Except cats."

"Cats?"

"Cats like sleeping and resting on intersections. There are many stories about magical animals but really, apart from the dragon, the cat is the only creature which can absorb the force. No one knows why a cat absorbs it and what it does with it . . . What's the matter?"

"Oooo . . . There, in that direction! I think there's something there! Behind that tree!"

"Ciri, don't fantasise. Intersections can only be sensed by standing over them . . . Hmmm . . . Interesting. Extraordinary, I'd say. Do you really feel the pull?"

"Really!"

"Let's go then. Interesting, interesting . . . Well, locate it. Show me where."

"Here! On this spot!"

"Well done. Excellent. So you feel delicate cramps in your ring finger? See how it bends downwards? Remember, that's the sign."

"May I draw on it?"

"Wait, I'll check."

"Lady Yennefer? How does it work with this drawing of the force? If I gather force into myself then there might not be enough left down below. Is it right to do that? Mother Nenneke taught us that we mustn't take anything just like that, for the fun of it. Even the cherry has to be left on its tree for the birds, so that it can simply fall."

Yennefer put her arm around Ciri, kissed her gently on the hair at her temple.

"I wish," she muttered, "others could hear what you said. Vilgefortz, Francesca, Terranova . . . Those who believe they have exclusive right to the force and can use it unreservedly. I wish they could listen to the little wise ugly one from Melitele's Temple. Don't worry, Ciri. It's a good thing you're thinking about it but believe me, there is enough force. It won't run out. It's as if you picked one single little cherry from a huge orchard."

"Can I draw on it now?"

"Wait. Oh, it's a devilishly strong pocket. It's pulsating violently. Be careful, ugly one. Draw on it carefully and very, very slowly."

"I'm not frightened! Pah-pah! I'm a witcher. Ha! I feel it! I feel . . . Ooouuuch! Lady . . . Ye . . . nnnne . . . feeeeer . . ."

"Damn it! I warned you! I told you! Head up! Up, I say! Take this and put it to your nose or you'll be covered in blood! Calmly, calmly, little one, just don't faint. I'm beside you. I'm beside you . . . daughter. Hold the handkerchief. I'll just conjure up some ice . . ."

There was a great fuss about that small amount of blood. Yennefer and Nenneke did not talk to each other for a week.

For a week, Ciri lazed around, read books and got bored because the magician had put her studies on hold. The girl did not see her for entire days – Yennefer disappeared somewhere at dawn, returned in the evening, looked at her strangely and was oddly taciturn.

After a week, Ciri had had enough. In the evening, when the enchantress returned, she went up to her without a word and hugged her hard.

Yennefer was silent. For a very long time. She did not have to speak. Her fingers, clasping the girl's shoulders tightly, spoke for her.

The following day, the high priestess and the lady magician made up, having talked for several hours.

And then, to Ciri's great joy, everything returned to normal.

"Look into my eyes, Ciri. A tiny light. The formula, please!"

"Aine verseos!"

"Good. Look at my hand. The same move and disperse the light in the air."

"Aine aen aenye!"

"Excellent. And what gesture comes next? Yes, that's the one. Very good. Strengthen the gesture and draw. More, more, don't stop!"

"Oooouuuch . . ."

"Keep your back straight! Arms by your side! Hands loose, no unnecessary moves with your fingers. Every move can multiply the effect. Do you want a fire to burst out here? Strengthen it, what are you waiting for?"

"Oouuch, no . . . I can't—"

"Relax and stop shaking! Draw! What are you doing? There, that's better . . . Don't weaken your will! That's too fast, you're hyperventilating! Unnecessarily getting hot! Slower, ugly one, calmer. I know it's unpleasant. You'll get used to it."

"It hurts . . . My belly . . . Down here—"

"You're a woman, it's a typical reaction. Over time you'll harden yourself against it. But in order to harden yourself you have to practise without any painkillers blocking you. It really is necessary, Ciri. Don't be afraid of anything, I'm alert and screening you. Nothing can happen to you. But you have to endure the pain. Breathe calmly. Concentrate. The gesture, please. Perfect. And take the force, draw it, pull it in . . . Good, good . . . Just a bit more . . ."

"O . . . O . . . Oooouuuch!"

"There, you see? You can do it, if you want to. Now watch my hand. Carefully. Perform the same movement. Fingers! Fingers, Ciri! Look at my hand, not the ceiling! Now, that's good, yes, very good. Tie it up. And now turn it around, reverse the move and now issue the force in the form of a stronger light."

"Eeeee . . . Eeeeek . . . Aiiiieee . . ."

"Stop moaning! Control yourself! It's just cramp! It'll stop in a moment! Fingers wider, extinguish it, give it back, give it back from yourself! Slower, damn it, or your blood vessels will burst again!"

"Eeeeeek!"

"Too abrupt, ugly one, still too abrupt. I know the force is bursting out but you have to learn to control it. You mustn't allow outbursts like the one a moment ago. If I hadn't insulated you, you would have caused havoc here. Now, once more. We're starting right from the beginning. Move and formula."

"No! Not again! I can't!"

"Breathe slowly and stop shaking. It's plain hysteria this time, you don't fool me. Control yourself, concentrate and begin."

"No, please, Lady Yennefer . . . It hurts . . . I feel sick . . ."

"Just no tears, Ciri. There's no sight more nauseating than a magician crying. Nothing arouses greater pity. Remember that. Never forget that. One more time, from the beginning. Spell and gesture. No, no, this time without copying me. You're going to do it by yourself. So, use your memory!"

"Aine verseos . . . Aine aen aenye . . . Oooouuuuch!"

"No! Too fast!"

Magic, like a spiked iron arrow, lodged in her. Wounded her deeply. Hurt. Hurt with the strange sort of pain oddly associated with bliss.

To relax, they once again ran around the park. Yennefer persuaded Nenneke to take Ciri's sword out of storage and so enabled the girl to practise her steps, dodges and attacks – in secret, of course, to prevent the other priestesses and novices seeing her. But magic was omnipresent. Ciri learned how – using simple spells and focusing her will – to relax her muscles, combat cramps, control adrenalin, how to master her aural labyrinth and its nerve, how to slow or speed her pulse and how to cope without oxygen for short periods.

The lady magician knew a surprising amount about a witcher's sword and "dance." She knew a great deal about the secrets of Kaer Morhen; there was no doubt she had visited the Keep. She knew Vesemir and Eskel. Although not Lambert and Coën.

Yennefer used to visit Kaer Morhen. Ciri guessed why – when they spoke of the Keep – the eyes of the enchantress grew warm, lost their angry gleam and their cold, indifferent, wise depth. If the words had befitted Yennefer's person, Ciri would have called her dreamy, lost in memories.

Ciri could guess the reason.

There was a subject which the girl instinctively and carefully avoided. But one day, she got carried away and spoke out. About Triss Merigold. Yennefer, as if casually, as if indifferently, asking as if banal, sparing questions, dragged the rest from her. Her eyes were hard and impenetrable.

Ciri could guess the reason. And, amazingly, she no longer felt annoyed.

Magic was calming.

"The so-called Sign of Aard, Ciri, is a very simple spell belonging to the family of psychokinetic magic which is based on thrusting energy in the required direction. The force of the thrust depends on how the will of the person throwing it is focused and on the expelled force. It can be considerable. The witchers adapted the spell, making use of the fact that it does not require knowledge of a magical formula – concentration and the gesture are enough. That's why they called it a Sign. Where they got the name from, I don't know, maybe from the Elder Speech – the word 'ard', as you know, means 'mountain', 'upper' or 'the highest'. If that is truly the case then the name is very misleading because it's hard to find an easier psychokinetic spell. We, obviously, aren't going to waste time and energy on something as primitive as the witchers' Sign. We are going to practise real psychokinesis. We'll practise on . . . Ah, on that basket lying under the apple tree. Concentrate."

"Ready."

"You focus yourself quickly. Let me remind you: control the flow of the force. You can only emit as much as you draw. If you release even a tiny bit more, you do so at the cost of your constitution. An effort like that could render you unconscious and, in extreme circumstances, could even kill you. If, on the other hand, you release everything you draw, you forfeit all possibility of repeating it, and you will have to draw it again and, as you know, it's not easy to do and it is painful."

"Ooooh, I know!"

"You mustn't slacken your concentration and allow the energy to tear itself away from you of its own accord. My Mistress used to say that emitting the force must be like blowing a raspberry in a ballroom; do it gently, sparingly, and with control. And in such a way that you don't let those around you to know it was you. Understood?"

"Understood!"

"Straighten yourself up. Stop giggling. Let me remind you that spells are a serious matter. They are cast with grace and pride. The motions are executed fluently but with restraint. With dignity. You do not pull faces, grimace or stick your tongue out. You are handling a force of nature, show Nature some respect."

"All right, Lady Yennefer."

"Careful, this time I'm not screening you. You are an independent spell-caster. This is your debut, ugly one. You saw that demi-john of wine in the chest of drawers? If your debut is successful, your mistress will drink it tonight."

"By herself?"

"Novices are only allowed to drink wine once they are qualified apprentices. You have to wait. You're smart, so that just means another ten years or so, not more. Right, let's start. Arrange your fingers. And the left hand? Don't wave it around! Let it hang loose or rest it on your hip. Fingers! Good. Right, release."

"Aaaah . . ."

"I didn't ask you to make funny noises. Emit the energy. In silence."

"Haa, ha! It jumped! The basket jumped! Did you see?"

"It barely twitched. Ciri, sparingly does not mean weakly. Psychokinesis is used with a specific goal in mind. Even witchers use the Sign of Aard to throw their opponent off his feet. The energy you emitted would not knock their hat off their head! Once more, a little stronger. Go for it!"

"Ha! It certainly flew! It was all right that time, wasn't it, Lady Yennefer?"

"Hmmm . . . You'll run to the kitchen afterwards and pinch a bit of cheese to go with our wine . . . That was almost right. Almost. Stronger still, ugly one, don't be frightened. Lift the basket from the ground and throw it hard against the wall of that shack, make feathers fly. Don't slouch! Head up! Gracefully, but with pride! Be bold, be bold! Oh, bloody hell!"

"Oh, dear . . . I'm sorry, Lady Yennefer . . . I probably . . . probably used a bit too much . . ."

"A little bit. Don't worry. Come here. Come on, little one."

"And . . . and the shack?"

"These things happen. There's no need to take it to heart. Your debut, on the whole, should be viewed as a success. And the shack? It wasn't too pretty. I don't think anyone will miss its presence in the landscape. Hold on, ladies! Calm down, calm down, why this uproar and commotion, nothing has happened! Easy, Nenneke! Really, nothing has happened. The planks just need to be cleared away. They'll make good firewood!"

During the warm, still afternoons the air grew thick with the scent of flowers and grass; pulsating with peace and silence, broken by the buzz of bees and enormous beetles. On afternoons like this Yennefer carried Nenneke's wicker chair out into the garden and sat in it, stretching her legs out in front of her. Sometimes she studied books, sometimes read letters which she received by means of strange couriers, usually birds. At times she simply sat gazing into the distance. With one hand, and lost in thought, she ruffled her black, shiny locks, with the other she stroked Ciri's head as she sat on the grass, snuggled up to the magician's warm, firm thigh.

"Lady Yennefer?"

"I'm here, ugly one."

"Tell me, can one do anything with magic?"

"No."

"But you can do a great deal, am I right?"

"You are." The enchantress closed her eyes for a moment and touched her eyelids with her fingers. "A great deal."

"Something really great . . . Something terrible! Very terrible?"

"Sometimes even more so than one would have liked."

"Hmm . . . And could I . . . When will I be able to do something like that?"

"I don't know. Maybe never. Would that you don't have to."

Silence. No words. Heat. The scent of flowers and herbs.

"Lady Yennefer?"

"What now, ugly one?"

"How old were you when you became a wizard?"

"When I passed the preliminary exams? Thirteen."

"Ha! Just like I am now! And how . . . How old were you when . . . No, I won't ask about that—"

"Sixteen."

"Aha . . ." Ciri blushed faintly and pretended to be suddenly interested in a strangely formed cloud hovering over the temple towers. "And how old were you . . . when you met Geralt?"

"Older, ugly one. A bit older."

"You still keep on calling me ugly one! You know how I don't like it. Why do you do it?"

"Because I'm malicious. Wizards are always malicious."

"But I don't want to . . . don't want to be ugly. I want to be pretty. Really pretty, like you, Lady Yennefer. Can I, through magic, be as pretty as you one day?"

"You . . . Fortunately you don't have to . . . You don't need magic for it. You don't know how lucky you are."

"But I want to be really pretty!"

"You are really pretty. A really pretty ugly one. My pretty little ugly one . . ."

"Oh, Lady Yennefer!"

"Ciri, you're going to bruise my thigh."

"Lady Yennefer?"

"Yes."

"What are you looking at like that?"

"At that tree. That linden tree."

"And what's so interesting about it?"

"Nothing. I'm simply feasting my eyes on it. I'm happy that . . . I can see it."

"I don't understand."

"Good."

Silence. No words. Humid.

"Lady Yennefer!"

"What now?"

"There's a spider crawling towards your leg! Look how hideous it is!"

"A spider's a spider."

"Kill it!"

"I can't be bothered to bend over."

"Then kill it with magic!"

"On the grounds of Melitele's Temple? So that Nenneke can throw us out head first? No, thank you. And now be quiet. I want to think."

"And what are you thinking about so seriously? Hmm. All right, I'm not going to say anything now."

"I'm beside myself with joy. I was worried you were going to ask me another one of your unequal grand questions."

"Why not? I like your unequal grand answers!"

"You're getting impudent, ugly one."

"I'm a wizard. Wizards are malicious and impudent."

No words. Silence. Stillness in the air. Close humidity as if before a storm. And silence, this time broken by the distant croaking of ravens and crows.

"There are more and more of them." Ciri looked upwards. "They're flying and flying . . . Like in autumn . . . Hideous birds . . . The priestesses say that it's a bad sign . . . An omen, or something. What is an omen, Lady Yennefer?"

"Look it up in *Dhu Dwimmermorc*. There's a whole chapter on the subject."

Silence.

"Lady Yennefer . . ."

"Oh, hell. What is it now?"

"It's been so long, why isn't Geralt . . . Why isn't he coming?"

"He's forgotten about you, no doubt, ugly one. He's found himself a prettier girl."

"Oh, no! I know he hasn't forgotten! He couldn't have! I know that, I know that for certain, Lady Yennefer!"

"It's good you know. You're a lucky ugly one."

"I didn't like you," she repeated.

Yennefer did not look at her as she stood at the window with her back turned, staring at the hills looming black in the east. Above the hills, the sky was dark with flocks of ravens and crows.

In a minute she's going to ask why I didn't like her, thought Ciri. *No, she's too clever to ask such a question. She'll dryly draw my attention to my grammar and ask when I started using the past tense. And I'll tell her. I'll be just as dry as she is, I'll parody her tone of voice, let her know that I, too, can pretend to be cold, unfeeling and indifferent, ashamed of my feelings and emotions. I'll tell her everything. I want to, I have to tell her everything. I want her to know everything before we leave Melitele's Temple. Before we part to finally meet the one I miss. The one she misses. The one who no doubt misses us both. I want to tell her that . . .*

I'll tell her. It's enough for her to ask.

The magician turned from the window and smiled. She did not ask anything.

They left the following day, early in the morning. Both wore men's travelling clothes, cloaks, hats and hoods which hid their hair. Both were armed.

Only Nenneke saw them off. She spoke quietly and at length with Yennefer, then they both – the magician and the priestess – shook each other's hand, hard, like men. Ciri, holding the reins of her dapple-grey mare, wanted to say goodbye in the same way, but Nenneke did not allow it. She embraced her, hugged her and gave her a kiss. There were tears in her eyes. In Ciri's, too.

"Well," said the priestess finally, wiping her eye with the sleeve of her robe, "now go. May the Great Melitele protect you on your way, my dears. But the goddess has a great many things on her mind, so look after yourselves too. Take care of her, Yennefer. Keep her safe, like the apple of your eye."

"I hope" – the magician smiled faintly – "that I'll manage to keep her safer."

Across the sky, towards Pontar Valley, flew flocks of crows, croaking loudly. Nenneke did not look at them.

"Take care," she repeated. "Bad times are approaching. It might turn out to be true, what Ithlinne aep Aevenien knew, what she predicted. The Time of the Sword and Axe is approaching. The Time of Contempt and the Wolf's Blizzard. Take care of her, Yennefer. Don't let anyone harm her."

"I'll be back, Mother," said Ciri, leaping into her saddle. "I'll be back for sure! Soon!"

She did not know how very wrong she was.

extras

orbit

meet the author

Andrzej Sapkowski was born in 1948 in Poland. He studied economy and business, but the success of his fantasy cycle about the sorcerer Geralt of Rivia turned him into a bestselling writer. He is now one of Poland's most famous and successful authors.

introducing

If you enjoyed **BLOOD OF ELVES**,
look out for

THE LAST WISH

by Andrzej Sapkowski

V

The mare flattened her ears against her skull and snorted, throwing up earth with her hooves; she didn't want to go. Geralt didn't calm her with the Sign; he jumped from the saddle and threw the reins over the horse's head. He no longer had his old sword in its lizard-skin sheath on his back; its place was filled with a shining, beautiful weapon with a cruciform and slender, well-weighted hilt, ending in a spherical pommel made of white metal.

This time the gate didn't open for him. It was already open, just as he had left it.

He heard singing. He didn't understand the words; he couldn't even identify the language. He didn't need to—the witcher felt and understood the very nature, the essence, of this quiet, piercing song which flowed through the veins in a wave of nauseous, overpowering menace.

The singing broke off abruptly, and then he saw her.

She was clinging to the back of the dolphin in the

dried-up fountain, embracing the moss-overgrown stone with her tiny hands, so pale they seemed transparent. Beneath her storm of tangled black hair shone huge, wide-open eyes the color of anthracite.

Geralt slowly drew closer, his step soft and springy, tracing a semi-circle from the wall and blue rosebush. The creature glued to the dolphin's back followed him with her eyes, turning her petite face with an expression of longing, and full of charm. He could still hear her song, even though her thin, pale lips were held tight and not the slightest sound emerged from them.

The witcher halted at a distance of ten paces. His sword, slowly drawn from its black enameled sheath, glistened and glowed above his head.

"It's silver," he said. "This blade is silver."

The pale little face did not flinch; the anthracite eyes did not change expression.

"You're so like a rusalka," the witcher continued calmly, "that you could deceive anyone. All the more as you're a rare bird, black-haired one. But horses are never mistaken. They recognize creatures like you instinctively and perfectly. What are you? I think you're a moola, or an alpor. An ordinary vampire couldn't come out in the sun."

The corners of the pale lips quivered and turned up a little.

"Nivellen attracted you with that shape of his, didn't he? You evoked his dreams. I can guess what sort of dreams they were, and I pity him."

The creature didn't move.

"You like birds," continued the witcher. "But that doesn't stop you biting the necks of people of both sexes, does it? You and Nivellen, indeed! A beautiful couple you'd make, a monster and a vampire, rulers of a forest castle. You'd dominate the whole area in a flash. You, eternally thirsty for blood, and he, your guardian, a murderer at your service, a blind tool. But first he had to become a true monster, not a human being in a monster's mask."

The huge black eyes narrowed.

"Where is he, black-haired one? You were singing, so you've drunk some blood. You've taken the ultimate measure, which means you haven't managed to enslave his mind. Am I right?"

The black-tressed head nodded slightly, almost imperceptibly, and the corners of the mouth turned up even more. The tiny little face took on an eerie expression.

"No doubt you consider yourself the lady of this manor now?"

A nod, this time clearer.

"Are you a moola?"

A slow shake of the head. The hiss which reverberated through his bones could only have come from the pale, ghastly, smiling lips, although the witcher didn't see them move.

"Alpor?"

Denial.

The witcher backed away and clasped the hilt of his sword tighter. "That means you're—"

The corners of the lips started to turn up higher and higher; the lips flew open . . .

"A bruxa!" the witcher shouted, throwing himself toward the fountain.

From behind the pale lips glistened white, spiky

fangs. The vampire jumped up, arched her back like a leopard and screamed.

The wave of sound hit the witcher like a battering ram, depriving him of breath, crushing his ribs, piercing his ears and brain with thorns of pain. Flying backward, he just managed to cross his wrists in the Sign of Heliotrop. The spell cushioned some of his impact with the wall but even so, the world grew dark and the remainder of his breath burst from his lungs in a groan.

On the dolphin's back, in the stone circle of the dried-up fountain where a dainty girl in a white dress had sat just a moment ago, an enormous black bat flattened its glossy body, opening its long, narrow jaws wide, revealing rows of needle-like white teeth. The membranous wings spread and flapped silently, and the creature charged at the witcher like an arrow fired from a crossbow.

Geralt, with the metallic taste of blood in his mouth, shouted a spell and threw his hand, fingers spread in the Sign of Quen, out in front of him. The bat, hissing, turned abruptly, then chuckled and veered up into the air before diving down vertically, straight at the nape of the witcher's neck. Geralt jumped aside, slashed, and missed. The bat, smoothly, gracefully drew in a wing, circled around him and attacked anew, opening its eyeless, toothed snout wide. Geralt waited, sword held with both hands, always pointed in the creature's direction. At the last moment, he jumped—not to the side but forward, dealing a swinging cut which made the air howl.

He missed. It was so unexpected that he lost his rhythm and dodged a fraction of a second too late. He felt the beast's talons tear his cheek, and a damp velvety wing slapped against his neck. He curled up on the spot, transferred the weight of his body to his right leg and slashed backward sharply, missing the amazingly agile creature again.

The bat beat its wings, soared up and glided toward the fountain. As the crooked claws scraped against the stone casing, the monstrous, slobbering snout was already blurring, morphing, disappearing, although the pale little lips which were taking its place couldn't quite hide the murderous fangs.

The bruxa howled piercingly, modulating her voice into a macabre tune, glared at the witcher with eyes full of hatred, and screamed again.

The sound wave was so powerful it broke through the Sign. Black and red circles spun in Geralt's eyes; his temples and the crown of his head throbbed. Through the pain drilling in his ears, he began to hear voices wailing and moaning, the sound of flute and oboe, the rustle of a gale. The skin on his face grew numb and cold. He fell to one knee and shook his head.

The black bat floated toward him silently, opening its toothy jaws. Geralt, still stunned by the scream, reacted instinctively. He jumped up and, in a flash, matching the tempo of his movements to the speed of the monster's flight, took three steps forward, dodged, turned a semi-circle and then, quick as a thought, delivered a two-handed blow. The blade met with no resistance . . . almost no resistance. He heard a scream, but this time it was a scream of pain, caused by the touch of silver.

The wailing bruxa was morphing on the dolphin's back. On her white dress, slightly above her left breast, a red stain was visible beneath a slash no longer than a little finger. The witcher ground his teeth—the cut, which should have sundered the beast in two, had been nothing but a scratch.

"Shout, vampire," he growled, wiping the blood from his cheek. "Scream your guts out. Lose your strength. And then I'll slash your pretty little head off!"

You. You will be the first to grow weak, Sorcerer. I will kill you.

The bruxa's lips didn't move, but the witcher heard the words clearly; they resounded in his mind, echoing and reverberating as if underwater.

"We shall see," he muttered through his teeth as he walked, bent over, in the direction of the fountain.

I will kill you. I'll kill you. I'll kill you.

"We shall see."